For Eric, Theo, Dahlia and Lyla-Rose. xx

If you train your mind to find the positive in every event you will banish worry and feel empowered.

Jacqueline Gold

THE CORNISH BEACH
HUT CAFÉ

JANE LINFOOT

One More Chapter
a division of HarperCollins*Publishers* Ltd
1 London Bridge Street
London SE1 9GF
www.harpercollins.co.uk
HarperCollins*Publishers*
Macken House, 39/40 Mayor Street Upper,
Dublin 1, D01 C9W8, Ireland

This paperback edition 2024

2

First published in Great Britain in ebook format
by HarperCollins*Publishers* 2024
Copyright © Jane Linfoot 2024
Jane Linfoot asserts the moral right to be identified
as the author of this work

A catalogue record of this book is available from the British Library

ISBN: 978-0-00-853706-7

Printed and bound in the UK using 100% Renewable Electricity
by CPI Group (UK) Ltd

APRIL

Just outside St Aidan, Cornwall
Sequins and a following wind
Wednesday

Wouldn't you know it? After three hundred miles of trouble-free driving since London, half an hour before St Aidan I opt for the short cut down the lanes, and now my trusty Mini convertible is at a standstill, stuck behind a line of cars.

I groan at Shadow the dog, who lifts his big brown head briefly, then settles back across the back seat, buoyed up by the bags I couldn't fit in the boot. 'It's only April, it's not even warm enough for us to have the hood down. Surely the holiday hold-ups can't have started already?'

As I smack the flat of my hand on the steering wheel, even singing along to Miley Cyrus's 'Flowers' doesn't help any. I hope this first snowflake of doubt about moving back to Cornwall doesn't become an avalanche of all the downsides I've forgotten in the decade since I left. As I look over the hedge to the expanse of pale blue sea beyond the fields, and catch my first glimpse of St Aidan, its picturesque pastel-coloured cottages stacked across the hillside in the curve of the bay, I hang on tight to the wave of wild optimism that brought me here.

When my mum rang me at the end of January to ask if I would like to buy the beach hut her friend Ivy was selling for a knock-down price, it felt like serendipity. True, a dilapidated shack on the sand dunes in a village at the edge of the world wasn't anywhere on my radar at the time, but with my life in London crumbling around me, it felt like the lifeline I'd been waiting for.

Four years earlier I was in my late twenties and everything I'd ever wanted had finally clicked into place. I was a team manager at a buzzy post-industrial bar called The Circus, where the only things loftier than the drink prices were the high-wire performers. I was in love with my adorable boyfriend, Dillon, a hot-shot engineer and childhood friend with whom I'd reconnected with in St Aidan town centre the New Year's Eve I was twenty-three. Home was a swanky rental in N16, and we were sure enough about our future to have secretly made our own wedding rings. There we were, researching honeymoon destinations, debating whether to spend the savings on a flat deposit, a fabulous elopement or the wedding of the decade. Speeding towards the public announcement of our engagement. And then one routine cervical smear test result blew all that out of the water.

Except that's not entirely true. My cancer diagnosis knocked the breath out of us, but after that I threw everything at it, and Dillon was with me all the way. When I wasn't able to work, I couldn't have asked for better support. When I went back to waitressing and it wore me out, I even managed to reboot my career, and started doing audio-book narration instead.

But it was as if that battle used up an entire lifetime of love. Before I was ill, we couldn't keep our hands off each other. But by the time I had the tentative all-clear, our relationship was over too.

Dillon took the fabulous promotion in Dubai he'd been holding off on and paid a year's rent on our flat to give me some breathing space. For spending money, I let out the spare room to an Estonian PhD student called Elise, who was mostly out at the lab. Then I threw myself into my work.

And for a few quiet months it felt like I'd cracked it. Then one minor surgical procedure left me with a throat rasp from the breathing tube, which means my voice now gives out a few pages into the manuscripts I read, so working my new job wasn't possible. And sadly, however big the tips, I'm way past picking up my old job, because I'm simply not that extrovert, life-of-the-party woman who persuaded revellers to buy round after crazily priced round. As I feel now, I doubt I could *give* cocktails away.

When I first arrived in London in my late teens, I vowed I'd stay for ever, but lately my luck has run dry, which is why, when the beach hut came up, I jumped at the opportunity. A place so sleepy that nothing ever happens might once have been my private nightmare, but it's the perfect refuge for where my life is now. Four walls and a roof are all I need; they might be a million miles away from the fifth-floor luxury living with a basement gym I'm giving up, but at least they're mine. If I hide myself away and live very quietly, I should be able to make my savings last until I'm able to ease back into my audio-book work again.

There's a sympathetic snort from Shadow in the back seat, but before I can thank him for his doggy solidarity on traffic issues, I catch sight of the signage on the car in front of mine in the queue and my sinking heart gives a skip.

The Little Cornish Kitchen! Delicious afternoon teas and events, Seaspray Cottage, St Aidan!

My fairy godmother must be looking down on me more than I know!

The Little Cornish Kitchen is run by Clemmie, one of my older sister's besties, whom I've known my entire life. As a figure in a blue flowery dress appears around the back of the car, pushing back a mass of auburn curly hair, I'm already out on the road and grinning.

'Clemmie! This is the best surprise ever! What's going on?'

Her cheeks are flushed as she nods at the child asleep in the back seat of her vehicle. 'Bud and I were out delivering a traybake order. Everyone stopped because a dog was out in the road, but a driver in front caught him and now they're all zooming off.'

I tense as I think of Shadow running loose in traffic, then relax again as Clemmie's arm flops onto my shoulder. Since Shadow and I rescued each other, he's done a great job at plugging the gaps that opened up in my life when Dillon and I parted. Who needs a partner when you've got a large hairy dog who sneaks on the bed the second the light goes out, and shares your addiction to custard creams?

Clemmie's beaming. 'You're the surprise here!! Who'd have thought we'd ever see London devotee Florence May moving back to St Aidan?'

Definitely not me, that's for sure. But I keep that to myself, go in for the hug then pull back when I collide with her bump. 'Nice work, Mrs Hobson! You're already bigger than when you had Bud!'

Clemmie clutches her stomach. 'It's a boy this time. He's due in a month, which is why I've been having these practice contractions all week.' She blows out a breath and leans back on the car wing. 'Between us, Flossie, when the traffic in front stopped, I was pleased to get out and rub my aching back.'

Clemmie, my sister Sophie, Dillon's sister Plum and a lovely woman called Nell are a group of friends who go all the way back to when our pregnant mums met at the Mums and Bumps group thirty-six years ago. Obviously, Dillon was already there, and I came along a bit later, but even as we've moved elsewhere, we've always all met up back in St Aidan.

Wall-to-wall weddings go with our age group, and some summers there was one a month. Around the time I was turning up here bloated from the steroids, having lost every bit of hair including my eyebrows with the chemo, Clemmie and her partner Charlie were trying for a baby and being endlessly disappointed. And Nell was another one who thought kids were never going to happen for her and her partner George.

When you're thirty and struggling to conceive you're right on the outside, especially at parties, and as my own chances of ever having a family of my own dwindled too, Nell, Clemmie and I stuck together. Being alcohol-free, we couldn't even console ourselves by necking the free booze and getting off our faces. We sat through so many receptions, waving our mocktails and rolling our eyes at those lucky women who'd stopped taking their pills and caught on the first try.

But eventually Clemmie got lucky. Her and Charlie's last-chance IVF baby, Bud, arrived last year. The whole village had shared their struggle to become parents and was equally delighted when Clemmie's surprise second pregnancy turned up out of the blue last Christmas.

Clemmie brightens and pushes herself upright again. 'Nell's baby's due around the same time.'

Anyone other than Clemmie and Nell, I might have found their pregnancies hard to watch, but no one deserves a happy family more than those two. From Clemmie's screwed-up face, it's clear she's still not ready to get back into the car, so I put my urgency to see my new home to one side, and carry on with our catch-up.

'Did Bud enjoy her first birthday?'

Clemmie opens her eyes and blows again. 'You bet!'

When I look again, she's turned and is holding onto the edge of the car roof. 'Everything okay there, Clems?'

She waves away my concern. 'I've rung Charlie, he's on his way to drive us home.' She tenses again, then smiles. 'Enough about babies. Tell me about this beach house you've bought. Sophie pointed it out from across the bay when we were at theirs.'

What I haven't said yet, is that Sophie is 'Sophie May', *the* multi-national cosmetics magnate who began her business on her kitchen table as a single mum in her twenties and now advertises in *Good Housekeeping* and dresses in pale aqua to match her products. She's as tiny, blonde and polished as I am sprawling, dark and messy. She also has a gorgeous husband, Nate, four kids and a clifftop castle called Siren House. It's good that I never make comparisons; the only thing I ever did better than her was being a teenage goth.

I'm not sure how much Clemmie's taking in, but I say it anyway. 'It's more a shed than a house, but I'll be over the moon if it's half as pretty in real life as it looks on Google Satellite.'

Clemmie stops and stares at me. 'You haven't *seen* it yet?'

'It was fully checked out by Mum.' What's not to like about a beach hut? – especially one at the tired, deserted end of town I prefer. 'I fast-tracked the sale because of the dog-friendly garden. It'll be Shadow and me, and seclusion by the sea.'

Clemmie frowns at me. 'You do know St Aidan won't be *that* peaceful with us lot here...?' She clamps her hand to her stomach again. 'Fuck! Sorry, Bud!'

As students in a flat-share in my early twenties, we watched every episode of *One Born Every Minute*, so I know the signs. I don't want to panic, but if she's swearing like that this baby could be here a lot sooner than next month.

'Would you like to sit down, Clemmie?' I reach into my car for a rug and as I shake it out on the verge another car's drawing up.

By the time the driver gets out, Clemmie's on all fours in the field gateway.

'Everything okay here? Do you need any help?'

I'm staring up into slate-grey eyes under dark curly hair, breathing in the kind of sophisticated aftershave that makes my knees go weak. *Add gin and kiss thoroughly ... is not any thought I should be having when my bestie is doubled up in agony on the grass and I'm starting my new single life.*

I pull myself together. 'I'm Florence. My pregnant friend

Clemmie is having contractions. Could you possibly phone 999 and say the words "rapid labour" while I check she's okay?'

Clemmie lets out a wail. 'No one needs an ambulance, Floss! A few minutes down here and I'll be... Arrrggghhh!'

As the guy gets straight through and starts giving the details of our location, the echo in my head tells me it's not the first time I've seen those dark curls and that half smile. Then it hits me that I'm not in Stoke Newington anymore with nine million strangers – in St Aidan everyone local looks familiar because they all are.

He catches my eye. 'The nearest ambulance is fifteen minutes away, they're doing their best to get someone here.'

As he returns to his phone Clemmie grabs my hand. 'I'm so sorry, Floss, you're the *last* person who should be helping me through this.'

I kneel down beside her and dab the sweat off her forehead. We both know she's right. Before I was ill, having kids had never crossed my mind, but when the chemo snatched that possibility away from me, it changed my mindset in ways I couldn't have predicted. I try not to make a big thing of it, but when I know I won't ever be pregnant or give birth to a child of my own, keeping babies at a safe distance is a self-preservation instinct.

But Clemmie didn't plan for this – I have to dig deep, and get on with it. 'I might be *the best* person to help! A woman at The Circus went into labour once, so it's not my first time!'

That puts a stop to her contractions, and she turns to look at me. 'Don't leave me hanging – tell me what happened?'

I shouldn't have started this. 'An off-duty paramedic leaped into action and caught the baby in his T-shirt.' I call up to the guy on his phone. 'You're not a doctor by any chance?'

He shakes his head. 'Sorry, I'm a metallurgist.'

Damn. It was worth a try.

Clemmie's eyes are level with my boobs as she pants. As she reads the logo on my chest, her face clears with the recognition. 'The Libertines at Reading, 2010 ... *I was there, with Sophie!*'

I grin. 'This used to be her T-shirt.' It felt like an auspicious choice to wear for coming back. When I dressed the part and slung it over my spangly bikini top this morning I didn't intend being out in a force ten gale blowing off the sea.

Clemmie's gasp turns to a wail. 'Sophie will have kittens if you catch Arnie *in that!*' Her calling the baby by name makes him sound alarmingly like a living, breathing person rather than a bump.

I laugh because what people forget is, if you stand up to Sophie she'll usually back down. 'It's my top now, she shouldn't have given it away.' Then the full weight of what Clemmie said sinks in. 'How close *is* this baby?'

The guy kneels down on the grass beside us. 'I'll put the emergency centre on speakerphone. They're asking, can you see the head yet?'

I wait until Clemmie opens her eyes again. 'Is the head there, Clems?'

There are damp strands of her hair sticking to her forehead as she lets out a whimper. 'I think it might be.'

'Shouldn't we be waiting for Charlie?' I'm playing for time here, but I untuck my vest from my shorts just in case. 'He can't be far away, he's going to be devastated if he misses this.'

'I might need to push...'

I'm all about the practicalities here. 'What about your pants, Clems?'

'I gave up on those weeks ago...' Her next groan is so loud it obliterates any relief her answer just gave me.

The guy is keeping up a running commentary into his phone as Clemmie's face turns redder. 'She's on her knees, pushing now, and her friend Florence is beside her, steadying her hips.'

The sound of a siren might be blowing on the wind, but I could be dreaming that. And I might be the one steadying *myself* as I grasp Clemmie's waist, not the other way around.

A woman's voice is echoing across from the phone. 'You and your baby are going to be fine, Clemmie, we'll talk you through... Grasp the baby as it comes, Florence... Hold on to it firmly...'

I peel off my vest, drop back behind Clemmie, and push past the flowery fabric of her dress. My most valuable cargo to date was a tray of diamond sparkle champagne cocktails someone paid thousands of pounds for, but the small body I'm reaching for with my outstretched fingers is so much more precious.

I gasp as the full weight of a baby lands in my hands. He's warm as I pull him tightly against the skin of my bare midriff. I should be shouting, so everyone can hear, but the most I can manage is a whisper. 'I've got the baby, Clems! He's really heavy!'

As she collapses sideways onto the rug, I move in beside her. 'You've done it, Clemmie, Arnie is here!'

What the hell happens now?

The next seconds stretch to an age, then there's a small splutter, and a cry that turns to a wail. I take in a crumpled face and tiny fists as I sit back on my heels and try to pull the vest around him.

As I slide him onto Clemmie's chest her cheeks are wet with tears and she's shuddering. 'Thanks, Floss. I d-didn't expect this when I set off!' She looks down at the bundle in her arms. 'He's beautiful, isn't he?'

I swallow back a sob. 'Another redhead too.'

Her eyes go wide as if she's had another thought. 'If you want a custard cream blondie, help yourself from the car!' She clasps my hand. 'They are still your favourite?'

Then there's a blur of bright red vehicles and blue lights further along the road and as the tyres skid to a halt on the gravel I'm thinking this must be a mistake.

'Didn't we call for an ambulance?'

The first two men are already kneeling down beside us. 'We firemen are the local first responders; you're in safe hands with us.' He pauses to grin. 'If in doubt, Blue Watch will sort you out!'

The second one frowns at me. 'We'll fill in until the paramedics arrive. The next bit is the umbilical chord, then the placenta.'

I drop a kiss on Clemmie's cheek. 'I'd better make room for the professionals!'

As I hear the emergency centre hand over to the crew on the ground a third guy is looking down at us. 'Clemmie Hobson! Having a baby by the side of the Truro road is taking natural childbirth to extremes!' He does a double take as he sees me. 'And Florence Flapjack-face too! Back to set the town on fire, I presume?'

As I scramble to my feet it's not lost on me that I'm surrounded by enough talent to fill a uniformed worker calendar, but my goosebumps are all down to the person in the dark suit trousers and white shirt standing back by the hedge.

I have nothing to lose here, I might as well own what

everyone knows anyway. However old I grow, there will always be someone in St Aidan to call me by my childhood nickname and remind me of the time I was trying to smoke a paper towel for a dare in chemistry and accidentally set the school alight. It's hard to re-compose myself as a sensible thirty-something, when my boobs are falling out of a bra top with diamond trim that's two sizes too small and my cheeks are sticky with tears, but I give it my best shot. Then another car draws up, and as Charlie jumps out, I run off to prepare him.

'Clemmie's-by-the-hedge-she's-had-the-baby-they're-both-fine!' I race to get to the end part, but Charlie still turns the colour of the Green Fairy absinthe cocktail we used to serve at The Circus.

Then an ambulance pulls to a halt behind the fire engine, and the paramedics come towards us carrying a stretcher. Charlie drops to join the group on the rug, and I dash round the cars to check on Bud and Shadow, who are both still asleep. I'm wiping my hands on a paper towel someone gave me, when I look up to see the guy who called the ambulance shaking a T-shirt at me.

'Have this if you're cold.'

'I couldn't possibly...' Asking how to give it back could be misread as a chat-up line.

'It's old stock. "White XL" isn't a judgement, it's the only size left.' He squeezes my shoulder and glances at a very sleek wristwatch. 'I'm Kit, by the way – that was a perfect catch you made there. If we're all done here, someone is waiting for me in Penzance, and I have a long drive home after that.'

I'm hugging the T-shirt to me, aware that he's backing away. 'We couldn't have done it without you, Kit.' I'm also aware how much I'd like to stop him from leaving, which is completely ridiculous. I'm pointing at his legs. 'Your trousers are covered in mud. Charlie will have some to lend you if you have time to drive to the village?'

He raises an eyebrow. 'I have three more clean pairs in the car, I can soon change.' His eyes widen as he reads my face. 'Being impeccable is part of my job description.'

I block the image of him stripping off on the verge – or hotter still, struggling into a new pair in the passenger seat – and force my mind onto the task in hand. 'If you could give me your deets, I know Clemmie will want to thank you herself. If you're going to help deliver anyone's baby a cake maker is a good choice. You're pretty much guaranteed a lifetime supply of Little Cornish Kitchen chocolate brownies. I *will not* be holding back on mine!'

I'm hearing myself going full-on with the confectionery bribery. *Who is operating my mouth here?*

I should simply ask what his aftershave is, so I know to avoid it in future, and shut the eff up.

There's a beat of silence. 'Is home *far away*?' I can't believe I was the one who said that too, but now I have I may as well sort out if I know him. 'You're *not from round here?*'

He hesitates and turns, with a perplexed expression. 'Home is a little fluid right now, but I'm definitely not local. Not yet, anyway.' He's almost back at his car. A few minutes more and he'll reverse away and be gone.

'And your number?'

'I'm really not expecting thanks.' As he opens the car door, I have a sense he may be testing me. Or teasing me. Then he gives in. 'Nice to meet you both, anyway. If you want to get in touch, it's all on the merchandise.' His face breaks into a smile for a moment as he waves. Then his engine turns over, and he's gone.

I push my arms into the T-shirt sleeves, look down to straighten it, and when I read the words printed on the fabric my heart turns to stone.

tOgether fOrever
www.KitAshton@Love2LoveAtelier
Covent Garden

Of course! He's from my London past, not here!

If anyone can understand someone looking totally different a few years on it should be me. What's unexpected is that losing the man bun and being so much more lean and wasted has made him so sexy. What's more, his 'together' promises are total bollocks! He's the metallurgist who made the wedding rings Dillon and I never got to use, and we had the very same T-shirts in the right sizes. '*Forever apart*' would have been a better epitaph for us.

I whip my arms out of the sleeves and spin the T-shirt round so I don't have to see the words, but when I look down this time there's that calligraphy that was everywhere four years ago.

ALL YOU NEED IS
LoVE

Looking at that I actually get a bit of sick in my mouth.

As I stare out and watch the parallel lines of surf etched across the blue of the bay, I thank my lucky stars that Mr Forever-Together is already a dot on the horizon. I'd just hate anyone here to know that Dillon and I ever went down that road.

I sniff and stamp my foot, wanting to shout at the wind because I've had it up to here with couples and love. 'Some of us are committed to futures alone – there's nothing wrong with that!' I mutter to myself.

As I hurry back to Clemmie, and the start of my brand-new solo life in St Aidan, I'm hoping this will be as exciting as it gets.

But obviously, having bought a beach hut without seeing it first, there is plenty of potential for more surprises.

The beach hut, St Aidan, Cornwall
Orange boxes and a view from space
Tuesday

'So where did the new hotel next door spring from?'
It's almost two weeks later by the time Clemmie, Nell and the gang come to call on Shadow and me, and once they've had their tour of the hut, and are clustered onto the veranda, that's my most pressing question.

Just like me, they looked straight past the weathered clapboard outside of the hut in dire need of paint and the wobbles on the rickety tin roof, and saved their gasps for the lovely outdoor decks, and the unexpectedly airy spaces inside.

When I first arrived and glimpsed the picket fence at the back, and the little gate with its very own postbox, I started to cry and carried on for the next few days. Mostly they were happy tears at what a wonderful place I'd stumbled on by accident, but it was also a reaction to the shock and eventual happy outcome of Clemmie's ten-minute labour. Even someone not sensitive about babies would have found that traumatic.

It's only since I've arrived that I've had time to ponder what exactly made me make that split-second decision to come back to the childhood home I'd been so happy to leave all those years ago, and it's about a lot more than The Hideaway. I'm here because my instincts told me to run to somewhere safe. Somewhere with no complications or challenges. A place where I can pull the metaphorical quilt over my head and have no need to leave. And so far, it's proving to be a perfect fit. But even in a seaside idyll that seems to be the answer to all my problems, where I'm already perfecting the art of becoming a hermit, there is an undercurrent of worry.

At eighteen it was a thrill to move to a city where there was no one I knew to judge me, and I adored the freedom, the excitement of being an anonymous stranger in a huge metropolis. Adored that there were wild new people to party with, a different club to go to every hour, that I could walk for a day, a week, a year, and still the streets wouldn't run out.

It was only when things got tougher that I found comfort in more familiar things and surroundings that I wound my way back, to draw on the unconditional love and support of friends and family who've known me my whole life. Perhaps the reason I've really come back is to be close to the people with whom there's no need to explain myself.

For someone who founded so much of my identity on the wonderful city I lived in, alongside the relief of finding sanctuary, it's also terrifying to know my world is shrinking. Now I'm back in a place where it takes fifteen minutes tops to walk in at one end of town and out of the other, I'm frightened that I will shrink in proportion. Not that I'd done too much to be proud of in my life compared to Sophie, Clemmie and the gang. And not that I'd mention this to them – *but now I'm back in this tiny place, what if I disappear altogether?*

Clemmie and I shared our best and worst bits of her grass-verge birth by phone as she waited to be discharged from hospital. I've cooed over pictures of Bud holding baby Arnie back at home on Messenger and she's sent me brownies too. I've kept the others happy posting photos of Shadow looking out from the rain-drenched windows on the WhatsApp group they named 'Flossie May is back in town, woohoo!'. And according to Clemmie, Kit's 'thank you' cake hamper was delivered to an address he gave in Dorset, so that's drawn a line under that one too.

As far as beach huts go, this one is as battered as they come but bigger than I could ever have hoped, and thanks to its position up on the slope above the tide line, the views around St Aidan Bay are fabulous in the day and at night the lights fade into the distance in a wide starry arc. The wind might drive the raindrops along the window panes in horizontal lines when it blows off the surf, but the way the hut nestles in the dunes is why it's called The Hideaway. There's even somewhere to leave the car alongside the track that runs behind the sandhills, and a tiny cabin with an outside loo.

The inside is the same weathered white planks that were in the photos Mum had sent me, and Ivy had cleaned the place from top to bottom and even left basic furniture with a few extra bits. I'd put most things from the London flat into storage, and as I only brought with me what would fit in the car, the unpacking here was minimal. Sure, Dillon was older than me, but when it came to buying swanky sofas and designer pieces he was light-years ahead, which is why most things we had belonged to him. He and his mates vied over who could spend biggest, outdoing each other with their hard-edged masculine vibe. As in most areas of our life together, Dillon was in charge, and I was happy to let him get on with it. But because I've never been a home-maker, when it comes to making this place cosy, I haven't the first clue where to begin.

During our first few days in St Aidan the non-stop rain turned the sea and the sky to a dark, gunmetal grey, and the bleached plank floors were covered with Shadow's soggy paw prints, but at least the rain bought us some settling-in time.

And now the sun has come out, the sea has turned to shivery aquamarine and Sophie, Nell, Plum and Clemmie have come for tea. Now they've had their tour I'm hoping they'll fill me in on the biggest surprise after Arnie's arrival.

I carry on with my explanation. 'The plot next door was still a sand dune when I looked at the beach hut on Google Maps.'

Nell pulls a face. 'It's total donkey-droppings that they update those satellite pictures every hour.'

Every expectant mum carries their bump differently, and Nell looks very much as she always did, with her tummy concealed between the sides of a padded waistcoat she's borrowed from George.

Plum's sitting on the steps that lead up to the front deck. She tosses her dark ponytail and fiddles with the strap on her paint-splattered dungarees. 'Your new neighbour is the High Tides Serenity Spa Resort, Floss; it's so exclusive it refuses to call itself anything as downmarket as luxury.' The disparaging shake of her head she gives is unnervingly like Dillon's. 'They started building last year, and they're opening as we speak.'

Plum is awesome, with her huge seascape paintings and the gallery she converted from a disused chandler's store, but however close we once were, lately I tread more carefully around her. Even though Dillon and I parted as friends, it's only natural she'd feel protective of her brother.

Sophie, who is leaning against the wooden side rail surrounding the deck in her usual head-to-toe pale aqua, joins in. 'Those Italian Cypress trees might look out of place, but it's certainly pulled this end of town up by its boot strings.'

Clemmie shoots a sideways grin from the director's chair where she's cradling a sleeping Arnie. 'Those lawns look so neat I'm expecting La La and Po to come running over the hill.'

We've pulled a wooden armchair outside for Nell, and she stretches back against the cushions. 'With the prices they're charging we mermaids won't be wallowing in their salt splashes any time soon!' These four first called their friendship group 'the mermaids' as kids, and they've never given up using the name.

Clemmie turns to me. 'How do you feel about it, Flossie?'

I'd hate them to know that as I've watched the builders add the finishing touches to some super-swanky beach huts at this end of the site, my heart has sunk further every day, so I make my voice bright. 'Mine's bound to look scruffy next to it, but there's nothing I can do – so let's move on to cake.' As I carry the tea tray out there's a chorus of cries. 'Nice cups!'

I laugh and hand round the brownies they've brought. 'The cupboards are full of them. There's no saucers, plates, or dishes, so Mum's friend Ivy must have drunk tea and nothing else.' Then I add an afterthought. 'With three gables and two covered verandas, I'm definitely not grumbling! People in St Aidan fight to get their hands on places half as pretty as this. I'm very lucky.'

'Too right you are!' Sophie's retort is a second too quick.

Like most sisters, we fought fiercely as kids, but as adults we usually have each other's backs. No one's more kind and generous than Sophie, she also works like a demon, and we all know not to be fooled by those baby-blue chinos – when she's set on something, she's ruthless. But there has to be something I'm missing here.

'You *had* turned this place down before Mum offered it to me?' My heart drops as I take in the shake of Sophie's head. 'She didn't tell you?'

She sniffs. 'It's fine, I've got a castle with steps down to the sea. This way it's in the family *and* we get to have you living here full-time.'

'I still wish you'd known about it.'

Sophie squeezes my hand. 'It was only a shock because we thought you were so committed to the city. But a beach hut is very "you" – wonderfully airy and impermanent.'

I can see where she's coming from; if she's accusing me of seeing London as the unrivalled centre of the universe these last sixteen years, I'm guilty as charged. St Aidan's never been in my top ten places to rock up, it's more my desperate last resort when all else has failed.

But Sophie is the last person I'd share my problems with because she'd be straight in with the handouts, and I'd hate her to feel she had to help me. 'Well, I'm here now, so let's make the best of it!'

Sophie's smile warms. 'It's great if your narration work is paying well enough for you to afford a place like this.'

Sophie's one of the few people who could get away with a statement like that, due to the fact her company's worth so much she could buy and sell St Aidan several times over. But where I found the money for my hut is another topic I want to steer her away from, and if I want to move on fast the new baby is the obvious choice.

'Anyway ... Shadow and I are very honoured that Arnie has come to see us for his first trip out.'

Clemmie's smile widens. 'As if I'd go anywhere else after what you did for us both.'

Plum looks up at me. 'You know, Flossie May is still St Aidan grapevine's hottest topic. Your nerves of steel in the face of an arriving baby may yet eclipse your reputation as a fire raiser.'

Everyone laughs at that, then turns to look at Arnie, so it's job done, and the pressure's off me.

As I move to smile down at the baby Clemmie squeezes my hand. 'Don't worry, Flossie Flapjack-face. When the time is good, I know it'll all fall into place for you too.'

She's trying to be reassuring, but it's funny how far behind she is with my game plan. I know exactly what she's talking about; for someone in my position, I'm very lucky that I got to freeze my eggs.

The whole of St Aidan knows about this because that's just the kind of place it is, but I owe it to Plum to give credit where it's due. 'That's how lovely Dillon was, leaving me with enough to pay for a surrogate.'

When we divided everything up, even though most of our savings had come from him he insisted I took the lion's share, so I'd have enough to pay to have a baby if ever the time came. But after the pain I went through separating from Dillon, I can't ever see a time I'd want another partner. And I saw enough of Sophie coping on her own with her first baby, Milla, when she got accidentally pregnant as a student, to know I'd never want to go it alone. All of which is how I came to change my forward planning and put my faith in a different kind of future for myself.

Arnie snuffling into his fist is compelling to watch but Sophie's gaze drifts. A moment later she turns on me, realisation on her face.

'Please tell me you haven't, Flossie?' Even though I don't flinch a muscle under her scrutiny, a second later she blinks again, and punches the air. *You used Dillon's surrogacy money to buy The Hideaway!?*'

My heart is plummeting that they've found out so fast, but I'm going to have to stand my ground.

Plum's forehead wrinkles. 'No judgement, Flossie – but you may regret that decision down the line.'

Clemmie lets out a wail. 'Now I feel *so* much worse that you had to deliver Arnie!'

Nell's looking at me over the top of her bump. 'You chose to invest in what was most important to you now, Floss, and we should all respect that.' She hesitates for a second and when she carries on, she's cocking an eyebrow at Plum. 'And *however* we talk about the money, it's hers to use as she wishes, not Dillon's.'

I'm truly grateful that Nell is so down to earth, holding steadfastly to her accountant's view of the world, while clearing up that last point too.

I need to reinforce what Nell's said. 'I agonised long and hard, but now I'm here it feels right.' It's as if wiping out the possibility of a surrogate baby has taken away the pressure I didn't realise I was feeling. I wouldn't say it out loud in case Sophie's still miffed, but a few months of total rest here in this fabulous place are going to be wonderful. Amazing even. But however good it is, it's only temporary. My plan is, when my voice comes back I'll pick up my work again, and tiptoe back to town.

Sophie's brownie is still untouched on the upturned orange-box next to her cup. 'You do know there's a catch?'

I have *no* idea what Sophie's grimace is for, but I can't let her know that.

Clemmie and Nell exchange glances, but Sophie carries on. 'The council own the land these huts are built on, and when they granted permission for the hotel, they re-designated the huts at this end of the beach as live-work units.'

'And that's important because...?'

Nell huffs and sits up straighter. 'You're only allowed to stay overnight in the huts along here if you're running a business too.'

Damn. I was so caught up in checking the picket fence could stay, I totally missed the significance of the what the 'live-work' bit of the contract meant. 'Does anyone even care?'

Plum frowns. 'They certainly will once the visitors arrive.'

Sophie shakes her head at my gaffe, then visibly mellows. 'It's absolutely *not* a problem. We'll simply set you up as a Sophie May outpost, testing our products in the field.' Her arm slides around my shoulder. 'St Aidan Bay is renowned for its complexion-wrecking westerlies, you'll be our researcher on the beach!'

She's trying her best, but I'd hate her to feel she *has* to step in just because I've screwed up.

Clemmie's watching as I ease out from under Sophie's arm

and she catches my eye as my bottom lands on the step next to Plum.

'A Little Cornish Kitchen at this end of the beach might work, if you're more comfortable with cake than cosmetics?'

I can't believe that she's offering. 'That might be ... more visible.' I'm jumping at this because any offer from Clemmie will come with fewer strings than Sophie's.

Clemmie's beaming. 'There's no one I'd *rather* help out, Floss. If I lend you a few bits, you'll look like the real deal by tomorrow.'

I catch my breath. 'I don't want to be *too* authentic!' Blondies are one thing, customers are something else entirely.

Sophie sniffs. 'No worries on that score, this part of the village is deader than Elvis – paying footfall is non-existent.'

I smile up at her. 'That's a perfect fit for me. We both know I have zero business ambition and even less aptitude.'

While the rest of them have striven for success, achievements have passed me by. My rule with work was it had to be fun, and even though I had responsibilities at The Circus, in everyone's eyes I was still only a waitress.

Nell nudges me. 'Never say never, Florence! No experience, and you did fine delivering Arnie over there.'

My hopes and dreams are in tatters and I know I should wrap this up before anyone drops any more bombshells. 'If you've got to hurry Arnie home, Clemmie, that's fine – we can catch up more when I call round for the props.'

But Clemmie's oblivious, staring out across the dunes.

Plum taps her knee. 'What's so interesting, Clems? If Chris Hemsworth is in a High Tides hot tub, don't keep it to yourself!'

Clemmie's craning her neck. 'Floss, over there by the glossy new beach huts...'

Nell's rubbing her bump again. 'I may be nine months pregnant, but I still know a hottie when I see one – not that I'm objectifying.'

Plum stands up to get a better view. 'Nothing like Chris, but the calibre is equally high.' She laughs. 'Someone here must be doing something right, he's heading this way and he's waving!'

Clemmie's voice rises in excitement. 'It *is* him, Floss, isn't it? That's Kit who phoned the ambulance!'

I can't *begin* to imagine what he's doing here, but it fits with the general downhill trajectory of the afternoon. Giving up on men has been easy so far, so I'd rather not see one who makes it feel hard.

I look up and catch Sophie's eye in an effort to make up. 'How would it be if I promise to give you first refusal if ever I sell this place?'

Let's face it, I'm not going to be here for ever, it's only until I sort myself out. In reality, it isn't *if* I sell, it's *when* I sell, and Sophie knows that as well as I do.

A curious look of satisfaction spreads across her face. 'Thanks, Flossie, that makes me feel a lot better. I can definitely work with that.'

I wasn't expecting these undercurrents of animosity to come out with the first cup of tea! There I was, wafting around, talking about coming back for family support, and I should have brought my boxing gloves.

But it could be about the transition. Before I was a visitor. Now I'm a resident, and the territory has shifted.

But now for the next job of the afternoon: finding out what the hell Dr Love2Love is doing in town.

3

The Hideaway, St Aidan
Happy returns
Tuesday

'Did Ian Somerhalder lose his way on *The Vampire Diaries* set and get teleported to St Aidan?'

As Plum leans round the veranda corner post for a better view of Kit my lips are pursed, but the others chorus their agreement.

It's not only that the guy is so well put together. He might be looking a little overdressed with his sharp trousers, snowy shirt and dark tie, but his smile and laid-back warmth literally radiate as he strolls towards us. I only hope the audience stifle their shrieks *before* he comes into earshot.

It's ridiculous for me to feel the kind of attraction that pulses through my body in thousand-volt bursts as I watch him skirting the picket fence. He's the man who made my wedding ring, and he was engaged himself at the time too, both of which take him right off the table.

As he swings up onto my sand deck my involuntary gasp is huge. Then one whiff of his aftershave blows every bit of my hands-off resolve off the beach.

Somehow I manage to say, 'Hey, it's you! Who'd have thought? Guys, this is Kit.'

After that Clemmie steps in. 'Kit was our heroic helper by the roadside, and this is Plum, Nell and Sophie, and of course, baby Arnie.' She adjusts the bundle in her arms and Kit comes closer for a better view.

'Hello again, Arnie, you've grown since we last met.'

Guys talking to babies are heart-melting at the best of times, but watching this one blasts my heart into a million tiny pieces. As he stretches out his left hand, I see there isn't a wedding ring. Not that I'm looking. Or even curious. It's just useful to know sometimes.

Even if he was there at the birth there's only *so* much to say to a newborn. Once Kit compliments Arnie on his cute turned-up nose that's just like his mum's and steps back, I brace myself to find out the worst.

'So, Kit, you're back in St Aidan! I assume you've dropped in for a super-fast look at the new place next door on your way home to Dorset?'

Kit turns to me, and squints into the sun. 'High Tides?' Up close his hair is tangled by the wind, and as his smile widens, he gives us the full benefit of his dimples through his stubble. 'I'm hoping I'll be here slightly longer this time than last.'

The laugh he gives is so low it reverberates right through my chest. I can't honestly remember the last time my nipples perked up this much. It has to be that mix of wild and tamed that makes him so irresistible, but with words like that flashing through my head I need him out of my orbit ASAP, if not sooner.

I'm making bargains with myself, trying to focus on the best possible outcome here. I could probably handle him sticking around for afternoon tea. Overnight would be trickier. I'm desperately banking on the millionaire-retreat-prices stopping him from checking in for any longer, because an entire week waiting for him to appear over the horizon might actually blow my mind.

I make my smile really huge and bring out a medium worst-case. 'Let me guess – you're staying for dinner?'

There's that laugh again. 'Keep going...' One eyebrow goes up. 'I've actually booked in to High Tides for the next two years, starting today.'

My stomach drops like a high-speed lift. 'B-b-b-but...' *Surely he can't have?*

Sophie fills the space where my words should be. 'Don't keep us in suspense – have you won the lottery, or are you just plain loaded?'

Plum's eyes are bright with excitement. 'Wait, I heard about this at the Chamber of Commerce! Are you the artisan jeweller working in collaboration with the hotel?'

Kit nods. 'That's me! My Love2Love Atelier is expanding into Cornwall! I'm in the newly built beach huts over there!'

Nell's not one to let a chance go, so she immediately launches in with 'If you're sticking around, you'll *have* to come to our singles club events.' Nell's so obsessed with the St Aidan singles club she founded, which has now expanded to be St

Aidan's main social hub, we're not quite sure how she's going to step away for long enough to get to the labour ward.

My mouth is like sandpaper, but I force myself to beam. 'Congratulations, they'll make wonderful workshops.' On the bright side, even if he does sixteen-hour days, he has to go home at night.

His smile widens. 'And the best part about this particular package – I'll be living here too!'

In my mind I'm thumping my head with my fists, jumping about the beach like Basil Fawlty with his worst meltdown ever. But somehow I manage a grimace and a happy voice.

'Fabulous news. You and I will be neighbours!'

'Awesome!' He looks out at the horizon, then looks back at Clemmie and me. 'For those of you who missed the T-shirt, couples come to me and we design and make their rings together and document their journey. The sunset-over-the-sea shots here will be out of this world!'

My nausea has grown so much I feel like I need a vomit bucket.

'The ultimate romantic experience you can Instagram for ever!'

Paraded in front of me every single day. I'm fighting to keep the irony out of my voice as I turn to Nell. 'If ever there was a singles club hook-up made in heaven, it's this one!'

Nell claps her hands. 'Absolutely, Kit! Why didn't I think of that? We'll do a special event for you to sponsor!'

I was hoping Kit might look terrified at the prospect, but he's still beaming as brightly as I am.

'So what's *your* work speciality, Florence?' He turns on me so fast I almost fall down the steps.

'*My what?*'

He tilts his head. 'For the live-work zone?'

Clemmie steps in. 'Floss will be working under the Little Cornish Kitchen umbrella, adding her own – very special – beach-hut spin.'

This is so absurd, I'm biting my lip trying not to laugh. 'In summer it'll be a parasol rather than an umbrella, obviously! All I can divulge for now is ... I'm all about the sugar rush, *and there will be custard!*' I have no idea where that came from, but I do keep a large carton handy for my Mr Kipling apple pie habit. It's a little-known secret that it works wonderfully with ice cream too.

Sophie coughs. 'And Floss is very keen to sponsor some singles club events too! You could even join forces!'

'Thanks for that, Soph!' I thought I'd placated her earlier, but barbs like that mean I'm not completely forgiven.

I hear a snuffle from Clemmie's arms, so I dash across the deck. 'So sorry, Kit, we're going to have to get the baby home, he's already had a very long first outing.'

Nell gets up from her armchair. 'Very true. Come on, Clemmie!'

And a second later we're all trooping off over the dunes towards the track and their cars.

And the moral to that story is: however far downhill an afternoon has gone – it can always go further.

I'm going to have to put in a lot more effort than I imagined if I'm going to get a quiet life!

4

The Hideaway, St Aidan
House parties and writing in the sand
Wednesday

St Aidan may not be as tranquil or trouble-free as I'd imagined, but I'm hopeful it will soon calm down. I won't be rushing into anything either. It hit me as I waved the mermaids off along the track behind the dunes that however kind Clemmie's offer, there have to be better work options to hide behind than parading myself as an outpost of her events venue and tea garden. So this afternoon, as I set off along the sands with Shadow, I'm determined to use our walk to come up with a more appropriate solution.

Unfortunately, the tide is running high up the beach and Shadow, who's still not completely at home with the sea, takes each rush of water as a personal affront. By the time we get back half an hour later my ears are ringing from his non-stop barks, but I'm no nearer to finding the brainwave I need. Then, as we make our way up the dunes, what I see in front of The Hideaway ends all hope of a change.

'Plum and Nell! We've only been gone thirty minutes! You've been very – er – busy!'

They're waving at us from the main deck, and the three unfolded café tables and stack of chairs beside them suggest they're a long way ahead of me here.

Nell's standing with her hands on her hips. 'We must just have missed you! How's this for a surprise?' Her beam is so wide as she nods at the crowded deck, all I can do is to pretend I'm delighted too.

'Wonderful! I hope you're not overdoing it, Nell?'

She laughs. 'Plum's done the work, I'm under strict orders to keep my hands in my pockets.' She frowns down at her bump. 'To be honest, I'm pleased to take my mind off the waiting, these last few weeks are taking for ever.'

I go in and give her a hug. 'Not long now.' It must be hard for Nell to see Clemmie already home with Arnie when they were originally due around the same time.

She looks down at Shadow as she scratches his head. 'How's this guy settling in?'

At least I can be honest about this. 'You'd think miles of empty sand would be a treat, but he sees ghosts behind every pebble. Some days he's so nervous I get the feeling he preferred the city.'

'We definitely heard you coming!' Plum shuffles the chairs into position and stands back to assess. 'Will six seats be enough for starters?'

'So many?' I stifle my choke. However cute and pretty they are, I can't imagine them with strangers sitting on them.

Plum turns to me, her hand on my shoulder. 'Is that still the same cough you had at New Year?'

Nell lets out a chortle. 'With a voice that low and husky, no wonder they can't get enough of you for those love stories you read.'

Little does Nell know, but she couldn't be more wrong. My mum's the only person with any idea about my recent difficulties, and as I'd hate Dillon to find out, I need to be careful with my answers.

It was a huge surprise to me when the partner of one of Dillon's colleagues who worked at a studio suggested I should try out for the audio-books as I recovered from one of my later rounds of chemo, and an even bigger surprise to find I could do the work. Accents have always come easily to me, my part-finished drama diploma meant I can read without stumbling, and it turned out that my voice had the resonance and range that meant it recorded well. Best of all, the listeners found my cosy tone easy to listen to, and their positive feedback meant my bookings built quickly for a beginner. The trouble now is that my voice gives out. One minute I'm croaking, the next it's a whisper, then I'm squeaking. When the listeners need consistency, I'm no use at all as I am.

I've worked out an official version. 'I'm taking a break from the reading work. It isn't fair to leave Shadow until he feels more confident.' I smile up at them both. 'It'll give me a chance to sort this place out too.'

That's another porkie. Everyone keeps saying how much there is to do here, but when it comes to homes I'm low-intervention; with a location this perfect there's very little I want to add.

Plum's smile widens. 'I may have another surprise to help with that.' She pulls a folding blackboard from behind a table. 'Ta-da!'

The curly writing in everlasting-white marker saying '*Welcome to the LCK, FlorenceMay@TheHideaway*' seals this in a way that's so permanent my stomach seems to leave my body. 'Wow! My own signage, *so fast!*'

Plum's smiling. 'One I made this morning. Clemmie insisted we got straight onto it.'

Nell's nodding. 'Your car's fully corporate too! We went a bit overboard, but those customised branding magnets are easy and instant, and Clemmie had lots to spare.' My stomach is dropping lower with every new revelation.

Plum props the blackboard next to the steps. 'There's no hiding now! The Little Cornish Kitchen has officially arrived at the Beach Hut.'

Nell's unrolling some PVC fabric. 'All that's left now is the hanging sign!'

My throat is constricting in panic. 'Won't that attract unwanted attention?'

Plum smiles. 'It's important it feels genuine. Clemmie used this on her stall at the Christmas market.' She takes the end of the string from Nell and jumps up on a chair. 'We'll hang it between the posts supporting the veranda roof, nice and high. How's that, Floss?'

I'm blinking up at the sign. As it swings in the breeze against the deep blue sky beyond, it couldn't be any more conspicuous. 'That's fabulous. Absolutely brill! Thanks for all your help with this!' Every part of that is true. I just wish this feeling of misgiving wasn't weighing like a stone in my gut.

Nell's punching the air. 'Great job, Plum, it really is the dog's bollocks!'

I send Shadow an apologetic glance for that, and slide onto a chair because as the full effect sinks in my legs don't feel as if they can hold me.

Plum's frowning at me. 'Everything okay there, Flora-Dora?' Her hand is on my shoulder again. 'Don't worry about Sophie and her older-sister green-eyed monster, she always deals with it eventually.'

In the thirty-three years I've spent tiptoeing in the shadow of my go-getting sibling I've never considered myself worthy of jealousy before. 'Apart from The Hideaway, what have I ever had that she'd have wanted?'

'You name it...' Nell laughs.

'Pretty much everything.' Plum's counting off on her fingers. 'Your name, your beach party Polly Pocket, the way your dark hair was right down your back and shone when hers didn't, your entire life in London – especially the last flat – your long legs, big boobs and tiny waist...'

I sigh. I've been so unaware. 'At least the flat, the long hair and my tiny waist are out of the equation now.' I try never to blame things on the cancer, but realistically, without it I'd probably still have all three.

Nell blows out her cheeks. 'You've always got on better with your mum, so maybe that's a part of it too.'

Our dad left home when we were young, but Sophie was a daddy's girl, so she always took it harder than me. I was closer to our mum, and that's how it stayed, but I can't believe how much me getting this place has stirred it all up. I can't believe I assumed coming here was going to be an easy answer when it sounds like Sophie's waging full-out war!

'It isn't actually Sophie I'm worried about.' With so many home truths flying around, I may as well come clean myself. 'I'm *so* grateful for all you've done, but I'm not sure this is the long-term answer. Even with the stage set and my hygiene training from my days at The Circus, I'll struggle if the council come to check me out.' I hesitate, and finally get to the real truth. 'When I'm here to get away from it all, with a bag of nerves for a dog, I'd rather not have Joe Public tramping onto my deck.'

I should know by now that Nell always grabs the proverbial bull by the horns.

'So what were you thinking instead?'

I'm floundering, then another glance at the tables strengthens my resolve. 'Those mice made out of stuck-together shells?'

Plum's joining in. 'St Aidan's already drowning under the weight of shell animals, but if you can sew you could do beach bags?'

Damn. They must have forgotten my second claim to fame at school was machining my oven glove project to my school skirt. 'Scrap that idea – I can't.' I look along at the other larger huts nestling in their plots along the dunes, and the line of smaller huts beyond them. 'What else do people do along here?'

Plum frowns. 'There's a digital pet portrait artist, someone paints words on stones and sells them on Etsy, there's a stylist, and a couple of guys customising paddle boards.'

Nell's leaning her shoulder against the door frame. 'Sophie wasn't being mean about the beach being quiet here. No one's been past in the last hour. In the unlikely event a customer finds their way to the deck, will it be so hard to bung them a brownie to take away?'

Plum's nodding. 'If you did want to raise your profile, the kitchen here's not huge but it's got everything you'd need.' She takes in my appalled grimace, and carries on anyway. 'You always served up amazing meals when we came to stay in London.'

We're on very shaky ground here talking about the past, but we've got to yet another crux. 'Serving I can do. The food was mostly down to Dillon.'

Nell lets out a guffaw. 'Well, stone the crows, you both kept that secret!'

It's just one of those rules of my life, and it was always the same with Dillon as it was with Sophie – wherever I am, whatever I'm doing, there's always someone who can do it better. Except for being a goth, obviously. And persuading people to buy mahoosive rounds of cocktails. Those were *my* superpowers. And I might have got good at the audio-books too if it hadn't been for that last operation scuppering my chances. But for the rest, I'm completely reconciled to being bottom of the class and stepping back to let the superstars get on with it.

Plum looks at the sky, then carries on. 'It's a big mistake to let Sophie's success undermine you, Floss. You're sparky and creative, you put in the effort, and if you ever *do* decide to have a new-style Little Cornish Kitchen, you're *more* than capable.'

Nell reaches out and squeezes my hand. 'We'd all be here to help you too – *you do know that*?'

I close my eyes and repeat under my breath, '*Quiet life, quiet life, quiet life.*'

When I look again Plum's nodding. 'Clemmie's even offered to show you her gran's recipe cards.'

Mum wasn't the kind of mother who'd sent us out into the world without cooking skills, and she was especially strong on her homely puddings. But my sherry trifle and apple crumble didn't cut it once Dillon moved up the career ladder and his tastes went upmarket too.

I'm biting my lip as I look up at the concern in their faces. 'I really appreciate your honesty and support; it means a lot.' I have zero intention of selling eighties-style quiches from my veranda, but it's still heart-warming to know they've got my back.

'And talking *of Dillon*...'

My eyes snap on to Plum's face, because unless I'm the one mentioning him, he's the last person I want to discuss.

'You know he still cares about you?' She's fiddling with her dungaree strap again. 'A lot...'

I have no idea why she's brought this up now, but I have my answer ready. 'Dillon and I will always stay friends.'

The strap is knotted around her finger. 'He still hasn't moved on ... not at all...' The pause is for what we both know to sink in – Dillon, given his freedom and who he is, should have. That was the plan anyway. 'I wanted you to know.'

I'd trusted Dillon would have let me know himself had there been a change, so I'm not sure where to put this information, or how to react to it. My heart was so wrung out by the time he left, I'm not sure either of us have fully processed it even now.

All I know is, every decision I made back then came from a place of love – I was desperate to do the right thing for both of us, especially him. In the end you have to go with your gut instinct in the instant, stand by that – and hope you're giving the person-you-loved-the-most-in-the-world wings to fly, rather than a detonator and a bomb that shatters their life for ever.

'As far as I'm aware, Dillon's enjoying Dubai.' I gather every ounce of my strength around me, to underline the situation that Plum should already know too. 'It's only Shadow and me now, and I don't intend to change that. But thanks for telling me anyway.'

I can only hope she understands the same as I do from what I've said here, and doesn't add a spin of her own. I have no plans to add in anyone new. But it also means I won't be considering a reconciliation either.

'Hey, Floss, it's your neighbour. He's waving again!'

Nell's nudge is so hard she almost knocks me off the chair.

I already know what Kit's friendly wave from the front of his hut looks like, because I saw it when I came out onto the deck first thing this morning. It's just a shame he isn't further away; a few more yards and he'd be out of waving range. As it is, there's this unspoken pressure to acknowledge each other every time he pops up in my eye line.

I turn to give a twitch of my wrist across the expanse of dune and realise he's not alone.

Nell's hip collides with my elbow again. 'There's three of them, the other two are holding hands.'

For eff's sake. 'He's not losing any time. Second day here, looks like he's already up and running with real live customers!' I put a hand on Shadow's collar as I hear the rumble of a growl in his throat. 'You can't go running after them either.'

Plum's frowning as the couple dash along the natural path below the deck, and down onto the beach. 'Kit's got his camera out. There's not much sand to run on when the tide's in, but they're going for it anyway.'

I already know the drill. After Dillon and I had sorted out our rings, Kit had us posing all over Neal Street to round off our record of the day with romantic shots of Covent Garden. We'd actually chosen a picture he took of us by a line of red phone boxes for the save-the-date cards we never got as far as printing.

I glance at my phone. 'If he's hoping for shots at sundown, he's going to have a long wait.'

Nell's grinning at me. 'With David Bailey and his happy couples prancing around down there, you won't be short of entertainment.' She lets out a huge guffaw and her next shove is so strong I almost land on the floor. 'Play your cards right, you could be serving them afternoon teas!'

I laugh. 'The High Tides Hotel or my beach hut? I think I'm safe there.' But seeing Kit waving his Nikon, I'm kicking myself. 'Why didn't I think of opening the sand deck as a photo booth?'

Plum laughs. 'Too late now! The Little Cornish Kitchen at The Hideaway is here to stay!'

It's not as if you can look away when it's playing out right on your doorstep. Kit's directing the happy couple from pose to pose along the dune edge. Back-to-back, side by side, face to face. As they hurl themselves down on the sand, chins propped on elbows among the reed clumps, they're barely twenty feet in front of us. Kit comes to a standstill above their horizontal bodies then turns to look at us. As his gaze meets mine, he grins at me, shakes his head and rolls his gaze up to the clouds. Then a second later he's down on his knees, going in for the close-up shots.

Plum looks across at me. 'Did you see that eye-roll? What the hell was that about?'

'I've got absolutely no idea.' But I could do without the goosebumps it brought on.

She frowns. 'Are you shivering? You need to wrap up with that cough of yours.'

Another nudge from Nell brings me back down to the deck. 'I know you're averse to customers, but what's a thirsty woman got to do to get a cup of tea round here?'

And a second later I'm inside putting the kettle on.

5

The Hideaway, St Aidan
Dancing queens and breakfast telly
Thursday

'I f you're barking at the sea again, it's too early.'

It's the next morning, and my shout is muffled by the duvet clamped over my head to keep out the morning light that floods in through the windows in the sloping ceiling above the double bed. I'm puzzling because I usually have to prise Shadow out; our mutual love of cosy mornings is another reason we're so in sync.

When his noise doesn't stop, I stagger across the living area, rub my eyes awake and hope his wave-chasing will subside before it becomes a habit. It's only when I reach Shadow, his tail wagging furiously by the French window, and pull back the white muslin curtains to look out that I understand.

'Sorry.' I pat his head. 'Good boy for letting me know we have visitors.'

Except the people I'm looking out at seem more permanent than that. Two women in puffer jackets are outside on the deck, their knees already firmly under a table, ankles crossed under their chairs. When they notice me, one raises a hand and the other gets up and comes towards me.

I open the door a crack. 'Can I help you?'

'We saw the sign and came to see if you were up and running.' She's looking achingly expectant. 'We rather hoped we might be your first customers.'

At seven-thirty my groan is entirely justified. 'I'm still in my pyjamas.'

Which is shorthand for *fully shut, do not disturb*.

It's my own fault. A 'Closed' sign across the blackboard was all it needed. I add it to the top of my mental to-do list, which I'm much less on top of now than when I was working.

She studies the palm trees on my PJ bottoms. 'They're very pretty for nightwear, we'd never have guessed.'

It's not as if I'm wearing one of those swanky satin sets the fashion editors are already pushing to double up as office-wear in summer. A chrysanthemum-print top with a starry sweatshirt added at midnight to keep out the chill wouldn't make it into *Cosmopolitan*, but in Cornwall at dawn I'm warming to the compliment. Which I shouldn't be at all when I brought them up as my excuse for closing the door immediately and diving back into bed.

'So what were you hoping to order?'

Her eyes brighten. 'What have you got?' As I hesitate, she comes closer. 'So long as we get a pic for the socials, we're happy to make do.'

Her friend calls from the table. 'Before you say it, old people do Insta too now.'

They remind me a lot of my mum, with their early-morning lippy and their buttery blonde balayages. 'You both look in great shape. Definitely not old.'

The one at the table carries on. 'That's thanks to the 5:2 diet, and lots of walking. We never say "no" to puddings though.'

I have to tell them. 'You do know our Seaspray Cottage branch is serving a very wide menu only *a short walk* along the beach?' As well as doing functions, lately Clemmie's place is open from early 'til midday.

'But we're *here*.' They sound as determined as my mum. 'We're Jean and Shirley, by the way. It's lovely to meet you, Florence.' Just as clever as Mum too, using my name off the sign so I feel more obligated.

I lay down some ground rules as I try to think what I've got inside. '*My* Little Cornish Kitchen branch will usually be open by prior arrangement only, with occasional takeaway cake days, and it'll never serve drinks.' There's not enough milk for tea, no bread for eggs on toast, I don't have bacon. Then it hits me that Clemmie began by serving desserts, and I have my solution. 'It's never too early for chocolate, so today – *as a very special conces-sion* – how about a lucky-dip medley?' I'm thinking cheesecake cubes and mini scoops of vanilla ice cream all topped off with a Coco Pop garnish. If I give them my left-over slice from tea and the last of my cereal, that's breakfast and lunch gone, but at least I'll get my deck back.

Their smiles widen. 'We'll have two of those please.'

'They'll be eight pounds each.' The price I pull out of the air is to scare them from ever coming back. Then I remember most of my dishes are dirty. 'This particular sweet comes in a cup.'

Their eyes brighten. 'Better and better.'

It's so unbelievable, it's surreal. I murmur down at Shadow as I pull the door closed behind me and head to the kitchen area, 'I *promise* this is a one-off.'

Even I can do this. I push the boat out with a couple of cocktail umbrellas of Ivy's I find in the drawer and a slurp of carton custard, and I'm back out in no time. With a tray in my hand I even manage a flourish as I deliver the pieces of kitchen roll I have to run back for.

We get as far as their teaspoons being poised over Ivy's mismatched cups, then they pause and look up.

'Yes?' I should have known it was a *big* mistake to start this, I only hope I can save myself before I trash Clemmie's reputation completely.

Shirley coughs. 'Do you have a card reader?'

Jean joins in. 'We only have plastic, and we'd hate to start if we couldn't pay.'

'Is that all?' My relief whooshes out of me. 'You're my first-ever customers. Even if you did have cash, I don't have any change. Have these on the house!' As if I'd argue over a handful of Coco Pops, when all I want to do is wave them on their way.

Twenty minutes later, I've managed to let Shadow out for a wee by the door at the back, and then he's joined us on the deck for ear scratches, and we've got all the way to our goodbyes.

Jean squeezes my arm as she heads for the steps. 'Thank you for opening for us, the sweets were delicious.'

Shirley looks up from the dune. 'Much too tasty to be free. We'll drop in when we're passing and pay for them.'

I have to be firm about this. 'Really, you don't have to.'

Jean turns as she reaches the sand. 'No time to argue, there's another customer arriving. We may be the wrong side of seventy, but we can still appreciate pecs in a wetsuit fresh from the waves.'

I glimpse what they're talking about, die of a small heart attack and still manage to reply. 'That's my neighbour, I'd better see what he wants.'

I watch them head off along the beach towards St Aidan. When I turn to look the other way again Kit's stubble shadow is close enough to snag my gaze. When he smiles, the bottom falls out of my stomach. Then Shadow yelps and rushes down off the deck, and as he leans in for another round of head-scratching, I get a grip of myself.

My commitment to staying solo isn't only because of getting over Dillon. Dating is bad enough if you're well, having had cancer adds in a million other complications. I mean, why would anyone choose someone who's been ill when there are so many healthy people out there? If you do happen to get a guy as far as a date, the quandaries begin... Do you drop in the C-word on the first outing and watch them run? Or do you save it until the twenty-first and risk a broken heart when they ghost you? When your confidence is already in tatters, the rejections are especially hard to take. Add in explaining about the scars and the infertility, and it's easier to forget it altogether.

I don't even know why I'm obsessing over this now when I'm ninety-nine per cent certain, despite the still-missing wedding ring, that the guy next to me is already spoken for.

I glance at my watch and see it's barely eight. 'Does everyone in St Aidan get up before they go to bed?'

Kit rubs his fingers through his damp hair which tousles it even more. 'It's hard to sleep with the noise of the sea. Do you find that too?'

I half wish I did. 'I'm not having any trouble.' It may change if the weather is more stormy, but as it is the constant roll of the falling waves lulls me. 'Sleeping was what I found hard in Stoke Newington. The sirens on the High Street would always wake me.'

'This London refugee is a lot more out of his comfort zone than you are,' he says, gesturing at Shadow.

It already feels like another lifetime. 'Shadow is from Hackney. He's doing it tough.'

Kit smiles at him. 'I thought I recognised his accent.'

'You've heard him barking?' The last thing I want is to be a local nuisance.

'Now and again.' Kit's lips are twitching. 'He's a dog, it goes with the territory.' Then his smile breaks free. 'You've got your legs covered up today.'

I'm blinking. 'For someone wearing neck-to-toe neoprene, that's a strange observation. Seriously though, the water must be arctic out there?'

'I'm here so I figure I may as well make the most of it.' He pulls a face. 'I'm told it gets easier when you get used to it.'

I laugh. 'The first lesson of living in St Aidan – don't believe everything the locals say.'

The corners of his mouth pull downwards. 'I'll bear that in mind.' Then he grins again. 'Every other time I've seen you recently, you've been wearing shorts.'

I have to tell him. 'If you're only here to diss my PJs, I'm going back to bed.'

His hand is on the deck rail. 'There is something else...' His pause is so long and ominous there's time for us both to listen to my heart as it bangs against my chest. 'I recognised you straight away on the roadside – you and Dillon came to me for your rings...?'

'That's right. We did.' The question is hanging in the air like a lead weight. 'Dillon's not here. We didn't get to use them.' I'm astonished by his powers of recall, but this works two ways. 'We aren't the best advert for your brand, but don't worry, it's not a thing I broadcast.'

His eyebrows rise. 'Say no more. Your secret's safe with me.'

I twist the hem of my starry top around my waist and pull hard. 'Tip number one for living your best life – leave the past behind and make a new start.'

Seeing he's taken the similarly extreme step of abandoning the city for a beach hut, I'd expected this to resonate enough to get a come-back. Not that I have any interest in his situation *at all*, which is good because his attention has moved to the china stacked on the table. 'Are you serving *breakfast?*'

I hesitate. 'I had a special request.' Then I remember I'm charging so much it's worth giving up my own serving. 'There's one portion left if you're interested?'

'I have clients due very soon, so I'd need that to take away. I'm also swimming without cash.' He slaps the non-existent pocket on his buttock, then smiles hopefully. 'I could pay when I returned the dish.' My eyes sting as I watch his palm collide with the place where his back pocket should be.

'Cup. It comes in a cup.' It's well worth me being hungry if I can wave him off and get on with the rest of my day. 'And it costs ten pounds.' It's not just inflation due to being the High Tides end of the beach. This really has to be a one-off. ' I'll get it now.'

And as I press the orange and brown cup into his hand and watch him dash across the dune a few minutes later, I promise myself this is my last-ever transaction.

Then my phone pings, and the message from Nell takes my mind to another level entirely.

Singles club pub and pie ramble tomorrow night! 7.30 at the Yellow Canary! I've told Kit about it!

When it comes to singles events, Nell doesn't take 'no' for an answer. How the hell can I get out of this?

A fake business, customers at dawn, a smoking-hot neighbour, and singles club to dodge – I'd have had more peace if I'd set up camp in Trafalgar Square.

6

The Hideaway, St Aidan
Runaway trains and things in drawers
Saturday

'Customers, so quickly!'

'Coming back for seconds, too!'

So much for low footfall at this end of the beach. With Nell, Plum, Clemmie, Sophie *and* three of her four kids joining Shadow and me for our early-morning beach walk, it's like high summer by the donut stall.

It's Saturday morning and the wind coming straight into our faces blows most of our conversation away, which means we pass the hotel without comment. It's only as we reach the castle at Comet Cove and turn around that we start to chat properly. As we head back towards St Aidan, suddenly no one's holding back with their enthusiasm for what's been happening on my veranda since Nell and Plum were last here. Secrets are hard to keep in St Aidan at the best of times. With Jean's #CocoPopswith *FlorenceMay@TheHideaway* Insta posts, my stealth mode was blown in two seconds flat.

And when Jean and Shirley promised to drop by again with their cash, no part of me thought they meant they'd come again today, even less that they'd be pleading for a second round of daybreak desserts. Shadow was still in bed and didn't bother to stir when they appeared at the French windows today, and me hopping around, pulling up my shorts, opening the door chewing on a toothbrush, finger-drying my hair trying to get ready for the gang to arrive wasn't my best look.

I have to protest before they get properly carried away. 'They're *not clients*, they're acquaintances. Ephemeral ones.'

Nell lets out a snort. 'Say that again in Cornish please, Mrs.'

I laugh. 'They're simply friends passing through, who *won't* be getting loyalty cards.' If I get my way, they won't be coming again either.

When did my life get this complicated? Here Shadow and I are, tripping over seaweed strands, kicking through salty shingle, when we should still be snoozing under the duvet. All because the only way I could distract Nell from her singles club event last night was by suggesting a morning outing with her and Clemmie instead, which everyone else decided to join in too.

Plum gives me a sideways glance. 'So what exactly is *toffee crackle?*'

I'm not even sure what she's doing here when she should be opening her gallery. It's hard to sound like a bake-off contestant when I threw today's mix together even faster than yesterday. 'Teensy scoops of salted caramel ice cream, and Crunchy Nut Cornflake garnish. With a plastic flamingo to finish and a dribble of carton custard – in a cup, because that's all I had.' And even though I was rushing, I did ask about allergies.

'If I hadn't had three bacon baps at Clemmie's already, I'd have needed one myself.' Nell's licking her lips as she strides along the tide line, pausing every now and then to throw sticks for Clemmie's dog Diesel, while Shadow looks on with a mix of disdain and disbelief, except when the waves come too close, and then he starts barking at the sea.

Clemmie's grinning at me over the top of Arnie, who's tucked in a sling on her front. 'I can't fault you on the embellishment.'

I can't take all the credit for that. 'Ivy's drawers are bursting with them. The best part is they're reusable.' Not that I'll be exploiting that, because this was definitely my last hurrah.

Milla, Sophie's teenage daughter, re-ties her silky blonde hair in a scrunchie, then catches her younger sister Tilly's hand, and they fall into step beside me. 'Would we be able to hold Shadow on the way back?' Her broad smile is as persuasive as her mum's. 'Tilly's never led a dog before, and I think she'd love it.'

Milla's very hard to say 'no' to, and why would I? She's always been an easy child who's shown emotional intelligence beyond her years and is endlessly patient and helpful with her three younger half-siblings. I can't ever remember a time when she's been naughty, and she's slid into adolescence like a dream.

I smile at her. 'The sea makes Shadow so jumpy that I bought him a long leash.' So far, it's stayed coiled in my hand, because he's glued to my knee so he can dive for cover if he meets anything scary. I unwind the lead, keep hold of the loop and hand the rest over to Milla. 'There, you can both lead him.

Hang on tight though, he might tug suddenly if the waves come up the beach.'

Sophie is laughing. 'I never thought you'd be a helicopter parent, Flossie!'

I pull a face because she's right. 'I've only had Shadow a few months, I'm a very anxious mum. The move has unsettled him – he never barked in London!'

Nell throws another stick for Diesel. 'Don't worry, he'll soon find his sea-paws.' She gives a sniff. 'He's not the only reluctant new resident – Kit passed on the singles' pie night yesterday too.'

I can't knock him for that. Me not wanting to go is why we're all here now.

Plum laughs. 'Being realistic, he'll hardly want to leave his swanky hotel hut to hang out at the Yellow Canary, even if their pies are award-winning.'

Sophie looks dreamy. 'Their sweets are amazing. And the sticky toffee pudding is to die for. Just saying.'

Clemmie gives a low moan. 'The ginger cheesecake too...'

By the time they've worked their way down the entire dessert menu and gushed over the stupendous cherry Bakewell tart and the out-of-this-world lemon meringue drizzle, the hotel is coming into view again.

Hand on heart, I'm concentrating more on the icing sugar dusting on puff pastry cream slices they've just described than on Shadow, who's been happily trotting beside Tilly and Milla, without any of his usual barking because the rest of us have blocked his view of the scary sea. So when a freak wave rolls up the beach and we all scatter as it crashes over our feet, the tug on the lead in my hand takes me by surprise. A moment later there's one loud bark, and Shadow is gone, haring off into the dunes, his lead trailing behind him.

I curse under my breath, and when I see his bounding shape weaving between the skinny cypress trees that edge the hotel lawns I groan. 'The last thing I want is him running loose in the High Tide grounds!'

I start to run and a few yards later my chest starts to burn, reminding me of how unfit I am. Plum, Sophie, Milla, Tilly and Maisie have joined the chase too, all dashing along the sand beside me. As we come to the wide walkway that marks the hotel's path to the beach, I catch sight of a familiar figure up by the buildings, and before I can stop myself I'm yelling, 'Kit! Shadow's escaped! If you see him, please can you grab him?'

He pauses to scan the space, then as he hurries across the slope above the beach Shadow comes into view again, galloping across the grass. Kit makes a beeline for him and launches himself at the dog. For a moment Shadow's held in Kit's full-length rugby tackle, but a wriggle later he bursts free, and zig-zags through the box bushes, his lead still trailing behind him. Kit springs to his feet, and as Shadow heads for the flat gravelled parking area another figure appears. Kit yells, 'Get the dog, Rye!'

Shadow hurls himself down the steps, sending box plants in pots flying in all directions, and simultaneously the man Kit was calling to steps out from between two parked cars, and into Shadow's path. A second later he's scooped Shadow up, and he's clutching him to his body, laughing across at Kit.

'Nice tackle there, mate, bad luck for missing him.'

As we come closer, I'm taking in a jacket with epaulettes and trousers with creases. I'm kicking myself for letting Shadow go as I wail, 'Just my luck to rock up next to a hotel with a dedicated dog warden!' A strong one too, from the way he's holding forty kilos of dog as if he weighs nothing.

Plum rolls her eyes. 'Get real, Floss, a uniform that snappy in a luxury establishment car park? It's clearly the man who does the valet parking.' She turns to him and flashes a hundred-watt smile. 'I'm right, aren't I?'

It's not only her smile that's lighting up. She's wiggling too, tossing her ponytail, and sticking out her chest for all she's worth, which is completely unlike Plum.

As Kit hurries across to join us, I let out another wail. 'And look at you, with your shirt covered in mud! I'm *so* sorry!'

He rests his hand on my shoulder and shakes his head. 'No worries, I have a hundred more back at my beach huts, all clean and ironed.' A smile spreads across his face as he lets his hand fall again. 'Joking there, obviously.'

The guy holding Shadow laughs. 'He's not. They're why he needs two huts.'

Kit shakes his head. 'Stop giving away my secret vices! Parking valet, that's a good one!' He smiles at us. 'This is Rye Radley, another London escapee, who has known me long enough to count my shirts and judge my wardrobe.'

Plum's voice is breathy. 'Good to meet you, Rye Radley. Nice alliteration you've got going on there.'

Nell, Clemmie and Diesel arrive in time to catch the tail-end of that crazy comment, and Nell chimes in. 'Stuff alliteration, this is the best news ever for the singles club! Two new guys in town means double the excitement! Old friends, too! You can come to events together.'

I'm holding my breath. If there are partners around, or back in London, this would be the moment to mention them.

Milla puts her finger up. 'You don't have to be single either, in St Aidan everyone joins in, regardless of status.'

Damn.

Kit pulls a face. 'We'll get back to you on that.'

Rye Radley grins. 'Come on, Kit, you promised you'd stop being a workaholic and start being an extrovert once you came to Cornwall.' He rolls his eyes. 'And to set the record straight, I'm not an animal trainer. I'm heading off for my induction as a part-time fireman, which is why I'm in uniform.'

Nell's eyes are shining. 'Better and better! There's a lot of love in St Aidan for our emergency service workers.'

Sophie's muttering in my ear. 'Especially ones who are "built" and could work as Matt Damon's body double. Have you seen Plum? We need to get out of here before she melts into a puddle at his feet or starts licking his face.'

Clemmie's taking a lead on this. 'First things first. Rye, how about you put Shadow down, and let Floss get hold of him.'

Whatever Sophie says about Plum, I can't get out of here soon enough either. I'd intended to keep as far away from Kit as possible, not become inadvertently indebted to him and his bestie, while looking like an irresponsible dog owner to boot. I step forward and take a firm hold of Shadow's lead. 'Thank you so much for your help, gentlemen, we can take this from here.'

Then I step back, and as Rye puts Shadow back on the ground, in the split second before he launches himself at me, I notice the sand and sea-water stains all down Rye's front.

'Here, let me brush you down.' Plum steps forward, hands outstretched.

But before she makes contact Sophie comes in sideways and

shoves her out of the way. 'I'm sure Rye can manage that on his own, Plum.'

I'm in a full body hug with Shadow, but even his paws on my shoulders can't stop me dying inside for the mess I've caused. 'Obviously I'll pay for the cleaning.'

Nell joins in. 'Go to Iron Maidens and ask for Jenny; she'll speed it through for you.'

I'm doing some shoving of my own, to move everyone on. 'Give me a shout about the bill. We'll let you get on with your day.' I turn to the gang and murmur the words guaranteed to get them going. 'How about elevenses back at mine?' And the next moment we're back out on the sand, racing back to The Hideaway.

Milla falls into step beside Shadow and me as we kick our way past the seaweed piles. 'Did you sense a vibe back there, Aunty Florence?'

I smile. She's so perceptive. 'Plum's very picky with her men, but those muscles under that uniform definitely woke *something* up back there.'

Milla laughs. 'Not Plum. I meant you and Kit. They were high-voltage sparks if ever I saw them!'

'*Sparks? High voltage?*'

Whatever I said about Milla's emotional maturity, scrub that. She's got this entirely wrong.

7

The Hideaway, St Aidan
Dogs and bones
Saturday

'Mum, can *we* have a dog?'

Apart from Plum, who's gone off to open the gallery, half an hour later we're all crowded onto The Hideaway's front veranda, dipping into ice cream served in cups, which seemed a small price to pay to hurry us away from the hotel. But when Sophie hears Milla's question her spoon stops short of her mouth.

Being Sophie, she collects herself in two seconds flat. 'That's a lovely thought, sweetie. But we don't have the room.'

Milla tosses her head. 'We all know that's bollocks! I can see the castle from here, it's big enough to house a Husky pack.'

Milla's always been encouraged to be forthright and express her opinions, but there's an edge to her voice here that's new.

When I think of the teenage rebels Sophie and I were, I realise it was bound to happen.

Sophie's eyes snap open wide. 'Can you *please* watch your language in front of the babies! We simply don't have *space in our life* for a dog.'

Sophie's never had much empathy with animals. As kids I was the one with the rabbits running round the kitchen while she was the one complaining about the poop on the bottom of her ballet shoes, so I sympathise with Milla.

'Why not share Shadow with me, Mills? We're always up for company on walks.'

'Thank you, Floss.' Sophie gives a relieved eye-roll. 'So now that's sorted, are the guys next door besties or a couple? And did anyone else notice Plum?'

The small matter of Kit's super-attractive fiancée – now possibly wife – Violetta, whose name crashed back into my head at three this morning, could be the decider. But I'm not about to throw that into the public domain now.

Milla grins at me. 'I'd love to help with Shadow.' Her smile widens. 'And Kit might be prissy with his shirts, but judging from his reactions earlier, he's definitely into girls.'

Clemmie sighs. 'Let's hope for Plum's sake Rye's the same.'

Milla's still looking at me. 'Your beach hut is great, Aunty Floss, but you could take it a lot further with the right accessories.'

This time it's my ice-cream spoon halted in mid-air, but put on the spot, I'm reacting as fast as Sophie did. 'Moving is an expensive time, I'll do more when I've saved up.'

Milla's rolling her eyes at me. 'Mum spent a fortune

zhuzhing the castle, but you don't have to buy new. Everything in my room came from charity shops and Freecycle.'

Sophie sticks out her chin. 'Before you start banging on about repurposing, Milla, I'm recycling an *entire building*, remember.'

Milla's shaking her head. 'No need to get your Spanks in a knot, Mum, I'm only saying if my friends and I come *here* for our girlie get-together next weekend instead of ours, we can give Aunty Florence some practical suggestions.'

I can't help interrupting. 'You wear *support pants, Soph?*' Of all of us here, there's not an inch to spare on her neat, trim frame. As for baby weight, she's that rare kind of woman who snaps back to her pre-pregnancy shape the second she jogs out of the maternity ward.

Sophie rolls her eyes. 'Believe me, after four babies I need them.' Then her face falls as she turns to Milla. 'Your pampering day was about trying out *my* new teen range *at home!*'

Milla blows out a breath. 'But it's so pretty here. And there are the landscape guys next door at the hotel too...'

Sophie does a double take. '*Gardeners?*'

Milla lets out a sigh. 'The hot sixth formers all got Saturday jobs tidying the grounds.' She doesn't leave space for a reply. 'Don't make it a big deal, Mum. Aunty Florence is the new face of the Little Cornish Kitchen and we'll be helping her make the beach hut the best it can be.'

It seems no time since Milla was Arnie's size. I was finishing sixth form and Sophie was in her final year at uni when she had her, and holding Milla in my arms the day she was born is one of the most wondrous moments of my life to date. I'm blinking back the tears as I think of how small she was. How I held her on my chest, all snuffly in her stripy Babygro.

Milla's sensing Sophie's weakening. 'I ran it past Aunty Florence earlier, and she's fine with it.'

I'm opening and closing my mouth, not wanting to betray either of them.

Sophie looks up at the sky, then relents. 'So long as you promise not to entertain hotel staff at the beach hut – okay, we can relocate here.'

Milla winces. 'You don't *actually* need to be here *in person*, Mum.' She hesitates. 'Weren't you the one telling Aunty Flo *not* to be a helicopter parent?'

Sophie's sending me the kind of 'what the hell?' glance I'm not used to. 'Aunty Floss might not be strong enough to manage six of you. She has been ill.'

Milla gives a defiant glance. 'And she's fully recovered and cancer-free! She doesn't want to be an invalid for ever!'

I'll never be as robust as I was before, but she has a point – all I want now is to be normal.

Sophie rolls her eyes at me. 'I'll ask Mum to give you a hand.' She hesitates. 'Or better still, you ask. She always responds better to you than me.'

We both know our mum's unlikely to be free at short notice, but if it gives Sophie a sense of control, that's fine.

Clemmie leans across to me. 'If your mum can't make it, the rest of us will cover.' She turns to Milla. 'How many are coming?'

Milla counts on her fingers. 'Now the venue's been upgraded, probably ten!'

I grin around at them. 'So many girls on my deck, what a great way to spend a Saturday!'

Milla squeezes my hand as tightly as she did when she was three. 'We'll obviously need to come inside too. *That will be okay?*'

'Of course.' The words are out before I have time to think if Shadow and I *really* want to share our space with that many excitable adolescents, but we have a whole week to get used to the idea.

Milla's spikiness has melted away as she smiles at Sophie. 'Don't worry, we'll come home for our sleepover. Then we can binge-watch *Emily in Paris*, *Sex Education* and *Happy Feet*.'

None of this is what I'd planned, but listening to that list, I suspect I got the easy part of this bargain.

MAY

8

The Hideaway, St Aidan
Bumpy roads and rocky mornings
Wednesday

Ten girls at The Hideaway for a day? When I'd intended to be winding down not up! Not that I'm panicking when I rush off to Penzance to buy art supplies, it's more that I'm investing in a bit of forward planning. Back in the day Milla would fold paper for England – it might be too much to hope she'd be thrilled to do it again, but if they're feeling crafty, I could warm to a few origami seagulls strung across my wall.

I'm just edging my Mini past the hotel and along the lane on the way home, thinking that if paper birds were the extent of my accessorising, I could live with that too, when a figure leaps out in front of the car, waving their arms.

I mutter to Shadow as I wind down the window. 'I'd recognise those snow-white sleeves anywhere.' Then I arrange a suitably bright smile for the man himself. 'Kit, how can I help? If there's a woman in labour, I'm happy to take off my T-shirt.' *What the hell made me say that?*

He runs his hands through his hair, which is more dishevelled than usual. 'I'm afraid it's way worse than unplanned childbirth – my ten o'clock appointment has gone AWOL.'

I glance at my watch, thinking he's being overdramatic. 'As it's almost eleven they could be a no-show?'

'People pay so much upfront, they always arrive. These two checked in at reception and *then* disappeared.' The groan he lets out is very unlike him. 'I *so* need this to go well, they're influencers, with a massive following...'

'High stakes then. You can't afford to lose these two in the dunes.'

He frowns at me through the window. 'Can I put my number on your phone, then you can ring me if you see them?'

I pass him my mobile. 'Any distinguishing features?' I'm not sure if the butterflies in my chest are due to the hollows under his cheekbones, or the novelty of someone giving me their deets, which hasn't happened in a hundred years.

'Man and a woman, in their thirties, impossibly cool – that's as much as I know.'

It could be worse, at least they're not fanny flutters I'm getting. 'And very much in love, no doubt.' I look at him over my sunnies and try not to sound cynical. 'I'll be in touch the moment there's a sighting.' But as I take back my phone, I'm not holding out any hope.

By the time I've wound up the window he's running back towards the hotel and I carry on to my parking area, which is as windswept as usual, but otherwise empty. As I drag my shopping bags across the sand hills, Shadow is tugging ahead on his lead and I'm regretting buying so many heavy baking ingredients. Hands in the air, I admit I'm more worried about Saturday than I'm letting on – but if all else fails, M&M cookies will be my fall-back position.

As for our mum coming to help, she's as overstretched as any of us – obviously not including my leisure-rich self in that sweeping statement. She's been a single mum for almost my whole life because our dad left when I was so young I barely remember him. I have a picture in my head of Sophie sitting on his knee in the armchair by the fire in the tiny fisherman's cottage up on the cliff where we lived at the time; they were both blonde and Sophie liked to press her temple next to his to compare their hair colour. Mum was blonde too, but she never did it with her.

It must have been hard for Mum, on her own with two small girls. But she was fiercely independent and worked as many jobs as she needed to make sure we never went without, and she's never really stopped since. Eventually she did up the cottage, sold it at a profit and stumbled on a way to marry her artistic side with her business savvy. Since then she's done up a handful of properties up and down the coast, but because she's so driven, she's more likely to be up to her ears in building rubble than out enjoying herself.

Between us, I think our dad walking out put her off relationships. Even though she scrubs up great once she takes off her overalls, much to Nell's frustration with her singles club agenda, Mum's more likely to be out hunting the perfect colour of Annie

Sloan chalk paint than chasing down a perfect guy. She decided thirty years ago that men were a waste of time and space, and no one since has given her reason to change that opinion. When it comes to dating, she insists that she has an open mind – but we all know she hasn't. Even though she doesn't go on dates, I'll still be lucky to pin her down for next weekend.

As Shadow and I make our way towards the little gate in the picket fence I juggle the bags to let us through. 'Every time we come back it feels more like home, don't you think?' Shadow wags in agreement, although to be fair he's the kind of dog who wags at most things I say, and pulls towards the back veranda entrance that faces the lane. Just before we go in, I take a look along the dune tops and the reed clumps moving in the breeze. 'No lost couples on this horizon.'

As the bags thud down on the kitchen floor, I'm pondering if I should text Kit to say I *haven't* seen anyone, or is that an unconscious ploy to get my number into *his* phone? Then Shadow's bark at the front window puts an end to my agonising.

I shout through. 'Come on, Shadow, the sea isn't *that* much nearer than it was when we went out. I'll show you as soon as I've put things away.' As his barks get more frantic, I abandon my bags of flour and sugar, but when I join him by the doors and look beyond the front deck railings I'm apologising. 'Sorry, mate, you're right again! I wonder if these are Kit's lost clients?'

They certainly look beautiful enough to be. *And* they're holding hands. I try not to let either of those things make me cross, because I can do without prickles on the back of my neck. Even if they've booked into the High Tides, they still look like they're trying too hard for a blowy day in St Aidan.

The guy's in an undeniably gorgeous vintage Burberry mac, and as he holds out his hand to greet me, his smile is warm (tick one) and he hasn't got a hipster beard (tick two). 'We're Victor and Amery, what a wonderful place you have here.' (Tick three, and that unexpected compliment confirms I'm going to do everything in my power to help them.)

The woman pulls her choppy blonde hair into a knot on top of her head, but it immediately escapes and blows across her face. 'We thought there was no one home. I hope you don't mind, we've been taking a few selfies by your fence.' I hope her lovely foundation and perfect pink lippy are driving-rain-proof, because that's what's on the forecast for later when they should be lolling on the sand with Kit capturing their happy moments.

The guy joins in. 'The boarding on your hut is so weathered and authentic, we had to come and inspect it up close.'

I shrug and glance at the peeling paint. 'You don't get any more genuine than this.' Being praised for The Hideaway's shabbiness is a whole new thing for me. 'I hope you don't mind me asking – do you have an appointment at the hotel?'

They exchange glances, then the guy begins. 'We do, but it's a bit shiny for us there. We headed straight over here for a breath of fresh air and a burst of reality.'

The woman picks up the theme. 'Neat isn't really our thing.' She takes a breath. 'We run the V&A Vintage & Awesome social pages, so we're all about old and battered.'

I can't hold it in. 'I love your cowboy boots.' I've drooled over the same style myself on eBay. This pair are well worn and the hem of her swishy flowery cotton dress is billowing around them.

She pulls her bleached denim blazer close around her body. 'Genuine Russell and Bromley Rockafellas.' As she looks down at the scuffed suede and coils of studded straps she gives a shiver so big I have to ask.

'Are you cold?'

She pulls a face. 'My bad, gale-force winds were another not-so-good surprise.' Her sigh is loud enough to hear above the crash of the iron-grey breakers. 'When I talked Vic into this I was looking at pictures of a topaz sky with sea to match. With clouds and the ocean both black, I feel like I've made a horrible mistake.'

It bursts out of me. 'Hell, no! Truly, you haven't! Even on cloudy days Kit's rings are amazing!' I can sense these influential influencers are about to run, and however much I'd rather he wasn't parading his lovey-dovey couples under my nose, I'm still going to work my socks off to stop these two slipping through his fingers. 'Why not come in and warm up by the stove? You can have a hot chocolate while I locate him.' It's the last thing I want, but now it's out there's no going back.

With the promise of heat Amery's tense expression eases. 'If you're sure you don't mind, that would be amazing.'

Vic smiles too. 'Could I take a few more close-ups of the beach hut too?' He gives a grimace. 'I'm not sure the hotel will give us the kind of shots our followers are after.'

Amery gives him a nudge as she follows me into my living room. 'I know today should be about us, but sharing our life's details are what we do, and our honesty makes us popular.' Her face breaks into a big smile as she sits on the corner sofa and holds her hands out towards the wood burner. 'Now *this is* the kind of place I imagined we'd be designing our rings.'

I message Kit as I heat up the milk in the kitchen.

Your ten o clocks are at mine.

I don't want to be disloyal to Victor and Amery, but it's only fair to warn him so I add:

They're a bit cranky.

His reply pings back.

I'll be straight across.

I don't want to tell him what to do, but I can hint.

On my sofa waiting for hot drinks AWS. Suspect High Tides isn't their bag – maybe bring your work stuff here?

Another ping.

Gotcha. Be there in two.

Let's hope he means seconds not hours.

I take in Shadow's look of horror as he watches me put a plateful of our newly bought favourite biscuits on the tray beside a jug of frothy hot chocolate and two mismatched cups. 'Don't worry – we'll get more this afternoon,' I say to him quietly.

Victor's eyes light up as brightly as Shadow's do when he spies the plate arriving on the table in front of Amery. 'Teatime

Assorted! The perfect retro choice for this mid-century home! Don't touch anything until I've snapped them!'

I laugh. 'Don't take too long, or Shadow may expire.' I give him a hard stare because he knows the rules. 'No begging when we have visitors! And definitely no dribbling on their nice boots either!'

If I didn't know better, I'd swear that he's frowning. Then, beyond his eyebrows, I spot movement on the deck. 'Here's another visitor!' I smile reassuringly at Vic, who's finally settling down beside Amery, and heave my own silent sigh of relief. 'Kit's here now. I knew he wouldn't be long.'

As I open the French doors Kit strides across to meet the couple. He drops his laptop and camera bag on the bleached plank side table and shrugs off a dark overcoat he's added since I last saw him. Cashmere on the beach? What is the man thinking? Except he's right because it's perishing for the time of year, which is the first thing he's commiserating about with Amery and Victor.

I might as well step in and see if I can help to salvage the situation. Push Victor and Amery into committing before they have time to pull out. 'As it's blowing a force ten out there, why not discuss your designs and take any initial photos here?' I already know the process. 'Fingers crossed, the wind will have dropped by the time you get to dash across to Kit's workshop to deal with the practical side.'

It definitely won't, but no one needs to know that.

Amery takes my bait and jumps in. 'We were hoping for matching rings with a hammered finish, in recycled gold, if that's possible?'

'Absolutely.' Kit's already next to Amery, his laptop open,

the screens flashing up super-fast with the hotel's superior WIFI signal. He looks up at me. 'Great plan, Florence. And thanks for lending us your lovely beach hut for this morning.' He smiles then turns back to Amery, who looks like she's bursting with another question.

'We will be able to come back here for afternoon tea?'

Kit's agonised expression says it all as he turns to me. 'How do you feel about that, Florence? Does that fit with you?'

I'm peering at the one teapot in the kitchen, thinking on my feet. 'Obviously anything I'd do here would be much more simple than you'd get at the hotel – or you might enjoy the main branch of the Little Cornish Kitchen, which is very much your style and just along the beach.'

Amery's eyes are open wide. 'I know I'm biased, but your place is *so* cosy, and Vic's photos are *the best*! You'd feature on our blog even more if we had tea here!'

It's years since I baked, but there's something about their sheer enthusiasm that pushes me over the edge. 'Would warm buttered scones and strawberry jam work for you? And a nice pot of Yorkshire Gold?' Even I should be able to manage that. 'I'll work my alchemy here while you do yours next door.'

Kit's eyebrows shoot up. 'Making wedding rings is science, Florence, not alchemy. There's a big difference.'

It strikes me he might need to chill. Hang more loosely. Ditch the trouser creases and get that tight, gorgeous ass of his into a pair of ripped, bleached jeans.

And in case anyone saw that shudder, it was definitely a shiver due to the cold draughts seeping through the cracks in the hut, not a flutter where there shouldn't be one due to that last unwelcome image in my head. I jump again as I hear my phone ping. It's from Kit.

I owe you for this, big time. Name your price.

I blank out the vision of him lying on my bed as fast as it flashes in. My sex drive left the building years ago when I lost my ovaries, so that's a doubly crazy thing to imagine. Yet another reason from the very long list of why dating for me is firmly off the table. When you've had surgery in the places that I have, in the unlikely event you did feel the urge, the practicalities were problematic too. If I wrote on my Tinder profile, *Sex can be excruciatingly painful, I prefer to avoid it,* I'd get swipe left every time.

I dip into the kitchen and hide behind the outsize double fridge so no one sees me tapping the reply.

You haven't tasted the scones yet.

There's another ping.

I'm sure they'll be delicious.

Which is more than I am.

FFS Mr Ashton, stop texting me and deal with your clients!

Another ping I didn't want to hear.

*If this is you being assertive and professional I'm
impressed. Or are you St Aidan's secret dominatrix?*

There's no easy answer to that, so I change the subject.

My prices are astronomical, don't forget.

Yet another ping.

*Amery says please can we have sultana scones. I'll go
with that too.*

I'm rolling my eyes.

YOU want a cream tea?

*How else am I going to know if the baking is worth the
extortion?*

WTAF? This man is too much.

*Get back to me tomorrow if it all goes well. Shadow and I
are off to buy clotted cream.*

*Thanks! That last thought will see me through what
could be a very stressful day.*

Damn. I did not think that one through!

Don't worry, Floss, you're going to nail this x

I can't be the only one who *has* to have the last word in a text exchange?

Back at ya x

As for those pesky *x*'s, how did they come into this? And why did I follow suit?

But there's no time to worry about that now! I need to get on Google and find some scone recipes!

9

Trenowden Trenowden Trenowden, The Harbourside, St Aidan
Home truths and a sweet tooth
Thursday

The morning after what I'm now calling 'the V&A debacle', Kit came around first thing and pressed a bundle of twenty-pound notes into my hands. And later a card and a lovely hand-tied bouquet arrived from Amery and Vic too. So even though I've put that day behind me, I'm still smelling the roses, real and proverbial.

Later that afternoon Nell drags me to her other half's office down on the harbourside, saying she's gasping for a cup of tea and that George needs to see me too. As George was acting for Ivy with the sale of the beach hut, I used a solicitor from Stoke Newington High Street, so I'm assuming George has something else to pass on from Ivy – fingers crossed it's a key for the padlock on the little outside toilet behind the hut, as that's the only thing still outstanding.

Lucky for us, Trenowden Trenowden Trenowden, Solicitors, is a dog-friendly office. The minute George sees that we've come with confectionery he brushes away my concerns about Shadow's trail of sandy paw marks on the deep-pile carpet and shows me to a smart leather tub chair while Nell commandeers his huge executive swivel.

She rubs her bump then slides a cardboard box from the bakery down onto the gigantic oak desk. 'Is it daft how much I'm longing for George to have a picture of our baby to put on here?'

George gives her a hug, steps back as his assistant brings in some mugs of tea, then nods at me. 'Would you like to open the cakes, Floss?'

When I undo the string, pop up the box lid and breathe in the smell of confectioner's custard and fresh strawberries I give Shadow a run for his money with my drooling. 'I'd forgotten how delicious Crusty Cob's fruit tarts are. I don't know why I struggled to make scones the other day when I could have bought them from there or Clemmie's.'

Nell grins. 'Now you've done your first home baking, you won't look back. Something tells me those customers were pretty picky and you came through for them.' She watches me closely. 'They wouldn't have sent flowers if they weren't happy.'

I pull a face as I remember. Considering how small and crusty the scones looked, Vic and Amery were remarkably kind about them. 'Next time I'd use a bigger cutter, roll the mixture thicker and make more of them.'

'More?' George's left eyebrow goes up. 'If you're making them again, let us know when, and we'll be there!'

I need to make myself clearer. 'I was talking hypothetically.

Those scones were a one-off in someone else's emergency, there *won't* be a repeat performance.'

Nell lets out a shriek. 'There you go again, Mrs, spouting your fancy London bollocks that no one understands.' Her eyes twinkle. 'If George doesn't stop eating for two he's not going to fit behind his desk.'

I laugh. 'I won't be baking for the public again, so you don't need to worry about your waistlines.'

Nell helps herself to a profiterole, George takes a cream horn and I sink my teeth into a tart and decide to move this on.

'So, Nell says you may have a key for me, George?'

George brushes a pastry flake off his chin and gives me a hard stare. 'I didn't ask you here to talk about locks.'

'Damn.' I can't help myself. 'I don't know why I'm disappointed, I don't even use the outside loo.'

George clears his throat. 'If it's the toilet door you're worried about, I'll send a locksmith along tomorrow. This is another matter entirely. Something quite unexpected, in fact.'

Nell's eyes are like saucers. 'Well, don't keep us in suspense, George! Hurry up and tell us what it is!'

George presses his fingertips together. 'David Byron, from the High Tides Hotel, has asked me to let you know that he is interested in buying your beach hut and the surrounding land.'

My gasp doesn't express the kick-in-the-guts feeling this has brought on. 'Excuse me?'

George's tone is measured. 'He would have tried to buy it previously, but it didn't ever reach the open market.'

I give a sniff. 'You mean Ivy wouldn't sell to him?'

Nell's eyes are flashing. 'And good for Ivy for selling to someone local.'

'I'm hardly...'

Nell shushes me. 'David Byron is from Australia and so long as we overlook your fancy London expressions, you're Cornish through and through.'

George's nod is hardly perceptible. 'He claims to have lived here at one time, though I've yet to meet anyone who remembers him. But the sum Mr Byron is offering for your hut is substantial. It would be more than enough for you to buy a much larger, more comfortable cottage in the town.'

Nell's flapping her hands in front of her face. She's an accountant, and she can't hide that there are pound signs flashing through her head. 'Stone the crows! You'll triple your money at least! That's better than a key to an outside carsey!'

I'm not sure I'd agree. 'A place in town?' I should be delighted. In fact I can't understand why I'm not. Then I look down at Shadow, curled up on my foot, and think about the way we run along our bit of the beach together. How gloriously empty it is. The way the grasses bend on the dunes. How he's gaining his confidence a little more each day. There is one thing I can concede. 'It's true, when the wind blows straight off the sea, the living room lampshade spins – but I'm just not sure town is where I want to be.'

George is nodding. 'There's no pressure. Mr Byron simply perceives that your land is worth much more to him than to you, and in view of that he's willing to be extra generous. What happens next is entirely up to you.'

Nell reaches for my hand across the table, and her squeeze is reassuring. 'We can have a look at what's out there. Your mum can help too. See if there's anything that catches your eye.'

'Absolutely.' I'm bullshitting. All I can see in my head is

acres of Teletubby grass stretching right along the dunes, because if I give in here, the other huts will no doubt fall like dominoes, too. And most annoying of all – I'm also sounding like bloody Kit.

Nell's leaning across the desk. 'I've lost count of how many years I've been trying to get your mum out on a date with the director of Hansons and Hansons estate agents. This could be our big chance.'

This is St Aidan. Nothing is straightforward, everything is multi-layered, and there are ulterior motives around every corner. But as a native I should know that.

'Great!' I say. It isn't at all. 'We'll get onto it after the weekend. But first things first – we've got Milla's pampering day to organise.'

And with the complication that's just been thrown into my path, being over-run by teenagers intent on making the beach hut into something it isn't should be the least of my worries.

10

The Hideaway, St Aidan
Colour swatches and quick changes
Saturday

It's funny what you dread. I've been quaking inside for an entire week, and now Milla and the girls are all here, wafting in and out, so far it's going without any major hitches. The best thing is that as they arrived this morning, the sun burst from behind a fluffy white cloud and warmed the beach and gave us a taste of the endless summer we hope will soon be here.

It's also funny what you forget. I was totally unprepared for them storming through into the living room, all stripping off, and five minutes later appearing in entirely different clothes from the ones they arrived in.

I frown at Milla as they file back out into the sun, some of them still doing up their buttons. 'What just happened there?'

Milla looks at the sky and takes a breath. 'We all like each other's clothes better than our own and swapping for a day saves us having to buy new stuff.'

I'm staring at their feet. 'You even changed shoes?'

Milla grins. 'We do that at school too. You must have done it when you were our age?'

I laugh. 'I was too much of a beanpole to swap jeans. But now I think about it, I was in love with Fiona Cameron's velvet frock coat, and she'd happily wear my beaten-up biker jacket.'

Sara gives Milla a nudge. 'Any sign of Tyler or the crew next door?'

Milla pulls a face. 'Ty's younger sister said they're on afternoon shift this weekend, so they won't arrive for *hours* yet. Let's concentrate on Aunty Florence's beach hut make-over.'

Thanks to the gardeners only starting work at High Tides at two, we spend a very relaxed and homely morning, with everyone spreading through the hut and out onto the decks. Sure, they dip in and out of activities, but even Sophie on a critical day wouldn't find fault with their focus and productivity.

By the time Clemmie arrives with picnic hampers of sandwiches and sausage rolls for lunch there are paper bluebirds hanging on a bunch of driftwood twigs gathered from the beach, propped up in a reclaimed clam basket filled with stones, with their more colourful relatives strung in loops across the central wall. Several girls have impressive new hair styles, nails have been buffed and polished in a rainbow of colours, enough chocolate brownies have been made to feed everyone for elevenses, and still leave enough for a big stack by the steps to the veranda, nestled on a tray under a large glass dome.

Obviously these are for personal consumption, but such is the dedication of our women-of-the-future that they leave nothing to chance. So there's also a price ticket and a pile of serviettes under a stone and a Bonne Maman jam jar, for any passing person who's brave enough to part with their cash in return for the stickiest cakes this side of Southampton.

Once all the empty sandwich bags have been collected up and tidied into my recycling bin, Shadow has a shampoo, blow dry and groom, which I *think* he enjoys, in spite of the side-eye. And then they set to work filling in score sheets for all of Sophie's products. Shamed by all the activity I slide into the kitchen and make a double batch of M&M cookies, joined by two of Milla's friends for moral support and washing up. It's such fun we actually make another batch of brownies too.

I can't remember exactly when I stopped baking, but it must have been around the time Dillon changed to his job as a specialist loss adjuster. He and his colleagues had so many expense-account meals in ever more upmarket venues that nothing made by a normal person cooking in a humble flat kitchen stood the remotest chance of getting a second glance, let alone getting eaten. The moment he got that promotion, food had to be as obscure and rarefied as Heston Blumenthal's or forget it. It was quite a transformation; the night we met under a bush in the St Aidan pleasure gardens, he was happy to eat chips and curry sauce out of a polystyrene tray.

I remember his new-style mates all being round at ours before some sporting event where they were heading for a hospitality box. I was dipping into the fridge, grabbing a quick snack, and not wanting to be selfish I inadvertently offered round my New York cheesecake. Wrong! If I'd asked them to eat a cow pat from Nell's parents' farm they couldn't have looked more dismissive.

Talking of men with more money than manners, that leads me on nicely to the offer to buy the hut. Despite it looking like a cracking opportunity for someone who – let's face it – is living in a house with a roof that looks like it may lift off in the next big gust, I'm less delighted than people think I should be.

If anything I'm angry that Ivy went to all this trouble to keep the hut out of the wrong hands, only to find the local magnate is trying to buy me off. It's like someone – i.e. Dave Byron – thinks money will open any door. But it's not going to open mine! Not if I can help it.

The other thing it has done is make me prickle with rage every time I see Kit. I know he's not involved directly, but as part of that whole next-door set-up, he's implicated. I can't help thinking of him as just another incomer, here on the make – so until he shows me otherwise, it's probably best if I avoid him. Fine, his friend caught Shadow, but as I saved his social media stars from going rogue, that pretty much makes us quits. I can carry on my life without feeling I owe him anything.

As two o'clock approaches and the girls head down to the beach their screams go up a notch. The tide is out so they set up a volleyball net, using the excuse of firmer sand and a more level pitch to edge as far as they can towards the hotel grounds. Then they strip off their hoodies and start hurling themselves around, diving after the ball.

I murmur to Shadow as we watch them from the dune edge. 'If they carry on shrieking this loud, I'm going to be back in Kit's debt again before we can say "barking dog".' Not that I ever intend to think of him again.

As if to prove how wrong I can be, there's a ping on my phone, and dammit, it's Kit.

Any chance of some of those scones you made the other day?

I roll my eyes.

They were hard and rocky. Why would you want more?
We have very tasty brownies, for sale by the steps.

Rye's round, and he's hungry. For the record, we've
already demolished your brownie pile.

I turn around and see he's right.

Why aren't you working?

Ping.

Last minute cancellation due to illness.

Bad luck. Why not get scones from the hotel?

Ping.

Have you seen the menu? Lava cake and seaweed
pancakes won't touch the hunger pangs of a ravenous
part-time fireman. Will it help if I beg?

What the hell?

My niece is here with nine friends.

Ping.

So that explains the crowd. We thought it was Netflix casting for extras for a Baywatch *remake.*

No way I'm rising to that.
Ping.

You're not that busy if you're on the beach, playing with your phone. Not stalking, just saying. Please PLEASE PLEASE save us from hotel cakes. What kind of person wants sugar-free sponge?

I'm close to breaking.

It's going to cost you.

Ping.

Big numbers don't scare me – I deal in diamonds, don't forget.

Sometimes it's more effort to resist than to cave.

With sultanas?

Ping.

An unequivocal yes to dried fruit, and we'll take as many

as you can give us, Rye is a scone fiend. Pop round to pick them up in thirty?

That gives no time to mess up.

Make that an hour.

Ping.

We may have expired by then. But carry on anyway and if necessary our estates will settle on our behalf.

He's so up himself. It's going to take at least three M&M cookies to psych myself up for this. It's lucky I still have the recipe in the drawer from the other day, scribbled on the back of an envelope, just like Mum used to do. And this time I'll try to get them lighter and fatter.
   Ping.

Thanks, Floss x

It's going to take more than x's to get round me. For the record. Just saying. And I really don't want him calling me Floss. After what happened this week, he's nowhere near my friend category.

11

The Hideaway, St Aidan
Chelsea buns and other tight corners
Saturday

When Mum arrives at four o clock, I'm stacking the last of Kit's scones on a cooling tray in the little kitchen.

She breezes in and swoops me into a hug. 'Baking? Ivy will be so happy to hear you're using the kitchen.'

She's petite and blonde, like Sophie on speed, with a few more wrinkles and a lot less pale turquoise in her wardrobe. I'm assuming that like Nell and Plum earlier, she's only popping in briefly, because she's wearing her second-best painting overalls.

I'm frowning down at my scones. 'They're still not as fat as I'd like, but at least they're golden this time.' A lot less like rocks too.

'They smell delish.' Mum closes her eyes and breathes in the scent, then she snaps her eyes open again. 'I hope you're not upsetting yourself over that message you got the other day!'

'What's this?'

She pushes her fringe back off her forehead. 'Your offer from the hotel of course! It's scandalous, the whole of St Aidan is up in arms!'

There's no point asking how they know. Information here whistles down the wind faster than you can say 'pinot noir'.

My mum frowns. 'Ivy was clear, it's yours to sell if you wish. But if a sale *is* what you want, hold out for more and drive up the price!'

Wheeler-dealer isn't my style, but I need a clear reply to feed back to the village. 'I've already said no. I'll be staying where I am, and keeping the hotel at arm's length, along with everyone in there too.'

There's no point offering my mum a scone, as she's super strict about not eating between meals. But as she moves out into the living room she nods. 'Nice bird strings, Flossie! Wall-to-wall white is overrated, those dashes of colour make the place feel much more "you".'

'I've hardly done enough decorating to have my own style, Mum, but you're right.' I let my grin go. 'How can a few scraps of coloured paper make a place feel like home?'

She rubs her nose. 'I never felt the flats you and Dillon shared reflected you at all.'

I laugh. 'That's because they didn't. Dillon wouldn't have let paper birds within a mile of any place of his.'

Twee and whimsical were his pet hates – his idea of accessories was vintage Land Rover bonnets, random engine parts and large fossils. Dillon was also hooked on what he called his 'sand palette'. My one stand was to slip in a snowy White Company duvet cover, but that was buried under a mountain of baked-earth-coloured quilts and throws.

Looking back I feel like I spent the last ten years living in the kind of landscape the Dakar Rally crosses. That was another macho event on all of their bucket lists, although, between us, the extreme endurance and desire to rough it were all a bluff. I doubt they'd have lasted a day on the dunes here, let alone a fortnight driving across deserts, living like nomads.

Mum's moved to look out across the front deck to the sea. 'You were quirky though – back in the day.'

I stop to consider. 'When we first got together it was because Dillon liked how skinny I was.' He always went for thin women, which definitely isn't how I am now, but I can't help noticing the wistful tone in Mum's voice. 'Do you miss him?'

She agonises for a second. 'The family definitely feels smaller since you separated.' As she hesitates and fixes her eyes on the horizon, it's like she's trawling for the right words. 'What I miss most is having his parents and Plum round on Christmas Eve, and us going to Dillon's parents' on Boxing Day. And the get-togethers whenever you came home.' Her stare is still searching when she turns to me. 'How about you?'

I wasn't expecting the question to bounce straight back, but I might as well be honest. 'I miss being loved.'

She comes over and slides her arms around me. 'My poor baby. We need to teach you to love yourself better, and then you can look for someone else.' This is Mum through and through. She doesn't talk endlessly about emotions, but she gets straight to the heart of the problem.

I have to protest. 'Definitely not! From now on I'm going to learn from you, and fly solo.'

She purses her lips. 'Except I've never been *truly* on my own – I've always had you and Sophie travelling with me.' She draws a breath. 'There's a big difference.'

And that's so profound, I don't have an answer to it. I do have one more question though. 'Please tell me you aren't holding out for a reunion?'

She draws in a long breath. 'I know all the mermaids are, and for a long time I was too. But since you've been back here again, I'm less sure.' She squeezes my hand. 'From what Plum says, it sounds like that door is still open.'

None of them know the full truth about our split. So far Dill and I have been learning to live without each other with that get-together-again safety net always there but I know jumping into it wouldn't be right.

I shrug. 'I can't see myself in Dubai.' To be fair, I never saw myself in St Aidan either, but I don't want to get into that now.

There's another squeeze. 'If you're with the right person, where you are isn't important.'

And dammit for how wise my mum is considering how long she's been on her own. 'Are the girls okay down there?'

She nods. 'Are you expecting anyone, Floss? Because you seem to have Men in Black approaching your veranda.'

I shake my head in disbelief. How many guys does it take to carry a dozen scones? And whatever happened to kicking back when the client didn't show and losing the white shirts? 'It's the guys from next door, come to collect their baked goods.'

Mum frowns. 'I thought you'd cut ties with that awful place.'

I pull a face. 'I succumbed to extortion. It won't happen again after today.'

As they come in through the French windows their eyes are bright with expectation. I take the rolled-up note Kit presses into my hand, then move on to introductions.

'Kit and Rye, meet my mum, Suze. Mum, Kit is High Tides' resident goldsmith, and Rye's a newly arrived groundsman with a side-line in fire extinguishing.'

Rye laughs. 'What she means is that I'm helping out down at the fire station.'

Mum has visibly perked up. 'If you're ever giving out free smoke alarms, you're very welcome to knock on my door – I'm up at The Hermitage.'

Rye's smile is wide and friendly as he takes in her overalls, cinched so tightly at the waist that she looks like she might snap in the middle. 'Another painter? I was hoping last week's painter might be here too?'

I smile. 'Mum's a perpetual decorator rather than an artist. And I'm afraid you've missed Plum, she and Nell dropped in earlier.'

'That's a shame.'

I take pity on Rye because he's visibly deflated. 'Plum has the Deck Gallery, just above Crusty Cobs bakers. If you ask nicely and pay her a few thousand pounds, I'm sure she'll paint you a seascape to cheer you up.'

His expression brightens. 'Maybe she could do some for the hotel?'

I assume from that he has the hots as badly as she does. 'You'll have to ask her that, although you might need to run it past Mr Byron first. Apparently he has more money than sense, so I doubt you'll have any trouble persuading him.'

Rye's eyes are wide open, and Kit seems to be choking into

his sleeve, so it's a relief when Milla comes bursting in from the deck.

'I thought we agreed *not* to entertain hotel staff at The Hideaway, Aunty Flo?'

I grin at my mum. 'They're just leaving. Is there anything you girls want? I've hardly seen you!'

Milla nods. 'There's some Fanta chilling in the fridge.'

I turn into the kitchen, bring out the drinks tray for Milla, then go back and wrap the scones in a clean tea towel. When I get back to the living area I'm surprised to see Milla's still there.

As I push the scones into Kit's hands Rye gives a cough. 'To show how much we appreciate Florence's baking, we've come with gifts.'

Kit shuffles. 'A few hotel freebies, they're nothing much.'

Milla's eyes open wider when she spots the fan of cards in Rye's hand. 'Vouchers for a High Tides Spa session. How awesome will that be! Thanks, guys!'

Rye turns to Milla. 'I'm afraid these are midweek evenings, for over-eighteens only, although we do offer facilities for babies and nursing mums.'

Milla gives him her best Disgusted-of-St-Aidan snort. 'I hope you realise you're being extremely discriminatory there, Rye?'

Kit smiles at her. 'High Tides is very much a sanctuary, the guests don't want to be disturbed by rowdy teenagers.'

Milla's nostrils flare. 'Adolescents being noisy is a complete myth perpetuated by fun-sucking adults who can't bear to see young people enjoying themselves.'

The rest of us are so taken aback by that, for a moment we

all stand there with our mouths open. But as we do the silence is broken by a series of piercing shrieks from the beach.

Kit puts his hand behind his ear. 'As the screams in the distance don't appear to be coming from pensioners, I rest my case.'

Ever the diplomat, my mum reaches across and takes the cards from Rye. 'Thank you, this is very kind.' She narrows her eyes, as she always does when she tries to read without using her close-work glasses. 'Complimentary spa treatments, including hot stone massage, facials, mud wraps and pedis, and a hot tub for twelve with fizz! There's a lot to like about this!'

Kit nods. 'The hope is to trial the hen party package, if you and your friends wouldn't mind helping?'

Mum is purring. 'Bring it on! Reporting for duty and ready to be pampered!'

I can't quite believe what I'm hearing, or how fast she's changed her tune. Before this gets any more out of hand I take the cards from Mum, stack them into a neat pile and push them back at Kit. 'Thanks for thinking of us, but I'll be severing ties with the hotel from now on. I'm sure you won't have any problem finding other volunteers.' I give a sniff because I may as well make myself clear while I'm here. 'That includes baking orders too. I won't be doing those either.'

Kit's brow wrinkles and his voice is full of concern. 'What's happened, Floss? Is something wrong?'

As his hand falls on my arm I twist away. 'I came here for sanctuary too. I'd rather not compromise that.'

Kit pulls away. 'Absolutely, it's your call. In that case, we'll say thanks for the scones, and leave you and your guests to your...' he hesitates for a second '...quiet afternoon.'

I'm shouting over the yells from the beach. 'Great! Goodbye, then.'

As they make their way back onto the sand, Mum watches them all the way down the steps. Then she turns back to me. 'Well, those two were nice!'

I let out a wail. 'No they weren't! They're the enemy, remember? Not that I'm paranoid, but anyone as determined to get what he wants as Mr Byron may well attack on several fronts. Kit and Rye could well be the sneaky team, wriggling in with the freebies.'

Mum pulls a face. 'Fine, thanks for reminding me. But if lovely Rye comes round offering free smoke alarms, I *am* going to take them. Is that okay?'

I can't believe she just called him lovely. 'So long as he calls round in his capacity as a fireman...' I stop to grin at her for how incorrigible she is '...knock yourself out.'

Milla chimes in. 'Mum would like Kit's bum, it's a dead ringer for Bruce Springsteen's.' Her face breaks into a grin. 'I was actually checking him out for you, Aunty Flo. Did you notice he was looking at you like he wanted to eat you?'

I'm not taking this lying down. 'The man was ravenous for sultana scones!' I need to move this on, and fast. 'Talking of being hungry, as soon as you're ready for tea, we'll put your pizza order in. How does that sound?'

Milla nods. 'We *are* ordering from the place with the hand-stretched dough, wood-fired oven and vegan options, not the rubbish one down by the harbour?'

I can tell she's Sophie's daughter. 'Absolutely.'

Her face breaks into a smile. 'There you go, Kit said that too!

One of the biggest giveaways of attraction is accidental mimicking of language.'

I let out a squeak. 'Where on earth did you get that from?' I could do with knowing so I can keep one step ahead of her.

She shrugs. 'I think we read that in *Grazia*. Tallulah gets it when her older sister's finished with it. It's great for sex tips too.'

'*Sex tips?*' I'm mouthing the words, and nothing's coming out. I make my smile very bright and thank my lucky stars they're only here for another couple of hours. 'I was thinking we could make mocktails later?'

Milla smiles. 'The girls will love that. But you do know they're called alcohol-free craft-beverages now?'

'Absolutely. Thanks for reminding me.' I kick myself for that the second it's out. And even worse, when did I get *so* left behind with the trends?

She laughs. 'We've been saying, next time we're round we could have a driftwood fire and toast marshmallows by moonlight.'

I'm opening and closing my mouth. 'You want to come *again?*'

She pulls me into a hug. '*Absolutely!*' She digs me in the ribs to make sure I get the joke. 'Everyone adores it here, and you're such a great hostess! Will next Saturday be okay for you?'

I stare across at my mum for help.

She wades in. 'We'll have to see what your mum says first, Milla.' Phew to that! Sophie will hate the idea. 'But it's good for Aunty Flo – you're like a breath of fresh air – so I'm sure your mum won't mind.'

Damn!

Did I mention sanctuary earlier? Because it's not. It's more like St Pancras on a Friday teatime. One more crazy Saturday, then I've promised myself I'm going back under my 'duvet'.

12

Clemmie's Little Cornish Kitchen, Seaspray Cottage, St Aidan
Slush puppies, pom poms, and request slots
Wednesday

'Sounds like you wowed Milla and her friends on Saturday if they're wanting a return visit so fast?'

Sophie, Plum, Shadow and I have popped into Clemmie's Little Cornish Kitchen for lunch. We're actually crashing the St Aidan Mums and Bumps group, which have regular get-togethers in Clemmie's café, just along the sands from St Aidan harbour.

Clemmie's doing well to comment. Not only has she got Arnie in her arms, she's also spooning jelly into Bud's mouth as she sits on the floor by her feet.

I shrug. 'I'm not under any illusions about Milla and her crew. The hotel gardeners are the major attraction, not me.'

As Nell and Clemmie were going to be here anyway, the rest of us decided to brave the sticky-fingered toddlers and drop in too. Today the furniture has been pushed back to make room for toys, but on normal days the space is spectacular, with its floor-to-ceiling windows on three sides giving a view right around the bay.

The place is filled with a riot of bright clashing colours, set off by the deep blue of the sea beyond the windows, which today is striped with parallel lines of white breakers frothing towards the shore. As I look around at the painted wooden chairs in pinks and blues and yellows and reds clustered around bright-coloured wooden tables, and the fuchsia velvet sofas, it's making me realise what Mum meant about minimalism being boring.

Sophie leans across, tapping my shoulder to get my attention. 'Don't worry, Floss, teenagers turn faster than the wind. The second something more interesting comes along, you'll have your deck back.'

I'm very aware I might be treading on her toes with Milla and her impromptu invitations. 'So long as you don't mind them being at mine?'

Sophie's voice is shrill. '*Mind? Why ever would I mind?*' Which means she does. A lot. She gives a rueful sniff. 'At least when they're at yours I still know what they're doing.'

Nell chortles. 'By the way, Floss, I bumped into Kit earlier in Hardware Haven.'

I pull a face. 'I'm keeping well out of his way.' I've dodged his early-morning waves, and if I'm missing him dropping in every morning after Jean and Shirley, I'm not about to admit it. I wanted him out of my orbit, and I've got my wish. It's not as if we were close. A month on I still hadn't found a time to ask after his fiancée. For all I know she might be holed up in the beach hut that I don't see, although somehow I can't imagine her putting up with sand between her toes.

Nell ignores me and carries on. 'He's well up for a singles night. I said you'd join in.'

I groan. 'But I've cut ties with next door!'

Sophie frowns at me 'I still can't believe you knocked back a free spa night.'

I sniff. 'I refuse to deal with people who are dishonest or underhand, and Shadow's the same.' I'm giving his ear a tickle, as the door opens and Mum walks in.

She perches on the edge of a chair. 'I saw Rye in town earlier. Has he dropped anything off for me?'

Plum sits bolt upright as she hears Rye's name. 'Will it be a big package or a small one?' She gives a cough. 'So Clemmie's prepared.'

I'm shaking my head. 'I expect it will be a box of smoke alarms.'

Plum's sitting up even straighter. 'I could do with some of those too. If I can catch Rye at the fire station, I'll grab yours while I'm there, Suze.'

I'm looking round the circle of eager faces. Whatever happened to friends and family solidarity? 'If you're *that* desperate, I'll go to B&Q myself and treat you both.'

Mum frowns at me. 'Take a chill pill, Floss. Smoke alarms will make us all safer, no one needs to lose their shizzle.' 'No one' meaning very specifically – *me*.

I'm realistic enough to know there are bigger fires to fight than this one. 'Right. I take your point. They're free, with no link to High Tides other than Rye. Why *not* grab them?'

My mum smiles at me. 'Good girl.' She pats my hand. 'I'm

on my way to the paint shop, shall I get some for you while I'm there?'

I can't help smiling that her way of expressing her affection slash appreciation is to offer to buy me some decorating materials.

She turns and looks at the walls. 'You're in the right place for inspiration, with all Clemmie's different colours. A feature wall would look fabulous at yours behind the paper swallows.'

I'd never have thought of it myself, but now she's said it I know in my gut she's right. 'Okay. Dark, dark navy blue with a hint of green, like the sea when it's angry and the sun comes out. And deep cerise please.' I'd say Sophie's nails but a shade lighter, except I don't want to sound demanding.

Mum looks at me patiently. 'The whole point of a feature wall is that it "features" one colour, not two, Floss.'

Clemmie laughs. 'From where I'm sitting in my rainbow interior, I'd say all the best decorating rules are made to be broken. Pink plant pots would look awesome!'

That encouragement fires me up. 'You'd better get me some brushes too, Mum! And a painting gang.'

Mum's pushing back her hair. 'Best avoid a crowd in a small space, sweetheart. You and I will nail this ourselves.'

It's too weird to admit the thought is giving me butterflies because it's years since I last had those. Apart from Kit obviously. Except what I felt that first day when Kit walked across the beach towards us, and every day since if I'm honest, has more to do with huge beating gull wings and feeling so sick it's almost as bad as chemo. Nothing to do with nice associations at all.

'So lots to look forward to!' I'm beaming round the group.

Nell nods. 'Don't take too long to pick a date for the joint singles night. If it goes well, we could do more!'

Maybe I spoke too soon about looking forward to things – Plum chasing Rye all over town is fine for her, but I draw the line at liaising with Kit.

And then Sophie chimes in too. 'I'll bring you some old towels for Saturday. Tallulah and some of the others want to dye their hair.'

This sounds like a secret plan of Sophie's to put a stop to my Hideaway days. 'What colour are they thinking? Some subtle blonde on blonde?'

Sophie grins. 'They're not sixty, Floss!' My mum winces at that. 'They're mostly going shades of pink!'

Clemmie grins. 'They'll match the plant pots!'

Sophie nods. 'So long as she's painted them by then.' She turns to the others to justify this comment. 'Floss tends to prevaricate with her interiors. Don't you, *sweetheart*?'

It would be more accurate to say, 'Floss doesn't do homes, full stop,' but I'm not going to argue. And the second comment is her long-running gripe with our mum, for calling *me* pet names when *she* doesn't have any. Between us, it's her own fault for never tolerating them back in the day.

Mum sends Sophie a look. 'Give her a chance, please, for once in your life.'

'Fine.' Sophie's sticking her chin out. 'For once in your life, *sweetie* would be nice.'

Clemmie jumps to my defence to move this on. 'With *those* colours and *that* blank canvas, I doubt Floss will be hanging back this time.' She gives Sophie a placating pat on the knee. 'And the hair dye sounds wild!'

Sophie turns to me. 'So long as Milla doesn't come home with pink hair, everything will be fine.'

Plum says, 'Can you handle that, Flo? If not, I can always come and help.'

And we all know why that is.

How come I feel like the most popular woman in the village, *and* the most unpopular, all at the same time?

13

Clemmie's Little Cornish Kitchen, St Aidan
Raised voices and personal assistants
Wednesday

'Floss? What are you doing at Mums and Bumps?'

Running headlong into a guy in a dark cashmere over-coat as I exit the loos ten minutes later is never a good look. When it's the person I *least* want to meet and I'm still tucking my sweatshirt into my over-sized boyfriend jeans, ideally I want the ground to open up and swallow me.

'It's not Floss, it's Florence, Kit.' Now I've got over the shock of him being here, I'm not taking any prisoners.

He stares down at my stomach, his face falling. 'You're not...?'

Even though he hasn't said the 'p' word, we all know what he means, and the silent eye-rolls from Clemmie and Nell across the room acknowledge the irony.

'Pregnant? Me?' I may as well fill in the gaping hole in the air. 'Hell no! And Sophie, Mum and Plum aren't either – we've just popped in for lunch.' Well, flapjack, in my case, but he doesn't need to know that. I look back up at him. 'How about you?'

He smiles. 'I'm here because I'm expecting cake.' Then he nods towards a tall stack of parcels on the counter. 'As your beach hut bakery is out of action Rye and I followed your recommendation – I'm here to collect our bake boxes.'

Clemmie points to the tower. 'That pile there is yours, Kit. Help yourself, there's nothing more to pay.'

As Kit peers over the top of the boxes he's swept into his arms Nell's frowning at me. 'Orders that size, Floss, I can't believe you haven't grabbed the business with both hands!'

Kit nods in agreement. 'Me neither, Nell!' His brow furrows as he hesitates. 'You would tell me if something was wrong, Floss? It feels like you just pulled up the drawbridge and cut us off for no reason.'

I close my eyes and count to ten, but the second I open them again my indignation bursts out like an explosion. 'How about the hotel trying to push me out of my home so they can expand right along the beach! *Is that enough of a reason?*'

I'm hissing so I don't upset the kids, but I can tell from the way the mums are sitting bolt upright in their pink velvet chairs right around the room that they've all heard every word.

Kit's frown deepens. 'If this is about David's offer, you've got him very wrong.'

'A rich guy exploiting people for a quick profit? Someone who wants to replace the wild beauty of the dunes with box bushes and Bentleys? *Which bit of that isn't right?*'

He inhales so deeply the bake boxes heave in his arms.

'David's honest and fair, he's the last person who'd want something for nothing.'

The way Kit's talking, Byron sounds like a best friend not a business associate.

Kit's not giving up. 'You might have been desperate to sell, but without asking David didn't know. As for his plans to extend the complex, he's been talking to the council about his dreams for a salt-water lido ever since he arrived.'

The whole room is aching to catch his response. This time I can't help my screech. 'Why does he want *another* swimming pool? The hotel's already got at least two.'

Kit smiles. 'This one's more special. It would be carbon neutral and chemical-free with sand filters. But best of all, it would be available *for local people to use – at highly subsidised rates!*'

There's a beat of silence as the last part sinks in. Then the room erupts.

For a few moments there's a rushing in my ears like the sound of the sea, and I feel like I'm going to faint. Then as I grasp the corner of the counter to steady myself I'm hearing cries of 'Wow!', 'I'll have some of that!', then, more worryingly, 'How good would carbon neutral swimming lessons be for the children?'

Whatever I imagined Kit was going to come out with, it wasn't this; impeccable credentials *and* community inclusion make it so much harder for me to argue against. If it's a choice between a gorgeous natural outdoor swimming area that everyone can enjoy, or a beach hut so insignificant and scruffy the breeze from the sea might blow it away, there's very little for me to add.

'Yay, Kit! What's *not* to like?' Apart from me losing my home, which the entire room seems to have overlooked. All I can think of is how unpopular I'll be in St Aidan if I'm the one responsible for depriving everyone of this lido-of-a-lifetime.

Clemmie's giving Kit a glacial stare. 'You do realise a pool where Floss's beach hut is would mean you'd lose your local brownie stop?'

I mutter under my breath. 'He's lost that anyway.'

Plum's in there to back Clemmie up. 'If Floss goes, who's going to catch your runaway influencers, or talk your reluctant customers round with scones and hot chocolate?'

Nell's joining in. 'And where are you going to get your breakfasts? No one else in St Aidan serves ice cream and custard complete with pink plastic flamingos at seven a.m.'

Sophie's in there too. 'Floss promised to give *me* first shout if ever she sold! I hope David Byron's ready for a fight!'

Even Mum's having her say. 'Sophie's got a castle *and* the best credit rating in St Aidan. Byron won't get a look in!'

Now it's Kit's turn to look bemused. 'Nothing's been decided. I was simply making the *private* point to Floss that High Tides isn't as bad as she perceives.'

Clemmie smiles at him. 'I think we've got that now, Kit. It might be a good time for you to leave us to take in what you've told us.'

Kit's staring around the room, like it's sinking in how many people he just shared this secret with. He gives a cough. 'I trust I can count on everyone here to be discreet?'

No one looks up in acknowledgement, because they're already glued to their phones passing on the news to anyone and everyone they can think of.

Which is my cue to say goodbye and remind him this is St Aidan, not Hackney. 'Good luck with the privacy policy, Kit! Enjoy your cakes.'

There won't be any more for him from my kitchen, that's for sure. What's more, I'm kicking myself for rushing out of the loo. Two more minutes redoing my eyeliner, he'd have been gone, and this showdown would never have happened. With something so beneficial for the village I'm tempted to give up now.

But then I think of my coloured birds hanging from their arc of string. Now I've had a glimpse of how comforting a place can be when it feels like home, I don't want to give that up. And I might be standing on my own, on a very wobbly tuft of dune grass – but at least it's mine.

If I'm going to give this fight everything I've got, I need to come out from under the duvet! I need to stop pretending I'm not here and get my act together. Ideally, I need to become something everyone would miss if it weren't here. I just don't have the first idea how I'm going to achieve that.

14

The Hideaway, St Aidan
Pony tails and dark horses
Saturday

'Is this pink too bright?'

Tallulah's newly coloured hair swings in front of us in a luxuriant arc. Having emerged from this afternoon's dedicated blow-dry area by my bed for her 'ta-da' reveal, she's scouring the circle of faces in the living room searching for approval.

'It's fab – the most vibrant yet.' I'm leaning out from the kitchen, talking through my chocolate brownie.

Tallulah nods. 'That's why I went last. We've been winding up the dose.'

With nine newly coloured heads, there's so much swishing of hair it's like being in the dunes when the breeze sweeps through the marram grass. Except here in the beach hut every version is a different shade, all the way from pale oyster to pulsating crimson.

Milla laughs. 'With magenta, there's no such thing as *too* much, Tallulah.'

I smile at Milla. 'Not feeling left out? I'm sure we could persuade your mum to let you have a pearl-blush version?'

IMHO Sophie might need to flex a little more now Milla's getting older; if she holds her reins too tight, it could blow up in her face. But what do I know?

Milla twists a flaxen tress between her fingers. 'Pink doesn't really suit who I am now.' Her sigh is fraught with frustration. 'If I struggle to be taken seriously as a woman with mayonnaise-coloured hair, I doubt that looking like I've collided with a raspberry milkshake will help any.'

That's stopped me in my tracks. 'Wow!!! Good point well made.'

She pulls a face. 'I know I'm letting the pink-hair fundraiser down, but I *am* planning to support it – just in my own way.'

'Great!' It's good she's being true to herself. 'I've only ever seen the world as a dark brunette – except when all my hair fell out, obviously.'

That was so traumatic, I've been glad of any hair at all ever since. When I was ill I tried never to grumble, but my first chemo round hit me like a freight train. I should have known what was coming – after all, the cocktail of poison was designed to kill the worst cells invading my body, so it wasn't going to do much for the rest.

Everyone responds differently to treatment; some people lose their hair, other luckier ones don't. Looking back I wish I'd bitten the bullet and been brave enough to have a pixie cut straight away; at least then I could have done some good and donated my locks to wigs for kids. Instead I clung on to my optimism and my long hair simply because it was so much of who I was.

Milla grasps my hand. 'You were super pretty with a shaved head. But it must have been hard.'

Chemo knocked me so low I didn't brush my hair for a week, and when I finally did it came out in clumps that made me feel sicker still. My hairdresser was so kind – she was round with scissors in the hour – not that there was much left to crop. But at least that way I wasn't the one picking my hair up off the floor.

Milla hesitates. 'I promise whatever I do with my hair won't be that extreme.' She smiles. 'You look so fab with the choppy style you have now – and it's almost down to your shoulders!'

These days I have my hair cut into layers because since it came back it's been more like wire than silk, but I'm not sure who I'm kidding. It's an achievement that it's long enough to catch into a ponytail with a scrunchie. But I have to admit it's so fabulous to have. 'I love it too.'

With so many girls to get through the bathroom they arrived extra early this morning, then headed straight off along the beach. We all knew collecting driftwood for this evening's fire was just a ruse to scope out the hotel grounds, and the woodpile by the front deck is big enough to roast a hog, not toast a few marshmallows.

Between us, I'm not a fan of crispy pork. Any celebration Dillon's friends had, from weddings to an '*I got a new BMW*' party, invariably included a hog roast. As someone with animal rights sympathies, the sight of a pig on a spit has always sent me running to find the veggie burgers, so I'd rather not encourage my own beach version.

It was dry when they arrived earlier, but it's one of those

mercurial St Aidan days where one moment the sun is shining from a cornflower sky, and the next it's the colour of a dungeon, and the rain is thrashing down so hard it's drilling holes in the sand. But far from us feeling cooped up, the day has flown by.

There was a moment of disappointment when a text arrived to confirm that the hotel groundsmen's shift had been called off due to bad weather. And I could have done without the graphic descriptions of Kit and his loved-up couple-of-the-day, even if it was great news that he's switched his preferred location for photo ops to further along the beach. I know I'm not supposed to look that way, but there's still no sign of his fiancée shepherding the couples along the beach. Then a few moments later, the girls were diving in the towel pile and deciding who was next for the shower.

Our little chat over, Milla turns from me, back to her friends. 'Okay, so I'll take the last turn in the bathroom. Tallulah and Scarlett are coming to help with my styling, Aunty Flo needs help with more baking. And someone needs to break up some sticks so the campfire is ready for later.'

There's a flurry of discussion, then Shadow, me, Sarah and Sadie head for the kitchen. In a beach hut bursting with teens, a pile of M&M cookies goes a long way to keeping everyone chilled. We're sliding the third batch onto the cooling rack when the call finally comes from the bedroom alcove.

'Stand by, everyone come in from outside! Milla's ready for her reveal!'

They've been so long they must have done a deep condition *and* a fancy style. I grab a last handful of broken biscuit and step out for a better view.

'Surprise!' Milla does her jazz hands, then steps forward into the living area.

After so long I'm expecting braiding, and for a second I think she's still got a towel over her head. It's only as I blink and look again that the awful truth sinks in. Instead of Milla's pale blonde waves cascading over her shoulders, the dark glossy mane I'm looking at makes me choke on my cookie.

'What...' *the hell?* I strangle that mid-phrase and try again. 'What ... a transformation!'

If it weren't for the stains around her hair line, I'd think it was a wind-up, but there are tell-tale dye marks on her scalp too.

Milla tosses one inky tress over her shoulder. 'I've taken a leaf out of your book, Aunty Flo. I'm rocking the raven shimmer.'

Not that I've ever had hair the colour of shiny coal. I'm more dark coffee, but compliments where they're due. 'You've got it beautifully even.' It's not easy with blonde hair. The tone is so solid it's wiped away every bit of Milla-the-nymph and instilled her with a different force altogether. If Sophie was dead against pink, this will send her ballistic.

I cough. 'Not wanting to spoil the party, but...' it's a pertinent question a savvy brunette should be able to answer, no problem '...what's your mum going to say when she sees you?'

Milla tosses her head. 'I feel ten times more kick-ass than before.' She turns to the girls. 'Let's FaceTime her now!'

Milla's phone is already in her hand, and as Sophie picks up on the second ring, everyone crowds around Milla and choruses 'Ta-da' again!

There's a beat of silence, then Sophie's voice. 'Who's this? What are you doing on Milla's phone?'

Milla giggles. 'It's me, Mum, I'm showing you my make-over! Ebony suits me so much more than cerise would have, don't you think?'

Sophie's voice jumps up an octave. 'You *are* joking me? Milla? *Milla?*' As Milla lets a curtain of black hair drop across her face, Sophie's squeal turns to a roar. 'This is *not* funny. Put Aunty Florence on. *Now!*'

Milla holds out her phone to me. 'While you deal with Mum, we'll be outside sorting the campfire and the fairy lights.'

'I'll ring you on mine, Soph.' I wave away the phone, then listen to the footsteps tramping out onto the deck.

I take in Shadow's side eye. 'At least that will give me the time to find a hard hat and a flak jacket.'

I know from back in the day, Sophie on the warpath is never a pretty sight. This may be my cue to leave town, and fast.

15

The Hideaway, St Aidan
Guilty parties and good impressions
Saturday

'How *could* you let this happen, Floss?'

We're on sound only but I don't need to see Sophie's face to tell she's apoplectic. She's also holding me a hundred per cent responsible for Milla's hairdressing mishap slash act of wanton defiance.

As kids, the only way to deal with Sophie's wrath was to run. But she was always faster than me, and her signature move was to catch hold of my ponytail as I fled. I can still feel the searing pain in my scalp as she wrenched out a handful of hair, right up to the time my legs grew longer than hers and I could outrun her.

But there's no point me arguing about this. Milla and Co. aren't babies, and for me to watch them every second would be impossible *and* inappropriate. I'm desperately hoping Sophie won't use this as an excuse to stop them coming round to the hut because the thought of a Saturday without them is dismal. And that's nothing to do with the ten-pound notes they each insisted on giving me to put toward my expenses. When I put that with the payments from my Insta ladies, who pop in for a 'lucky dip' breakfast more days than not, I'm getting quite a haul.

I hold the phone away from my ear until I hear Sophie's shouts subside, then I tiptoe in with my apology.

'If I'd had *any* idea what was going on I'd have watched them more closely. I'm sorry that I didn't.' I'm looking out watching the girls running across the sand taking wood from the pile. 'You should see how hard they're working with the fire-building.'

Sophie lets out a long sigh. 'It could be worse. Google says one wash with *Head and Shoulders* and it should be gone.'

It's my turn to take a deep breath. 'I'm afraid the dye Milla's used is permanent. But her blonde hair growing out will look amazing.' I can't help laughing. 'This is karma coming back to bite you. You dyed *your* hair black, remember, and Mum went ape?' I'm looking down at Shadow, his nose stretched in the air. 'You could be pleased Milla's expressing herself?'

I'm watching sea mist drifting across the front deck, knowing that if Sophie comes down too hard it will only make things worse. Except how come the mist is rolling from the direction of the hotel rather than off the sea? Then a tickle in my nose makes me look again.

'Is that smoke?' As I walk over for a better view, Sophie's mulling which of Milla's privileges to withdraw. 'Typical! High Tides choose the one day when the wind is blowing in this direction to light a bonfire. And it has to be huge if the smoke's carrying this far.'

As I cross to the side window there are prickles of anger rising up my neck. But what I see as I look out across the dunes turns my stomach to stone.

'We weren't supposed to light the campfire *this* early.' It comes out as a whimper. 'And who decided to build it *right next to the hut?*' Here I am, blaming High Tides, and meanwhile my home is about to go up like an incendiary device.

'What's that about camping?'

I cut Sophie off. 'I have to go...' There's no easy way to say the teenagers are about to raze the place to the ground. 'I'll ring you back.'

Even as I'm running for the door, pushing Shadow out in front of me, I can see the flames darting upwards beyond the side windows.

I hare off the deck and round the hut, press Shadow's lead into Sarah's hand and take in Milla and Tallulah, eyes wide, their hands flapping behind the roaring pile of driftwood.

'We were trying to use a tampon for kindling like Bear Grylls does, Aunty Floss...'

'*What?*'

'We used a boxful and the whole lot went up.' There's a second of stunned silence. '*What shall we do?*'

For a terrible moment all I can see is the fire stretching outwards, licking towards the planks of the side wall, ready to engulf the whole place.

Tallulah's shout breaks my trance. 'Phone 999! Quick, Sadie!'

However fast they respond, by the time the fire engine arrives from St Aidan, my precious beach hut will be ashes.

Milla joins in. 'Rye! He's a fireman. We need Rye!'

That kicks me into action. 'Kit!' I'm stumbling across the soft sand of the dune, waving my arms, yelling so loud my lungs feel like they might burst. '*Kit ... help!*' He's the last person I want to call on given the way we parted. But before I reach the second hump, I catch sight of a figure tearing towards me. One glimpse of that crisp white shirt, my heart gives a lurch and the world stands still.

For a few crazy seconds in my head we're running towards each other in slo-mo like lovers on a cheesy advert. And then as I catch a blast of his cologne on the breeze, then draw in a lungful of smoke, I crash back down to earth. We almost collide, then I whip around and I'm running beside him, panting to keep up.

'What the hell are they doing, Floss?'

Trust Kit to have enough breath to talk, run *and* lug a massive fire extinguisher. Even so it takes an age to make it across the last fifty yards. By the time we slide to a halt, the searing heat coming off the fire is scorching our cheeks. He balances the extinguisher on his knee, rips out a pin, and a second later he's spraying foam like he just won a Grand Prix.

Then the flames are gone and when we stand back and find we're staring down at a pile of charred logs, it feels like a bit of an anti-climax.

'Thank frig you came, Kit, we were moments away from The Hideaway going up like a fireball. You've saved me again.'

He shrugs and raises one eyebrow. 'All in a day's work for a superhero.'

I'm staring at his Adam's apple, then the sooty smudges on his collar. 'Can I wash your shirt?'

Why am I even thinking of burying my face in it? Of keeping all the doors shut, leaving it out on the sofa and capturing his smell for a day.

He shakes his head. 'The hotel will do that. No point having a laundry service and not using it.'

Being crazily indebted when I'm not even supposed to be speaking to him makes me so uncomfortable, I'm being absurd. 'Would you like some Fanta?' Even mentioning something as small as that feels like an insult when he's just saved my home. 'Or a cup of tea?' Now I sound like I'm ninety.

He shakes his head again. 'I'm with clients, so I'll leave you to get on.' He frowns. 'Just so I know for Rye, what happened here?'

I think on my feet. 'Some unfortunate tips on kindling.'

He looks suitably unimpressed as he backs away. 'You might like to invest in an extinguisher if the kids are going to play with matches.'

He has a point, but the way he puts it sounds so judgmental. I fix my gaze on the girls. 'We'll get straight onto that now.'

He's backing away, then as he stares at the crowd of faces, he pauses. 'Is it my eyes, or have you all been hit by a cherry bomb?'

Milla clears her throat. 'Not *quite* all of us, Kit – I've gone from vanilla to bitter chocolate.'

Kit's blinking. 'So you have! For a moment there I thought you were Floss!'

I mutter, 'Florence.'

The grin on Milla's face is as wide as the bay. 'Right answer, Kit! That's exactly the look I was going for.' She smiles across at me. 'Once Scarlet's mum gives me a choppy cut, you won't tell us apart.'

However badly this afternoon is going, it just got a hundred times worse. And then, as Kit turns and I watch his back disappearing over the dunes, I'm kicking myself for not being more grateful. Before I know it, I'm calling out.

'Anything I can do in return, just shout.' Not cakes obviously. I already owe him brownies for life. I'm talking about far bigger stuff.

He turns and shouts over his shoulder. 'I'll get back to you on that.'

And then he's gone, and I'm left with a stomach whizzing around like a washing machine on fast spin.

16

The Hideaway, St Aidan
Heroes and happy Mondays
Monday

'Floss, you're there!'

When Kit's name flashes up on my phone two days later, the moment I pick up I can tell there's a problem.

'Are you free to come to the studio – like now?'

'This sounds urgent!' It's a surprise he needs me so soon after my own emergency, but I want to arrive prepared. 'Shall I bring an extinguisher?'

Not only did my own three arrive by next-day delivery, but every time I've dropped a box of 'thank you' brownies on the doorstep of Kit's hut, he's brought me a pile of firefighting equipment in return.

I sense his sigh. 'You may need one. One half of this morning's couple is having a meltdown. I hoped you could talk her down.'

I've never actually been in his studio, but if it's anything like his trousers it's going to be well upmarket so I'd better check. 'Is there a dress code?'

'Smart but speed is more important. She's quite upset.'

Most of my clothes are cast-offs or from charity shops. At The Circus we could wear what we liked so long as it was outlandish and vaguely on theme, which suited me down to the ground. When I reached the dizzy heights of team leader I took to wearing a ringmaster's outfit, and ran around in a red long-tailed jacket with a nipped-in waist, with a baton in my hand and velvet shorts or silk breeches, depending on my mood. So there's no point looking to my work clothes is what I'm saying – and the rest of my wardrobe resembles a jumble sale.

I flip through the pile of clothes on the chair, pull on the least flouncy midi dress and some cowboy boots, grab a spritz of Miss Dior and run. By the time I jump onto the veranda of Kit's studio with Shadow two steps behind, I'm gasping ... and not just because I'm out of breath. Out in the sunlight my boots look like they belong in the wild west, there are so many creases in my tiered denim dress it looks like crinkle fabric, and a loop of cream lace is dangling from the hem. And eff my life – I haven't brushed my hair today!

I'm leaning up against the doorframe, with two minutes to elevate myself to High Tides standards. As I unknot the hair tangles with my fingers and try to tie up the trailing trim, an image flashes into my head of the day Dillon and I went to Kit's place in the city, and I know I'm so far below Kit's level that I've already lost the fight.

His fiancée, Violetta, was the one who welcomed us, and she was impeccable; statuesque and spare, groomed within an inch of her life, her sheath dress so classy you knew it had cost more than I'd have earned in a month, and that's including tips. I've revisited this memory a lot lately, trying to second-guess where she is, because she was so dynamic and present, she's not the kind of person who would simply drop out of the picture. Hair piled up, every sweep of bronzer highlighting her incredible cheekbones. I'm trying to recall her nail colour when the support behind my shoulder gives way, and a second later I'm diving headfirst into the studio, the wooden floorboards flying up towards me.

First impressions don't come much worse than me sprawled with my nose an inch away from Kit's shiny black brogues, my boobs spilling out of my scoop neck, while Shadow licks my ear. But as Kit helps me up and I hurriedly drop his hand and rearrange my dress instead, it sinks in that no one is taking notice of me.

The space I'm staring into has the sharpness you'd expect from a designer who just landed from London, but there's a serious lack of warmth. The walls are painted in blocks of grey, with occasional tall glass cabinets and angular steel furniture artfully arranged. Seeing Kit still hanging on to the same signature flourish of significant quotes written on the walls, all these years on from Dillon's and my visit to Covent Garden, gives me shivers of the wrong kind. And if that hadn't already turned my blood to ice, the young woman sitting on the long suede sofa beyond the desk, crying buckets into her tissue, finishes the job.

'Is she okay?' I mouth the words at Kit, but it's obvious she's not.

Her partner is standing beside her, his hands jammed into

the pockets of his chinos, staring upwards like he's trying to bore holes in the ceiling.

Kit hisses in my ear. 'Bianca and Salvador walked in, looked around and this started...' He steps back and shrugs, then comes back in again. 'If you'd like to take it from here? For context, I've told them you're my partner...'

My stomach does a giant leap. As it hits the floor, I screech, 'Your *WHAT*?'

'Business not sleeping...' The flicker of a smile goes and he blows out a breath.

Okay, I put my hands up. Weeks scanning the area without a single sighting of Violetta should have been the clue, but it's still come as a shock to march in and find she's definitively not inside.

I hurry on to check my mission statement. 'Do you have a preferred outcome?'

'No expectations, do whatever you can. A smile as she leaves would be a bonus, but I accept that's unlikely.'

I glance along the studio then mutter down to Shadow. 'Fire-fighting would be a hundred times easier.'

I stare down at my feet, think of Violetta's Manolo Blahniks, and it hits me – the way forward might be to channel a bit of the woman whose shoes I'm filling. I close my eyes, imagine I'm wearing *that* dress, and give a mental gasp as, in my mind's eye, my thigh slides through the waist-high side-split. The breath I drag in to summon my courage adds six inches to my height. As I take four immense strides down the room, I force my face into a smile as confident as Violetta's and it takes all my inner willpower not to add in her gorgeous Eastern European accent too. Whatever I've done, something must have worked, because as I open my mouth, I feel ready to boss the world.

'Kit!' In my head I'm teetering on stupendous spikes. 'While Bianca and I get to know one another, why not show Salvador your alchemy equipment?'

His eyes widen in surprise. 'It's not alch—' My frown kicks him back into line. 'Great idea, thanks for that, Floss.'

I aim a super-sophisticated beam at the woman on the sofa. 'What are men like? This one doesn't even remember his partner's proper name.' I roll my eyes at Kit, then turn back again. 'Lovely to meet you, Bianca, this is Shadow and I'm *Florence*.'

Kit's already steering Salvador past the desk. 'Come next door to the workshop...' he sends me a meaningful stare '...also known as the atelier or the *metallurgy* department.'

And a second later they're gone.

Now I'm closer I get the full benefit of Bianca's blonde pixie cut with the blue blaze that matches her faded denims. As she twists her cropped biker jacket tighter around her waist and crosses her feet in Doc Marten sandals it hits me how young she is.

I scrunch up my skirt, prop my chin on my fist and turn to look at her. 'No pressure – *at all* – but if you'd like to tell us what's going on, Shadow's a very good listener.'

That makes her smile. Then she heaves a sigh, and she leans back to look at me. 'It's completely stupid. If I hadn't been certain about this, I'd hardly have got up at dawn so we could get here.' She sniffs and dabs her nose. 'Then I get in the door, read the words on the wall and two seconds later I'm in bits.'

As I scan the blocks of painted script searching for a clue, I can't see that Albert Einstein's famous quote about attraction would push anyone over the edge. 'Which words *exactly*?'

She points at the wall above the desk. 'It was your slogan – *tOgether fOrever*.'

It's ironic she's attributing me ownership of my most hated phrase, so I try to distance myself. 'That's one of Kit's favourites. Me, not so much.'

'I love being engaged. I can't wait to be married.' She scrutinises the tiny solitaire on her left hand. 'Then I got here, read that and...'

I fill in for her. 'You did the maths?'

She nods. 'I'm twenty-two. All that flashed through my head was, it sounds like a *very* long time to be with one person.'

I'm going to have to put a different spin on this. 'How did we get that so wrong? It's not meant to scare the bejesus out of you, it's supposed to remind you that ... *forever isn't long enough*.'

Shadow's sideways glance tells me my improvising hasn't convinced him, so I can only hope it's helped Bianca.

She shakes her head. 'That's what I'd always felt until now. The worst thing was, I blurted out how scary it sounded to Salvador. He looked *so* gutted and the next thing I knew there were tears flooding down my cheeks.'

I put my hand on her arm. 'The run-up to a wedding is a very emotional time.' Then I notice how pale her cheeks are. 'You say you had an early start. Did you have breakfast?'

She winces. 'That was another disaster. We were running late, then when we did arrive the hotel menu was so weird, we didn't bother.'

'One thing I do know, you can't make rings when you're hungry!' Gently reinforcing the idea of what they're here for, I dial Nell, hoping she's in town and available for a dash to Crusty Cobs. 'How about we reset with some bakery pastries?'

Bianca's face brightens. 'Could we have coffee with those?'

'Absolutely.' I stand up and head for the row of three doors across the room, in search of a kettle. It would be more than I'd hoped to hit the kitchen straight away, but I dive into the walk-in cupboard in front of me, trying to look like that's where I meant to go. When I come out of the gloom five minutes later, Nell's up to speed on my new role and location and on her way. And Kit's replied to my texts to say the coffee machine and fridge are one door along, and that they'll give us another twenty before they come to join us.

As I emerge from the kitchenette with a tray of mugs and a large pot of coffee ten minutes later, Nell is already pushing her way through the front door, puffing with the exertion.

She shakes her head. 'Latitude One and Two? What's all that about then?' Trust Nell to pick up on Kit's shiny new name boards.

I grin at her as I put the tray on the coffee table in front of the sofa. 'They're the official addresses of the beach huts.' Before she launches into a tirade about poncy Londoners, I get in first. 'Latitude is a play on the navigational position and the sense of freedom.'

She drops a large cake box down beside the tray and leans back and stretches. 'Well, who'd have thought?' She turns to Bianca. 'I'm Nell. I'm eighteen months pregnant which is why I'm the size of a ferry boat. And I don't know about you, but I'm gasping for a drink!'

I smile at Bianca and pull up a leather chair for Nell. 'Nell runs the St Aidan singles club, and she's promised she'll share her insights on romance in return for a Danish.'

As I open the lid of the cake box Nell closes her eyes and breathes in the smell of vanilla and jam. Then, as I hand round the drinks and they pull out an almond croissant each, Nell turns to Bianca. 'So what's he done? They can all be knobheads sometimes.'

Bianca replies straight away. 'We hardly ever argue, but this morning we had our first tiff.' Her frown deepens. 'We were already behind, and I'd just been back into the flat to change my shoes for the *third* time, because I wanted today to be perfect.'

I look down at my toes, realising the issue. 'For you the important thing was your feet feeling right, but for Salvador it was being on time. Him hurrying you along could be a sign of how much he cares too.'

Bianca's nodding. 'That's true.'

Nell chortles. 'It's also normal to throw wobblies when you get to the parts like the rings – because that's when it hits you how real it is.'

Bianca's nodding hard. 'That's it too!'

I'm the last person who should be persuading people to tie the knot, but there's no going back now. 'But if you're more comfortable with that person than anyone else, it's a damned good sign.'

Nell pushes the cake box towards Bianca and takes a cinnamon whirl for herself. She brushes the pastry flakes off her bump. 'If you feel like you'd like their baby sometime, that's even better!'

Bianca breaks a corner off her pain au chocolat. 'He wants two kids, I want four – so we've settled on three.' Her eyes go wider as she stares at Nell's expanse. 'Not *straightaway* though.' She relaxes again. 'The nursery is going to be Farrow and Ball babouche yellow.'

'You've obviously thought it through.' I sigh at the bliss of her certainty. That they have so much planned out, with no concept of what might lie ahead to derail those dreams. I widen my smile. 'You still need to be brave. It takes a lot of courage to commit.'

Nell chortles. 'The trick is, don't overthink it. Listen to your heart and trust your own judgement.'

I have something more to add. 'Kit doesn't only make wedding rings. He does eternity rings, and promise rings, and groups come to make them to celebrate friendship.' Our time is running out, so I'm throwing it all in here. Playing it down, but playing it up too. 'Your rings simply embody whatever you feel in the moment you create them. They can even just be a lovely way to celebrate a day by the sea.'

Bianca's eyes are bright. 'We want the ones with our finger-prints on in dark shadow. In gold, with inscriptions on the inside.' She pushes a spike of hair off her forehead and gives her nose a last dab. 'Or at least, we did. So long as I haven't blown it with my howling.'

I hardly dare to hope, but Bianca sounds like she could be back on track.

'You'll be fine.' As I push the pastries towards her again, there's the sound of footsteps on the deck. As Kit and Salvador come into the room I jump to my feet and turn my smile on the guys. 'Once Salvador's had a cream horn, I'm sure he'll be happy to carry on with the day?'

Salvador nods. 'Definitely.' He drops a kiss on Bianca's

cheek and takes her hand then turns back to me. 'I explained to Kit earlier, nothing's quite as beachy as it looked in the photos. I'm guessing that's why Bianca was upset.'

Maybe this isn't in the bag after all.

I'm straight in with the excuses. 'We're very new here, which is why it's still a bit bare.'

Kit's staring at me like I've fully lost my marbles.

Bianca's biting her lip. 'Victor and Amery's pictures on the Vintage & Awesome site were the reason we booked.'

My heart drops down to my boots; I never imagined their publicity would backfire so spectacularly.

Kit steps forward. 'Victor and Amery had a *special advance arrangement* to take photos at Florence's *antique* beach hut next door.' He raises his eyebrows. 'They also chose the afternoon tea option.' There's a pause as he lets that sink in. 'You've opted for the six-course plant-based Ocean Wonders hotel dinner, which means your venue is *slightly* different from theirs.'

Another place entirely, in other words.

As Nell sees their faces fall, she jumps in too. 'Brave choice having the seaweed-central menu! But I'm sure Florence can think of some other way to make your day more what you were hoping for?' She and Kit are both staring at me.

The local joke is you come out of High Tides more hungry than when you go in ... and that gives me an idea. 'If you're up for eating two puddings, I could serve you a selection of mini sweets on my veranda after your meal? Give you a quick taste of vintage-by-the-sea before bed.'

They'll have to bring their own fizz and glasses, but I'm sure Kit can sort that out. More important still, if I'm trying to make the beach hut more significant, this is a gift of an opportunity and I need to seize it!

Bianca looks at Salvador, then he nods. 'That would be a game changer. So long as it's not too much work?'

Nell beams at him. 'Don't worry! Florence has a gang, we'll all pile in.'

It already feels more like a party than a chore. As I grin at Nell, I know with their help I can do this standing on my head. And in my mind I'm punching the air because with this as a decider, I've pulled them on board for the whole day. And for me that's a result!

Kit holds up his hand. 'Thanks all the same, Nell, but Florence and I can handle this.' He raises one eyebrow. 'Can't we, Floss?'

Why the hell is my heart racing when it should be plummeting? As for this being a walk in the park, we all know everything gets a hundred times more difficult when Kit is around.

Nell laughs. 'Good thinking, Kit! Put in the practice for your joint singles club event.'

Damn damn damn! I'd assumed that was off now I'm distancing myself – which admittedly could be going better seeing as I'm technically on High Tides ground *now*.

And this is my life in St Aidan: two steps forward, twenty-five steps back.

As for my worries about my conscious self getting lost in St Aidan, they're completely justified. The person who arrived here is disappearing, but not because I'm shrinking. I'm being buried beneath the mountains of interference.

17

The Hideaway, St Aidan
A spoonful of sugar
Monday

Sophie might still be in a razz about the hair dye, but that girl has more candles than Jo Malone, and once Nell spread the word about tonight, she didn't hold back on lending me lanterns. When Plum arrived mid-afternoon it took us four trips to bring them all from the parking area. We put the big ones on the steps and around the side of the deck, and the smaller ones went on the side tables with some for the main table, which we put in the centre of the veranda.

Once Bianca and Salvador started poring over ring designs with Kit, I spent the rest of the morning back home making favourites from my old repertoire to cut up and use in the sweets. My mum heard too and dropped by with a posy of flowers for the table, then she rushed off again with a random promise to come back and paint my wall blue tomorrow. Nell, Clemmie, Bud and Arnie arrived soon after Plum, and while Plum strung lights around the deck Clemmie and Nell helped by tasting my sample concoctions and tweaking the mixes.

While the others go home for tea, Plum stays long enough to help light the lanterns and see the full impact of the fairylight strands swaying in the wind as the day fades to dusk. Inside I've opted for my relaxed playlist, and I'm swaying along to Roxy Music's 'Dance Away' as I wait for Bianca and Salvador to work their way through their High Tides meal.

Kit is bringing them over afterwards, and my phone pings repeatedly as he messages with news of their progress. As the Pet Shop Boys ease into 'Always on My Mind', there's yet another ding.

And we have lift off, Floss. Be with you in five.

And this is it. As I step outside, the distant rush of the tide and the gentle flap of the white linen tablecloth feel like the perfect backdrop for lovers coming to the end of a romantic day by the beach. I hear their voices in the distance along the dunes before I see them, and then a torch flashes and their figures appear out of the shadows.

As they clamber up onto the deck calling their hellos, Bianca is already clapping her hands.

'It's amazing, Florence! The veranda is even more beautiful than it looked on Insta!'

Kit squeezes my elbow, drops an ice bucket with a bottle on the table, then puts his camera bag on the floor. 'Okay kids, let's take a few more for the album before you settle in.'

I give the rugs on the director's chairs a last pat, and step back towards the door. 'And while you do that, I'll prepare the goodies.'

It couldn't be a better night. As I carry out the tray later the velvet blue sky is studded with diamond pricks of stars, the warm breeze along the dunes is ruffling the sand as it passes, and the sea is dimpled with the shimmer of moonlight.

I arrange the full cups on the table, Kit takes yet more pictures, he pops the champagne cork, tops up the flutes, we both chorus 'Enjoy!', then we slip inside and I point Kit towards the sofa.

'So what are you treating them to?' Even after a full day with clients, as he sits down the only sign that he's kicking back is his shirt cuffs pushed up his forearms.

'I've done a selection…' That's as far as I get before I breathe in that familiar scent of his and lose my thread. I wasn't ready for his presence in my living room to be this unbalancing.

'Keep going.'

I make myself concentrate. 'Sticky toffee pudding with ginger ice cream, lemon cheesecake with sorbet and popping candy, chocolate fudge cake with double chocolate chip ice cream, Coco Pops, and dark chocolate sauce, and Victoria sandwich with jam, fresh raspberries and vanilla ice cream. All with my usual additions and embellishments.' Custard, cereal sprinkles and flamingos, in other words.

He's leaning forward so eagerly I take pity on him. 'You aren't hungry?'

His face splits into a grin. 'I could eat a horse.'

I bite back my smile. 'A cupful of ice cream won't do the job then.' I watch his face fall, and then I relent. 'Don't worry, there's an extra-large serving waiting for you in the fridge and one for me too. I made a guess at your favourite flavour.'

Two moments later, as I hand him the cup piled high with chunks of brownie cake and scoops of dark chocolate ice cream, he murmurs, 'You know me so well.' Then he takes the spoon and instead of digging into the cake pile he points it straight at me. 'You do know you're extraordinarily good at all this, Floss?'

I pop a piece of jam and sponge into my mouth and laugh. 'What? Putting people at their ease then watching them eat their body weight in ice cream?'

He shakes his head at me, then he nods towards the deck. 'Those two were ready to walk this morning – it's entirely down to you that they stayed.' He pauses to let a spoonful of double chocolate chip Häagen-Dazs melt on his tongue. 'And whatever unique and memorable processes they did earlier with their rings, I know this will be the highlight of their day.'

I shrug and get ready for an admission. 'Making people relax and have the best time is one thing I *can* do.' It's what I lived night after night at The Circus. 'Hospitality used to be my thing – a few years ago.'

He frowns. 'I only realised today what a difference it makes having a woman in the studio with me.'

I nod as I remember. 'When Dillon and I came in as an engaged couple it felt super-romantic that you were working with your fiancée.' It feels like he's left this wide open for me to ask what I've been aching to know. 'So is your "real" partner looking after the London end?'

He blows out his cheeks. 'I'm afraid there isn't a London end to the business anymore. After Vee and I went our separate ways, I handed the studio on to a friend and moved everything down here to Cornwall.'

Somehow saying I'm sorry sounds too negative. 'A perfect place for a new start.'

And I'm not sure why my heart feels like it's left my body and started to orbit the earth either. Knowing he and Vee are no longer an item has absolutely no bearing on anything to do with me.

He lets out a sigh. 'Vee wasn't ever my fiancée. We were *together*, but she pretended the rest for the sake of the client experience.' He pulls a face. 'She insisted that so long as she wore a big enough diamond no one would be any the wiser or any worse off.'

Now it's confirmed, I can't ever imagine Vee kicking back in St Aidan. But at the same time, thinking he was fully committed was useful because it's much easier being around someone hot when they're spoken for. This way means I'll need to put a lot more effort into keeping any unconscious – inappropriate – thoughts under control.

This throws up a lot more hypothetical stuff too. It would be bad enough for me trying to date someone ordinary. Imagine if it were someone I really liked. How much worse it would be if they knocked me back. This is why I'm right. Why I can never go there.

I need to smooth over about making our rings. 'Vee gave us a great day at the time. You both did. I mean, us never using the rings had nothing to do with her faking it.'

He laughs. 'That's good to know.'

I hesitate for a second knowing he's not going to push. But

having got myself in this deep I might as well explain. And this is the plus side; if I'm fully decided that I'm not going to put myself through the dating, I don't have to think of drip feeding the information. I can just be honest, put it out there, and move on. 'I was ill for a while, and by the time I was over my cancer we wanted different things.'

He nods. 'I'm sorry. Illness can change everything, but it's good you're better.'

I'm grateful he hasn't asked more. But I do feel better that he knows. Even as a friend slash colleague, it's a relief he hasn't gone all weird about it, because a lot of people do. I give a rueful smile. 'Running west to St Aidan wasn't anywhere in my original life plan, but here I am.' I pull a face. 'Believe it or not, I came here hoping for solitude.' It feels strange now to think how certain I was that I wanted to be left alone and do nothing.

'I can see that's working out for you.' He laughs and looks at the ceiling. 'I'm having a similar level of success. I assumed relocating the business to the beach huts would be easy, but with two couples close to abandoning in as many weeks, I may need a rethink.' He frowns into his cup, then he looks up hopefully. 'Do you have any ideas?'

I have approximately a million, but I stick to the basics. 'It could be about client expectation?' We were all over this in the cocktail job. 'Your buzzy urban cool might not work in this location. When people travel to a sleepy seaside village, they're buying into something more relaxed and laid back.'

'Okay.' He's nodding. 'So what do you suggest?'

I swallow. 'If you tried dressing for the beach not the city, that would be a start?'

He gives me a sideways glance. 'I'm *not* wearing my wet suit.'

'*Obviously* not.' I take time for an eye-roll. 'Shorts or surf pants might put people more at ease.' I see his doubtful look and try again. 'Jeans and a T-shirt then? A linen jacket instead of a suit one?'

'Jeans?'

'You do have some?'

'Of course.' He pulls a face. 'At least one pair.'

I exchange glances with Shadow.

Kit lets out a long breath. 'I'll have to give this some thought.' He runs his finger along the crease in his chinos. 'Like what the hell would I do with two hundred redundant white shirts?'

And he's definitely got me there.

I take a spoonful of cake and ice cream, close my eyes and let the sweet tang of the jam melt onto my tongue. When I open my eyes again a long time later his gaze is locked on my face.

My stomach turns three somersaults before I manage to speak. 'Is something wrong?'

'Not at all.' He shakes his head and drops his eyes.

I follow his sightline. 'You're looking at my cup.' It takes a moment to figure out what he's thinking. No need for the cart-wheels after all then. 'You'd like to try the Victoria sandwich?'

He holds out his own cup. 'You can have some of mine in return?'

As I look across at him I can see the wrinkles at the corners of his eyes when he smiles and I'm trying not to think about Milla's *Grazia* articles. If his eyes are blurred and slightly out of focus, it's only because he's enjoying his pudding, or he's totally knackered after a really long day.

'You've got more than me. If we split fifty-fifty, I get the better deal.' I'm trying not to enjoy this. Then my practical mind catches up. 'Shall I go and get more spoons?'

He frowns. 'Why?'

It spills out before I can stop it. 'Anyone with more shirts than minutes in the day is likely to be germ obsessed too.'

His low laugh resounds through my chest. 'I don't give a damn about contamination. The numbers are outrageous because I'm naturally messy and prone to spills.' He laughs again. 'If we talk about it much longer the ice cream will have melted.'

'So you're good to share?'

'Absolutely. I am.' He pushes his chocolate pile towards me, I hitch my stool closer, and a second later we're dipping into each other's sweets.

As I watch him scoop one of my raspberries and shiver as it slips between his teeth, I wonder what *Grazia*'s take on this would be. So long as we aren't feeding each other, I reckon we're okay. But this close up his scent is overlaid with entirely different notes and as we work our way down our portions, I can see the pores on his skin where the stubble grows. And each individual dark eyelash.

As expected, mine runs out first, then a few moments later he's scraping up the remnants of his.

I shake my head and let out a sigh of relief that it's over. Then instantly regret that too. 'Leave the glaze on the china, Kit.'

When he finally raises his spoon from the cup it's loaded to the max. Then he pushes it towards *me*. 'This last one is yours.'

My tummy drops. 'You have it.' Any excuse *not* to cross that line of him putting food into my mouth. I try again. 'You're missing that my kitchen is *bursting* with chocolate fudge cake.' And I'm missing that he might have saved my house from burning, but he's technically still on the enemy side. This is so much closer than the distance I intended to keep.

'No really – you made it, it has to be for you...'

Oh my. I pull back, then decide it's quicker to get this over than protest and go forward, parting my lips. An inch before I reach the target, I totally lose my nerve and veer off. As my cheek collides with his wrist it jogs the spoon and sends the large dollop of melting chocolate ice cream sliding straight down his shirt front.

'Shit, I'm *so* sorry!' How can so little ice cream go so far? 'You look like you've been mud wrestling! I'll get the kitchen roll.'

He's on his feet. 'No worries, it's fine.'

A nanosecond later Kit pulls the shirt over his head and as he scrunches it up, I'm left gaping at a tanned torso that's nothing like Dillon's much narrower, gym-hardened version. Not that I'm comparing. These shoulders are large and naturally muscled. Wide and strong enough to throw me over them. Not that I'd let him. *Not in a thousand years.*

I'm opening and closing my mouth, grasping for words. 'Can I lend you a T-shirt?'

He unzips his camera bag, and a moment later there's a flap of white fabric. 'This is why I always carry spares. Luckily, I have one last clean shirt.'

I let out a sigh because he's so full-on. 'And a hundred and ninety-nine in the wash?'

'Thank you for doing the counting.' He catches my eye and

18

The Hideaway, St Aidan
Undercoats and overcoats
Tuesday

By the time Shadow and I get back from our after-breakfast walk next morning, my mum has arrived as promised and she's ready to go.

'As soon as we've spread out the dust sheets, we'll do the painting right away.'

Kit sent me some photos from yesterday, and I'm pleased I forwarded them on to the gang and saw their comments and flashing heart emojis before going out, because there won't be any time now. Mum's in her hundred-per-cent painting overalls, and the stack of Hardware Haven carrier bags and paint rollers she's piled across the deck obliterate every trace of last night's romance.

I can forget about basking in the praise from Bianca and Salvador too, because my mum is like a tornado. I'm struggling to get to grips with the change of pace, hoping I'm not rushing into this. 'Should we do a tester square first to check the colour?'

She waves away my concern. 'One coat should cover it. If you don't like it, we'll paint it again.'

'Would you like a coffee before we begin?' As I play for time I'm waving at Jean and Shirley in their red puffer jackets further along the beach. Now we know each other better we've reached an understanding that they can pop in whenever they like to have whatever's in my fridge, and pay at the end of every fortnight.

Mum pulls the tie belt that's nipping in her waist even tighter. 'We can have a drink later.' She follows my gaze along the beach. 'If your friends are coming over, I'll get everything inside while you see what they want.'

As Jean and Shirley climb the steps, I call to them, 'Sorry, we're busy decorating this morning.' I know better than to get in Mum's way while she's working.

Shirley pats my arm. 'Don't worry about that, we've just come from Seaspray Cottage.' She looks up at the light strings blowing in the wind. 'We couldn't help overhearing Clemmie and Nell looking at your photos. So you're moving into evening entertaining?'

Jean peers past a carrier bag with paint rollers spilling out and stares pointedly at a lantern. 'As the secret's out we came straight away.'

It was one couple for barely an hour, but with the St Aidan bush telegraph, who needs advertising? 'Do you have something in mind?'

Shirley beams at me. 'Six of us, on Thursday. A little

surprise to toast our friend's seventieth. Seven until nine would be perfect.'

'We know it's short notice.' Jean is frowning. 'But we'd love to be the first to help you expand your horizons.'

Telling it like it is isn't a problem with these two. 'I could do you a selection of sweets on our usual terms if you provide the Prosecco and glasses?'

'Lovely. We'll let you get on.' They're already going back down the steps. 'Can we bring our own birthday cake?'

'Absolutely.'

My mum comes out for the last bag. 'Another booking?'

It's not what I intended or wanted, but with a lido on the horizon it's sink or swim. I might need to go forward with my instincts a bit more.

I nod. 'If I make the beach hut matter to people, even in a small way, then they won't want to see it demolished.'

'Spoken like a true May! Don't let anyone walk over you! Come out fighting!' She hands me a paintbrush. 'Now, let's get inside and we'll do that wall.'

19

The Hideaway, St Aidan
Cornets, chimes and bright ideas
Tuesday

'There's no point looking at the colour when it's wet, it changes as it dries.'

Mum and I spent quite a while wandering round the beach hut before we settled on how much wall to include in the feature area. We've painted the edges with small brushes, and the first inky aquamarine lines of the midnight ocean paint we're using are already looking dramatic. And so far there's more paint on the wall than on my threadbare shorts and old shirt.

Mum's throwing out her thoughts as we work. 'This is one of my favourite go-to shades. It'll fly on once we start, which is why we only need two of us.'

I turn to check that Shadow is keeping his distance and see the wag of his tail get wider until it's waving in large circles. By the time he's jumping up and down on the spot barking his head off, Mum turns around too.

'What's Sophie doing here? And Maisie!'

I'm wondering the same. 'She may have come to pick up the lanterns?'

My mum sniffs. 'She probably wants input on the colour. You'd think she was the only person in St Aidan who'd ever made a mood board.'

'Mum!' I'm firing a warning shot. When it comes to interiors, she and Sophie get oddly competitive.

Decorating is still a mystery to me, so I need to check. 'Haven't Sophie's houses all been white?'

There's a knock on the French door, and Sophie's already in the room answering. 'Cream, actually, but I still know the Pretty Green chart inside out.' She smiles at me. 'Nice top, Floss.'

I grin. 'Not my usual, but St Aidan's pushing me to explore my wild turquoise side.' She has so many this colour I can't blame her for not remembering this was once one of hers.

Our mum is still tutting. 'This isn't a painting party, Sophie, there's barely room for Floss and me as it is.'

Sophie pulls a face. 'You'd better get used to a crowd, there are more coming.' Then as my mum's face falls as there's a clattering on the deck steps, she backs down. 'It's only Nell, Clemmie and the children. We're on our way to Busy Bee Storytime, but there's important business to see to first.'

Mum puts down her brush. 'We only have half an hour of painting to do, and I'm busy elsewhere after that, so this *better* be special.'

Clemmie leads Bud in, and by the time I uncover a chair for her and Nell, there's another knock at the door.

'Plum, too! Lovely to see you all.'

Clemmie sits down and arranges Arnie, then she squints at Sophie and me. 'What's with the twin vibe? You're usually like chalk and cheese, and today you look very alike!'

I couldn't have hoped for a better cue. 'I'm wearing a Sophie cast-off top. It's Ted Baker.'

Sophie's eyebrows shoot up. 'Why did I give *that* away? It's gorgeous!'

It's not often I get to tease her, so I laugh. 'Different clothes suit different people.' Then I laugh even more at her indignant look. 'I'd give you it back, but you'd drown in it. It's from when you had Marcus and Tilly.' Only Sophie could be pregnant with twins and still be smaller than I am now.

She recovers herself. 'That's all right then.'

I stare around the circle of faces. 'So what's this about?' Then, as Shadow starts to whine again, I check the deck and I turn to my mum with a sinking heart. 'I'm sorry, I have no idea why Kit should be here, he knew we were painting.' My heart sinks even further. 'With Rye too.'

Sophie opens the door, and beckons them in. 'We asked Kit over so we could share the news with you both at once.'

Yet another disadvantage of living so close. And when I glimpse Kit's rear view in inky blue jeans, it hits me that dishing out advice to neighbours is another bad call that's come back to bite me. Who'd have thought a simple swap from flannel to denim would elevate a disgustingly hot tush to off-the-scale can't-keep-my-hands-off status? All in the most politically correct, unobjective way, obviously.

Mum must be thinking of her free smoke alarms more than she resents the disruption, because she greets the guys like long-lost friends, plants a kiss on each of their cheeks, then makes space for them on the dust-sheet-covered sofa.

As soon as they're settled Clemmie begins. 'So guess what? We've been offered a vintage ice-cream van for the evening this Sunday!'

'Great!' I have no idea what the fuss is about. 'And that would interest me because...?'

Nell slaps her hand on her knee. 'For the joint singles club evening you and Kit offered to do! What else would it be for?'

I take it from Kit and Rye's broad yet entirely unsurprised smiles that they've known this for hours, if not days.

'But Sunday is so soon?' I'd counted on having at least a couple of months to build up to this. I'd actually hoped everyone would forget about it altogether.

Nell stares at her stomach doubtfully. 'I needed a distraction.' Then she perks up. 'So many people have signed up to come, we couldn't possibly send them all onto The Hideaway veranda, so we've gone to Plan B.'

The more I hear about this, the more it sounds like it's been going on for ever.

Clemmie's eyes are bright. 'We thought an open marquee and bar next to Kit's, then people can take their drinks into his to browse and have a tour of the studio. If we park the ice-cream van close by and put out your beach hut signs, you will have an independent base. That way you're free to add in whatever else you're comfortable with, and serve from there.'

Plum's somehow manoeuvred herself right across the room and onto the slice of the sofa next to Rye, who is sitting there like a beach god in his Aztec trousers and sun-bleached T-shirt. She's staring at me as she squeezes her shoulder in next to his.

'You don't even *have* to be there, Floss. But if you gave out teensy ice-cream cones and a few flyers, at least it tells the world that your business is up and running.'

Rye coughs. 'Or, better still, how about a cake halt?'

Plum's fuzzy adoring eyes as she stares at Rye could have come straight out of a *Grazia* piece, but even though her swishing ponytail keeps catching him under the chin, the inch of air between them suggests that she hasn't progressed to the hands-on phase yet. Which unfortunately leads my gaze three feet to the left, where it lands on denim, stretched tight across Kit's thighs. For a fleeting moment I regret my decision to be a thoroughly committed singleton, then I remember who I am, and redouble my resolve. It still takes a full ten seconds to unstick my own eyes from that view and get back to the business in hand.

Ducking out of the singles night might be my preference, but however much I'd rather have a hundred miles between me and High Tides, with the challenges ahead it would be rash to waste this opportunity. I need to embrace it and make it work for me.

'So how many people are we talking?'

Kit raises an eyebrow. 'Definitely less than a hundred and ninety-nine.'

'Thanks, Kit.' I can't cope with jeans *and* attitude. I turn back to Nell.

She's looking at her phone. 'Forty to fifty. Sixty max.'

My chest implodes. There's no way I can do that number. *But then, I can't afford not to.*

Nell carries on. 'The more you give them the more we'll charge – and the bigger impact you'll make.'

I stare around the expectant faces and screw up every bit of my courage.

'I'll do lucky dip puddings.' I'm so far out of my comfort zone here, as I turn to Nell again it's like some entrepreneur from *The Apprentice* has taken me over. 'In mini ice-cream tubs to keep on theme. One tub per person – or two?'

Nell brings her fist down on her knee. 'Call it three, and we'll really put you on the map.'

'Three it is!' It's like someone else is operating my mouth. It takes a minute to do the sums and when it hits me what I've agreed to, my blood runs cold. But it's out there! It's too late to turn back now.

As I see Rye's smile fade, I take pity. 'And there will be chocolate brownies too. For the purists.'

Rye gives the air a punch as he stands up. 'Great! Now everyone's on board and up to speed, we'll leave you to your decorating.'

Kit sits forwards on the sofa edge and holds up a fan of tickets. 'One last thing...'

Sophie's like a terrier on a scent. 'Are those ... High Tides Spa vouchers?'

I can't believe he's brought this up again. 'It's more a girls' night in a hot tub, with seaweed crisp snacks and salt-water fizz. Florence wasn't sure last time I offered.' Kit's looking at me, querying.

Clemmie's looking at me too, her eyes full of concern. 'It's always worth a second try, Kit. No pressure, Floss, but if you fancy giving it a go the rest of us will all be there to support you.'

Mum's nudging my arm and Plum's nodding so hard her head might drop off.

Sophie fixes me with her significant, hard-headed stare. 'We have to admit, it would be *so good* to check the place out.' And she has a point. Knowing what's inside High Tides may well give me an advantage in the future. In fact, it could be another gift I'd be mad to turn down.

I drag in a breath, then I cave. 'Absolutely,' I say in a totally ironic way. 'Why not?'

I can't believe I've agreed to two nightmare evenings in the space of five minutes. But as they all troop off across the deck, I know it's a measure of how scared I am. However much I dislike my neighbours, I don't want to be pressured into losing my home.

And before I even get to think about this, there's another party to get ready for too.

The Hideaway, St Aidan
Open mouths and bright sparks
Thursday

Kit ambling across the dunes and swinging up onto the deck isn't ideal at the best of times. When there's barely half an hour left for the last-minute jobs before the guests arrive for Jean and Shirley's mini birthday 'do' on Thursday it's definitely bad timing.

At least the light strings are lit, the flower posies are on the table with the glasses they brought around earlier, the fridge is bursting with their Prosecco, and the ice bucket is waiting in the freezer. If I carry on hanging the blankets over the chair arms, he should get the message.

'Nice shirt, Kit.' I assume that's what he's come round to show me. The dark blue check could be wilder, but at least it's a start and the colour suits him way too much. It's not his fault the extra open button where his tie usually is lets me glimpse the indentation at the base of his throat, and sets my heart banging against my chest. 'Great with those jeans too.' I'm lying. From the point of view of my pulse rate the whole outfit is a total disaster. 'I'm sure your clients will appreciate your vibe.'

He grins. 'I hope it's not too casual for tonight. I came early to help light the lanterns.'

'Early – to what?' I have zero idea what he's talking about, but now I've given his outfit the thumbs-up, I'm wishing he'd hurry up and leave.

He frowns. 'The birthday get together – *it is this evening?*'

My mind is racing. He can't possibly be coming. I can't stand another night of him at The Hideaway. 'Since when do you know Shirley and Jean and their friends?'

He gives a shrug. 'We met on your steps and bonded over Coco Pops. They asked a lot of questions about my wet suit, and it grew from there.'

Unbelievable. 'They implied it was a women's night, that's all.'

He pulls in a breath. 'Apart from me it is. I'm not under any illusions – I've been invited to pour the drinks and look pretty.'

He's here as toyboy totty! My jaw is on the floor. 'Do you mind that?'

His mouth twists into a smile. 'There are incentives. If I eat enough puddings it saves me cooking dinner. There's birthday cake too...'

That's the downside of letting people pay to use my veranda – I don't get to choose the guests. Even if I have more parties, I seriously doubt Kit will turn up at any others, so I need to concentrate on the good bits, like the happy whoosh I'll feel if everyone has a good time. And how much this will add to the roll of notes in my kitchen. Every day my throat stays husky, I look up at that roll more often.

But back to tonight, it's happening, so I need to suck it up. I thank my lucky stars it ends at nine and start acting like a hostess.

'In that case, welcome to the party, Kit! I probably should get on, so if you're sure you don't mind helping...' I hold out the candle lighter.

'So long as I get to finish the leftovers?'

'You might have gone home by then.'

'I probably won't.' He laughs. 'Leave it with me.'

Like so many things in St Aidan, the reality when it happens is nothing like as bad as I fear. Jean, Shirley and their three friends come along the beach from the harbour, and Jean and Shirley have been here so often they're immediately at home, pointing out the landmarks in the distance around the bay. As soon as I bring the ice bucket out Kit pours the drinks and hands them round.

While they stand and watch the sea rolling up and down the beach and drink more fizz, I get busy with the ice-cream scoop, and in no time they're sitting down, gasping as I deliver the first trayful of goodies to the table. As the evening passes, they have more wine, and more puddings.

As they work their way through even more wine, and even more sweets Shadow and I are sitting quietly inside, listening to the chatter and the laughter, and watching the light strings swing as the grey sky beyond turns to charcoal.

I break off from making lists of new sweet ideas to take out more fizz, and serviettes and plates, and then I light the seven and the zero candles, and carry out the cake. I stay long enough to sing 'Happy Birthday', then slip back inside again.

Even though I'm here every day, I never stop thinking how amazing it is. And because the sky and the wind and the sea change from second to second, no two moments are ever the same. It's such a special place, everyone here tonight will remember this evening for ever. It's not just about making people think The Hideaway is important. It's so unique here, it's a lovely feeling to be sharing it with other people, even for a short time.

As they cut up the cake the door opens a crack, and Kit comes in carrying some for both of us.

'How's it going? Still in one piece?'

He laughs. 'I did my uni placement in a jewellers on an upmarket cruise ship so I'm used to this crowd. Their generation are great company.'

This man is full of surprises. I glance at my phone. 'There's still half an hour and a few more bottles to get through. If you give up now, they'll call you a lightweight.'

'I'll take that risk. I was wanting a chat with you anyway ... about Sunday.'

I put my hands over my ears. 'I can't think about that until this is over!'

From his smile he thinks I'm joking. 'It's about the timings.'

'And?'

'With the numbers Nell's talking, it would be great if you could come and help me with the hosting and the tours at mine.'

'Me?' It's the end of a long day. *Why me?*

He blows out his cheeks. 'You've lived the ring-making experience, you know enough to talk about it confidently. No one else here can do that.'

'And the ice-cream van?' I can't actually bring myself to mention the hundred and eighty puddings.

'That can be part two, once everyone has been through the studio.' He smiles. 'Then I'll be around to help you.'

I'm mentally shaking my head. The van was so I could stay right away from the High Tides people; this way means a hundred per cent exposure. If Kit insists he needs my help with his part I'll come through with that, but he doesn't need to be involved with mine.

'The van will be full of mermaids – they'll all want to help, they always do.'

'Nell in the ice-cream van? *Really?*' He sounds doubtful.

I have to be realistic, she won't want to be on her feet all evening. 'Maybe not Nell. *Or* Clemmie.'

He carries on. 'If Rye's on the bar, Plum may prefer to be with him.'

And good luck to anyone who tries to prise her away. It shouldn't be a shock he's noticed. He'd have to be blind not to have done.

Which leaves Sophie. Who is also doubtful. 'Milla may come. Or my mum.'

I'm bluffing. Singles club is the last place she'd want to be, and if Milla is still grounded it's likely this will be me on my own.

Kit stares down at the curls of buttercream in his hand. Then he grins at me. 'I had a lot of practice working small spaces on the cruise ship, I promise not to tread on any toes.'

That's the best reason of all to say no. Me in the confines of an ice-cream van with Kit's denim-clad butt is a very bad idea. That rear and I need to be properly socially distanced at all times. Two metres clearance is nothing like enough.

I cram a handful of cake into my mouth and try to sound airy. 'I'll get back to you on that.'

He nods. 'You can always use my place for prep. We'll need a run-through of the tour, and we can talk through your strategy at the same time. You can let me know then.' He swallows a buttercream rosette.

'Fabulous. Absolutely.' It's totally not. What the hell does he mean by strategy? All I have this far are paper ice-cream cups in pastel colours, a pack of two hundred biodegradable mini spoons, and a promise of trays and containers from Clemmie.

He flicks a cake crumb off his cuff. 'I can run a few shirts past you too.'

'Better and better.' Like there'll be time for that!

'Will nine tomorrow be okay?'

This isn't me! I'm not a caterer or a fashion expert! Before now I've always been the kind of person who goes to parties, not someone who puts them on. I'm also someone who throws things together and wings it. It's not like I've ever done anything this big or important before, which is why I must be mad to even try.

I hate to admit that Kit's right – but that mahoosive number of puddings aren't going to materialise on their own. If I want to avoid falling flat on my face in a puddle of soft scoop, I'm going to have to seriously up my game here. All while trying not to rip the clothes off the metallurgist.

It's an enormous challenge – I only hope I'm up to it.

21

Latitude One, High Tides Hotel, St Aidan
Cereal boxes and forward planning
Friday

Shadow and I are up at the crack the morning after Jean and Shirley's party, not that there's any clearing up to do. By the time the friends wandered off back to St Aidan any crumbs had long since blown away, and then I washed a few dishes, stuck the bottles in the recycling and it was job done. All that was left was the glow of pride in my chest, and the echoes of their effusive thank yous carried by the wind along the beach. If it hadn't been for the Kit complication, that would have been the easiest roll of twenty-pound notes I'd ever earned.

As arranged, on the dot of nine Shadow and I settle into Kit's sofa area and watch a catwalk show of clothes mostly borrowed from Rye. We go for the least tight jeans, and a blue shirt with a dark blue flower print, worn outside the trousers to give maximum bum coverage. Like everything in life, you have to choose your battles. We give up on trainers and settle for deck shoes without socks because anything is better than black leather city brogues and we don't have all day.

Once we move onto the proper stuff, I follow Kit around and nod while he delivers his tour. I only interrupt to remind him he needs a single angle as well as his usual one, when it hits me that the couple stuff isn't making me want to scream quite as much as it once did. Having happy couples paraded non-stop under my nose for weeks has taken the edge off me wanting to throw up the instant I see them. It helps that I've seen from the inside that even the most loved-up ones have their difficult moments. Don't get me wrong, I still hate that the world is built for pairs, but I'm more at peace coexisting beside that as my own person.

I offer to get flowers. We send out for crates to stack artfully in the studio, fishing nets to drape over them, and two blue deck chairs for the front of each hut. I'm thinking we're almost done here when Kit comes out with the showstopper: 'So what about *your* plans?'

As it was a choice between reluctant family members and Kit, I didn't have much leeway. I rang Sophie and apologised for the very last time for Dyegate, then I committed to future baby-sitting out of all proportion to the crime. But at least I secured her services.

'We'll use your second hut for storage of the prepped cups, as you suggested.' I can't quite bring myself to give it its full title. 'Then Sophie, Milla, Mum and I will run them across to the van and finish and serve from there. And you can have a second serving station with the brownie stack and extra sprinkle supplies at a table outside.'

He looks doubtful. 'Is that the best balance?'

I try to stop my worst fears from breaking through my calm exterior. 'It's one night! Sophie and Milla will have to suck it up and get on!' That goes for Mum and Sophie, and me and Sophie, too. 'Given the friction it's not ideal, but it's the best I can do.'

He looks out at the sea. 'I was talking about numbers, not personalities.'

Damn. 'Let's not overthink it. I'll juggle as it happens.'

If it sounds like a recipe for disaster, it probably is.

22

Latitudes One and Two, High Tides Hotel, St Aidan
Bouncy castles and lines in the sand
Sunday

We couldn't have wished for a more perfect night. For once the wind has dropped, and as the sun sinks across the bay the singles club members arrive and cluster around the gazebo bar. Nell is there, welcoming everyone from her steamer chair as Rye pours mojitos for a wide range of guests. The ladies from Iron Maidens cleaners are here, there are a couple of young barmen I recognise from Jaggers bar, some people in gym gear who look like they've come straight from aerobics, and Jean and Shirley have brought a gang from the walk-and-talk group.

Plum bounces around, giving out cards for tonight's icebreaker, which is how most singles club events begin. If you find someone with the same picture as yours, you have to yell 'Together Forever' at the top of your voice, kiss them on both cheeks, and then you both have to down your mojitos and go and get a refill. As there are only four different cards the noise soon drowns out the sound of the waves, and Rye is wielding his jug as if he's been doing this for ever rather than only half an hour.

I'd been dreading the bit where Nell introduced Kit and me, but it's over in seconds and no one seems to give a damn that I gave up ironing my ditsy print dress halfway round the skirt. Before I know it, I'm in the studio, answering a thousand and one questions about jewellery as if I've been doing it my whole life. Kit's working the crowd at the other end of the room, and as I catch only glimpses of his dark curls over other people's heads, this is definitely the kind of teamwork I can cope with. Before I know it, part one of the evening is over, and the spotlight is turning onto me.

When it comes to my own team, a van was a great idea to separate us from the High Tides gang, but I knew cramming my mum, Sophie and Milla together to assemble the sweets was a risk. In ten seconds flat Sophie and Mum have clashed over whether to stick the flamingos in the cake chunks or the ice cream, and my mum flounces off down the steps to help Kit with the flyers.

'Two firm orders for wedding-ring days and a definite maybe! For a singles event that's a result.'

Sophie's carrying on as if nothing has happened, as she and Milla add the ice cream, Rice Krispies and custard to the syrup sponge themed desserts, and I pass them through the serving window to the queue of customers snaking past Latitude One's veranda and out towards the sand.

As my supply runs out, I turn to get the next trayful. 'There were some very wistful "When the time comes" sighs, too.'

Sophie nods. 'You can't look too far ahead in business. These are all potential future clients. After all, Nell loves to give her singles goals to aim for.'

It was a good move to light up The Hideaway too, so when people ask where I'm based, I can point. It looks magical with the warm glow of its windows, and the hanging bulbs splashing light across the decks as they swing in the breeze.

As we come to the end of the queue and I give the last of the sweets to Nell's partner George to take to the helpers, I let out a sigh. 'Sixty down, only another hundred and twenty left to go!'

Milla puts the top on the caramel ice-cream tub. 'So what's next?'

I take a breath to clear my head. 'White chocolate cheesecake, fresh mango and grated coconut.'

Sophie nods. 'If people like them *half* as much as the last ones, you're onto a winner.'

I hold up my crossed fingers, and wriggle past them. 'They're in Kit's fridge. If you two get the vanilla ice cream out, I'll go across and grab them.'

The front of the van is darker as I head for the open sliding door. As I squeeze past the driver's seat, I'm so busy looking over the crowd working out the best way to avoid Kit at the outdoor table that I launch myself off the top step without looking down. I'm in mid-air in full trajectory before I sense someone step right into the space where I should be landing.

All I can do is let out a cry. 'Hey, look out!'

It's a cross between a collision and a full-blown attempt to squish the person on the ground into oblivion, *and it's all my fault*. As I come to a halt rammed up against some stranger's chest I'm dying of shame, wondering how I'll ever begin to apologise. Then, as a familiar scent engulfs me, and a very low voice reverberates all around me, I'm dying all over again.

'Floss? Are you okay?'

'I'm fine, Kit.' I'm not. 'Totally.' In fact, I couldn't be any worse. Of all the people here, he's the last person I'd choose to crash into. The entire front of my body is crushed against his, his arms are wrapped around me holding me up, and there's no escape backwards because my spine is rammed against a bloody ice-cream van.

The most hideous thing of all? My body feels like it's woken up after a hundred years asleep, and every nerve end is jangling. My sensible brain is telling me to get the hell out of here, but another part of my head is overruling, forcing my legs to stay exactly where they are – rooted to the spot, so I can soak up the electric pulses that are surging through me for the maximum time possible.

I close my eyes and allow myself to sink against him. Then as my sensible self takes over again, he turns and now instead of being rammed against him I'm standing looking up into his eyes and they're laughing.

'That's what's known in the trade as a happy landing.'

Considering he took my full weight, he's taking this very lightly. 'I haven't broken your legs?'

That makes him laugh even more. 'I doubt it.' He steadies me and I take a step sideways. 'I was on my way to tell you your mum had to rush off unexpectedly.'

I hope she's all right. 'Was she called away?'

He shrugs. 'She caught sight of someone in the distance, said to tell you she couldn't stay, then she bolted.' His hand is on my elbow. 'Everyone's wanting your cards, but I'll manage on my own.'

However much my feet are opting to stay here for ever, I need to get a move on. 'Great! I'll let you get back to it.'

It's not all bad news – at least I don't have to go a long way round to his fridge to avoid him now.

I do two trips to Latitude Two, and by the time Sophie meets me at the van door to take the tray the second time, her face is like thunder.

'Everything okay in Mr Whippy paradise?' I ask.

She looks up at the van roof as I follow her inside. 'Listening to Absolute 80s on the radio *isn't* a crime, Milla. I've always loved Madonna.'

Milla shakes her head. 'We aren't even talking about music. You had a go because my T-shirt didn't have any sides, and I asked why you never wear proper clothes. If you won't buy me the styles I like, I have to customise with scissors. So what's your excuse?'

Sophie pushes her back against the freezer and points down at her trousers and top. 'It's jeans and a sweatshirt, sweetheart. What's not to like?'

'The colour!' Milla gives a snort. 'As an ex-blonde with loaded parents it's hard enough to maintain my credibility as it is. When my mother *insists* on dressing like a mint mousse every single day, I may as well give up.'

Our entire life, Sophie has always come out fighting, but this time she looks beaten. And however much I secretly agree with Milla about the aqua-blue overkill, part of me knows I have to throw Sophie a lifeline.

I'm smiling into space, but my mind is on why we're here.

'Could we possibly talk about this *after* we've prepped the next sixty desserts?'

Sophie's tugging her apron strings and a second later she hangs it over the back of the driver's seat. 'I'm sorry to run out on you, Floss, but I'm going outside.'

I'm recalling what someone else said as I let out a wail. 'But that will upset the balance.'

Milla's already got the top off the ice-cream tub. 'We've got this, Aunty Flo. You make them up and I'll go to the serving window.'

Except we haven't got any part of it! The two of them had trouble keeping up first time round and when people have to wait too long it kills their enjoyment. I'm resigning myself to the earlier success turning into dismal failure when there's a tap on the van side. A moment later a face appears next to the driver's mirror.

'Kit! If you're here for second helpings, we're a bit busy.'

Kit smiles. 'I haven't had *any* yet, I gave mine to David.' He takes in my blank stare. 'David ... *Byron*.'

My jaw drops because this wasn't in the plan at all. 'David Byron's eating my dessert? What *the hell* is he doing here?'

Kit shrugs. 'I'd guess because he owns the hotel and wants to support our event.' His face cracks into a smile. 'He is single too. And he probably heard how good your sweets are and wanted a piece of the action.'

I'm shaking my head. 'If that's all...'

'It isn't.' He holds up a finger. 'Sophie mentioned you might need a hand. I'm scrubbed up and ready, just point me to where I'm needed.'

The minute space beside me would have been fine to rub

along with Sophie, but can I cope with Kit that close? It takes a nanosecond to decide.

'I'm just on my way to get Plum.'

He raises his eyebrow. 'I'll save you a journey. Someone else took over on the bar, and Plum and Rye were last seen heading off along the beach.'

Milla lets out a whoop. 'Another coup for Nell!'

I give Kit a look. 'And two more rings for you down the line? The singles club could be a whole new market!'

Milla laughs. 'No arguing, Aunty Flo. If Plum's making out in the dunes, it looks like Kit's on custard.'

And for one time only I have nothing left to add to that.

23

Latitudes One and Two, High Tides Hotel, St Aidan
Revelations and incantations
Monday

L ast night in the ice-cream van... How did it go? *Honestly?*
Being crushed into a space the size of a shoebox with the most touchable body in St Aidan then having to dip and bend and swivel around him while simultaneously delivering perfect scoops of fudge brownie ice cream into cups was as tense and tantalising as playing Twister with an octopus.

Me having accidentally landed on him barely fifteen minutes earlier, knowing how delicious it felt to have my boobs rammed against his ribs and my hip bone grinding against his fly made it a thousand times worse. Imagine the most luscious dark chocolate cake, covered in lashings of buttercream, then put yourself two inches from it, and for an entire two hours, you aren't allowed to touch it.

Add in a running commentary from Milla at the serving

window, who had eyes in the back of her head when it came to seeing what was – *or wasn't* – going on behind her. Then you'll see why I'm really pleased that today is a brand-new day.

When I was ill and had my first operation, I didn't allow myself to worry in advance. I'd always imagined I'd be the kind of courageous woman who blasted her way through the hospital doors, punching the air while Sia's 'Titanium' pulsated through her ear buds. But when it actually happened, I crept into the surgical unit at six-thirty in the morning in total silence, whispered, 'See you on the other side' to Dillon, and slid into my gown. When the nurse brought me my elastic stockings, I was so scared my feet were shaking too much for her to put them on. But then the pharmacist came, and the anaesthetist, and after that there was so much going on there wasn't time to worry. And when I woke up afterwards all there was left for me to do was to recover.

But what that whole time taught me was that the fastest way to get over your fears is to live through them – and I feel I should be doing that now. Except I haven't really thought that one through. If I were applying that to the teensy problem next door, I'd simply breeze in, sleep with it and get the whole thing out of my system. That's what I might have done when I was twenty, but there's no way I'm up for that anymore. It's not only about my age. It's about my post-operative state, which is actually like a disability. And as it's relatively new to me, I'm meeting all these issues for the first time. Heading through life without my usual toolkit is like trying to fight a boxing match with my hands tied behind my back. But all things considered, I'll have to skirt around this problem, rather than deal with it head-on.

Not that I count this as a huge issue when there are other

much bigger ones around. I'm hoping this is one of the kind that will go away if I forget it. So when I hang around on the path by my deck, stretching my neck to watch until Kit's left his veranda and headed off towards the hotel, I'm definitely *not* stalking. There's simply no point making things more complicated by bumping into him when I'm going to pick up the remnants from yesterday.

The moment I see him amble off towards the car park, Shadow and I sprint across the dune, heading for the porch on Latitude Two, where we've agreed Kit will leave anything I didn't pick up last night. We're on our second trip, sweeping the last of the boxes into my shoulder bag, when a voice beyond the deck chairs makes me jump.

'Floss! Just the person I was hoping to meet.'

'Kit!' My heart sinks as I scramble to my feet. 'We thought you must be out.' Including Shadow in the statement makes me feel like I have backup.

Kit gives Shadow's ears a tickle. 'I went to run something past David. He said to pass on his compliments for your sweets.'

When Sophie phoned last night to thank me for supporting her with Milla, she mentioned this too. As if David Byron chugging his way through my chocolate chips wasn't bad enough, apparently he also took every opportunity to mingle and spread the word about his bloody lido.

I can't keep it to myself. 'That man has a damn cheek, hijacking our event for his own ends.' I know it's his hotel, but in my book this crosses the line to unacceptable behaviour.

He was also responsible for my sleepless night, but he accidentally did me a favour; by dawn I knew I couldn't sit back any longer. I wasn't intending on going public quite this soon, but hearing his name again is like yet another wake-up call.

Kit shuffles. 'He was very enthusiastic about my suggestions, which is why I wanted to talk to you.'

I hold up my finger because this can't wait. 'Let me give you my news first. As last night's feedback was so positive, I will *definitely* be doing more hospitality at The Hideaway.'

'That's brilliant. Your puddings are too delicious and original not to share them.' His eyes brighten, and he squeezes my arm. 'Will that extend as far as brownie stacks?'

I'm about to reply with a coy 'it may', but half-hearted won't do here. 'If you have orders, bring them on.' A thriving business in a beach hut will be so much harder to obliterate than a woman as invisible as a sand worm.

'That fits in very well with my ideas too.' There's a gap where he should be asking for three dozen, but he shuffles again. 'Everyone loves the beach vibe you've created at Latitudes, so I want to take that further.'

My mind is racing. 'You're adding in a sea shanty compilation? Or flip flops?'

There are crinkles at the edge of his eyes as he smiles. 'Better than that. I want to include a visit to The Hideaway as an option in my ring-making package.'

Hearing that last word makes me realise I'm staring at his fly, so I wrench my eyes upwards. 'Fabulous. If you have any takers, let me know and we'll get together with my appointment book.' I seriously doubt he will, so there's no need to get excited. 'Nice Levi's you're wearing there.'

Hopefully that explains what I was looking down at. If he does happen to get any bookings, I'll make sure he does his romantic poses and leaves me with the couple, because I'm seriously over him hanging round on my sofa.

My decision about my dating future didn't happen overnight; it took months of agonising, considering the pros and cons at every stage of a relationship, balancing the need for fun with the need to avoid disaster, and protect myself and any partners at a time when I'm vulnerable. But having finally committed to how I'm going to live my life, there's no point making it harder for myself than it needs to be. If there's someone messing up my long-term strategy, it's sensible to avoid them as much as I can.

Kit slides his thumb through the belt loop. 'I had to check that David didn't mind me diverting the business to you instead of the hotel.'

That thought fires me up all over again. 'We could always ask Vic and Amery if you could use their pictures of The Hideaway on your website.' There's no point doing this by halves. If I'm involved, I may as well go for it! 'You had some dreamy shots of Bianca and Salvador on the deck too.'

He nods. 'I'm on it. Last night brought up something else too.'

My heart rate falters. 'How great chocolate flakes taste when they're crumbled rather than stuck in?'

His face breaks into a smile. 'I was going to say how well it worked with the two of us in the studio.'

I can't believe I was worried he was going to talk about the static inside the ice-cream van when he probably didn't even feel it.

He tilts his head on one side. 'The atmosphere is transformed when we're both there. I wondered if you'd consider coming to help welcome the clients as they arrive. As a part-time paid position it would work in well with the visits to The Hideaway.'

I'm biting my lip. 'It's a great offer.' But when I've vowed to stay away from the hotel it's out of the question. And it doesn't sit well with me trying to spend less time with him either.

He's already searching my eyes for an answer. 'And in case it's a clincher, Shadow's welcome to come along with you too.'

I'm silently cursing that he's covering every angle. 'Can I see how it fits in with my other plans, and let you know?'

I already know my answer will be no, but this gives me time to work out a watertight get-out.

He claps his hands and rubs them together. 'Take as long as you need. It's the spa night tomorrow, so if I don't see you before I'll pop in then and check how you're all getting on.'

So much for me avoiding the hotel. The way things are going this week I might as well book a room and move in!

24

The spa night, High Tides Hotel, St Aidan
Fake nails and limp lettuce
Tuesday

'How are the curries working, Nell?'

As her due date came and went long ago, we've finally abandoned the diplomatic approach and as we laze on our enormous personal hotel hot tub terrace with the sound of waves lapping up the beach a little way below, we're back to talking about her baby progress. So far, the spa night party consists of me, Plum, Sophie, Milla – who blagged a late entry from Kit thanks to being so helpful in the ice-cream van – Clemmie, who's here with Arnie for the alcohol-free fizz but not the tub, Nell, and Mum who arrived and then disappeared just as quickly.

Nell lets out a snort. 'Three vindaloos and a rogan gosht last weekend *and I'm still here.* Draw your own conclusions.'

High Tides have provided us all with fluffy white bath robes to go over our own swimsuits, as well as a stack of towels the height of the Empire State Building, and we've been away in twos for our complimentary massages and pedis. And now we're resting our newly buffed toes on polished outdoor limestone tiles until we find enough energy to join Sophie and Milla in the barrel-sided tub.

Now we're here, sipping our fizz, soaking up the luxurious surroundings and nibbling from dishes of deep-fried kale, it's annoying that there's very little to find fault with. Plum leans over from the next steamer chair and points at the green mass on the plate Nell's holding. 'So what's that you've got there?'

Nell sighs. 'Emergency room-service to keep my blood sugar up. Seaweed salad, with a balsamic dressing.'

Sophie frowns. 'Was that the most appetising thing on the menu?'

'By a million miles.' Nell holds out her plate. 'Anyone like to try some?'

Sophie pulls a face and waves away the offer.

Milla rolls her eyes. 'Not being open to new things is why you're getting so left behind, Mum.'

I give Milla a warning look. 'You and your mum both promised – no arguing at the spa night!'

As Sophie flashes me a discreet thumbs-up, Plum joins in. 'If you're offering it around, I'll give it a go.' She helps herself to a sprig and lets out a shriek. 'Jeez, Nell, that vinegar's strong!'

Clemmie laughs. 'Which reminds me, is Rye around tonight?'

We somehow assumed he would be, but so far it looks like the new bikini Plum's hiding under her robe is going to go to waste.

Nell chews hard on another forkful then swallows. 'So far, you've been very cagey about what went on with you and Rye the other night, Plum. You need to confirm for my records.'

Milla's sniff is just like her mum's as she turns to Plum. 'Have you asked him what he does when he's not at the fire station?'

Plum wrinkles her nose. 'We didn't talk about stuff like that.'

Nell punches the air. 'Which answers my question about what happened on Sunday. If you weren't discussing careers, did he do well enough in "other areas" to warrant arranging another date?'

Nell is very systems orientated and she awards her singles events a cupid if a couple has a subsequent date, which is why she's pushing to get her facts straight.

Plum's pretty skilled at dodging. 'I was actually having a tour of the hotel grounds to assess the potential for outdoor sculpture commissions.'

Clemmie lets out a laugh. 'I bet that went well in the dark.'

Plum ignores her. 'So far there's no date in the diary for further discussions, but while we're waiting for that to happen, we need to talk about Floss's new initiative.' She turns to where I'm perched on the edge of Clemmie's steamer chair footrest. 'There must be masses of people we know who'd like to party at The Hideaway.'

I'd run this past Clemmie yesterday, before I met Kit, and by the time I got home our WhatsApp group was all over it.

Clemmie picks Plum up straightaway. 'I'll bring a group from Mums and Bumps along. With summer on the way, you could make that a regular slot.' There's a noise behind her and she turns to see Mum appearing from the room where we changed. 'Suze, at last! Where have you been?'

Sophie doesn't wait for a reply. 'You know you've missed your pedi, Mum?'

Mum shakes off her robe, goes up the hot tub steps and slides down into the water. 'Well, I'm here now.' She puts on a towelling headband and tucks in her hair, but for someone in a spa she looks a lot more troubled than relaxed. 'I was chatting to David Byron.'

Sophie's eyebrows shoot upwards. 'For *an hour and a half?*'

I'm right about her unease then. 'I didn't realise you *knew* him.'

My mum shuffles her position. 'If you go to over-sixties events, you know everyone by sight.'

We all know she wouldn't be seen dead there, but Mum brushes away our stares. 'He offered to show me around and it seemed rude to refuse.'

This isn't like Mum at all. She's renowned for speaking her mind and pleasing herself. She's also shut down most men in the southwest, so there's definitely something odd going on. There's a very long pause and when she continues her voice sounds almost hoarse. 'He's actually asked me to have dinner with him, next week.'

'Yes!' Nell's shout breaks through the horrified silence. 'That's a date! You were both at the singles event, so it has got a cupid after all!'

Sophie's shaking her head. 'But they didn't coincide. By the time David came Mum had gone.'

Milla frowns. 'Are we *sure* about that?'

Sophie's snapping. 'Yes, we are! Aren't we, Mum?'

Mum winces for a second, then she firms up. 'There's no point asking me if I wasn't there.'

Nell splutters on a mouthful of wakame. 'Bugger technicalities, a date's a date! The cupid's in the bag.'

I was too appalled to say anything at first, but I have to challenge Mum on this. 'So – this date with Mr Byron.' I may as well parade it for what it is. 'Will you go?'

Mum takes such a deep breath her chest heaves out of the water. 'I think I may.'

I can overlook Plum throwing herself at Rye because her hormones are ruling her head, but I thought I could count on Mum. I let out a shout. 'What about your sense of loyalty? Or does the offer of a fancy meal with the local billionaire mean family solidarity goes out the window?'

My mum looks wounded and when she finally speaks her voice is quiet. 'I was hoping it might help.'

That's so unbelievable, I'm bemused. 'Help – *how*?' Anything with David Byron is bad. Accepting his dinner invitation feels like the betrayal couldn't *be* any bigger.

Clemmie's stroking Arnie's head. 'A view from the inside is always useful, Flossie Flapjack-face.'

Plum nods. 'It's only an extension of what we're doing now.'

'Which, for the record, I was a hundred per cent against.' I may as well remind them.

My mum purses her lips and looks at me. 'That's why working with Kit is such a great opportunity for *you*.'

It's as if Clemmie's peering inside my head and picking up on my secret thoughts. 'You *are* going to accept the Latitude job, Floss?'

I came here tonight determined to refuse it, but if what

they're implying is *keep your friends close and your enemies closer*, I might have to think again.

Clemmie's tugging at the hem of my bathrobe. 'Word on the street says Kit was like a puppy dog in the ice-cream van. If you're holding off working with him because he's really into you, that's a valid consideration.'

'*Excuse me?*'

Milla calls from the hot tub. 'I've told you this all along, Aunty Flo.'

Clemmie grins. 'Whenever you're together it's obvious how much he likes you. But you finding that hard to cope with in a work situation would be a good reason to turn down his offer.'

My chest is imploding that she's got this completely back to front. I might have to take the job, if only to prove to everyone it's not true.

I'm desperately struggling to come up with a denial, then I realise Plum is looking at me. 'You *do* know Dillon's planning a trip here later in the summer?'

I didn't, but if she's bringing this up because of what Clemmie's said about Kit, it's bad news all round. 'That'll be nice for Dillon. That surely wouldn't affect my working at Kit's though?'

As she sees I'm not being drawn on this, she looks away. 'Kit's coming into view now, walking up from the beach, so we might want to stop talking about him.' Plum's gazing at the distant pools of light, two tiers down on the Teletubby lawn. Then her voice shoots up an octave. 'And Rye is with him too.'

If Kit and Rye are on their way, even though I'm in a one-piece under my robe, I'd still rather be submerged in the tub before they arrive. I'd also like to stop Plum from launching into her full seduction routine with Rye.

As Clemmie catches my eye, it's obvious she's thinking the same. 'Why don't you all get into the water, and I'll take some photos before it gets too late for Arnie.'

I skirt behind Plum. 'After you!' As she tosses away her robe, and I follow her into the tub I'm thanking my lucky stars that we've saved Rye from those barely-there bottoms.

As we take our places, our arms hooked around the tub edge, Sophie kicks my foot. 'So what about the job at Kit's? Are you going to think about it?'

'Absolutely!' It's out before I can stop it, and I avoid catching Milla's eye. 'You lot are right. It's solid gold, I *have* to take it.'

And just like that I've committed myself.

25

The spa night, High Tides Hotel, St Aidan
Clam shells and falling pennies
Tuesday

'Okay, one more shot to show me you're all having a splashing time!'

Clemmie's skirting around the hot tub with Arnie still asleep in his sling. She finally steps back, skims through the pictures on her phone and nods. 'Great, that's a wrap!'

There's a clatter as Nell puts her plate down on the side table and struggles to her feet. 'Excuse me, but I'm not even in any of them yet. I might as well dip my toe in, now I've finished my salad.'

Plum laughs. '"My salad" are two words we never thought we'd hear you say together, Nell.'

'If they had pork sandwiches with crackling they might have more guests,' Nell jokes.

I smile. 'If they ask for feedback that's one for the suggestions box.'

Clemmie's watching as Nell goes up a step at a time. 'Do you need a hand there?'

Nell shakes her head. 'No, but I'm so wide, you might want to switch the camera to panoramic.'

Sophie looks up at Nell. 'Sit on the top step and dangle your feet in.' She frowns as Nell hesitates. 'Everything okay up there?'

Nell's paused, standing still with her legs apart, leaning slightly forward. 'Stuff me! I might have accidentally peed!' She's staring down at her legs in bafflement. 'There's definitely something, it's still coming out, I can feel it!'

Nell's shaking her head as she drops back down to the ground. 'I know I'm broadminded because I grew up on a farm, but peeing on the High Tides pool deck? Some of it went in the water too! I don't think I'll ever live this down.'

Clemmie's still holding her phone. 'I'll just grab a couple more photos, then you might all want to come out onto dry land.'

Sophie climbs out of the hot tub and puts her arm around Nell's shoulder. 'Don't worry, Nelly-melon, I don't think it's wee, I think your waters may have broken.'

Nell's shaking her head. 'Why didn't they warn us about this at antenatal class?'

Sophie smiles. 'The good news is, once this happens, the baby won't be too far behind.' She takes in Nell's wide eyes. 'If you haven't got any pain yet, it'll probably be tomorrow rather than today.'

Plum stops at the top of the hot tub steps and waves towards the bay. 'Perfect timing! Kit and Rye are just arriving now.' Her shout is so loud they can't possibly miss it. 'G-u-ys! Come and join us!'

Back down on the ground, I'm handing out towels and passing round the robes. I've got as far as throwing a wrap around my shoulders when Kit and Rye bounce up the hill, hop over the last box hedge and come striding onto the terrace.

Kit gives me a grin. 'You don't mind us crashing the party?'

Unlike Plum, I'd rather not be caught with my nipples on show in a soaking wet swimsuit, with my hair in rat's tails, but I'm not going to say that. 'It's as much your party as ours.'

Rye hitches up his surf trousers. 'We'd have been here to see you earlier, but I was called away to the fire station.'

In my head I'm reliving the flames, roaring towards the beach hut. 'Nothing serious, I hope?'

Rye laughs. 'St Aidan's usual. A cat trapped in a bedroom with a broken door handle, obligatory tea and cake afterwards.'

Plum leaps down the steps and lands next to Rye. 'We were very well looked after by the staff on reception.' Her hands are on her hips, and she's in no hurry to cover up her goosebumps.

I shoot Mum a look. 'David Byron was very attentive too – wasn't he, Mum?' I stop short of saying the phrase *hitting on guests*, because even though that's technically what he did, I don't want to wreck the evening.

Rye smiles. 'I'm pleased you all felt the warmth of a High Tides welcome.'

Sophie jumps forwards and slides a robe around Plum's shoulders. 'Here, put this on before you freeze!'

Plum shrugs. 'I'm really not cold.' But she relents, ties the belt tight around her waist, and puts her hand on Rye's arm.

Sophie smiles. 'The good news is that thanks to your chef's salad, the baby should soon be on the way.'

Clemmie lowers her voice to the guys. 'Her waters broke. You'll have to do a clean-up operation, I'm afraid.'

Rye is nodding. 'No worries, dealing with the unexpected is what we're good at.'

Clemmie whispers in my ear, 'He must deal with crises like mole hills on the lawn all the time.'

Plum gives a shudder. 'That vinegar dressing was strong enough to strip paint!'

Rye looks concerned. 'We haven't had any complaints before.'

Milla laughs. 'Why would you if you're outside?'

Nell's voice pipes up from the lounge chair where she's reclining. 'I'll just luxuriate here for a few more minutes if that's okay with you?'

Rye smiles. 'Don't stay there *too* long. We'd rather not risk what happened when Clemmie had Arnie.'

Plum gives him a nudge. 'The fire brigade is already here this time.'

Kit laughs. 'I can see the headlines now! *High Tides manager delivers baby beside hotel hot tub!* might not be the publicity you're looking for.'

Plum frowns. 'The manager isn't here though. Reception said he'd been called away.'

Kit nods. 'Yes, called away – *to the fire station.*'

Plum blinks. 'So the manager is a part-time fireman too? How fabulous is that?'

'Well, yes – but no.' The lines on Kit's forehead deepen.

'There aren't two people, there's just Rye. Rye *is* the manager here. *How do you not know this?*'

I'm trying to get my head around this. 'But surely Rye is the dog warden...'

Milla joins in. 'Who doubles as a gardener...'

Sophie's not one to be left out. 'And gives out the parking tickets?'

Rye's biting back his smile. 'It's true, I do all of those, but I also run the place.'

'Well, blow me down, who'd have thought!' Nell explodes.

There are a few seconds of silence as we all readjust, then Milla exclaims, 'So you weren't making out with a manual worker after all, Plum. He's management!'

Sophie pulls a face. 'Muscles like that, anyone could be fooled.'

Plum shouts. 'For the last time, we weren't making out!'

Then Kit clears his throat. 'If you didn't get that Rye is manager, there's something else you might have missed.'

Plum rolls her eyes. 'Don't tell us – he's been abducted by aliens and brought back to earth?'

'Not quite.' Kit laughs. 'David Byron is Rye's dad.'

The rest of us are picking our jaws up off the floor as we take in what feels like a huge information dump, but Plum's straight on this. 'So how does that one work, Rye *Radley*?'

Rye rubs his chin. 'Radley is my stepfather's name; he brought me up. I only got to know my real dad in my twenties.'

I'm not sure why this is unnerving, but as I look around at Mum and Plum, it feels like everything suddenly got a whole lot more complicated.

Rye isn't just a random employee – as boss of the place his

father owns, he couldn't be any more involved. And as Rye's life-long friend, Kit is up to his neck in it too.

I turn to Kit. 'So is that everything? Or are there other surprises?'

He shrugs. 'No, that's it – for now.'

Except it isn't, because this changes everything.

Rye smiles. 'I can only apologise. If I'd been behind the desk in my work suit when you arrived, you'd have realised sooner.' He picks up an ice bucket. 'Let me get more fizz to make up for the misunderstanding.'

By the time he comes back we've had time to reset, and once he starts popping corks and filling the glasses, he's such a natural we can't understand how we didn't get it earlier. But the slicker Rye looks, the more doubts I'm having, and I know I need to get this straight in my mind.

I take a swig of my Fizzero to build my courage and look at Kit. 'In which case I assume your relocation to St Aidan wasn't entirely by chance either?'

Kit stares down at the bubbles in his glass before he looks up to answer. 'Rye wanted to make his dad's place a success. The deal they offered me on Latitudes was so generous it knocked all the other places I was considering out of the running.'

'You got a friends and family discount?'

Rye laughs. 'Given that it meant having a good friend like Kit around, the terms were bound to be preferential.'

Whatever I said to the gang earlier, it's obvious Kit is so much more involved than I imagined. Under these circum-stances I can't possibly work for him.

'Before we go on, we have a surprise for you too,' Nell says.

I can't think what she's going to say. Something about the baby's name?

She lets out a laugh. 'Flossie's made up her mind, Kit. She's going to take your job!'

There are whoops and squeals. It's only when I hear Rye calling, 'Let's drink to that! Welcome to the High Tides team, Floss!' that the full impact of what just happened sinks in.

It feels like there's no backing out. I'm on the inside, not the outside. And the game has changed. I just hope I can handle what's coming.

26

The Deck Gallery, St Aidan
Closed roads and space invaders
Monday

George Alfred Harry Trelawney Trenowden was born at Truro Hospital at ten-thirty the next evening, weighing in at nine pounds ten ounces. Two days later he and Nell were settled back home in St Aidan, and when George senior announced that they were ready for visitors we all went around to meet him.

Shadow and I took him a tiny sage green dragon suitable for newborns that I saw in Plum's gallery and fell in love with because the wings were so cute. And for a short time we all sat around marvelling that Nell and George are parents, and they have a tiny human who looks just like George but with a redder face, who will no doubt occupy every second of their thoughts for the next twenty years and longer.

I'd actually been worried I might cry, but the devastation in the kitchen caused by most of St Aidan calling for tea and cake wiped all the baby emotion away. By the time I'd loaded the dishwasher, put all the flowers into vases and narrowly stopped Shadow demolishing an entire tin of Scottish shortbread, I didn't need my tissues anymore. And then we all went back to doing what we were doing before, and life went on.

As Plum and I are the only baby-free ones left in the group, we felt a fleeting but significant connection, which led on to a crazy late one at the dog-friendly Hungry Shark karaoke night, and a suggestion that I should go along to hers with my next batch of sweets to taste once they were ready. So on Monday I arrive in the light, airy, very white Deck Gallery, carrying a bag of Ivy's cups and a basket of other random goodies, and we sit around Plum's long table on her arty metal chairs to finesse my concoctions.

As an international business magnate it's fortunate Sophie's good at delegating and can free herself up from office meetings for ones like this instead. Obviously once she and Clemmie heard Plum and I would be here with ice cream, they weren't going to stay away.

I look around the table, ready to tell them what I've brought for them to sample, but before I can Sophie cuts in.

'Before we begin, has anyone heard any more about Mum?'

Over the years Sophie and I have often gone out with the same crowd or ended up at the same parties, but I can't actually remember a time when we've deliberately sought each other out. But Mum's upcoming date with David Byron has drawn us together like we're magnetic.

The slightest whisper we hear around the town, it's pinged off in a text. When I called round to see Mum the day after the spa night and found her with her entire wardrobe strewn across her bedroom, Sophie was the first to know. When Fenella from Fish Quay Fashions rang Sophie to tell her Mum had been in later the same day, half an hour later she'd messaged me with photos of every outfit she'd tried on.

I pull a face. 'Her date is tonight, but every time I've texted her to check she's okay she rings back then cuts me short.' I've thought about this a lot. 'Mum choosing to go out with the most controversial man in St Aidan has forced us onto the outside. This all came from her and I feel excluded.'

Sophie sighs. 'She's always more open with you than me, but if she's shutting *you* out, it's worrying.'

I'm nodding in agreement as I hand round the loaded cups. 'I'm just glad we've got each other for this.' I can't remember ever feeling *truly* grateful for having Sophie before, but I do now. 'In the meantime, see which ice cream goes best with the apple crumble – vanilla, or toffee?'

Plum is peering into the next batch of cups as she dips in her spoon. 'You're getting adventurous! What else have you brought?'

I smile because I've had such fun doing these. 'Swiss roll, pink custard and rainbow sprinkles, an orange Eton mess with raspberries and mandarins, rainbow macaron pieces with vanilla ice and squirty cream, and a treacle tart special.'

Plum pops a cube of tart into her mouth, and nods as she chews it. 'Where did you buy that? The pastry is amazing.'

I try not to smile too much at the compliment. 'It's one I made earlier.' I laugh. 'It makes more sense to bake for myself rather than buying things in. I'm actually enjoying it too.' It's a huge surprise to me to find myself pouring over recipe blogs, and even more of a shock that I'm producing anything edible.

Clemmie's grinning at me. 'You're certainly raising your game here!'

'It's all down to David Byron. I was so angry at the way he stole the crowd at our event, but I'm not grumbling about the result.'

'Good for you!' Sophie gives a cough and looks at Plum. 'And while we're talking about David, have there been any developments with Rye?'

Since her bikini we've stopped pretending we hadn't noticed how much she likes him.

Plum pulls on her ponytail. 'There are plenty of sparks but that's it – I'd get more attention if I were a kitten trapped in a tree.' She lets out a sigh. 'Tell me something to take my mind off it.'

My other news is why I'm pushing ahead with so much enthusiasm. 'I had an enquiry from a hen party group, I got back to them with ideas and they've booked for five weeks' time!'

Clemmie and Plum both shout 'yay' and give me high fives, but Sophie's face falls. 'I suppose Milla will be helping you with that?'

I'm treading very carefully here. 'I told her I'd need to chat to you before I decided.'

'Thank you for that.' Sophie closes her eyes for a second. 'She still wants to cut her hair like yours.'

I smile as I think of how different the dark-haired Milla is. 'She was forceful as a blonde, but as a brunette she's something else.'

Sophie sighs. 'Don't I know it! As far as Milla's concerned, the sun shines out of your bum.'

Clemmie laughs. 'I can think of worse role models.'

Sophie shakes her head. 'It's so infuriating because all she does with me is criticise.'

Since I've seen more of Milla and her friends, I'm all over the adolescent problem articles. 'To become independent, they have to separate themselves from their family, and with a daughter, the mum takes the brunt.'

Sophie's mouth puckers. 'I'd seen it with other kids, but somehow I assumed Milla would be different. With it just being the two of us when she was small, we've always been like best friends.' She puts down her spoon and slumps back in her chair. 'I'm just so sad that I've lost her.' She gives a loud sniff and rubs her eye with her knuckle.

'Sophie! Are you crying?' There's no need for her to reply, the shining tracks on her cheeks are enough of an answer.

I can't remember when I last saw her in tears – probably when I coloured in her favourite Barbie's eyes with indelible Sharpie when she was ten. She's always been so tough and busy striving, it's a shock to see her breaking. But there's something so vulnerable about her that before I realise it I'm on my feet and my arms are wrapped around her.

Sophie gives a sob. 'I've worked so hard to be successful, but Milla's what has always made me proudest. Her turning against me makes me feel a complete failure.'

I'm patting her on the back like a child. 'It shows what a strong character she is. It's a sign she's taking after you.'

She sniffs again. 'That could be it.' She dabs her eyes with the tissue Plum hands her, and then scrutinises it. 'Mascara that's a hundred per cent tear-proof. At least I got *that* right.'

As I go back to my seat Plum pushes the ice cream towards her. 'Try the vanilla with macaron, that'll cheer you up too.'

Sophie gives a final sniff as she loads ice cream on top of the pastel-coloured biscuit fragments and swirls a mega helping of squirty cream on top. 'It's strangely satisfying having pudding out of cups.'

Clemmie nods. 'It's a small helping with a big volume, but you can still eat three or four!'

Plum licks her spoon and turns as the gallery door opens. 'I'll just check if this customer is okay to browse.'

Clemmie gives me a nudge. 'Not just *any* customer either, Florence Flapjack, it's your new boss.' She calls out as Shadow jumps up from under my chair and shoots off towards him, 'Someone's pleased to see you, Kit.'

Sophie calls out too. 'If you want to see the latest from Floss, it's over here.'

Whatever Kit's wanting, I'm hoping it's quick. As I hurry down the length of the gallery to get Shadow, I give a silent cheer as I see Plum is already ringing up the till and passing him a paper bag.

I get hold of Shadow's trailing lead. 'We were just having a quick tasting session.' I'd rather the others didn't get the chance to scrutinise us together. 'It's pretty much finished.'

Kit holds up his bag. 'I have my sister's birthday card in here. I need to catch the post.'

'Lovely!' I'm giving more silent hurrahs. 'Don't let us hold you up.'

Sophie calls again. 'Any more news on Mum's date with David this evening?'

'You haven't heard?' Kit's voice falters. 'They brought it forward and had it yesterday.'

'What?' My mouth is hanging open.

Sophie is quicker to recover herself. 'It's barely afternoon, no doubt we'll hear about how it went later.'

Kit frowns as he hesitates. 'It went well enough to arrange another, apparently.'

His words echo off the walls, as I try to take it in. What the actual hell is our mum doing? If once was bad judgement, twice is unbelievable. As for leaving us to find out what's going on from someone else – it's humiliating. As I march down the gallery, I'm stamping my feet so hard, the clatter of my footsteps is bouncing back off the ceiling.

'Good for them!' I say sarcastically over my shoulder. I can't say to Kit it's the worst news ever.

'I'll be in touch about tomorrow, Floss,' he calls.

'Absolutely.'

My first stint at my new job just got a whole lot harder. But my determination to prove myself just got a whole lot stronger.

I lean back in my chair and eat a handful of macaron pieces. Then I look across at Clemmie. 'Okay. How about fixing a date for that Mums and Bumps session at mine?'

27

The Hideaway, St Aidan
Answerphones and overtones
Monday

'Mum! How did your early date go?'

Sophie and I agreed that I'm the best one to make the call to Mum and I'm home again before I finally decide how to approach it. When she picks up on the third ring, I'm not out to trick her.

'So you know?'

I'm trying to be minimal with full transparency. 'Kit mentioned it.'

There's a beat of silence before she responds. 'I knew he'd be good for you to work for.'

Of all the answers, I wasn't expecting that. I ignore it and press on. 'And the date went so well that you're doing it again?'

Another beat. 'David lived in Australia. It's a continent, there's a lot to cover.'

'I'll take your word on that.' She had no interest in the place previously. When we watched *Neighbours* when I was a kid, she'd sneak off to the kitchen and listen to current affairs on Radio 4.

'You know how first dates are? We barely scratched the surface.' She takes a breath. 'If a job's worth doing, it's worth doing. Otherwise what's the point?'

'Once they're gone, they're gone.' If she starts saying she's doing this for me, I might just scream.

She picks me up straight away. 'What's *that* got to do with anything?'

I smile. 'Nothing. It's another of those sayings that doesn't mean anything.'

I can sense her eyebrows going up. 'On the contrary, they say "once they're gone, they're gone" all the time in those upmarket bakeries to make their over-priced cakes sell faster.'

'In which case, I might have picked it up subliminally on Stoke Newington Church Street. Or in Islington.' Now she's nudged my memory, it was actually Hot Cakes, in Notting Hill, at a time when I was randomly wandering around London trying to find anything to make the time pass after Dillon left. I queued for forty minutes outside a tiny backstreet shop for a feta puff dredged in icing sugar that lasted three bites and cost six quid. It was so unexpectedly glorious to find something delicious when it felt like I'd never enjoy anything ever again, I went back three Sundays running.

She carries on. 'They were talking about those bakery places in Force10 Hair when I had my last layer cut done. You could try that with your puddings – why not put them on Facebook?'

This is the thing about Mum. Not only does she effortlessly

pick up what's bang on trend. But over and over, she also cuts through the crap and gets straight to the heart of what matters.

'Genius, Mum, thanks. I might do that.' There's the small problem that the ice cream would melt, but it's nice she cares enough to make suggestions.

'Don't thank me, you're the one who brought it up.' She hesitates. 'I'll have to go, Michael's here measuring up for the plantation shutters.'

I can't help feeling a twinge of embarrassment that the stuff my mum is doing is so much cooler than me. She also has an army of super-skilled tradesmen she calls on who all ooze charm and good looks.

'Which one is Michael?'

'Like Robert Redford. But more sexy and achievable.'

As she ends the call I'm left with one burning question: if she wants a boyfriend and Michael is all that – *why isn't she dating him?*

28

The Hideaway, St Aidan
Stampedes and a sugar rush
Tuesday

Who knew nervous baking was a thing? Having had the thirty-second chat with Mum that told me nothing but left me so I can't sit still, I headed for the kitchen and made two batches of M&M cookies, and a double batch of brownies, and afterwards I felt a whole lot calmer.

Then I spend a soothing evening drooling over pictures of baking on Insta, and by nine I'm back in the kitchen. This time I do a blondie tray bake try-out and a carrot cake with a wiggly cream cheese topping and only then do I feel tired enough to curl up with Shadow and go to sleep.

It's only after our walk along to Comet Cove the next morning, as I'm slicing it into slabs, that the extent of my over-production hits me.

The cookies and brownies are destined for next door, but as

I'm off to Kit's shortly for my first morning of work the rest are homeless for now. As I get out my phone to take a couple of photos of the baked goods with Ivy's chequered linen napkins, I'm thinking about my chat with Mum. Clemmie and Nell are always raving about the St Aidan Facebook *For sale and wanted* page, and if I'm serious about getting myself out there, I have very little to lose. It takes a few seconds to write my post and upload my photos, and a moment later it's live.

> *Take a stroll to the Little Cornish Kitchen Beach Hut,*
> *and serve yourself.*
> *Today's treats: Bakewell blondies and pecan and*
> *carrot cake*
> *FlorenceMay@TheHideaway*
> *ONCE THEY'RE GONE, THEY'RE GONE!*
> *ENJOY!*

All that's left to do is to put them on trays under glass domes on the steps to the deck, with serviettes, price tickets and a money jar. And then I'm ready to go to Kit's.

As Shadow and I arrive at Latitude One ten minutes later the door opens for us as we cross the porch. I stride past Rye and down the studio, put my bags on the desk and smile at Kit, who is slumped in a leather sling chair balancing a pencil on his finger.

'So how are you guys this morning?'

Rye has followed me and peers over my shoulder. 'If those are brownies, I'm all good.' He wiggles his eyebrows as I slide the containers towards him. 'If it's not too much trouble, could we have the same again for two days' time?'

At first, after the campfire incident, I was bringing them as gifts but since they'd started insisting on paying for them, the orders had been ramping up.

I can't help commenting. 'Considering the mountains of cake you two eat you're both very slim. Would you like to share your secret?' I've always loved eating, but lately if I so much as look at a Danish pastry my jeans seem to shrink two sizes.

'Our *secret*?' Rye blows out his cheeks. 'Damn! I knew it couldn't last. Seeing as you're onto us, I'll come clean. I *have* been using brownies for staff meetings, but only because they put everyone in a better mood. And guests *might* have had the occasional one too, when they were in my office.'

'I was *joking*!' I'm shaking my head in disbelief. 'Why is a top hotel outsourcing chocolate cake?'

Rye gives a guilty shrug. 'Chef is a purist who refuses to make it and yours is an exceptionally tasty example.' He nods across at Kit. 'And ignore Kit, his face is as long as a wet weekend, but he'll cheer up now you two are here.'

I look from one to another and give a silent curse that Kit is even more beautiful with an expression like a storm cloud. 'Was it a heavy Thursday night?'

Rye pulls a face. 'I wish.'

Kit notices my querying gaze. 'Rye is dedicating a hundred per cent of his time to getting the hotel up and running, so late nights and socialising are off the table.'

I'm shocked. 'So you don't go out *at all*?'

Rye shrugs. 'Not unless it's linked to the hotel or the fire station.'

'So relationships are out of the question?' Asking for a friend here, obviously.

He nods. 'It's a small price to pay.' He must have picked up on my horrified expression. 'It won't be for ever. Once the occupancy rates rise the pressure will ease.'

I'm biting my lip, feeling bad for Plum. 'And how are those going?'

Rye takes a breath. 'Truthfully? It's been a slower start than we'd hoped, but we're working on that as we speak.'

Damn for Plum. But a silent thumbs-up for me, and another for Mum that her advice is already proving to be valuable. If I'd been at home instead of here at work, I'd have missed this conversation. I'm no expert on industrial espionage, but by St Aidan standards what I've just picked up feels like pure gold.

Kit takes an envelope out of his back pocket and slaps it on the table. 'And my reason not to be cheerful was some unfortunate post.'

I pull out a glass biscuit jar and push it towards him. 'Will cookies help? I hoped they might keep the clients happy.'

Kit gives a sour laugh. 'Only if they're big enough to sweeten a long and arduous separation.'

I pull the top off the jar. 'You'd better take two.'

Rye waves as he sets off down the studio, brownie boxes in hand. 'I'll catch you both later.'

As we watch him stride out to the porch Kit bites into his biscuit and lets out a long sigh. 'Some days it feels as if the unravelling is out of all proportion to the relationship. When I think back to what I had before Vee and I got together, then think of what I'm taking to the future, the comparison is dire.'

All I can do is put my surprise to one side and sympathise. 'I'm sorry, I'd assumed it was amicable.'

He tugs his fingers through his curls. 'I wanted to be fair and now I've been taken for every penny. I know if I'm bitter, I'm losing twice over, but some days, it's hard not to be.' He shakes his head. 'I'm sorry, this must seem like whining about nothing to someone who's had health problems.'

I rarely bring this up, but now he has I may as well say it. 'When you're ill the trick is to only think about the moment you're in, and make sure you enjoy the arse off it.'

Kit nods. 'I can't argue with that.'

It was a tough time, but at the same time it was rarefied and pure, because so much that wasn't important in life fell away. 'Someone sent me this poem, about not looking too far down the road. How there's no need to know what's around the corner until you actually get there.' I look up at Kit and hope he connects with the manly imagery. 'You could always give that a try?'

'I could.'

'So forget about whatever crap that letter is promising to rain down on you, throw yourself into making today's rings instead, and you might even have fun when you thought it was impossible.'

I can feel a smile spreading across my face as I remember. 'Being ill taught me to enjoy every day, but it turned out to be small things that counted more than big ones. Fresh bread in a sandwich, a robin coming to eat the crumbs in the park, clean laundry, an ice-cold can of Coke – they might sound like clichés, but they were what got me through, and I live for those same things now. Once you know they work, it's amazing how many you can cram into a day.'

'So that's why you're a happy bunny, Florence Flapjack-face?'

I laugh. 'Flapjack is another one.'

He taps his pencil on the glass. 'The ring of the jar. Better still when it's filled with baking.'

I smile at him. 'It's a game. The better you get at playing it, the more your mood lifts.' I dip into my bag and bring out a bunch of buttercup flowers from the florist I bought for the desk and the coffee table. 'Ranunculus are another of my things, especially when they're multicoloured like these.' The pinks and yellows and peachy oranges of the blooms are resonating in the shaft of sunlight coming in from the vertical window.

He smiles. 'With you and your flowers, it's already a better day.' He stops to look more closely at me. 'That's a great dress too.'

Down the line I'm aiming to move into shorts, but for this week I've dug out some bright floral mini dresses. As I give the hem a swirl there's a considerable expanse of thigh above the suede boots I chose to look smart. 'It's not too short?'

'Hell no!' Kit gives a cough. 'I mean, whatever you're comfortable with is good by me.' He blows out his cheeks. 'I feel such a hypocrite, pretending to believe in love with letters like this in my pocket.' He slides it back in and taps his bum.

I grin across at him. 'On the upside, if those are new jeans, you're looking the part.' Dark denim with rips might be great news for trade, but less good for my somersaulting stomach.

As he gets up he positions his hand for a fist pump. 'So, here's to a great morning!'

Our hands are about to collide when a tap at the door stops us in mid-air.

As a face appears from the porch, I know I'm on. I cover the length of the studio in three bounds, and thrust out my hand.

'Hi there, I'm Florence Flapjack, you must be the ten o'clock couple for Kit the metallurgist at Forever Together Love2Love?' It's not quite perfect, but it'll have to do.

The freckled face I'm looking into isn't showing any recognition, so I try again. 'You're here for your rings?'

The person looks hopeful. 'We're signed into the hotel on the liquid diet, and we're looking for cake?'

The second person looks equally pale but lowers her voice. 'We saw a note in the visitors' book saying if we were desperate to try at the beach hut?'

I point towards The Hideaway. 'Next one along, you'll find serve-yourself carrot cake and blondies on the steps. Just leave the money in the jar.'

They let out a collective groan of relief. 'Thanks, you're a life saver!'

It's only as they hurry off that I realise Shadow is curled up under the desk and hasn't even opened an eye.

'Did you say *blondies*?' Kit is coming towards me.

'I did. Bakewell tart ones.'

His pupils go hazy as he checks his phone. 'We should have a few minutes before the clients arrive. I'll go and grab us a couple.'

Now I'm here, about to start work, I'm thinking back to yesterday and all the unexpected insights I gathered. As a sudden stab of worry hits my chest I have to ask. 'You haven't only asked me to work here to further David Byron's quest to take over Cornwall?'

Kit's face falls. 'Why would you think that?'

I shrug. 'The stakes are high with property development. When it's my home David's set his sights on, I feel quite vulnerable.' After Kit's openness about his own problems, it's suddenly easier to share my concerns about this.

His arm slides around my shoulders, and he squeezes me into a hug. 'It's nothing to do with anyone else – I asked you because you're great at what you do and I like having you around.' He lets his arm drop and sounds more serious. 'Obviously it's a sound business decision too.' His face cracks into a smile. 'And then there's the baking.'

'Thanks, that's reassuring.' I can't argue with how sincere he sounds.

His smile fades. 'No one is trying to be underhand, Floss. How would it be if I promise to share any relevant news as soon as I get it?'

'Fabulous. Mum doesn't usually date, that's all.' I can't ask for more than that. 'If there are any left, the blondies are on me.'

His eyebrows go up. 'Is there a shortage?'

I laugh. 'There were only twelve – the first of my new "when they're gone, they're gone" selections.'

'Shit. Those people sounded desperate. I'd better hurry.' He's already across the porch.

JUNE

29

The Hideaway, St Aidan
Sandcastles and empty beds
Monday

I'm still getting used to how fast things move in St Aidan. After a quick look at the forecast to see that Monday was going to be sunny, all it took was a message on the Mums and Bumps WhatsApp, and the afternoon at mine was sorted. We kept the numbers small, so when Clemmie and Sophie came over the dunes from the lane, they were leading a column of six mums and their assorted small ones towards the picket fence. And since then they've been sitting on rugs and chairs at the bottom of the deck steps, while the little ones play in the sand with an assortment of buckets and spades.

Clemmie is on the deck with me, and while we've been taking out second helpings of trifle and sorting out ice-cream cones, we've been having our first catch-up about my week at work.

'It's hilarious that your bakes sold so well there weren't any blondies left for Kit.'

As she laughs, Clemmie sways Arnie, who's asleep in his sling. Sophie insisted on coming too, even though Maisie, her youngest, is at school, and she's keeping an eye on Bud. Even though the fizz is mostly alcohol-free it's going down fast, and I'm on my way to get more from the fridge.

I call to Clemmie on my way to the kitchen. 'Kit was beside himself when he arrived back at the studio empty-handed! We found out later that Jean and Shirley had come past with their walking group, and the hungry hotel guests had taken the rest.'

It might have been beginner's luck, but I did the same again on Sunday, with toffee Rice Krispies and lemon drizzle cake, and by the time I came back from Kit's at lunchtime, that had all gone too.

As for how it went at Kit's, Saturday's couple were in their fifties, on their second time around, and planning a modern elopement, and Sunday's were younger, but brought their kids along too. And thanks to Kit telling them all about The Hideaway, both lots added in an impromptu visit to mine for a pudding-on-the-deck photo opportunity at the end of the afternoon.

As I come back outside, Clemmie's looking down at the little ones running up to Sophie with her tray of ice creams. 'How have you coped, having all these little people around?'

I take a second to consider. 'When I first arrived, I might have found it hard to watch families, but what I care about now is The Hideaway's future, so it's great that the mums are here enjoying the place.' I can tell from her frown that she wants more reassurance. 'Moving was a gamble, but I haven't regretted it for a second. I don't feel there's anything I'm missing out on.'

For the first time ever I've got a home that's mine, and I'm earning in a way that makes people happy, too. To be honest, seeing Clemmie and Nell dealing with their newborns has been like a reality check for me. Their babies feed *all through the night!* I can't imagine putting myself through that. I love seeing them all, but it's a relief to curl up on the sofa after a peaceful supper and know the most I have to do before morning is let Shadow out for a late-night wee then dedicate myself to eight hours of uninterrupted sleep. As I can barely look after Shadow and me, I'm much better off as a star aunty.

Clemmie's face brightens. 'So you'd be up for another impromptu afternoon when the sun's out again?'

'Definitely.' As Kit apparently takes short-notice bookings too, last-minute works well for me. While I've got Clemmie on her own, I need to ask. 'So how did Plum take the news that Rye is off the menu? Was she devastated?'

Clemmie pulls a face. 'She was relieved to have an explanation for his lack of enthusiasm, but it hasn't put her off any.'

I laugh. 'If Plum is anything like Dillon she won't give in – it'll have made her ten times more determined.'

'Talking of the man himself...' Clemmie's eyebrows have gone into overdrive '...if he's planning to visit soon, does that mean he's not giving up on *you* either?' She takes hold of my hand and squeezes it. 'We mermaids are all hoping once you and Dillon have had time apart, you'll realise you belong together.'

When Mum mentioned this a while back I let it go, but I need to put Clemmie right before this express train runs away. 'I hate to disappoint you all, but there won't be a reunion for

Dillon and me because we didn't just drift apart, we broke – irretrievably.'

Clemmie's eyes go wide. 'I'm so sorry, we had no idea.'

There's no reason why they should have done. I've kept this to myself, but if they know more detail at least they'll understand. Even now it's hard to say the words out loud. 'It really wasn't Dillon's fault – but he slept with someone else.'

The colour drains from Clemmie's cheeks. 'Flossie, that's awful.'

I need to put it in context. 'Awful, but understandable. I was a wreck after my operations, and we hadn't had sex for ages. You know how Dillon throws himself at everything?'

Clemmie nods. 'Fast and furious is the only way he knows.'

I smile as I remember. 'His energy was what attracted me to him in the first place, but soft and gentle in the bedroom wasn't ever going to work for him. At first, I assumed our sex life would limp along until I got better, but then I realised he was only going to be properly interested when it got back to how it was before, which it actually never could. And it was only once the sex had gone that I realised how much that was what had glued us together as a couple. Without that there to keep us on track, we were adrift.' Even though it's horrible hearing myself say it, as I carry on it feels, once again, like what happened next was inevitable. 'We were trying to find a way through it all, and then Dillon was at this work party, some random woman hit on him, and boom. He was drunk enough to say yes, but sober enough to deliver the goods. And because this was honest, honourable Dillon, he came straight home and told me.'

That night is etched on my brain so clearly. What's more, I had so many chances to avert it and I missed them all. *If only* I'd put in the effort and gone with him, instead of letting him tuck me up on the sofa with an alcohol-free G&T and a packet of mini cheddars to binge-watch repeats of *Gilmore Girls*. *If only* I'd bothered to remember a cheeky hand job in the shower could be the highlight of his Saturday, especially if I made him a bacon sandwich after. I can't even blame it on the illness, because by this time chemo was a distant nightmare, and I was months into being officially cancer-free. But looking back, my eye must have been so far off the game, it almost felt like I'd given up playing it.

Clemmie's shaking her head. 'I'm so sorry.'

'I didn't blame him, it was just an awful mistake. I thought if I forgave him, we'd be able to carry on and get back to what we used to be.' I drag in a breath. 'But the problem was he couldn't forgive himself. He couldn't get past the guilt.'

He was sitting cross-legged on the end of the bed in the half light, waiting for me to wake up so he could tell me what he'd done, because he felt it wasn't respectful to come under the duvet before I knew. He was the one who cried while I sat there trying to work out if it was real or if I was still asleep. That was how absurd it was. For weeks after I couldn't shake off the feeling I was about to wake up and find the whole thing had been a bad dream. And after that he never stopped beating himself up about it.

Clemmie sighs. 'You two were such a perfect couple.'

I blow out a breath. 'Him knowing that only made it worse. We struggled on for a while, but we'd got to a place we couldn't get back from. However long we stayed together, he'd always know there was a time when he'd cheated. And however much I pretended, the post-op sex was never going to be what it used to be.' I shrug. 'In the end, I was the one who decided that we'd be best to separate.'

If I hadn't been ill, this would never have happened, so it felt like my responsibility to be strong, to try to make things right going forward. Dillon wasn't a bad guy, but as long as he stayed with me, in his own mind he would be. And that wasn't fair on him. Hard as it was, I loved him enough to know I had to set him free.

I'm agonising as I look at Clemmie. 'I'd hate anyone to think badly of Dillon, so please be sparing with what you tell the others. But I wanted you to know it all, so you'd know how to head them off. We always said we could still get back together again if we wanted to, but we both know it wouldn't work.'

Clemmie pulls me into a hug. 'Don't worry. I'll manage their expectations and if Dillon does turn up, I'll make sure they hold back on the matchmaking.' As she lets me go, she gives me a hard stare. 'So while Dillon's off having a ball in Dubai, what about you?'

While it's just me and Clemmie, I'm going to offload something else. 'The real reason I came to St Aidan is because I damaged my throat and haven't been able to do the reading work. But I haven't said anything because if Dillon or Sophie hears they'll want to step in with handouts, and I'd rather manage on my own.'

Clemmie's shaking her head again. 'Shit, Flossie, you've certainly had more than your share of things going wrong. I wish it hadn't happened, but at the same time it's lovely having you back.' Her eyes are shining. 'And you are managing, aren't you?'

I grin. 'Mainly thanks to Rye and Kit and their insatiable appetite for chocolate.'

She gives me a nudge. 'It's a lot more than that. Your sweets are incredible, they're completely unique.'

I wrinkle my nose. 'It's all down to you having me as an outpost! After that I just hit lucky. The strange thing is, I love what I'm doing so much it's becoming compulsive. I've never felt this enthusiastic about anything.'

Clemmie's biting her lip. 'And are you going to be as lucky in love?'

I shrink under her scrutiny. 'Shadow and I won't be adding to our cosy twosome any time soon.'

'Really?'

'Dating's a minefield at the best of times.' I don't often get this far down the road, but for once I'm allowing myself to think what would happen if there was someone I actually liked who liked me back. *Absolutely not* anyone in particular, you understand. Just trying the idea on for size. I drop my voice. 'I say I'm all better, but in some people just like me, the cancer does come back.' I shiver as I think about it. 'That's not something you'd put onto someone in the long term. Especially not someone you really, really liked. In fact, the more you liked them, the worse it would make it.'

Clemmie's mouth pulls down at the corners. 'It's a catch-22, then?'

'That's why the solo option is the one that works!'

She frowns. 'You not wanting another relationship doesn't mean you can't have fun. Not all relationships are long ones.' She takes in my horrified stare. 'As Nell would say, sleeping with someone else might be what you need to let you move on.' She grins at me. 'If a quickie in the dunes is ever on offer, promise me you'll grab it with both hands.'

I pull a face, both of us knowing it's never going to happen. If I couldn't manage to have sex with my long-term partner, I'm more likely to fly to the moon than do it with a stranger. But it's good she's pushing me to try this on for size too.

Clemmie gives me a scolding glance. 'Don't give me that look. St Aidan in summer ... the beach bursting with hot surfers ... you're bound to find *someone* on your wavelength!'

There's the shuffle of feet on these steps, and Sophie's blonde head comes into view. 'Have you heard from Nell?' She's holding Bud on her hip, and I'm hoping she didn't hear any of what came before.

I glance at my phone. 'She said she was almost ready to come, but that was two hours ago!'

Clemmie looks down at Arnie. 'If it's her first time out, she may not even make it.'

Sophie laughs. 'When Milla was a baby I didn't get dressed for a full four months.'

I'm sure that's not right, because I remember sharing my pint and a pack of salt and vinegar crisps with her outside The Slug and Lettuce when Milla was tiny, but it's the ideal opportunity for me to keep her on this subject. 'So have you bought any non-turquoise clothes yet, Sophie?'

Sophie's eyes are wide, and she's pointing to herself. '*How have you not noticed my new colourway?* My chinos are powder-grey, and my T-shirt is Alpine white.' She gives a grimace. 'I'm so far out of my comfort zone, I'm not having a good day.'

Clemmie stiffens as she hears my phone ping. 'Is that Nell now?'

As I read the message I only wish it was. 'It's Kit.' I turn to Sophie. Whatever she was saying about her day being bad, it's about to get a whole lot worse. 'He's just heard, Mum's going on *another* date with Byron.'

Sophie's suddenly shrieking. 'Don't just stand there, Flossie, *do something!*'

I pull a face. 'Like what?' There's another ping. 'It's Kit again.'

Florence Flapjack, if you'd be up for some low-key
parental surveillance at the High Tides bar, I'm happy to
come as your cover? Tomorrow night at eight would
work x

I'm trying to hide that my heart is banging against my ribs hard enough to be heard in St Aidan. 'He's suggesting we go for drinks at the hotel and do some covert monitoring.'

Sophie punches the air. 'A spying date! Brilliant!'

I wince at the words. 'Except we won't really be spying...'

Clemmie butts in. 'And you *definitely won't be on a date!*' She laughs. 'If you and James Bond grab every opportunity with both hands, I'm sure you'll get a great outcome.'

But by the time I should be replying to that I'm already down on the beach, filling up fizz flutes.

30

The Reef Bar, High Tides Hotel, St Aidan
Fried eggs and forced errors
Tuesday

'Can I get you a drink?'

Arriving at the Reef Bar early the next evening was meant to give me a chance to stake out the territory, so Rye behind the bar in his sharp suit loading up the glass-fronted fridges is a surprise.

I look along at the reed-woven stools tucked under the polished timber bar as I think about what to order. The creamy lime-plaster walls are punctuated with panels of exposed stonework, and the clusters of easy chairs and low tables in front of narrow vertical windows give views across the bay and reinforce the atmosphere of luxurious calm. 'I'll have a glass of Prosecco, please.'

Rye stows away the last bottle of sparkling water and turns. 'We have rosé or white, with alcohol or without?'

Spot the deliberate mistake. It's four years since I last drank, yet I'm so nervous I forgot to specify alcohol-free. Given how much my hand is shaking as I reach in my bag for my payment card, straight Prosecco might be exactly what I need to relax me. 'White, with, please.'

The place where I'm standing as I take my first sips of wine gives a three-sixty view of the bar area with glimpses of the lofty reception hallway beyond – good enough to keep an eye on incoming traffic. I pull out a stool, clamber onto it and start to arrange my dress. The silky dark-blue leopard print midi was the most discreet I could find, so now isn't the ideal time to discover that the full skirt has a hem-to-thigh split up one side.

'There you go, Floss. And Kit's here too now, so I'll put it on his tab.'

So much for surveillance. Given that Kit's only a couple of feet away without me having noticed him arriving, I may need to brush up on my observation skills.

Kit comes in for a kiss on each of my cheeks and whispers in my ear, 'Just so we look authentic.' Then he stands back and pulls out a stool for himself. 'Another nice dress, Florence Flap-jack-face.'

I look down to see my skirt has already slipped. 'Me showing a thousand acres of thigh was not intentional.'

He laughs. 'Once I sit down no one else will notice.' He glances at the one other couple at the far end of the room. 'As most people are in the restaurant, we pretty much have the place to ourselves.'

Rye brings Kit a bottle of Peroni he didn't order, and as he moves away I murmur to Kit, 'Is that where *they* are?'

Rye laughs and turns to us again. 'It's okay, I'm in on this too.'

Kit nods. 'Rye is as anxious as you are to know what's going on. That's partly why we suggested you came.'

This has thrown me. 'So are you saying your father doesn't make a habit of coming on to guests?'

Rye looks appalled. 'Absolutely. Which is why it's so strange your mum has got her hooks into him when others have all failed.'

'Hang on!' I need to put him right on that. 'My mum won't be the pursuer here – it *has* to be the other way around.' If this really was just about her getting an insider view for my sake, I might need to think up a smokescreen and fast. As for Kit and Rye, those two seem so close they're practically finishing each other's sentences.

Rye blows out his cheeks. 'I don't understand it. David was so devoted to his wife, he didn't even come looking for me until after he lost her, and he hasn't looked at another woman in the ten years since then.'

I glance at the lobby. 'Are he and Mum eating?'

Rye shakes his head. 'Not yet.'

My mind races and comes to a screeching halt in Byron's hotel suite. 'They surely aren't in his room?'

Rye pulls a face. 'No, nothing *that* bad. They went for a pre-dinner walk along the beach.'

Kit takes a swig from his bottle and gets hold of the bar menu. 'Anyone fancy a snack while we wait for them to reappear?'

Rye grins. 'Perhaps *not* the seaweed salad this time.'

I'd already eaten but I'm always hungry. 'Chips would be

nice to nibble?' I'm imagining how this upmarket bar will serve them. Maybe in a whelk shell? Or in a hand-hewn driftwood bowl?

Rye's straight in. 'I'm afraid Chef doesn't do chips.'

I let out a sigh of disappointment. 'If the restaurant is rammed, I can understand that.'

Kit frowns. 'Except it isn't. Given current progress with hotel occupancy Rye is going to be an OAP before he's free to go out.'

Rye rolls his eyes. 'That's sad but true. Since the first flurry of freebies we've been running close to empty. We aren't even picking up local business.'

I'm the last person up for helping High Tides, but this is such bad news for Plum, I'm going to push this. 'So can *you* make changes to help that, Rye?'

Rye purses his lips. 'It's entirely my responsibility, but when I've put in so much effort getting the place up and running it's hard to pinpoint where the problem is, let alone decide how to tackle it.'

I'm looking around, speaking as I've found it. 'The ambience is great, the staff and treatments are lovely, the hot tubs are fab, and the price point goes with the territory.' I hesitate as I work out how best to say it. 'Any negative comments I've encountered have centred on the food.'

Kit nods at Rye. 'That's true. It's great to have a cutting-edge kitchen, but there's very little on offer we'd willingly eat ourselves.'

Rye blows out his cheeks. 'David's vision was so pure, but clearly Cornwall isn't as ready to detox as we imagined.' He pauses as his phone beeps, then shakes his head as he reads the message. 'That was David. He and your mum are eating at The Harbourside, and they'll get a taxi home later. When the owner can't face eating at his own hotel, that says a lot.'

My heart goes out to Rye because he looks so crestfallen. 'You've nailed it for the people wanting an experience focusing on health and abstinence, but anyone visiting the website who's looking for indulgence will take one look at the photo of kelp flatbread, and book elsewhere.'

I've pored over both their websites these last few weeks, and I know how a single image can make or break a business.

Rye looks doubtful. 'The hedonist market might not be what David was aiming for, but it would certainly help our bottom line.'

'It would only be until you get going.' I'm working out how to make this better without completely ruining their concept. 'If you have a space that's slightly apart from the rest you could offer hidden treats there without compromising your original ethos. If you add even one mouth-watering photo to your website, it might translate into bookings.'

Kit laughs. 'A space at a distance – that sounds a lot like The Hideaway, Floss.'

This really isn't me touting for business. 'Hopefully you'll get a lot more guests here than I can fit at mine.'

Rye narrows his eyes as he looks at Kit. 'We could use the Shingle Studio as our "spoil yourself" area. It was meant for yoga, but so far they've been running that on the beach or in the Pilates lounge.'

Kit nods. 'That would work. It would make sense to test the idea before you make any big in-house changes. You could always get the scones from...' he stops to wink '...*our usual supplier?'*

Rye turns to me. 'Would you be interested?'

I'm opening and closing my mouth in shock at where we've landed. It might be the last thing I planned, but there's no time for wavering, I need to seize this before he changes his mind. 'Clemmie's the afternoon tea specialist, but I'm sure we'd be able to get the basics up and running pretty quickly.'

There's a smile lilting around Kit's lips. 'Cake stacks would go down well too. And you could design some special puddings to have in High Tides cups.'

I'm on a roll here. 'Why stop there? We could do cocktails too!'

Rye grins at me. 'This sounds a lot like me setting up my own personal pantry.'

I can't argue with that. 'You've got great taste. If you like it, the chances are that customers will too.'

Kit laughs. 'We'll have to rename it the Pleasure Dome.' He looks at Rye. 'See, I told you she was good.'

I hold up my finger. 'And chips! I don't care where they're served, but you have to have them. Triple cooked in teensy portions, served in clam shells.'

Rye reaches for a couple more glasses and fills them from the Prosecco bottle. Before I realise what he's doing, he's topped mine up, too.

He watches me hesitate. 'Sorry, if you'd prefer to switch to alcohol-free, it's only over here?'

The carefree bubbles from the first glass have already reached my head. 'One more will be fine.'

Rye picks up his glass and pushes the other towards Kit. 'In that case let's drink to good ideas and fully booked rooms.'

Kit nods. 'And undercover agents.'

I add my own. 'And parents who don't stay out too late.'

But even as I say it, it's so delicious sitting close to Kit with the heat from his body radiating across the space between us I realise I wouldn't care if we stayed here all night.

31

The Reef Bar, High Tides Hotel, St Aidan
Free style, line dancing and Archimedes
Tuesday

We stay at the bar for the time it takes for us to finish those drinks and a couple more, then Kit slides down from his stool.

'While you're here, I'll show you the place we're talking about.'

Rye nods. 'If you get a feel for the space, Floss, you might have even more suggestions.'

As Kit and I walk side by side along a wide corridor leading off the foyer past more vertical windows, I'm catching glimpses of the sea fading into the dusk, and the lights twinkling in the distance around the curve of the bay, and blaming any wobble in my legs on sitting on that high stool.

Kit is smiling down as he walks beside me. 'If we want to

look like authentic guests on a romantic getaway, I should probably have my arm around you.'

If he'd said that three drinks earlier I'd have laughed him off the beach, but I'm so full of feel-good fizz, before I know it I've tucked my shoulder under his arm and slipped my own arm around his waist. As I try not to expire from the shock, I find my voice is out of control too. 'So your break-up wasn't so bad that you can't be a fake incognito couple?' What the hell made me ask that? He can't mind too much because he laughs and I feel the vibration go through my body.

'I might have given you the wrong impression when you caught me moping about my letter the other day. It's frustrating that it's taken so long to finalise the finances, but when you aren't a hundred per cent committed emotionally, it's easier to carry on when things end.' He's taking this a lot more seriously than the accidental question intended. 'Sure, I've learned from my mistakes, I'm certainly keen to avoid repeat performance, but I'm not too traumatised to pretend.' He looks down at me. 'How about you?'

I give a twitch on Shadow's lead. 'There are too many complications for me to ever be a couple again, but if faking gets us the insight we want, it's worth it.'

Since I've been playing scenarios through in my head, it's reassuring to know that my dating strategy has held good every time. What's more, it means I can talk about it with conviction whenever it crops up. Where I was tentatively single before, I'm now more confident.

And finding someone else in a similar situation is useful, because I know he'll get where I'm coming from.

I stare up at Kit and watch his Adam's apple bob as he swallows.

'In case you're wondering, I haven't reached the milestone of sleeping with anyone else.' He clears his throat. 'Not because I'm not ready, it's just the time hasn't been right.'

My throat is suddenly so dry I'm croaking. 'Me neither.' I may as well be true to myself and add my mission statement. 'I actually plan to stay with Shadow for ever, and he's promised he'll stay with me until the custard creams run out.'

'I'd say we're all good then.' Kit heads towards a broad timber door and pushes it open. As we step into a large circular space, the lights on the floor come on automatically, and bounce back off the chalky white ceiling above our heads. 'Welcome to the new cake and kick-back zone. What do you think?'

There's the same pale cream stone floor as on the hot tub terrace, repeating windows right around the space like the ones in the bar, and the overall effect is enough to take my breath away. 'It's fabulous. When it's filled with tables and chairs it'll be like a modern orangery.' As I look up there's another surprise. 'A circular skylight! That's amazing too.'

Kit nods. 'It's there so you can see the stars.' He looks at me again for more recognition. 'Stargazing *is* how Cornish natives spend clear evenings – lying on their backs staring at the sky?'

I bite back my grin. 'Sorry to disillusion a city boy, but I moved away when I was eighteen, so my nights here were mostly spent on my feet partying. I only lay down when I passed out.'

He looks at me. 'Next time I want a wild night out in St Aidan, I'll remember who to come to for advice. And if we end up spending a lot more time undercover, I'm sure the stars are something we can discover together.'

I'm confused. 'So this isn't the end of it?'

Kit's eyes slide to the ceiling. 'Rye's stuck here at the hotel for now, but until Suze and David have run their course, we assumed you'd want to keep an eye on things as much he does?'

'Right.' My toes are curling at the way they already sound like a couple.

'Obviously any Hideaway events will take priority. In the meantime, if you're up for a dip, the next place on the tour is the thermal pool.'

I'm opening and closing my mouth. 'No one warned me secret agents had to swim!'

The corner of his eyes crinkle with amusement. 'It's not compulsory. But when you see how inviting the water looks, you may change your mind.'

Two more doors, and we arrive on the side of a pale blue, mosaic-lined pool surrounded by pine loungers, with semi-circular steps at one end and the kind of soft lighting that makes it feel like there's sunlight playing on the water.

I'm a wimp when it comes to true cold-water swimming, so I slip out from under his arm and bend down to test how the water feels. 'It's very warm.'

Kit runs his fingers through his curls. 'I knew you'd be tempted. The other hotel pools are colder, but this is kept at thirty degrees.'

I'm wavering. 'What about guests?'

He looks at his watch. 'They're encouraged to swim before dinner, so this is exclusively ours if we want to use it now.' He nods at a basket. 'There are plenty of hotel towels.'

My heart is racing. 'So ... skinny dipping?'

He laughs again. 'I'm keeping my boxers on, but feel free to strip off if you want to.'

My briefs and bra aren't a matching set but at least they're both black. 'My underwear will be fine, thanks.' My mind jumps to the patchwork of marks above my knicker line. 'I do have scars on my tummy.'

'They're simply a sign you've led an interesting life.' He's already kicking off his deck shoes, taking off his watch and throwing his shirt onto a lounger. 'The trick is to get in so fast no one notices.' A second later his jeans are off and his perfect racing dive slices through the water. When he surfaces a few moments later he's at the other end of the pool, his dark curls dripping as he scrapes the water from his eyes. 'I'll submerge and swim another length to give you a chance to get in.'

When the hell did the wild child inside me get this scared and tentative? I settle Shadow down by a lounger, shake out a towel to leave on the pool edge, step out of my sneakers and let my dress drop. As I slip off the side the water is delicious on my skin, and a moment later I'm doing a racing crawl up the pool, watched by Shadow, who is resting his chin on his paws. After three lengths I stop in the deep end with my back to the side to get my breath back.

Kit glides through the water and pops up beside me. 'The water temperature is too high for hard swimming; this pool is meant for relaxing.'

I'm in the most laid-back, luxurious place in St Aidan. It should be easy to float on my back, close my eyes, and reach my personal nirvana. But having the hottest guy in town stripped down to his undies, his wet, toned shoulders shiny and within touching distance, is blowing my cool into a thousand tiny pieces. I'm so thrown, my bilateral breathing is all over the place, and that's been muscle memory since I learned it at swimming club when I was twelve.

I've had four long years of living with a libido slightly less alive than a giant panda's – they're almost extinct, not because of a shortage of bamboo shoots, but because they have sex so rarely none of them know how to do it – so when I'm practically naked in the local hotel swimming pool it's not the ideal time or place to discover that my ability to feel fanny flutters has returned. Worse still, they've come back five times stronger than they ever used to be when I had them before.

I'd assumed I'd gone menopausal, and I'd never want sex again. But suddenly I'm aching for it so badly it's not just a want, there's this drive with the force of a bulldozer crashing through my body. There's only one thing for it, I'm going to have to swim my way through it.

I push off from the side and call to Kit. 'Just off for another few lengths.'

'Great, I'll wait here and watch.'

I'm storming through the water like a train. I'm on my sixth length when it finally hits me that I might be blaming the wrong thing. My raging out-of-control hormones are down to four glasses of Prosecco on an almost empty stomach. There's no need to panic after all because it's nothing to do with the man. *Damn*. Why didn't I think of that five lengths earlier?

By the time I arrive at the deep end, I've had a hard reset, and I'm gliding like a swan. I catch hold of the pool edge, shake back my hair and look up to test my theory.

There's an ironic twist to Kit's grin. 'This is why I love you so much, Floss. Who else would come in here and do an Olympic workout?'

This time it's so much worse. The bottom is literally falling out of my stomach. Then he bites his lower lip, and it's all over.

My hand makes contact with his jaw, and the stubble on his chin is rough against my palm, then my fingers travel and spread. Past his ear, through his damp curls, until I can feel the back of his skull, solid and certain beneath my fingertips. The breath I take is so deep my lungs feel as if they might burst. And for a while he doesn't move, and it feels as if the world has stopped spinning, and for an age time feels like it's standing still and I'm certain he's going to pull back. And then just as I'm about to give up hope, I feel his head dipping, slowly moving towards me, and then his lips brush lightly against mine. Then he comes in again, sweet and hot and tasting of wine, and my arm slides around his neck, and all I can hear is the rushing in my ears like the sound of the sea, as my slick wet skin slides against his. There's music, there are stars, there are rainbow colours zipping through my head and my pounding heart feels like it might be going to explode out of my chest. And when I finally pull away, I'm rubbing my lips and gasping. Then dying of shame for what I've done.

'I'm sorry, that was a terrible idea.' I'm disentangling myself, yet somehow still clamped against his chest.

He lets out a low laugh. 'There was nothing bad about it from my side.'

I'm lining up the reasons in my head, trying to find my best excuse for the outrageous behaviour. I'm at number five hundred and sixty-two when there's a splash somewhere behind me.

Kit's looking past my shoulder to the water, and his body tenses. 'Shit, that was Shadow. I'd better go...'

As he streaks off down the pool I pull myself up onto the side, and call, 'Try to bring him over to the steps. I'll get towels and catch him as he comes out.'

Shadow jumping in High Tides' best pool? It's thrilling and appalling, funny and shocking all at the same time, depending who you are. What more is there to say than 'Nice job, Shadow'? If I'd had to choose how to wind up our fake date, I couldn't have come up with a better ending.

Now all I've got to do is work out how to face the rest of my life.

32

Nell's house, St Aidan
All the pie
Monday

My first attempt at spontaneous, uninvited making out, and it ends with me standing poolside in my soaking underwear, while the unfortunate hero in question guides my admittedly very cute but very wet pet through the waves to safety.

I've learned from the experience – I won't ever try it again.

Okay, I admit I took a video of them both – they looked too hilarious for me not to. Shadow, his black nose breaking the water surface, legs paddling as doggedly as if he were running through treacle, tail straight out behind him like a rudder, puffing bubbles from the side of his whiskers as he panted his way up the pool. Kit, also very cute, emerging from the shallow end in his underpants, as he coaxed Shadow towards where I was calling from the steps.

I've showed the video to all the gang, and they see the funny side too. And me viewing it a thousand times is due to the comedy, and nothing to do with Kit and how ripped his shiny wet torso is.

That wasn't the end of the evening's drama either. As we were making our way back along the dune, we finally caught sight of Mum and David down by the water's edge, making their way back to High Tides for a nightcap at the hotel before Mum went home. A slight change of plan there then. At least Rye was around to confirm she'd left later.

So it wasn't a *total* waste of time, and we know more now than we did. First, that however hard you screw up your eyes you can't tell too much about people from a hundred yards away. Second, that people are spontaneously unpredictable – they rarely do what you expect, and they stick to their own plans even less than that. (I try *not* to put that down to new lovers being all over the place.) And third, if we're going to do this regularly, we'll need to invest in a pair of binoculars or some night vision equipment.

As for the detail, my immediate agonies after what happened in the pool were eclipsed by drying a dripping dog. By the time he was fit to walk back to reception, we'd all moved on. Since then I've done three mornings at the studio and the same number of afternoon teas on the deck with Kit's clients, and as neither of us has mentioned it again I'm assuming we never will.

Clemmie and I are at Nell's house the following Monday afternoon, and I've been filling them in on all the developments, except for my own blunder.

Nell's on the sofa tucking into the third sausage sandwich

from the bag that Clemmie brought round while small-George snoozes on her knee. She hands Shadow the last tiny piece and ruffles his ears. 'Well done, boy! We've both made tidal waves at the High Tides hotel now.' Her smile widens. 'So are you going to spill the beans about the rest, Flossie?'

My blood runs cold, and I know I have to tough this out. 'There are *beans*?'

This is St Aidan, everyone knows about everything, mostly before it happens, so more fool me for thinking it could be any other way. Me jumping Kit will have spread across the whole of the county, if not the world, and now it's out there, I'm never going to live it down.

Nell's staring hard at me. 'We all saw the video, but *what kind of undies was he wearing?*'

Clemmie laughs. 'Pants can speak volumes about a man. Is Kit an organic bamboo guy, does he shop at Primark, or was there *a label?*'

Nell chortles. 'Tesco ones are a great sign they know what a supermarket is.'

My accelerating heartbeats subside. As it sinks in that this is all they're asking about, I can't believe I've got away with it. 'I may have spotted the words "Calvin Klein" on the waistband...'

Nell nods. 'Stylish, yet *not quite* as up himself as a Ralph Lauren Polo wearer.'

Clemmie smiles. 'Charlie likes Calvin Kleins too.'

Nell rolls her eyes. 'Before grown-up George and I got together, his mum used to buy him his for Christmas and there's no changing him now. M&S cotton boxers, with checks not stripes, and he doesn't like red.' She looks at me again. 'What does Nate wear?'

I let out a shriek. 'I don't know, he's my brother-in-law, not my husband!'

Clemmie laughs. 'He used to wear Paul Smith, but lately he's been wearing Hamilton and Hare. It's amazing what you find out at Mums and Bumps!'

Nell takes a handful of Wotsits from the family-size bag propped next to little George's head. 'With this feeding lark I could eat an elephant, so talk me through your plans for High Tides while I build up to my last sarnie.'

Rye and I spent an afternoon at Clemmie's looking through her afternoon tea photo album and deciding on the best way to begin.

I clear my throat. 'I've already started supplying the hotel with freshly baked scones, cake, and puddings in teensy cups that guests can have as standalones, and for any proper afternoon teas the hotel will add in bite-sized sandwiches with astonishingly luxurious fillings, and delicately crafted miniature savoury pastries. They're working those up now.'

Clemmie's nodding. 'And they'll serve them on suitably impressive multi-tier glass platters once they buy them, but in the meantime, they're borrowing some of mine.'

I'm really excited about the next bit. 'They've already put a photo of one of my scones with a dollop of clotted cream and jam up on the website, so it looks like they're giving it a serious try.'

Nell runs her fingers through her hair. 'I could murder one of your puddings now, Flossie. But stuff anything minuscule, I'd need mine in a trifle bowl.'

It feels mean teasing someone who's so tired that they're

wearing their shirt inside out, but I can't resist. 'If you promise to come to the next get-together at The Hideaway, I'll make you one specially.' I take in the sudden downturn of her mouth, and backtrack. 'For now, you'll have to make do with a lemon and meringue pie that's so big it only just fitted through your kitchen door.'

Nell punches the air. 'Just what the doctor ordered, Floss!' Then her fist drops and her voice goes all small. 'The way things are going, I may never leave the house again. By the time I get baby George and me ready to go out, one of us is always too hungry to set off.' She blows out her cheeks. 'I can't ever see us moving past that.'

Clemmie rocks Arnie's baby seat with her foot and rubs Nell's knee. 'Is it any easier when grown-up George is home?'

Nell looks at the ceiling. 'He hasn't been back to the office yet; he's still working from upstairs!' She pulls a face. 'At least I'm dressed. He's still in his pyjamas with a shirt on top for Zoom calls.'

There's a tap on the living room door and a face appears.

I swallow my surprise. 'Milla! What are you doing here? And Tallulah, too!'

Milla swings her rucksack off her shoulders, and they each pull up a pouffe. 'We pop in most days after school to check Nell's okay.' She puts a large box down on the coffee table. 'We've come via the doughnut stall today. Six iced, six sugared, six jam. I hope that won't be too many?'

Nell laughs. 'I'm eating for two and George is eating for three, so we'll soon blast through those.'

Milla purses her lips. 'I couldn't help hearing what you were saying as we came in.' She leans towards Nell and squeezes her hand. 'The first few weeks with a newborn are very full-on. It *will* get better.'

It's not lost on me. However rebellious Milla's being with Sophie, she's still amazingly empathetic with everyone else.

Clemmie picks up on what she's saying and adds, 'Don't worry, Nell, it gets easier as they grow.'

Milla pushes a strand of dark hair off her forehead. 'Even my superwoman mother stayed at home with her babies! When she had Marcus and Tilly, *and* Maisie, Nate took me to places for ages.'

Nell's still clinging to her fingers. 'Thanks for reminding me, Milla. Somehow I thought I'd be straight back out there.'

Milla's eyes flash. 'I seriously hope Mum didn't tell you that! She's so full of crap at times, it's very irresponsible!'

I have to call her out on this. 'Milla! Let's try to be nice.'

Milla rolls her eyes. 'You asked her to meet me halfway, Aunty Flo, and she's still dressing like a mint mousse.' Milla's voice rises to a shriek. 'She pretends she'll change, then doesn't. That's what's *so frustrating*!' She drops her voice again. 'Sorry, George and Arnie, I didn't mean to disturb you.'

I've been pondering this a lot lately. 'We're going to have to step in!' I'm pretty happy with what I've come up with. How Sophie will feel about it is something else entirely. '*I'm* going to re-style her wardrobe!'

Milla's clapping her hands. 'Brilliant!'

Clemmie's smiling. 'Inspired! All we've got to do now is to persuade her to join in!'

I still have to put my mind to that one. 'That's settled then. We're all agreed we'll give it a try?'

'Totally!' Milla's frowning. 'I've got one other question...'

I'm hoping it's less exacting than Milla's usual ones, because I'm still very hazy on the detail, but I make my smile enthusiastic. 'Yes?'

Milla gives a cough. 'If the rumours are true that you and Kit went for a midnight swim at High Tides in your underwear – how did you keep your hands off him, Aunty Flo?'

The only way to deal with that is to go out to get the lemon meringue pie.

33

Sandpiper Books, St Aidan
Turning the pages
Monday

I've never been big on research or revision. If I go into a bookshop, it's for the cake or the stories, and Sandpiper Books has plenty of both of those. As I tiptoe up the creaky winding stairs later that afternoon to the non-fiction section on the first floor, the book-lined rooms I'm wandering through are like a whole new world.

The books I'm looking for are exactly where the assistant downstairs said they would be – in the third room along, on the left inside the doorway.

'Here we go, Shadow. Lots to choose from.' Dog-friendly is another reason we're in here. And the fact that it's tucked away along a narrow street at the top of town, so it feels like I'm less likely to meet anyone I know. It's nothing to be ashamed of, but I'd rather *not* be spotted poring over books about the night sky when Kit's the one who mentioned it first. Me being here is not about me wanting to make a good impression on Kit either. Ideally, I won't be looking at the sky with anyone, but if ever I can't avoid it, I'd rather not be totally in the dark.

The first small paperback I pick up has photos and charts and covers the basics. At £5.99, what's not to like? As we clatter down the stairs, I'm giving silent whoops that I'll have been in and out in five minutes, but when I step off the bottom landing I come to a jarring stop. There's only one person I know in St Aidan with blonde balayage and overalls. Standing next to the birthday cards, tapping her Chelsea boot as she waits for the till ... is my mum.

I'm pinning my hopes on a super-silent retreat back to where we've come from, but at that moment Shadow falls off the step behind me and crashes into the rotating postcard rack, and the best I can do to save the situation is to fold my arms and hide the book under my boobs.

It takes Mum a nanosecond to clock us. 'Floss! What are you doing here? I didn't know you read books!'

I give a sigh. 'It's what I do for a living, remember, when I'm not feeding ice cream to happy engaged people?' Now I come to mention it, it feels like another life altogether. 'You don't usually have time for anything other than paint when you're halfway through a project either!'

She winces. 'I'm actually buying a reference book.' She holds it out and I pick my jaw up off the floor.

'50 *Things to See in the Night Sky*. The hardback version with the glow in the dark cover!' I went for the less fancy one and saved myself a tenner. 'I didn't know you were interested in stars?'

'I'm not.' She shuffles. 'But I might be. I'll give it a try and let you know.'

I make my smile bright. 'It's great you're exploring new areas.'

'I'm not the only one, am I?' She reaches out and tickles Shadow's ears. 'Who's been having late night dips in the hotel pool?'

My mouth drops open. 'How come you heard about that?'

She gives a shrug. 'I expect it's on the CCTV.' She smiles. 'I'm pleased you're going out with new friends – Kit and Rye are especially nice.'

I give a cough to cover how appalled I am. 'We were actually having a work brainstorming session.'

She smiles. 'That clearly went well too. I tried one of your new afternoon teas earlier; your scones were delicious and David is delighted. They could be just what the place needs to draw in more customers.'

My voice is high with surprise. 'But you *never* eat lunch!' If she did it would be a salad.

She laughs. 'Never say never! That could be my new motto.'

Now I look more closely she's not in actual overalls either. 'You're looking extra smart today too.'

She stares down and gives her belt a tug. 'You don't think a French Connection jumpsuit is too young for me? Somehow it feels important for me to be myself.'

'You look fine – lovely, in fact.' It's a silky version of her usual long-sleeved boiler suit, but together with her platitudes *and* a new shade of lippy the whole effect is so unnerving I have to call her out on it. 'What's going on with you, Mum?'

I'm not about to credit David Byron by name in all of this, but I'm confident he's at the centre of the storm.

She half shakes her head. 'It's something and nothing, a few loose ends that need tying up. I promise you'll be the first to know if it's ever anything more.' Then the till drawer rings and my mum steps forwards. 'This is me! I'd better go.'

As I watch her hurrying out of the shop door a few minutes later I'm no wiser.

The sales assistant is helpful as ever as she takes my payment. 'Would you like a set of postcards of views of bygone St Aidan? They're a fundraiser for the local care home, we'll all be old one day after all!'

My fingers are crossed tightly for that.

'Why not?' They cost slightly more than my book, but Milla helps at the care home, so I know it's a lovely place and worth the support. As for the future, I've learned to focus on the present, but I've promised myself to be fiercely optimistic about the rest until there's a reason not to be. If I make it to old age, I'll be whooping.

The assistant rings it all up and tucks the cards inside the book. 'It's always lovely to see a mother and daughter enjoying the same hobbies. If you're starting an astronomy club, I can put up a poster for you?'

I take my paperback. 'Thanks, I'll get back to you on that one.'

It's not lost on me that Mum and I were in the same shop buying practically the same book, but we might as well have been in parallel universes.

Shadow and I head out onto the street, take a gasp of sea air to clear our heads and run straight into St Aidan's other overall wearer. At least Plum's are reassuringly paint-splattered.

She points at my book. 'Ooh, you're taking up astronomy?'

'It's only a precaution, I'm hoping not to.'

Her eyebrows go up. 'I'm pleased I've met you, because something's come up – one of those things that have to be discussed face-to-face.'

'If it's about Dillon...'

'No!' Her hand goes up. 'This is something else entirely. I can't tell you who told me, but – David Byron has made an informal approach to the planners, asking if they'd be in favour of putting a lido on your land.'

My heart goes into free fall. Talking about Dillon would have been manageable, but this is like Pandora's box opening. 'Can they do that without telling me?'

Plum's involvement with the Chamber of Commerce not only means she's in the front line for receiving information, but also that she understands it too. She takes a breath. 'An informal approach is a way for people to find out the kind of development the council would allow without going to the expense of drawing up a full scheme. They'd only inform all the landowners involved if a proper application was made.' She bites her lip. 'If they work out what they need in advance, when the full scheme is submitted it goes through faster.'

I blow out a sigh. 'It lets developers get all their balls in a row so they can take the little people like me by surprise.'

Plum blows out her cheeks. 'At least now we know what's going on behind the scenes we can decide on an action plan.'

I'm working out what she's getting at. 'A plan for what?'

She pulls me into a hug. 'I know we mermaids are a bit

depleted with Nell and Clemmie on maternity leave, but we can't take this lying down. *We have to fight it!*'

'We absolutely do!' I punch the air so hard, I drop my star book on the pavement.

And to think that my biggest worries up until five minutes ago were how to dodge staring up at the sky with Kit, and how to get Sophie to agree to a makeover.

34

The beach at High Tides Hotel, St Aidan
Postcards from another planet
Tuesday

'Let's be clear – we're not stargazers, and this is definitely surveillance. Anything else we do is simply a way of passing the time.'

As Kit and I stamp through the soft sand up the dunes on the far side of the hotel the next evening with our arms overflowing with supplies, it feels like a good time for me to lay down some ground rules. Whenever there's a man there's always a risk an outing will turn into an expedition, but who knew we'd need so much gear? By the time we've got rugs to lie on, covers to put over us, flasks of hot chocolate, mugs and marshmallows, an ice bucket, glasses and a bottle of fizz, a dog bed, dog water and emergency bone biscuits for Shadow plus snacks for us, we could have done with some sherpas to carry it all.

'So remind me again why we're here?'

Kit throws down a rucksack and spreads out a travelling rug. 'Suze and David have walked along the beach to Comet Cove for a gin-tasting event at the castle distillery. Our job is to lie low in the shadows *pretending* to stargaze while *actually* seeing whatever we can as they come back.'

'After what David's doing with the lido plans, I might be tempted to run out and shove him into the water.' I've already ranted about this to Kit earlier, but I'm so wound up, it keeps spilling out.

Kit blows out his cheeks. 'I admire how fiery you are, but I hoped if we gave this more thought we could come up with a more effective way to divert him than losing him at sea.'

It takes me a moment to fully take in what he's saying. 'Hold on. You're on *my side?*'

'Of course.' He shrugs. 'I'd hate to see your hut go.'

I'm mentally punching the air that my instincts at making The Hideaway indispensable are paying off. 'It definitely helps your business.'

He gives me a strange sideways glance. 'There's more to life than the bottom line, Floss.'

I have no idea what he means by that, but it's funny how things go. 'I used to want you to call me Florence, but Floss feels okay now.' I take a moment to let that sink in for me as well as for him. 'So what's in your bag?'

'Our new binoculars.' The orange sun has slipped out of sight on the line where the sky meets the sea, but it's still light enough to get the full benefit of Kit wrinkling his nose. 'I *might* have bought a star book, too. The woman in the bookshop said there's a local club starting up.'

'There definitely isn't.' This is how rumours in St Aidan get out of hand; you have to stamp on them straight away.

'If there was, we could go along.' He sounds hopeful.

'We'll probably be too busy playing look-out for Rye.'

Kit sits down and pats the sand to his left, and Shadow flops down beside him. 'You'll have to excuse Rye's hang-ups with David. Finding each other so late in life, there's a lot riding on their relationship. They're both over-protective of the other yet desperate to prove themselves too.' He shakes his head. 'David building the hotel was all for Rye.'

'That's a lot of pressure.'

Kit sighs. 'It's why Rye has to make it succeed. David left when Rye was a baby and they didn't see each other again for twenty-five years – there's a lot of making up to do.' He pats the rug on his right. 'Shadow's sat in your place so you'll have to come here. If we're spotting planets, we need our heads close together so we know we're looking at the same thing.'

Sometimes it's too much effort to fight the logic, but as I kneel down next to him there's an echo in my brain. 'We grew up without our dad.' I'm not sure why I'm sharing this now. 'Sophie remembers him more than I can, but after the effort Mum put in after he walked out on us, we wouldn't be up for any long-lost-father reunions.'

Kit's staring out at the lines of foam, running up the beach. 'Apparently Rye's parents' relationship broke down when David was ill.'

Another echo there. 'I know all about that.' I'm watching the shine on the sand by the waterline when it strikes me. 'Sophie, Mum and I were very self-contained as a family, so even as teenagers we didn't ask what had gone wrong.'

It's only sitting here now that it hits me how little I know about what happened. He was long gone, and we were fine without him. There was never any reason to ask any more.

Kit rests his elbows on his knees. 'Every family is different. I still have both parents and two older sisters and they're always on my case, but it's only because they care.' He rattles the ice bucket. 'Shall we have some Prosecco while we wait for it to get dark? I've brought flutes.'

I laugh. 'Or we could do it St Aidan-style, and drink from the bottle?'

He pops the cork and hands the bottle to me. 'I might be blaming Rye more than I should. I'm pushing for this as much as he is because I enjoy hanging out with you.' He takes a box out of his rucksack, pops up the top and pushes it towards me.

'If those are doughnuts, I'm very happy to be here too.' I tilt back my head, take a large slug and as the fizz goes straight to my head, I get a waft of his scent. 'If they're *custard* doughnuts I may have to kiss you.' As I hand back the bottle I'm kicking myself for letting that slip out, but I'm safe because the only shop that sells them is miles away, beyond the station.

He gives a low laugh and takes a drink. 'Five shops to find them was worth it then.'

My tummy does a somersault. 'You're joking me?'

He shakes his head. 'I'm not. Custard is your favourite. And Shadow's. And I might be on a roll here, but that could be a star...' His arm slides around my shoulder, and my hair is tangling against his cheek as my eyes follow his pointing finger to where a spot of light is shining against the fading sky.

'That could be Venus...' Don't ask me where that came from because I can't think any further than how hard my heart is hammering, and how the warmth of his body is spreading right through me, but I have to come clean. 'I bought a book too.'

He passes me the fizz again. 'From what I read earlier, I think you're right about Venus.' He runs his finger up my thigh and stops at the hem of my shorts. 'Are you cold?'

'No.' I suppress the delicious shivers that are zinging up and down my spine, drink some more and think of my mum saying it's important to be yourself. 'The photos of the Milky Way were awesome, but what I most like the sound of is watching for shooting stars.'

'Would you like to sit to do that, or would it be better lying down?'

As he stretches his legs out I snake my leg through one of his. 'As we've brought so many rugs it would be a shame to waste them.' A proper kiss would let me get him out of my system, but whatever I've said, I'm not going to be the one to jump him. I flop onto my back, and as I stare upwards, I notice he's looking down on me.

'How is the view from down there?'

I open my mouth to tell him there are already too many stars to count, but his face is dipping towards mine. I hold my breath, but he's coming so slowly that I'm going dizzy with anticipation. Then his lips graze mine and I taste the sweetness of his mouth all over again, and all I can hear is the sound of the waves as they crash on the beach. Then I close my arms around him, feel the muscles of his back give under my fingers as I pull him towards me, and after that the whole world goes blurry.

It's a long time later when we finally move, and that's only because there's a ping on Kit's phone right next to my ear.

He disentangles himself in the darkness and gives a grunt as he finds his phone. 'It's Rye saying David and Suze are back at the hotel.'

'We missed them!'

He laughs. 'I can't think how. They must have cut up the path behind the hotel.' He runs his fingers through his curls. 'When the evening's going so well, it's a shame to cut it short. There's more Prosecco at mine...?'

In case he means more, I might as well say it. 'Sex is a mine-field for me – since my ops.'

'I can imagine.' He leans over and pushes the hair out of my eyes, and drops a kiss on top of my head. 'There's no pressure or expectation – I'm just enjoying what we're doing.'

'We haven't even started the doughnuts yet.'

His smile is illuminated by the moonlight. 'We could begin with those and see where we get to?'

And a few seconds later we're on our feet hurrying towards the studio.

35

The beach by The Hideaway at first light
Evening classes and good vibrations
Wednesday

Kit and I are up at first light next morning so Shadow and I can get back to mine before St Aidan central grapevine wakes up for the day.

Kit's bed sheets? White Egyptian cotton, with pale grey waffle throws. How did we sleep? Solidly – but only for the last half-hour before the alarm woke us.

My arms are full and as I hesitate for a moment on Kit's porch to readjust the rug I'm carrying, he's at the door.

'I wish you'd let me walk you home.'

'I'm fine.' If he came to mine, I'm not sure I'd let him go again, but before I leave there's something I want to ask. 'What are we doing here? Just so I know.'

Kit's eyes narrow. 'Which bit? That part where you were

upside down hanging off the bed or the bits where it was so good I felt like I was going to expire?'

I shrug. 'All of it?'

'Do you want to give it a name?'

'Not as such. I'd like to put it into context – we both said we didn't want entanglements.'

'Will it work if we think of enjoying the moment? Doing it if we want, not if we don't.'

'Taking a day at a time?'

His face slides into a grin. 'We can take it minute by minute if it makes it easier? Any time it stops being fun, we'll think again.'

'No ties, no catches, just seizing the day.'

'That sounds like a St Aidan kind of plan.'

I'm glad we got that sorted. 'Great. I'll see you at the studio later.'

He looks at his watch. 'Three hours' time. If you come ten minutes early I'll make you a bacon subway.'

36

The Hideaway at lunch time
Full English
Wednesday

'I've made us mini cheese scones and salad, with meringue, strawberries and custard cups for pudding.'

When I ended up at Kit's last night I really hadn't thought through fitting in the hotel baking next morning, work at the studio and a lunch date at The Hideaway with the mermaids. As it turns out I'm running fine on half an hour's sleep because my body and my brain are still buzzing with the adrenalin rush of spending eight hours in bed with Kit.

Clemmie comes out onto the veranda with Arnie on one arm and an ice bucket and bottle in her other hand. 'I thought we could try this No-secco, it's Huntley and Handsome's wine of the week.' She stops and gives me a closer look. 'You're looking good today. Have you got new blusher?'

I try not to go scarlet. 'It's the St Aidan sun bringing my freckles out.'

She gives me a nudge. 'Whatever it is, order some for me!'

Plum's carrying a tray of plates and glasses. 'Nell's not made it?'

Sophie's following with Bud on her hip. 'Give her another month.' She sits down, settles Bud on her knee and opens her picnic box. 'I take it we're here for an update on all things High Tides?'

We're not. We're here so I can talk her into her makeover, with Plum and Clemmie here as my wingmen, but for now I'll play along. 'The best news is that the hotel is noticeably busier since word has got around they're serving cake.' Their scone and cake orders have doubled day-on-day this week. Rye marks it all on graphs, and has already shown me projections. 'If the orders carry on growing *this* fast I'll need to buy an industrial oven a week on Friday.'

Clemmie gives Plum a wink. 'You may only have to wait fifty years not a hundred before Rye comes out to play.'

I grin at Plum. 'I reckon you may get your chance before summer's over.' I give a silent groan. 'If only all the news were this good. Kit and I have missed David and Mum twice in a row, so we still aren't certain how that's going.'

Sophie's eyes narrow. 'If they know you're looking, they might be giving you the run-around.'

It's a good excuse to be seen out with Kit, so I won't close this down. 'We've promised Rye we won't stop until we find out what's going on.'

Plum's loading her scone with butter and grated cheese.

'Any ideas about how we can stop David taking over the dunes and the world?'

I fan out the pile of fundraiser postcards I bought in the shop. 'This is very new, but look what I came across while the scones were in the oven.'

Sophie glances at them. 'They're the Kittiwake Court bygone St Aidan cards.'

I pick out the most important. 'This one is from the nineteen thirties and it says it's a picture of a tide-fed sea pool. Doesn't it look gorgeous?'

Plum's looking at the photo. 'I've often noticed the remnants of it walking along the beach. It was on the rocky outcrop towards Oyster Point.'

Plum never ceases to amaze me. 'I had no idea it existed, but I've been Googling. It was abandoned in the seventies when a section of the wall collapsed, but the council had ploughed their money into the leisure centre so they never bothered to repair it.'

Plum pulls a face. 'That was the era when people were buying tumble driers and throwing away their washing lines. It's hard to imagine why people would abandon a sun-warmed sea-water pool to swim indoors in water filled with chlorine.'

'It wouldn't happen now, people love wild swimming.' Sophie's siting up straighter as she listens. 'You can see the tide running into it when you look down from Siren House. The water flows out again because of the hole in the wall.'

I'm thinking aloud. 'I came across that postcard completely by chance, but now I've seen it I can't help thinking – if it were there again to use it would be better for the community in every way than the lido David Byron's pushing for. This isn't just me wanting to save The Hideaway either, I do believe it's the truth.'

'I completely agree!' Clemmie's got a mouthful but she's waving her scone in the air for emphasis. 'It's closer to the town for everyone, it would be completely free to use, it's beautiful and natural, and so much kinder to the environment than acres more concrete at the so-called environmentally friendly High Tides.'

Plum slaps her palm down on the table. 'It's a fabulous idea, Floss. Everyone in St Aidan would love the idea of reinstating the sea pool. Anything *that* romantic and historically inspiring, they'd be bound to support it.'

'There are special grants and funds available for community projects.' I've been Googling this too.

Clemmie's expression is serious. 'If the community got behind an outdoor pool of their own it would leave David Byron and his horrible plans high and dry, and he'd be the only one to lose out.'

My heart is racing with excitement. 'So that's wins all round! We need to look into this further!'

Clemmie's beaming. 'Well done, Flossie May. I'll see if there's any way Charlie can help.'

Plum joins in. 'I'll ask around my contacts at the Chamber of Commerce.'

Sophie laughs. 'Looking ahead, Sophie May Beauty will definitely sponsor the opening party and in the meantime I'll organise the Friends of St Aidan Sea-Water Pool group.'

'So that's that for now.' I look around their eager faces and realise as they've known me my whole life, I might as well ask what's been on my mind. 'One question while you're all here – I realised the other night I had no idea what happened when Mum and Dad split up.'

Sophie's looking at me blankly. 'He walked out on us. There's nothing more to it than that.'

Plum chimes in. 'Everyone in St Aidan knows the story. Your dad was a long-distance bus driver.'

Clemmie carries on. 'One day he took a coach-load of holidaymakers to Chester le Street and didn't come back.'

Plum nods. 'We were six, because the day your mum came in to tell school about it I remember Mrs Banks, our Year One teacher, letting Sophie choose the story.'

It's awful when the village knows my family history better than I do. I suppose Clemmie lived in the same row of fishermen's cottages as we did, so she was bound to know.

I look at Sophie. 'But surely that can't be it? Had they argued? Was there someone else?' The questions flash through my mind.

Sophie shakes her head. 'He was away so often with his job, for a long time it didn't register with me that he'd gone.' She looks at me. 'Mum played it down. You were younger, and he always took more notice of me than you because I was an attention seeker.'

I grin at her for that admission. 'By the time we were old enough to ask it was ancient history.'

Sophie nods. 'It's similar with Milla. Her dad didn't want any involvement and that was a big thing before she was born, but we never think about him now.'

Which is the perfect opening to move this on. I give Clemmie a look and she picks it up and runs.

'You've given up on changing your colour scheme, then?'

Sophie stares down at her box-fresh turquoise hoodie. 'Whatever I choose Milla will criticise it.'

I look at Sophie. 'We've thought of a fun way to make Milla think again with her criticism.'

Sophie sits back in her seat. 'Don't keep it to yourself! I'll consider anything!'

Plum sits forward. 'We've all noticed that in Milla's eyes Aunty Florence can do no wrong.'

Clemmie nods. 'You're definitely up there with the goddesses, Floss.'

I take a deep breath and turn to Sophie. 'How would it be if we change you – by turning you into me?'

Clemmie's laughing. 'If you're wearing *Floss's* clothes, Milla won't criticise those.'

Plum's nodding. 'With a whole new persona it'll be easier for you to break free from your aqua habit too.'

Sophie's voice rises. 'Does it have to be *this radical?*'

I sense that she's wriggling. 'Two strong characters like you and Milla, anything less wouldn't work.'

She blows out a breath. 'Okay, I get that. But what about my hair? Much as I'd love to do this, I draw the line at dye.'

I wiggle my eyebrows. 'There's no need to change your colour. Luckily for you I still have my chemo wig.' This is the master stroke that will make it extra special.

Sophie lets out a murmur. 'I finally get the shiny brown swishy hair I always wanted.'

I laugh. 'To make it more of an event, I thought we could all go to the hairdressers and watch you have the wig styled into something slightly more like yourself?' I can't help smiling. 'We'll make a pact with Milla. Your challenge will be to last two weeks as me. If you make it, you can go back to being yourself afterwards, and Milla has to back off.'

Clemmie laughs. 'The more I hear, the more I like it.'

I carry on. 'After you've had fourteen days rocking the world in my colour-pop dresses and playsuits, you might see there's more to life than Sophie-May blue.'

Sophie groans. 'Playsuits? *Really?*'

'That's the part I'm looking forward to most. Especially my Day-Glo orange ones.' I take pity on her. 'Don't worry, they'll be a lot longer on you than they are on me, and we can hitch my mini dresses in with belts.'

Clemmie's eyes are bright. 'So what do you think, Soph? Are you in?'

Sophie sighs. 'Do I have a choice?'

Plum laughs. 'I don't think you do. It's already decided!'

I stand up and squeeze past Shadow, who's sitting up super-straight waiting for crumbs. 'I'll go and get another bottle from the fridge, to seal the deal, and I'll bring out a dress or two to give you a taster.'

I go to the bedroom and take a couple of dresses off the pile I've sorted, then go for the wine. As I'm bending down getting the bottle I hear footsteps on the living room floor, so it's not a complete surprise to find Kit resting his shoulder on the wall when I come through, with Shadow at his knee.

'Hey you! This is a nice surprise.' I make myself stop before I reach him.

'Good social distancing, Florence Flapjack-face.' He grins at me. 'I'm sorry to interrupt your lunch, but Monica and Ellie, whom you saw earlier, would love a visit to your veranda if you can fit them in later?'

'I'll make sure the mermaids leave them some meringues. Anything else?'

He drops his voice. 'Would you like to come over for supper later? Or a midnight swim? Or we could look for the Plough?'

Or we could just go to bed? I try to limit the width of my smile. 'Supper sounds good. Text me when you're ready for the deck visit.'

Kit's thumbs are hooked through his belt loops. 'Great, great and great. I'd better get back to Monica and Ellie. I could have messaged, but I wanted to see you in real life.' He's about to turn, but instead he steps forward and drops a kiss on my mouth. Then a second later he's gone.

I take a moment to steady my galloping pulse rate, then fix my smile in place, call Shadow to heel and saunter back out onto the deck.

'Today's couple want to come over later. That was Kit checking I had enough ice cream.'

Plum laughs. 'As if you'd ever run out.'

Sophie's staring at me. 'Am I seeing things? Did he just kiss you back there?'

Plum's eyes widen but she doesn't say anything. There's just a gaping hole of silence.

'Me? Kit?' I'm opening and closing my mouth but nothing more is coming out. 'W-whatever made you think that?'

Clemmie rubs her nose. 'It must have been the angle. There was no contact at all from where I'm sitting.'

I laugh and hold the dresses in the air. 'Nice try, Soph. It's going to take more than that to distract me from your transformation.' I toss the dresses over her chair arm. 'Here, take these. I'll go and get the seconds.'

37

Force10 Hair, St Aidan
Chop chop whoop!
Saturday

We've taken the last appointment on Saturday afternoon with Nikki at Force10 Hair, so apart from a couple of clients having their blow-dries finished we've got the place to ourselves. As Clemmie and I get Sophie ready in the hair-washing area, Plum is settling Milla, Tallulah and another five of their friends onto the burnt-apricot velvet sofas at the far end of the salon that overlook Nikki's cutting chair and handing out the non-alcoholic fizz in bright pink flutes. I peep through to the neon sign on the wall above the seating and give Sophie a nudge. 'I hope you're ready to *find your wild side?*'

Sophie looks at me through a curtain of dark hair. 'Is Nell here yet?'

I shake my head. 'It's a shame she's going to miss out on the fun.' I've been waiting as long as I could to break this next bit to

Sophie. 'Mum's not here either.' I didn't go into details when I invited Mum along because I didn't want the St Aidan grapevine to get hold of it, but I said enough to expect she'd be here.

Sophie sighs. 'No surprise there! All I can say is, she'd have come if it were you.' And strange as it seems, I think Sophie's right. All these years I've been oblivious, but now I'm looking for the signs Mum definitely does things more readily for me than for Soph.

As for my wig, Nikki could easily have styled that on a stand, but there would have been no drama in that, so Clemmie's making last-minute adjustments as Sophie puts it on.

'One more piece of blonde hair to tuck out of view.' She looks down at Sophie, who's running a long dark brown strand of hair through her fingers. 'With those two capes on, there's no sign of what you're wearing underneath either, so we're good to go out for the first reveal!'

All Milla and her friends know is that Sophie's having a bit of a trim to go with her brand-new self. I'm hoping I'm not tempting fate, lending her the wig I wore when I lost my hair with chemo, but it makes more sense for it to be used than for it to sit at the back of my sock drawer. I covered myself by telling the gang that if I do need it again, I'll simply wear it in whatever style Sophie has it cut into. Watching Sophie tossing those long glossy tresses over her shoulder, I acknowledge that they're part of the past and how I was before I was ill; they bear no relation to my hair as it is now.

Sophie stops in front of a mirror opposite the row of sinks and peers at her reflection. 'I look so different, I barely recognise myself!' When we hurried her into my freshly laundered clothes earlier in the cloakroom she said the same thing, but we covered them over before she could back out.

Clemmie winks at me. 'That's what we're aiming for!' Then she catches Plum's eye and gives her a thumbs-up to let her know we're on our way.

We walk through the salon towards the crowd, and as we call the word 'Surprise!' it reminds me of the day in The Hideaway when Milla came dancing into my living room with her new black hair.

Milla's first to call out. 'What the heck?' She stands up to get a better view. 'Is that you, Mum?'

I can't help but laugh now that the tables are turned. 'She's joining us on the dark side, Milla. What do you think?'

Milla leads the chorus of shouts and laughter.

'Sick.'

'Wowsers!'

'Good job, Mrs May!'

Nikki's waiting with her combs and scissors in her pockets. She shows Sophie to the chair, then stands behind her and runs her fingers through the waves as she studies her reflection in the huge wall mirror they're both looking into. 'We're doing a dry cut for you today. How about I put some layers in and follow on with some face framing at the end?'

'Great!' Sophie may look like someone other than herself, but she's still in charge here. 'And while Nikki's doing that, we can talk about what's happening with the sea pool.'

Clemmie's rolling Arnie's buggy back and forth, lulling him to sleep as she talks. 'Charlie found out the council did a design and costing for the restoration work on the pool, but the project was shelved due to budget cuts after the pandemic.'

Plum's perching on a stool watching Nikki part Sophie's fake hair into sections, scoop it up onto her head and secure it with clips. 'If there's a scheme that's prepped and ready to go, we're way ahead of the competition. And if we kick off some local fundraising right away, we'll soon persuade the people of St Aidan to get behind our pool, not David Byron's. And once that's up and running we can look into grant funding to make up the shortfall.'

The shop doorbell rings and we all turn to see whether it's Nell or Mum arriving.

A second later a very dishevelled George steps into the main salon area. 'Sorry to disturb you, ladies, I'm here to deliver a message from Nell.' His normally well-combed hair is sticking out in such random directions he looks like he should be next in Nikki's chair. 'She said to tell you she's set up the social media pages for the sea pool project, and she's got a fundraiser in the pipeline that's so awesome she won't be able to resist coming out to it. She's suggesting a Barbie and Ken fancy-dress roller skate on the prom!'

The sofa erupts with excitement. 'Nice one, George.'

I wrap up some of the blondies from the tray and push them into his hands. 'Would you like a glass of No-secco while you're here?'

He's already backing towards the door. 'It's Nell's first time on her own with little George, I'd better hurry back.'

'Send our love to Nell!' Sophie's clapping her hands as she calls after George. 'Let's keep those fundraiser ideas coming, ladies!'

Plum starts. 'How about a sea pool-themed art competition!'

Milla's got her hand up. 'We're hoping Kit would donate a

silver friendship-ring-making day, and we'll all go to that!' She's looking directly at me. 'You'll talk him into that for us, won't you, Aunty Floss?'

'I'll see what I can do.' This is Milla putting me on the spot again as Kit's public loyalty could lie with David, but I've already started my own effort. 'I've already done some sea pool *Once they're gone, they're gone!* Mars bar brownies.' It sounds so puny compared to everyone else's ideas and before I know it my mouth runs away with me. 'And how about a sponsored jump into the harbour?'

Plum's eyes light up. 'Brilliant! That's just the kind of head-line-grabbing event we need. You could have stalls and make it like a mini-harbourside festival!' She has her book and pen out and to my horror she's taking notes. 'I'll put you down for that, Flossie.'

And just like that I'm in over my head – again! But honestly, if it gets David Byron off my case, I won't mind.

Nikki has been cutting and combing all this time, and as more hair is released from the clips, there's a surprising amount of dark hair appearing on the floor around Sophie's chair. Nikki bends down to trim the hair either side of Sophie's chin, and then she gives the tresses a final comb-through with her fingers and stands back with a mirror in hand to show Sophie the back.

'Is that okay for you?'

The hair is glossy but much shorter at the front than before. Cut into layers it's thicker, falling around her shoulders and slightly longer down her back.

Sophie beams at her reflection, and Clemmie pushes me forward. 'As this whole makeover idea was Floss's, we'll let *her* take the capes off, and reveal the Sophie we're going to see for the next couple of weeks.'

I clear my throat. 'Just a recap of the rules here – Sophie can wear anything at all, *so long as I'd wear it myself.*' I've actually toned my own clothes down today, so my denim cut-offs and navy polka dot shirt won't compete with her outfit.

'If everyone's ready, I'll say, ta-da!' I take hold of the corners of both capes and tug. 'So, what do you think, Milla?'

Milla lets out a whoop. 'A bright pink playsuit with lime green flowers? Awesome choice!' She's frowning at her mum. 'You actually look like a mini version of Aunty Flo – which is weird but okay all at the same time!'

Only Sophie with her neat, tiny frame could carry off clothes sizes too big, and still make them work. It's only as I look at her face, framed by the dark side layers, that it hits me for the first time in our lives how alike our features are.

I sidle up to Sophie. 'Don't worry, there are lots of less dramatic dresses in the pile I have for you.' I laugh. 'I could even let you borrow your Leeds 2010 T-shirt back again.'

She flops down into the cutting chair, spins it round to face everyone. She's knocking back the glass of fizz Plum hands her when the bell on the shop door dings again.

A second later Mum hurries straight over to Sophie's chair. 'I'm so sorry I missed this, Floss. I've been saying for years that layers would suit you. I'll take you shopping in Falmouth next week to make up for being late and you can give me some advice on what to buy in the French Connection shop.'

Milla gives a cough. 'You might need to put your glasses on, Granny Suze.'

Mum blinks at her. 'Why, Muffin?'

Sophie shakes her head. 'Because I'm Sophie not Floss.'

Milla laughs. 'Don't worry, you're only getting confused because your brain is full of new-love hormones.'

'I don't know about that.' Mum is tutting.

Milla leans forward and smiles at me. 'The High Tides gardeners mentioned you have a new love interest too?'

Plums eyebrows shoot upwards, but it's Clemmie who jumps in. 'Don't believe everything you hear, Milla. Aunty Floss is the last person in St Aidan who'd want a boyfriend.'

Sophie rolls her eyes. 'Catch up, Milla! Aunty Floss can't go on dates when I've got all her clothes.' She stares at the huddle of girls on the sofa. 'I'll settle up with Nikki, then how about Plum and I take you all to the Surf Shack for ice-cream sundaes?'

Milla lets out a wail. 'But we'd promised to do your make-up?'

Sophie's already shepherding them off the sofas. 'We'll fit that in at home after ice cream, Milla.'

Mum is on her way before them. 'I'd better go too. I want to catch the paint shop before it closes.' Loved-up mistake number two. Even I know the paint shop isn't open on Saturday afternoons.

I call to Sophie over the clatter of feet on the wooden floor heading for the door. 'I'll collect your old clothes from the cloak-room.' Not that she'll be needing them.

She calls back. 'You'll have to come to mine for a bird's-eye glimpse of the sea pool too. Siren House is the best place in the village to see it from.'

As Clemmie and I fold Sophie's things I murmur to her, 'Thanks for saving me back there.' I screw up my courage to say what I sense she already knows. 'You saw Kit kiss me at The Hideaway the other morning, didn't you?'

She nods. 'I won't tell anyone.'

'It's completely insignificant to either of us. We haven't even ... you know ... yet. Just ... done other things.'

The corners of her mouth turn upwards. 'How is it?

I drop my voice. 'No one's ever made me scream like that before.'

She grins. 'I *knew* you looked happy!'

'It's good for me to tick the moving-on box, that's all.' It's nothing more than that. It'll fizzle in no time. I think of a better way to put it. 'What Kit and I have is like a shooting star. Pretty while it happens, but we'll be over in a nanosecond.'

She nods. 'Blink and you miss it?'

'That's the one. All stars die in the end, you know.'

She raises her eyebrows. 'Some will turn into a supernova first and that's pretty spectacular.'

I hold up my finger. 'Before we get onto that I need to read more of the book.'

'And while you're doing your research, google harbourside festivals. How huge did that sound?' She laughs. 'Don't worry, Flossie. We mermaids will have your back.'

I truly hope they do.

38

In Sophie's bedroom at Siren House, St Aidan
Tiger prints and forward thinking
Tuesday

I usually try to wriggle out of visits to Siren House, and it's nothing to do with being jealous. Every time I ring Sophie's original Georgian bell and step through the palatial front door it's a reminder of the chasm between us, though once I'm inside, the white walls and scrubbed plank floors always feel more down to earth and homely than the outside suggests it's going to be.

Today I've been summoned at four-thirty for a bird's-eye view of the sea pool, and Sophie waves Shadow and me in, lets the monumental door clunk closed behind us, then turns for the stairs.

'Nate's with the kids in the garden, so we'll go straight up and catch the tide at its highest before it turns. The best place to see it from is the master bedroom.'

It's Sophie's voice, but she's looking slightly freaky with her dark hair, and my leopard-print New Look dress cinched with her wide brown leather belt. When we step into it, I'm reminded that her bedroom is bigger than my whole house, including the decks, but I can't fault her white cotton bed linen, or the soft fawn cashmere throws and floor rugs.

I smile as we pass the colour-burst of my dresses hanging from a curly limed-oak coat rack.

'How's it going, living as me?'

She pushes a piece of dark hair behind her ear. 'Milla helps me decide what to wear each morning, so that's brought us together.' She frowns briefly. 'She's still full-on with the criticism in every other area, but it's bliss that she doesn't slag off my outfits.'

I laugh. 'She's a teenager, she'll need a few years to come through it rather than a few days.'

'You're right, Flossie.' Sophie does a twirl as she crosses the room. 'It's surprisingly liberating, being someone else.'

I catch hold of a dress I don't recognise. 'Is this one of mine?'

She looks guilty. 'We shopped for a few extra ones in smaller sizes. As it's short and orange I take it you'll approve?'

'Defo. Another playsuit too?'

A grin spreads across her face. 'What a revelation they are! Who knew they'd be so comfy or versatile.'

'And you're rocking the thick black eyeliner too.'

She shakes her head as if she can't believe it either. 'It takes me back to when I was a teenage goth, but if I'm in this for two weeks I might as well embrace it.' Her laugh echoes loud around the room. 'Poor Nate doesn't know what's hit him and Maisie's a little confused, but it's doing Milla and me a lot of good, so thank you for pushing me into it.'

She walks across to the enormous bay window with sliding sashes. 'Come and see the sea pool.'

Siren House is built on the clifftop, and its gardens run out to a cliff edge with steps leading down to the beach. From the first floor at high tide we're looking straight out onto a mass of shimmering blue water that melts seamlessly into the sky out on the horizon. To the left there's the harbour with the colourful village cottages stacked up on the hillside beyond. To the right where the cliff curves around a hundred yards further along the beach, there's an outcrop of rocks projecting into the water, which morphs into a man-made wall that surrounds a large space. As the tide rushes up the last part of the sand, it's spilling into the gap to form a pool.

Sophie's pointing downwards. 'You can see, from the line where the old perimeter wall was, the pool is quite a size. And the part at the front is where the dam has collapsed.'

I nod. 'So when that wall was in place, the water would flow right over and be held there when the tide flowed back out again.'

She nods. 'It's an ingenious blend of man-made and natural, only a short walk along the beach from the town, made all the more perfect because it's a sun trap so the rocks warm the water.'

I laugh. 'You sound like a tourist brochure – but that's exactly why it deserves to be re-born.' I've got good news for the fundraising too. 'Kit's agreed to do a day for Milla and the gang. He could fit them in next Saturday if they're free?'

Sophie's nodding. 'Great. I'll let them know! So long as you don't let them bully you into too many more things you don't want to do.'

As I'm taking note of that, I'm blinking at the sparkle of sunlight off the water. It's similar to the outlook from The Hideaway, in that it's looking out over an expanse of the same bit of ocean, but the height and the massive windows here make it more imposing. 'It's cute to see my beach hut nestling over on the far side of the bay. It's a phenomenal view from here!'

Sophie stares out into the distance. 'That view over the sea is why I went to hell and back to get this place when we really couldn't afford it.' She lets out a breath. 'It's all our dad's fault, of course.'

I'm taken aback to hear the word we rarely say. 'What's *he* got to do with anything?'

'Deep down I always felt that he left because I wasn't good enough; that if only I'd been better, he might have stayed.' She's wrapping her arms around her. 'That's why as an adult I've always had to strive – it's as if having the best company and the most amazing house was the only way I could safeguard against losing the people I love.'

My heart is breaking for the six-year-old Sophie and the loss she must have felt. Even more, that her outwardly solid appearance is founded on so many insecurities. 'It's remarkable how two children in the same family can have such different experiences. It sounds awful, but I can barely remember him at all.'

Sophie sighs. 'You and Mum got on so well, I always felt a bit of an outsider after he'd gone.'

I'm shaking my head. 'It's hard to believe I missed *that* my whole life too.' A few months back in St Aidan and it is literally hitting me in the face. 'I can understand why you'd feel jealous of that closeness.'

'It was never about material things.' Sophie shrugs. 'Much as I've always loved Milla, at times, when I saw the life you were living in London, I wished I was the one in the city.'

I laugh. 'I wouldn't have swapped you then, but maybe you were right all along. There's a lot to love about St Aidan.'

Her eyebrow goes up. 'There is?'

Sophie being so honest and upfront here is making me feel guilty for deceiving her, and I sense that she's waiting. 'You were right the other day too – Kit did snatch a kiss.'

Her smile widens. 'I knew it! Well done, Flossie! Of everyone I know, you're the one who really deserves your happy-ever-after.'

'It can never be that.' I choke at the long-term view. 'We're actually taking it minute by minute.'

'So long as you don't get your heart broken,' she murmurs.

I let out a forced laugh. 'Hearts don't come into this. In case you've forgotten, I'm out of the market for anything longer than a one-night stand.'

Her smile fades. 'When your outlook is so good you can't seriously be thinking about putting your love life on hold in case you get ill again?'

I pull a face. 'Dating is a nightmare for normal women. Add in being a cancer survivor who can't have kids...' There's a bigger reason too. 'Kit doesn't want to get involved either, so the H.E.A. is off the table.'

Sophie narrows her eyes. 'I was a single mum with a very opinionated small child, living beyond the end of nowhere, and I still found Nate. I refuse to let you give up that easily!' She laughs. 'As for being post-menopausal, that isn't holding Mum back any!'

'Poor Mum. I can't believe what happened when she turned up at the hairdressers.'

Sophie pulls a face. 'It was unfortunate, but illuminating – she's never asked me to go shopping with her.'

I have to take a stand on this. 'Mum always favouring me isn't fair. We need to tackle her about it.' I take in Sophie twiddling with the sleeve of her dress. 'If you can change your leopard spots, she can change hers too. It's never too late!'

Sophie nods. 'The problem is, she's changed so much lately we hardly recognise her.'

I think of the reason for that and let out a groan. 'Mum and Mr Byron are off to another thing at Comet Cove tonight and the secret agents are on standby, so I'd better be getting off.' I'm actually losing sight of what's going on here. Is it Rye giving Kit and me an excuse to go out, is it Kit wanting to show support for Rye, or do we all still want to know what's going on? 'With so much dancing around, it might be easier to go directly to Mum and ask her straight out.'

Sophie pulls me into a hug. 'My little sister who used to be so hesitant and tentative is suddenly so decisive. You're changing too and it suits you!'

I shrug. 'For the first time ever, there are things I care about – keeping The Hideaway is so important, I'm desperate to make the sea pool happen, I love baking and concocting puddings and at last I have a sister who needs my help instead of it always being the other way round.'

Sophie gives me a last squeeze. 'You *will* get your sea pool.'

'It's not *my* sea pool.'

She laughs as she lets me go. 'You were the one who redis-covered it. I think we all know it *is* yours.'

I'm laughing as I head for the landing. 'Thank you for showing it to me. I'll keep you updated tonight.'

A second later, Shadow and I are clattering down her stairs. And this time as I head towards the front door with my new inside knowledge and understanding, it looks a lot less swanky and in-my-face than it did on the way in.

39

On the beach at Cockle Shell Castle, Comet Cove
Cosy corners and sleepy heads
Tuesday

K it crosses his ankles and sits back against the dune. 'A string quartet in the castle gardens, gin cocktails and canapés on the lawn – maybe we should be there rather than watching from the sidelines?'

Cockle Shell Castle at Comet Cove is Mum and David's destination for this evening, and as we often come this way for walks, we've brought Shadow along the beach with us, and now we're lounging on the dry sand up above the tideline. Cockle Shell Castle claims to be the world's cosiest castle and as it's also where the famous gin is distilled. It has lots going for it.

I laugh. 'It all looks pretty starchy and upmarket. I'm not sure how Mum and David would feel about us being on the guest list.' I'm not sure I could handle meeting them face-to-face socially either.

The castle facade has a monumental nailed front door at the centre, symmetrical turrets to each side and lawns that run down to the shingle behind us. From where we're sitting, we can see the guests milling beyond the shrubbery, sipping their drinks next to white painted chairs arranged across the grass.

Kit gives a shrug. 'I'm not sure what Rye's expecting, but it doesn't look the kind of do where anyone's going to get their face snogged off.' He frowns into the distance at the ladies wafting around in their heels and impeccably ironed tea dresses, and gives me a sideways glance. 'Would *that* be your kind of evening? You do wear nice dresses.'

It's funny that he has to ask. 'Cocktails would be cool if they're made from alcohol-free gin.' I hope I'm not sounding too picky. 'If they swapped the quartet for dance anthems, I'd be up for that!'

He laughs. 'I personally feel that classical strings are best enjoyed drifting on the breeze.'

I'm with him on that. 'Ideally from a distance of at least a hundred yards, which means we're very well placed here.' I rest my chin on my hand as I stare out to sea. 'The funny thing is, if you'd asked me, I'd have said my mum was the same as us. And suddenly there she is, listening to Air on a bloody G string, and tilting her head like she's savouring every last note.' I can't actually see her, I just know it's what she'll be doing. And she's the woman who sands woodwork to Adele and rolls paint onto her walls to Queen's greatest hits.

Kit grins at me. 'You like dancing then?'

I nod. 'Doesn't everybody?' That was a stupid answer. Not that I'd ever compare, but Dillon always left the dancing to the women, while he hugged the bar with the guys.

He twitches his mouth. 'I was thinking how great it would be to have an evening of dancing on the harbourside after the sponsored jump.' His eyes are sparkling as he speaks. 'I'm not dumping this on you, but we could get Rye to bring along the hotel sound system. If we sorted out string lights and bunting, a bar and some burgers, we could dance the night away and get more cash rolling in too.'

It sounds perfect. 'Sponsored by Love2Love Atelier. You're on!'

'That's a date then!'

As it could be weeks away, I have to say, 'It's a long time ahead for people taking things an hour at a time.'

He grins. 'Luckily for us, you already talked me into taking an optimistic view.'

I'm thinking back to what Sophie said about not getting hurt. 'Summer's the best time for fun without a future.' I'm picking up a doubtful shadow passing across his face, and it sets off the doubts in me. 'You do still like it?'

His lips twist into a smile. 'Hell, yes.'

'Even though we haven't even gone all the way yet... You're still okay with that?'

He grins at me. 'There are no complaints from my side.'

Now we've got this far into this discussion, it seems like a good time to check. 'And if we *did* decide to stop the sleeping together, we'd still be okay to carry on working together and waving at each other across the dune?'

He raises his eyebrows. 'That's what no-ties fun is all about. It's completely separate from the rest of our life.'

I nod. 'The emotion box stays completely closed, so whatever happens, there's no drama or big deals.' Sophie would be proud that we've covered every aspect there. I laugh. 'Sorry for making this sound like more than it is. We can go back to the job we're doing now.'

'All good, Flossie Flapjack-face.' He laughs and pulls me towards him and into a very sweet but sexy kiss. 'I'm assuming Rye is hoping we'll catch a glimpse of the couple as they're leaving the venue. The next question, is what shall we do in the meantime?'

I rest my head on his shoulder. 'We could lie and watch for the stars to come out, then watch for shooting stars once it's darker.'

'How many of those have we seen so far?'

I stifle a yawn. 'That's why it'll be magical when we *do* see one. It's my mission of the summer, to see a shooting star.'

'Are you sleepy?'

'It's more that your shoulder is really comfy.' The truth is, since our first stargazing adventure on the dunes we've had every night together, and with the late nights and early mornings, I'm dead on my feet.

'If you need a little snooze, Shadow and I can chat amongst ourselves.'

I'm easing back and the worn denim of his shirt is soft against my face. 'Five minutes? Wake me up if I snore.'

The last thing I hear is the rumble of his voice under my ear saying. 'I will.'

When I next open my eyes, I know it must be a long time later, because the sky is inky blue. I say the first thing that comes into my head. 'Where are the stars?'

Kit stirs beside me. 'Welcome back! The stars are only showing in the gaps between the rather big clouds and the moon's gone in too.'

I'm rubbing my eyes and the only sound I can hear is the waves rushing up the sand. 'How long was I asleep? What happened to the music?'

He looks at his watch. 'I'm afraid you missed the performance. Most people left quite a while ago.'

I'm kicking myself for another total fail. 'Did you see Mum and David?'

'They were with a group who wandered back along the shore together. The moon was brighter then so I got a good view of everyone chatting and picking up shells. So, still nothing definite to report to Rye.'

I let out a long sigh. 'We're all thinking the worst and panicking, but maybe there's nothing going on after all. Mum's still going back to hers after dates as far as I know.' If it was anyone other than David B she was seeing, we wouldn't even be thinking about it, let alone running around St Aidan after her.

Kit laughs. 'She wouldn't want to share David's uberhealthy breakfasts. He's all about the protein shakes and chia seeds.' He scratches his head. 'Thinking back, when your mum hurried off from our singles evening, it could have been David she was trying to avoid.'

'In which case, apologies to Shadow, but we might have been barking up the wrong tree all along. Rye thinking my mum's here to seduce his dad is nothing short of bonkers.'

Kit gets to his feet. 'Do you need me to call us a taxi back?'

I smile. 'Thanks, but it's not too far to walk and the wind off the sea should wake me up.'

Kit offers me his hand and pulls me onto my feet. 'Tonight we should definitely catch up on our sleep.'

There's a twang of disappointment in my chest as he hands me Shadow's lead. 'Separately?'

His mouth twists into a smile in the half light. 'I'd prefer together – if you would?'

Relief floods through me. 'So a quick walk back to mine, and hot chocolate before bed?' Shadow looks up at me as he hears the word chocolate. 'There will be custard creams, Shadow.'

Our eyes are used to the dark, and thanks to the light of Kit's phone the worst we trip over is a couple of clumps of seaweed, and we can soon see the lights of the High Tides hotel spreading out across the sand.

Shortly before the marram grass scrub runs out to super-neat lawns, Kit guides me to the right. 'We'll take Rye's shortcut. It loops round the back of the hotel and comes out behind the Latitudes huts.'

I ease Shadow away from the beach and follow Kit off the sand and onto a neat gravel path hugging close to the buildings. We pass the backs of some rooms, and then I recognise the familiar circular shape of the next building with the repeating vertical windows with a pale glow coming out from inside.

'Is that the Pleasure Dome?'

Kit's nodding. 'And beyond it is your favourite swimming pool, Shadow. We can stop off for a quick dip if you'd like?'

I look down at Shadow. 'Like there's time to swim when there's a full pack of biscuits waiting at home!'

'Another short cut.' As Kit guides us onto another terrace and past a set of large doors the pale blue pool beyond the glass is luminous in the soft light inside.

As a movement beyond the water's edge catches my eye I stop and whisper, 'There's someone in there.'

Kit pauses alongside me and whispers back. 'Are you sure? It's closed to guests after dinner.' He looks again, then he lets out a choking sound. 'Shit. It's David and your mum.'

As I watch them running around the poolside, towards the deep end, then leaping high into the air, and catapulting into the water with a splash explosive enough to empty half the pool, it's one of those situations where I'm hating what I'm seeing, but I'm glued to the spot and I can't look away.

'Jeez!' I stifle a shriek and as the feeling comes back into my legs I break into a run and drag Kit off the far end of the terrace and only stop to gasp when we get into the shadows. 'Of all the things, I didn't expect that.'

Kit lets out a low laugh. 'Naked swimming at midnight! Good on *you*, Florence Flapjack-face's mum!'

I let out a groan. 'Whatever I do, I can't ever un-see that!' I'm blinking and rubbing my eyes, still questioning it was real. 'Please tell me this is Nell organising an over-sixties costume-free moonlight swim event?'

Kit shakes his head. 'I'm afraid this is a breakaway party of two, heady after an evening of gin and Vivaldi.'

I blow out a breath. 'If they're leaping nude into the deep end, they've definitely taken their relationship to the next level.' Not that I'm comparing, but this makes the night I jumped Kit in our underwear look like a nursery school outing. 'It was pure joy and abandon!'

Kit coughs. 'With no thought at all for the security system.'

My hearts skips a beat. 'There are cameras?'

Kit squeezes my shoulder. 'That's how everyone knew about

our swim with Shadow, but we were a lot more dressed than these two.'

My blood is running cold. 'Are you saying there was proper film of me pashing your face off?'

He laughs. 'There might have been.'

I'm hopping about on the spot. 'Stuff that! Did you delete it?'

He sounds more serious again. 'I wiped it from the system, but it was too cute not to save. I mean, what if we go the distance and end up with grandchildren? You'd want me to keep it to show them the night it all began?'

And this is exactly what I meant when I told Sophie that proper dating was too complicated. Two minutes of random conversation, and I'm so far out of my depth I can't even see the bottom let alone reach it. Sometimes you have to go straight in and say it like it is.

'We're never having grandchildren, Kit.'

His lips are twisting into a smile. 'Okay. Anything else I need to know?'

'We're supposed to be taking things a second at a time. Even if you're teasing, you're assuming way too much.'

He's biting his lip. 'I spend all day pretending I believe in love. My romantic side has a habit of leaking out. I'm sorry, it won't happen again.'

'And you'll show me the film when we get back?'

He nods. 'So long as you promise to let me keep it.'

I let out a groan. 'Whatever happened to snatching a fleeting moment? We're supposed to be here and gone, not stored on your iCloud for the rest of time.'

He's nodding. 'I know. I agree. It's just some things are too good to lose – viewed in my professional capacity.'

I've always believed you have to pick your battles. When it's one in the morning, given the choice between this and a hot chocolate, I'm giving up on the argument and going for the cocoa hit.

'What are we going to tell Rye?'

Kit sighs. 'I'll call him when we get back and he can delete the pool footage straight away.'

I just hope for Mum's sake no one finds it too cute or engaging, or *she* may end up on someone's iCloud too. But she's a big girl. I just hope she can look after herself.

40

Milla's ring-making day at Latitude One, High Tides Hotel, St Aidan
More splashes than Jackson Pollock
Saturday

R ule number one with Milla-the-brunette is to always anticipate a little extra, so when she and her ring-making group clatter up my steps at nine instead of arriving at Kit's at ten as arranged on Saturday morning, Shadow and I exchange a smile and carry on as we were. We've been up a good three hours already, so we had time to pull in a walk and baking for a busy weekend at the Pleasure Dome. Shadow's now back to napping, and I'm doing my last jobs in the kitchen before heading over to Kit's.

Milla leads the crew into the living room, where they drop their bags in a pile and then flop down onto every available surface. 'We thought we'd drop in at The Hideaway to put the finishing touches to our outfits and make-up, Aunty Flo.' Cue the usual mass clothes swap, in other words. 'And are we good to have Crunchy Nut Corn Flakes, custard and ice cream on the deck while we're here?'

I'm already in the kitchen loading a tray with cups and cereal boxes. 'Can you serve yourselves while I take my last batches of scones off the cooling trays?'

Milla wiggles her eyebrows at me. 'Of course.'

I'm covering every eventuality. 'And if Jean and Shirley come past with their walking group, can you point them to the "Once they're gone..." ginger cake and triple chocolate muffin stack by the bottom of the steps?'

She nods. 'All good, M— Aunty F.' She laughs. 'I nearly called you Mum there. By the time we all get our blonde wigs on for the Ken and Barbie fancy dress roller-fest it's going to be well confusing.'

It's funny to look back to that first day they came round and think how strange it felt then having people here. Now it happens so often that the beach hut happily expands to welcome whoever descends on us. Where I used to feel engulfed and overwhelmed, I now feel happy and fulfilled. It's as if by rediscovering my hostess role, I'm redefining myself.

Milla beams. 'And we're all coming back here later to finish off the afternoon with plant pot painting. As Mum says, someone has to use up that pot of pink paint Granny Suze bought you, it's a shame to let it go to waste. It's a good thing we're all in our ironic Barbie pink phase.'

This is another of Milla's brainwaves she sprang on me yesterday before I could say no. An hour later, when we roll into Kit's, it's a relief I've avoided being pushed into anything more. The doors between the studio and the veranda are thrown wide open, and there's a long wooden table placed across the beach hut.

Kit looks pretty relaxed as he grins at me and shows the girls to their places. 'Six of you each side, and there's a board and a set of tools for each of you. Floss will bring round some ring blanks to practise with first.'

I sidle up behind him. 'Nice cut offs.' It's the first time I've seen him working in shorts, and he's teamed them with my favourite Paul Smith T-shirt.

'Quicksilver flip flops too.' He looks super proud of himself.

I give him a discreet nudge. 'Well done for getting down with the teenagers.'

Milla's waving her finger in the air. 'I take it we're okay to put our playlist on to work to, Kit?' She pulls a speaker out of her bag and stands it on the table. 'No offence, but we'll be way more creative listening to Wet Leg and Olivia Rodrigo rather than The Beach Boys.'

I murmur to Kit. 'Don't take it personally, you've come a long way with your music.'

Kit gave them a choice of methods for their ring-making earlier in the week and the girls opted for the one where they carve hard wax blanks, leaving Kit to cast the rings in silver later, using the three-dimensional templates they've created.

As Kit starts to demonstrate what each of the cutting tools do, I take the box of blanks round to give them one to play with, then go round again giving them a second, letting them size them properly for their chosen fingers. Once everyone's got what they need, I leave Kit promising they can come back to make rings using the other methods another time, and I do a quick dash to drop off the last boxes of scones for the hotel.

By the time I get back, Sophie has arrived wearing the dress I spent a good ten minutes searching for at home earlier, and she's got herself a ring blank too.

She murmurs under her breath, 'After what happened with Mum and the pool, I thought I'd seize the opportunity to be on site.'

I lower my voice. 'Have you heard anyone mention it at all?'

Sophie shakes her head. 'Not a peep! But it's impossible to keep a secret in St Aidan.'

Behind us the girls are fully absorbed with their carving. As the conversation moves onto wedding rings Kit's answering their questions as fast as they fire them, showing them pictures on his phone.

Then Milla puts up her finger again. 'As you're the expert, Kit, we might as well ask – how can we tell when we've met "the one"?'

Kit gives an unbothered shrug. 'Sometimes you just know because it feels different from anything else that came before it.' He turns to me and grins. 'It can happen in an instant, can't it, Floss?'

I answer before I think. 'Totally.' Then I protest. 'Why have you brought *me* into this? I'm St Aidan's *most committed single person!*'

He laughs. 'I just wanted to see your cheeks go pink.'

I'm going to widen this out before they go scarlet. 'At any moment any one of us may only be a heartbeat away from finding that special person. The studio seems to be the kind of place that puts people in the mood for falling in love.' I'm kicking myself for how wrongly that came out too. Milla is opening her mouth to pick me up on it, but I'm saved on two fronts. First, Pink starts singing 'Just Give Me A Reason' and everyone immediately starts singing along, and then Rye strides in.

I jump forward. 'Rye! I dropped your personal brownies off at your office earlier so you didn't have to turn up to an opposition event.'

He laughs. 'Catch up, Floss! We've actually moved their afternoon tea from here across to the hotel. I know this is a sea pool fundraiser, but the word-of-mouth publicity we'll get for the Pleasure Dome more than makes up for that compromise.'

Sophie raises an eyebrow at me, then turns to Rye. 'I hear business is picking up nicely since Floss sweetened your range?'

He nods. 'We're proving a very popular destination for ladies who like cake, and they're coming for the treatments too.' He looks at both of us. 'And David is very committed to historic St Aidan because whatever local people think, he isn't a complete stranger; he actually remembers the sea pool as a boy.'

My mouth falls open. 'I thought he was from Australia?'

Rye purses his lips. 'That's where he made his fortune, but he was in St Aidan for the sea air for a short time in the eighties. He rented a cottage on the hillside above the harbour.' Rye's wave and description covers most of the houses in St Aidan. 'That's why he particularly wanted to build the hotel here.'

'Great.' I'm saying this as someone who should be grateful we're using his facilities, not because I think it is. In terms of historical dates, I often think of *The Crown*. Even if Byron spent a few weeks here while Charles was still married to Princess Diana, it doesn't change anything for *me*. In my book, due to his underhand methods and dubious aims, David Byron is still a first-class shit.

Rye murmurs to us. 'I'm here because I have news for the girls.' As he moves towards the table several of the faces are definitely appreciating his good looks. 'If I could have your attention, ladies! You'll be having refreshments later in the dedicated dessert centre at the hotel. And the special part is...' he pauses '...we've arranged for the High Tides gardeners to wait on you.'

The screams are so loud I have to clamp my hands over my ears. It's okay for Rye. He just says, 'You're welcome!' and a second later he's gone, leaving us to deal with the mayhem.

When the excitement finally subsides I turn to Sophie with a grimace. 'They're never going to want to come to mine to paint flowerpots after that.'

'Don't worry, I'm sure they will. I can help you if you'd like?'

I'm thinking the words came from Sophie, then I look behind her and see Mum walking in off the veranda. I make sure I get off on the right foot so I throw in a compliment. 'Another nice jump suit, Mum.'

This one's dark turquoise with a navy monstera-leaf print, and it really suits her.

Sophie mutters at me, 'We can only hope she keeps it on.'

I smile at Mum. 'Would you like to make a ring?'

She tenses a little. 'I'll probably just watch, and chat to the girls.'

It takes Milla a nanosecond to notice her grandmother is there. 'Granny Suze! That's lucky! Now you're here you can tell us first hand – is the goss true?'

Mum smiles. 'What's that, Muffin?'

Milla's straight back at her. 'Someone said you'd been skinny-dipping in High Tides' warm pool!'

My heart freezes mid-beat. It's bad enough us knowing. Other people seizing on it is too humiliating to think about.

Sophie's on it like a Rottweiler. 'Someone *who?*' She's talking through gritted teeth. 'Come on, Milla, this is *non-negotiable!*'

Milla shuffles in her director's chair. 'The High Tides gardeners have a WhatsApp group. It was all over school!'

I'm rigid, but I can't let Mum go under the bus like this – I have to save her! I give a cough. 'I'm afraid the WhatsApp group have got their wires crossed. If you're talking about skinny-dipping at High Tides last Tuesday, it was actually me and Kit.'

I'd rather not land Kit in this too, but it won't work without him.

There's a roar from the table, and Milla punches the air. 'So you two *are* an item! I knew it!'

I stand and waggle my finger. 'Honestly, Milla! Two people swimming naked doesn't *necessarily* indicate any kind of commitment. It just means they'd rather not go home with wet pants.'

Sophie's flashing me a secret thumbs-up.

Milla's turned on Kit. 'But you did feel that thing? *You do know she's the one, don't you?*' She turns to me. 'If you two get married, *I can be your bridesmaid!*'

Kit's looking a lot less mortified than he should, but the heat has skipped over him and onto me.

I hold up my hand before this express train runs away. 'Milla! I'm *not* having a wedding.' I'm trying to move the focus on. 'If Plum and Rye ever get engaged, you can always ask them.'

A moment later, they're talking about wedding outfits, and I'm left staring at Sophie, who's running her fingers through her fake hair, and Mum, who's tugging nervously on her belt. I've saved her from a lot, but she's not getting a completely free ride.

'So what do *you* think, Mum – if *you* were the one skinny-dipping would it be a sign of a significant relationship?'

She chokes, and then recovers herself. 'You know I've always liked Kit, sweetheart. Whatever name you decide to give to your attachment, I'll be happy for you.' She turns to Sophie. 'Your hair is still throwing me, I was about to call you sweetie again too!'

Which reminds me – while we're here, I may as well say. 'The other day Sophie and I were talking about when we were kids, Mum. Maybe we could all have a chat about it sometime?'

Mum slams closed faster than a laptop at home time. 'There's really nothing to talk about.'

I'm not letting this go. 'But there's so much I can't remember!'

She almost bites my head off. 'That's why it's called the past – because it's over and done with and there's no point digging it up.' She backs towards the veranda. 'My memory's like a colander, it's no use asking me, I'd better go.'

Sophie lets out a cry. 'But you promised you'd stay for Floss's cupcakes in the Pleasure Dome?'

Mum tosses her head. 'I can't be doing with lunch! Especially now.' And a second later, she's across the deck and hurrying back towards the hotel car park.

I blow out a breath. 'I didn't think that through. I should have asked her *after* the pot painting.'

Sophie comes across. 'You weren't to know she'd be so uptight. But thanks for putting yourself out there.' She pulls me into a hug. 'Don't worry about the pots, I'll help with them.'

41

At The Hideaway
Apple cake and shorthand notes
Monday

Two days later, it's late morning, and as I shake clouds of icing sugar over two raspberry and cream Victoria sponges and cut up a tray of Bakewell tart blondies I've made to take to the hotel I'm secretly congratulating myself on the complete lack of fallout from Saturday. I've moved on so far I'm actually thinking about my Barbie outfit for the fancy dress on the promenade, kicking myself for leaving my roller skates in storage, and hoping my neon-pink cycling shorts will still fit over my bum, when my phone pings with a message from Nell.

Yay to you and Kit! X

I message straight back.

What's that? x

One more ping is all it takes to blow my comfort bubble into a million pieces.

You're such hot news the St Aidan grapevine is melting. I'm claiming you two as another singles club success. Xx

I let out a sigh and type.

If we ever get to the exclusivity convo, I'll be sure to let you know. Xx

If we're as out there as this, I may need to check in with Kit. Since Saturday any spare moment we've been so engrossed in our own blend of blissful sex and eating ice cream in bed there's been no time to waste on everyday details.

I take his favourite pudding cup off the shelf, cube a piece of blondie, open the fridge and send him a message of his own.

Are you around for a quick sweet tasting? Xx

He pings straight back.

Appointment in thirty, I'll eat fast. Xx

Two minutes later, Shadow's skidding to a halt by the studio desk, and I'm putting Kit's mug down and being swept into a dizzying snog that I only emerge from a good three minutes later.

'I didn't know you had clients today?'

He picks up his dessert, takes a spoonful of raspberry ripple ice cream and closes his eyes as it melts in his mouth. 'It's only someone dropping by for a preliminary chat.'

I let him slip a lump of blondie into my mouth, then swallow and brace myself to say what I'm here for. 'Saturday was quite full-on – I hope me accidentally ticking the publicity box wasn't too much for you?'

He grins. 'Those first nights under the stars were very special, but we can't hope to stay undercover indefinitely.'

I sigh. 'Nell messaged earlier to say the news is all over St Aidan.'

He laughs. 'I hope they include that we were *allegedly* entirely starkers!'

'It's way worse than that! They're pretty much calling us a couple.'

He pulls me into a hug. 'As if we'd give a damn what other people say! What matters is that *we're* happy with what we have.'

I can't help my panic. 'But neither of us wants any more than a one-night stand!'

He's rubbing his thumb on his chin. 'At the moment that's true, but it's not inconceivable things may change.'

'What? Gossip turning into a self-fulfilling prophecy?' That's too weird to even think about.

When he starts again, he's looking at me really hard. 'You *are* happy, Floss?'

Obviously, there's the part where I can't keep my hands off him, and due to my situation I can't bear to look beyond the moment we're in because this can only ever be temporary. But within those tiny bites of time, whatever we're doing he makes me feel so comfortable and cared for and alive. He's so kind and hot and easy to be around and he makes me come all the time. When we're together I never want it to end, and when he goes, I can't wait to see him again. I know we're only taking it a nanosecond at a time, but each of those is filled with the kind of burst of pure joy that I've never really known before.

'Very.' It only seems fair to try to describe it. 'The kind of happy Shadow would be if he found a catering-size box of Teatime Assorted with the lid off, and I told him to eat every biscuit.' I take a moment to let that sink in, because the more I think about it, the more I realise I'd hate it if he didn't want to carry on. 'And you?'

He pulls a face. 'I'm the kind of happy Rye would be if you made him a brownie stack that reached to the ceiling.'

I can't hold my grin back. 'So minute by minute we're both all good.' As for things changing, he seemed pretty certain he wouldn't ever be up for being in a relationship again and nothing will ever be different for me – so if we both want warm nights with no thought for the future, we should be a perfect match. 'So what are you saying?'

He considers. 'How about we ignore the rest of the world and talk again when summer's over?'

I nod. 'October's so distant it's as comfortable as infinity, isn't it?'

I'm so pleased we're still on the same page with this. All the soul-searching I've done, and I'd never even considered a 'friends with temporary benefits' model, which seems to be where we are now.

As I wait for Kit to finish his mouthful and agree, I'm

looking out of the side window, idly watching a figure in brogues and a navy suit. It's only as he comes closer that two things become obvious: he's heading for the studio, and I know who he is. I let out a cry. 'I know it's his hotel, but *what the hell is David Byron doing here?*'

Kit looks at his watch. 'He's my one o'clock and he's early.' He blows out a breath. 'I was going to tell you about it.'

I hear myself shrieking. 'No! You absolutely mustn't. Whatever he's here for is completely confidential. Whatever it is, *I really don't want to know!*'

I call Shadow, dive past the kitchen, and a moment later we're out through the side door and heading back to The Hideaway.

JULY

42

The Deck Gallery, St Aidan
Secrets and pies
Monday

There are times when life gets so busy you don't have time to worry about the small stuff. Not that people calling us an item was tiny. When Nell's message first came, I was beside myself, but with two Hideaway hen parties with activities to deliver, most mornings at Kit's, baking for the hotel, and a lot of Kit's couples, not to mention St Aidan residents, ending up on my deck, I've been too flat out to worry about technicalities like my status. As for the bits in between with Kit, they've been like the buttercream swirl on the cupcake. The toffee brittle sprinkles on top of one of my desserts. The flake in the ninety-nine. If I'd never had it, I might not have missed it. But now I have it's so delish, I'm determined to devour it.

As for any doubts, I refuse to spoil it by overthinking. It may be atypical, it may be unconventional, but when you stop to think about it, it's completely in line with the minute-by-minute way I've been living for the last four years, so it's no surprise how easily I've slipped into it. It might not be for everyone, but if it's working for Kit and me, why knock it?

It's a measure of how full-on things are that it takes a couple of weeks to dawn on me that I haven't caught up with Plum lately. Whatever Kit and I said that day at the studio about not giving a damn about other people, as far as our non-relationship goes we're still very much 'under wraps'. We eat, take Shadow along the beach, then chill at mine or his. Thanks to the hotel being busier, we haven't even been along for another pool swim.

I must still be slightly uneasy about Plum's exposure to the local gossip factory, because not only have I brought Clemmie with me for backup today, but as she, Shadow, Arnie, Bud and I make our way up the hill to Plum's gallery, the bag of apricot crumble slices I'm carrying is almost as big as Clemmie's two-baby changing bag.

As I help Clemmie through the big glass doors with the double pushchair, I hold up my carrier and whisper to her, 'This is guilt cake.'

Clemmie shushes me. 'You have nothing to feel bad about.' She lets a wriggling Bud out of her seat straps. 'It looks like Plum's out on the deck in the sun. If I take this one, can you follow with Arnie?'

As we stroll the length of the echoey gallery and burst out onto the deck Plum looks up at us from her laptop. 'Hello, stranger. It's ages since we saw you in town, Floss.'

I couldn't have hoped for a better opening. 'I've been waiting for the skinny-dipping scandal to die down.'

She lets out a snort. 'You taking the hit for your mum has

pushed your swimming street-cred through the roof, which is great news for the sea pool. Has Suze recovered from the shock yet?'

This is still perplexing me. 'She'd been quiet for a while before that. Then, when Sophie and I tried to ask her about when we were kids, she lost the plot and rushed off and since then she's been even more elusive.' I give a sniff. 'If this is how she's going to be, we'll have to see what the other mermaids' mums remember about our childhood.'

Plum frowns. 'We were at the other end of town from you, but I'll definitely ask. Don't get your hopes up though because my mum has always been vague on details.' Plum's parents still live in the same Victorian house that seemed so cavernous when we were kids. The row of fishermen's cottages where we lived were like dolls' houses in comparison.

Clemmie's holding Bud on her knee. 'As we were in the same row my mum might know more, but she's on an extended bird-watching tour in Puerto Rico. We can certainly ask when she gets back.'

Plum smiles. 'So how's the romance going?'

My heart skips a beat and it's only when Clemmie jumps in that I realise she's talking about Mum's not mine.

'It's a wise move for you and Sophie to step back and give them space.'

Plum nods. 'However much you love your mum you'd be very lucky to love whoever she chooses as her new partner. And the same goes for Rye with David.'

There's a cough in the doorway. 'Am I too late to join in with this?'

We turn round to see Rye in faded jeans and a T-shirt, running his fingers through his already perfect hair.

Plum's practically purring. 'Rye had a spare half-hour, so he's come to see some pictures of sculptures on my laptop.'

It's not lost on us; she could have just as easily taken her laptop to his office, and as he's here as himself, not a fireman or a hotel manager, this is as close to a date as Plum's got yet.

Clemmie smiles. 'We were saying that grown-up kids rarely take to their parents' new squeezes.'

I grin at him. 'It's reassuring to know we're normal.'

Plum smiles at me. 'I take it the other romance in the family is all a storm in the St Aidan grapevine teacup?'

Shit! 'You're absolutely right.'

Clemmie jiggles Bud on her knee. 'Whatever the word on the street, our Floss is still determined to stay free as a bird.'

Interventions like this are why I wanted her with me. 'I'm St Aidan's eternally single albatross, destined to fly but never to land.' I give Shadow a nudge with my foot. 'We've promised to be soulmates for ever, haven't we, Shadow?'

Plum sits back in her chair. 'Talking of which, you know Dillon's here later this month?'

I knew this was coming, just not this soon. 'He said he'd be over but not when.'

Plum purses her lips. 'He wanted it to be a surprise, but with so much going on, I thought I'd better warn you.'

I appreciate that she has, and it's only fair to explain to Rye. 'Dillon is Plum's brother. He and I used to be together.'

He nods slowly and his eyes narrow. 'I know who Dillon is.'

Plum reaches across the table and squeezes my hand. 'Don't play it down, Floss, you two were an institution.'

I look straight at Rye. 'We're still good friends.'

Plum's looking at me searchingly. 'We all love that you still care enough to chat most days.'

We barely message anymore, but I'd rather not correct her. And however much this is making me wince, I'd rather it was out in the open than hidden.

Clemmie's eyebrow goes up. 'As if we mermaids would have it any other way!'

I seize my chance to move this on. 'You must have heard about *the mermaids,* Rye?'

He grins. 'St Aidan local knowledge is my specialist subject. Would you like me to tell you their names?'

We're all working out how to say we might be okay without the full list when the silence is broken by what sounds like a cross between a tidal wave hitting the shore and an elephant's trumpet.

Rye's eyes open wide. 'What *the heck* was that?'

Plum holds her nose. 'Time for a clean nappy, Bud?'

Clemmie reaches for the rucksack. 'That'll be a head-to-toe poonami. If you come with me, Plum, we can take them up to the bathroom and change Arnie at the same time.'

Plum's on her feet. 'If you don't mind making the coffee, Floss?'

Rye's up too. 'Did I see a machine?'

'Americanos all round?' As we move inside and head behind the gallery counter it's obvious I can't compete with Rye's barista skills, so I pass him the cups, and put some saucers on a tray. I'm counting out plates for the cake when he turns to me.

'You do know how much Kit likes you?'

I cover my horror with a joke. 'I should hope he does, the number of Bakewell blondies I make him.'

'It's way more than that.' Rye gives me a hard stare. 'It's the real deal for Kit. Always has been.'

My stomach has dropped like a high-speed lift with each successive revelation, but I know to take my time with this. 'Excuse me?'

'He's been head over heels ever since you moved here.' Rye looks at me more closely. 'You *must* have noticed, the guy practically took up residence on your deck. You surely didn't think begging for ice cream and cake at all hours was him just being hungry?'

I'm opening and closing my mouth, trying to take it in. 'But that was months ago! And he blamed the cake on you!' My mind races forward, and I finally land on a sensible argument. 'Kit and I talked about it and we both agreed – neither of us is up for commitment when we're still picking up the pieces after previous relationships.'

Rye shrugs. 'It's a big risk telling someone you care until you know they do too. But if you *don't* feel the same it's best that you know – there are definitely feelings on his side.'

How can I have got this so wrong when I've checked so often? Even if a tiny part of what Rye says is true, I can't leave things as they are. 'Kit getting hurt is the last thing I want.'

Rye gives a grimace. 'I'm pleased you think that too. I hope you don't mind me saying?'

This is the funny thing with St Aidan – every time I think things are going right, something happens and the bottom drops out of my life. I'm shaking my head. 'Not at all. I'm very grateful you told me.'

I put down the spoons I'm holding, whistle for Shadow and look at Rye. 'I need to go.' There are things I need to do. Places I need to be. Worse still, my chest feels like it's imploding. 'The milk is in the fridge under the counter. Can you say goodbye to Clemmie and Plum for me?'

This is all a terrible mess. There's only one way to make it right, and I have to do it as soon as I can.

43

The Studio, Latitude One, High Tides Hotel
Ninety miles an hour in reverse gear
Monday

That first evening Kit and I hung out at the hotel, when we talked about why we weren't up for attachments, my thinking was chaotic, my head bursting with a million random reasons – and I'd also drunk a lot of Prosecco. But as I walk back along the beach with Shadow and think about this solely in relation to Kit and me, with every footprint I leave in the sand my mind is clearing. This has nothing to do with hangovers from the past. What Dillon and I had doesn't even come into it. All that's left in very clear focus here is that if Kit and I ever *did* get to the stage of considering a future for the two of us, there is an elephant-sized obstacle standing in our way. I inhabit the present because the future is too uncertain to go there. However I look at it, I'd be short-changing Kit to ask for any more than we have now.

It was a completely accidental anomaly that we ever got off the ground at all. If my dating rules had been more rigorous, or even more tested, it might never have happened. I mean, you learn from experience, and reading between the lines this sounds like it could be shaping up to be an all-out catastrophe.

With that decided I go on to think about what Rye was saying about Kit. And when I put Kit's recent behaviour under a microscope, and look at his actions rather than his words, I have to admit there's a lot to support Rye's view. They're tiny signs rather than huge ones. A laugh here, a smile there. Looking comfortable, when he should have looked appalled. When I think back to the day Milla's group made rings, or when we talked about things later, I must have been blind not to notice them more. But if there's any doubt at all, I have to face up to it.

It's completely possible Kit's real feelings might be different from what he's actually said. I only have to think back to all the words of denial I've said to him myself, when every time my body was screaming the opposite. I've done a pretty good job of deluding myself, because I was selfish, and I liked what was happening, and I wanted to grab as much of it as I could.

When I think of hurting Kit by inadvertently leading him on, by accidentally implying that we could carry on for longer, it's the last thing I want to do. I'd hate to do wrong by him. Not only that, but the idea of causing him pain is abhorrent because I care about him so much. Which only goes to show how attached I have become, and how these things can grow while all the time I've been fooling myself that it's fine because I didn't give a damn.

And the final proof is when I turn the spotlight onto myself. When Rye said that Kit liked me, my tummy plummeted.

But in the split second before that, there was a moment when my heart leaped so high it could have cleared the moon. It was as if knowing Kit might like me more than we'd talked about was the most amazing feeling. As if that was all I'd been waiting for to let my own feelings explode. It's one thing having a rush of blood to the head every time someone appears. Recognising that crazy out-of-control sensation as something huge and real – a substantial, bona fide, straight-from-the-heart emotion – is something else.

What the actual eff have I done here? Falling in lust was fine, but falling in anything more is a total disaster.

Once I've thought all this, it's like fast-setting concrete in my head. I can't ever go back to how I was before. All I can do is sort it out for good. As fast as I can.

It's a good three hours before I look across from where I'm siting fixedly on The Hideaway's veranda, my eyes trained on the studio, and see Kit waving today's clients off towards the hotel. The second it happens, I have a large box of apricot crumble slices ready. I tuck it under my arm, call Shadow and we race across to Latitude One.

I burst through the door, slam the box on the desk, take a big jump backwards so I'm too far away to slide into Kit's arms, and open my mouth to deliver the speech I've made word-perfect.

'Is everything okay, Floss?'

I'm laughing inside at the irony. 'It actually couldn't be any worse, Kit. I'm sorry, but I can't do this anymore...' My voice dries to a croak.

Kit's blinking. 'Excuse me?'

I start again. 'In future we've got to stick to work and cake.' As his jaw drops I rush to continue. 'The rest has to end. Straight away.'

His brow is furrowed. '*What* has to stop?'

I'm struggling to make myself clear. 'The nice bits. We have to go back to being purely professional.'

He raises an eyebrow. 'So we're still good for supper?'

I need to be more specific. 'No! No more walks on the beach, no more meals, no more sleeping together, no accidental touching in ice-cream vans, and especially no kissing or sex.'

His voice deepens. 'Am I allowed to ask why?'

I have to keep Rye out of this. 'I should have been honest with myself sooner.' I take a breath. 'This way no one gets let down, no one gets short-changed and, best of all, no one gets hurt.'

He gives a snort. 'It's a bit late for that!'

There's a twang in my chest, and as I catch the anguished expression on his face I'm kicking myself for all of it. For being to blame. For starting any of it. If only I could wind back the clock I'd never have looked up at the stars. I definitely wouldn't have given him Coco Pops and custard at seven in the morning. I probably wouldn't even have come back to St Aidan.

My mouth is sour as I swallow. 'I've majorly messed up, but I'm doing my best to put this right.' As I push my chin in the air and dash towards the door the tears are stabbing my eyes. 'If there's nothing more, I'll see you tomorrow.'

Halfway down the studio he calls after me. 'I'm polishing the last of the rings for Milla's friends. We could talk now while I show you them.'

I steel myself and call over my shoulder. 'There isn't anything else to talk about, Kit. Show me in the morning.'

And a second later the wind off the sea is whipping my hair across my face as Shadow and I tear back to The Hideaway.

My world is in pieces, but life goes on for everyone else.

I'm halfway up the steps to the deck when my phone rings.

I gulp down a sob and pick up. 'Mum! How are you doing?'

She takes a second to answer. 'Are you okay? You sound like Gollum.'

'I'm outside. It's probably the wind.'

She carries on. 'I've been chatting with Judy.'

That's Plum's mum. I know things move at speed in St Aidan, but I still wasn't prepared for *that* circle to close so fast. I'm frantically working out how to play this, but before I get there Mum speaks again.

'I'm sorry I made you feel you had to go to other people, Floss. You and Sophie are *my* daughters, and however hard it is for me to look back on my life, it's still my job to give you the answers you're looking for.'

My heart goes out to her. 'Poor Mum, if we'd known you felt like this, we wouldn't have brought it up.'

She sighs. 'We should have done it years ago. Let me know when, and I'll be there.'

We know how booked-up she gets, and if it's difficult it's best not to rush her. 'Shall we do sometime next week?'

'Friday at yours? After lunch.'

It's the last possible day she could have chosen, but I'd still say that's a result. 'I'll let Sophie know straight away.'

Two rings later Sophie picks up and I fill her in. I'm thinking she'll be as delighted as me, but her voice rises to a shriek.

'I can't possibly wait *ten days*! Ring her back and make it sooner!'

Which only goes to show how different we are. I don't rearrange. For once Sophie will have to be patient.

For me it matters less because the second I broke things off with Kit it was as if I'd wandered into a time-slip. It's barely ten minutes since I left the studio and it already feels like a hundred years.

44

The Hideaway
Like holes in a string bag
Tuesday

After a month spending every night together with Kit, when I wake next morning my fingers are already stretching across the pillow searching to find the warmth of his skin, the curve of his shoulder, the prickle of the stubble on his jawline. It's only as I open my eyes and take in the soft pink light filtering through the muslin curtains that the realisation slowly seeps through my brain.

He's not here.

And he won't ever be here again.

There are a few seconds when I try to bargain with myself. Try imagining a parallel existence where it might work, where we could be together. By the time I've reminded myself it's a lost cause, Shadow is standing over me, a paw each side of my ribs, telling me he's ready to go. If we're talking about moving on, this sleepy city dog has definitely warmed up to country living.

And after that we're into our usual morning routine, which in some ways is more disorientating still. Walking, baking, showering, and rushing off to deliver three dozen scones and Mars bar brownie tray bakes to High Tides. Then because I woke a good hour and a half before I usually would, I'm so ridiculously early there's still time to bake an extra batch of cookies and to drive into St Aidan to pick up some flowers before we're due at work.

At least I've got things to hold on to as Shadow and I stride into the studio and crash around, splashing water into a tall glass vase, trying to act like we did before any of this began.

'Morning, Kit, have you heard carnations are having a resurgence? Especially the colour-pop ones.'

He looks so rough he might not have even been to bed. 'The orange is nice.'

I was up early enough not to have left this to chance either. 'They represent feelings of happiness, warmth, determination and creativity. They also signify health, balance and success.' We could both do with all of those things right now. Yesterday it was a struggle to find words, today I can't stop talking. And my heart is aching so much I feel like there's an axe embedded in my chest.

Kit puts a basket down on the desk. 'I've got the rings for Milla here.' He's holding a soft yellow cloth and some flowery bags with string handles. 'I'll leave you to give each one a final buff before you pack them up.'

I pick one with intricately carved flowers and look in at the rest. 'These are beautiful. The girls will be ecstatic.'

Kit ignores that and rakes his fingers through his hair. 'I heard you talked to Rye yesterday?'

I stop and look up to meet his eyes. 'Briefly.'

He frowns. 'I hope whatever he said wasn't what prompted your decision?'

I sigh. 'Kit, we agreed, if ever one of us wanted to stop, we could.'

He blows out his cheeks. 'The thing with you and me was that however temporary we were, it felt like we were both fully there, every single moment.'

I know he's right, but that's all the more reason for me to run for the hills.

He's biting his lip. 'I don't want to pry, but I'd like to understand what changed, because for me what we had is worth fighting for.' He rubs his thumb across his jaw. 'At the same time, however good it was, I don't want to push you into anything you're not comfortable with.'

He looks so rough, I'm kicking myself for the pain I'm causing. If he's hurting even half as much as I am, it will feel devastating. If only I hadn't started this.

However much I'm wavering, I have to put him first. 'I'm sorry, Kit. I appreciate what you're saying, but my decision won't change.' As I watch his face fall, my chest is aching.

He leans his shoulder on the wall. 'There's so much we haven't said yet.' He pushes back his hair. 'Rye mentioned Dillon's visiting soon. That isn't the reason you want out?'

'Definitely not.' Now the pressure's off I've got a sudden urge to overshare. 'Dillon and I broke up because I stayed home and watched *Gilmour Girls* instead of going to his après-Mud-Mucker party. There's no coming back from stuff like that.'

There's the hint of a sympathetic smile playing on Kit's lips. 'Vee and I broke up because she didn't want kids.'

It's random information that has no bearing on me whatsoever, but I feel like I've been stabbed through the heart. And where me putting Kit first and pulling away to save his feelings was my definite intention, finding out that Kit cares this strongly about having kids is like a guillotine slicing through every tie. This extinguishes every last remnant of hope that there could ever be anything between us. In endgame terms, I feel like a fly that got squashed by a mallet.

I've been playing with fire that I couldn't handle, and I should be ashamed of myself.

My voice comes out as a high-pitched shriek. 'Well, who'd have thought! Five hundred orgasms and we still know *nothing* about each other!' I look at my phone and then take in Kit, who has hollows in his cheeks so deep he looks like he could be about to expire ... and push on with the rest of my life. 'The future Mr and Mrs Lugieri-Walker will be here in exactly five minutes. I'd better get you a coffee to bring you round.'

45

The Hideaway
Clapperboards and double takes
Friday

'You're still dressed as me!'

As I watch Sophie climbing the stairs onto the deck she's looking so comfy in my favourite navy and white daisy print playsuit I'm starting to wonder if I'll ever get it back.

She flicks back her brown hair and grins at me. 'I thought I'd give it another week. Or if you can spare your clothes, I may even carry on until the Barbie bash.'

When I arranged this meeting with Mum ten days ago, I was happy to have a date in the near distance to work towards because it felt good to have a dot on the infinity of the future stretching out in front of me. And the Barbie day is the same. That's the weekend after this, and is my next way-marker in the wilderness of the rest of time.

It's not as if I'm going anywhere much other than to work or to walk on the beach or to make deliveries at the hotel. And yes, I'm disgusted with myself for letting a guy mess up my perceptions like this, but as it's never happened to me before I'm not sure how to tackle it. When Dillon and I separated that was awful in itself, but that was more of a shock that the comfortable couple structure we'd inhabited for so long was suddenly not there. This is more like being lost in a sandstorm of emotions I don't understand. Some days I feel like I need Milla to come round and tell me very firmly to woman-the-eff-up.

I feel awful and responsible for causing Kit so much heartache. The last thing I wanted to do was to hurt him. If only he knew that all of the boundaries and limits I'd put in place for myself were there so I'd save him from even worse heartache in the long run. I'd like to explain, but I'm not sure I'd be strong enough.

As Sophie tickles Shadow's ear and pulls out a chair, I nod towards a tall jug. 'Help yourself to iced lemonade, it's homemade.'

She grins at me. 'It's extraordinary. When you got here we all assumed you'd be changing The Hideaway, but it's as if The Hideaway has changed you to be exactly the owner it wanted.' She laughs. 'Don't tell me, any second, you're going to bring out cupcakes?'

I'm not sure how I feel about her reading me so well. 'As it happens, I am, but that's because buttercream melting on my tongue is my new addiction. What's in your envelope?'

Sophie taps the thick packet she's put down on the table. 'I've had ten days to prep for this meeting. My document runs to twenty pages plus supporting material, with copies for each of us. How about you?'

'My questions are all in my head.' Every time I got out my notebook I wimped out. 'If we want to get the best from Mum you might want to lose the wig?'

'Shucks, I almost forgot.' Sophie's own hair is less bright than I remember as she shakes it free, but she's definitely more herself now. She whispers under her breath, 'And here we go!'

Mum comes across the veranda and dips to kiss each of us, then holds out a bunch of cornflowers, sweet rocket and perennial geraniums bound with a raffia bow. 'I brought you a posy from the garden.'

'Thanks, they're lovely. Even Milla's given up on the flower growing here.' As I pour out a glass of water and put the flowers in, I see Mum tug at her belt. 'Your second-best painting boiler suit today.'

Sophie pours a glass of lemonade and pushes it towards her. 'I hope you're not rushing off?'

Mum clears her throat. 'No, there are things in life you hope you'll never have to talk about, but it's important that I say them now.'

I can see Sophie's fingers twitching on her papers. 'If an agenda would help, I have one ready?'

Mum reaches across and pats her hand. 'You need to do a bit of listening first, Soph, we'll deal with the rest after that.' She pauses and looks out at the horizon. 'When you were little, before Flossie was even thought about, do you remember where we lived?'

Sophie nods. 'In the row of fishermen's cottages out on the Rose Hill Road. You were still there when Milla was born.'

I wrap my arms around me. 'Clemmie lived in the same row.'

Mum smiles. 'The kitchen had quarry tiles on the floor.' She nudges Sophie. 'You had your first pair of tap shoes when you were three, and you didn't stop tapping until you became a goth.' She shakes her head. 'You had blonde curls just like your dad. He always hoped you'd be a dancer on a cruise ship.'

Sophie looks appalled. 'But I *hate* boats.'

'I know. It's ironic, isn't it? What I need to tell you both is about what happened then.' Mum watches the waves rolling up the beach, then she looks back at us. 'The thing is, your dad didn't leave voluntarily – I told him he had to go.'

The skin on my arms pebbles with goosebumps.

Mum purses her lips. 'All these years I let people believe what they assumed – that he'd walked out on us. I always meant to tell the truth, but it's always been easier to put it off.'

I take a deep breath. 'Until now.'

Sophie's opening and closing her mouth. 'B-b-but...'

'All I can do now is to tell you how it happened and hope you might understand.' Mum's clutching her collar. 'Your dad drove for a long-distance coach firm, so he was often away. There were a few cottages in our row, and at one stage a man took the end one on a short lease. He looked shocking when he arrived; he'd been ill with leukaemia, his marriage had broken down, and the women along the row rushed to look after him, taking him baking and popping in with meals.'

She pauses to look at the sky. 'He was very different from anyone I'd ever met before. He'd read a lot, he was interesting. Most of all, he was kind.' Her voice is distant and wistful. 'You don't plan for these things to happen, but with your dad away we became closer than we should have done. We barely acknowledged it to ourselves, but somehow your dad knew.'

She stops for a few moments, and when she starts again her voice has changed. 'And then Flossie came along, and it didn't feel right to go on as we were when I was pregnant, so I made a choice. I stayed with your dad, and the other man moved away.'

My heart is going out to her. 'That must have been hard.'

She nods. 'Looking back it was the only time in my life when I was properly in love. But it wasn't to be. His future was uncertain and I had two children to consider. It helped to know I was doing the best for all of us by keeping the family together. Then you were born, Floss, and you made everything worthwhile again.'

Sophie reaches across and squeezes my hand, and I hang on to her fingers.

Mum smiles. 'You were blonde as a baby, Sophie, and your dad idolised you, but Flossie took after *my* father. The morning you were born, Floss, your dad took one look at the dark hair and long legs that were nothing like his, and he barely looked at you ever again.'

Sophie's grip on my fingers tightens, and Mum goes on.

'I hoped that we could put things behind us, but he never shook off the jealousy. I could have coped with indifference, and I protected you as much as I could, Floss, but as you grew his animosity towards you became worse. Negativity like that is very destructive. It was no way for any of us to live.

'It was the hardest decision of my life, especially for how it would impact you, Sophie. But one day after he'd been especially mean, I told him he had to go, and not come back. He did what I asked, and that was that.'

Sophie's shaking her head. 'It sounds awful.'

Mum stares at her. 'It wasn't a good time, but it was a lot easier once I'd been brave enough to make the break.'

I may as well say it. 'That's probably why you treated us so differently.'

Mum nods. 'You were always bursting with confidence, Sophie, always certain you were right, whereas Floss needed much more reassurance. I meant you to be equal, but it doesn't always work out that way.'

Sophie wrinkles her nose. 'I've always felt indestructible on the outside, but since Milla's been challenging me, I'm a lot less sure of myself.'

Mum smiles at her. 'You've always been such a force. It's easier for other people when they see your vulnerable side.'

I'm hanging on every word. 'What happened to the other guy?'

Mum pulls a face. 'Treatments weren't what they are now, and his outlook wasn't good. To give our family the best chance we agreed to cut contact. He promised he'd write in his will that I was to be told if he died, but I never heard any more. And since then it has always just been the three of us.'

Sophie comes straight out without flinching. 'So whose child is Floss?'

Mum fiddles with her fingers. 'I've never been entirely certain, but it's unlikely a cancer patient would have been able to father a baby.'

They're talking about it like I'm not here. 'I've gone thirty-odd years without knowing either of them, so it's hardly relevant now.'

Mum's biting her thumbnail. 'My decision hit you the hardest, Sophie. I hate that I deprived you of the dad who loved you, but at the time it felt like the only way.'

Sophie scrapes away a tear. 'It helps to know it wasn't his idea to go.'

I put my arms around her and pull her into a hug. 'He didn't leave because of anything you'd done. I'm sorry it was me who caused it.'

Sophie sniffs. 'Don't ever think that, Floss. Even though you were on your own, Mum, you did a damn good job. We were happy. And thank you for telling us. It makes a big difference that I know.'

I'm surprised yet validated at the same time. 'I'm so proud of you for telling us, Mum. Those few sentences have completely reframed our childhood. Everything Sophie and I have been questioning lately has been explained.' I smile at her. 'If that's all, I'll get the cakes.'

Mum hesitates as I get up. 'It isn't everything. Not quite.'

Sophie's eyes are wide. 'If there's more than this, I need an icing hit.'

I slide the plate onto the table and slip back into my seat, and Mum gives a little cough.

'It's not the complete end of the story. For me love has always been about snatches of happiness, lucky coincidences of time and place. In my experience the secret to everlasting love is to let go and move on.'

Sophie takes a large bite of cake and smiles. 'That sounds like you, Mum.'

Mum sighs. 'If the man from the end cottage had come back after a few years, we might have made a go of it. When he turned up in St Aidan thirty-odd years later, my first instinct was to hide. And that's what I did for more than a year.'

I'm stunned. '*So he wasn't dead?*'

Mum shakes her head. 'He'd caught the wave of medical science, and gone on to live life to the full, as we'd agreed he should if he was lucky enough for that to happen. I'm not sure he was particularly looking for me when he came back, but St Aidan's pull is a bit like gravity – at times we've all ended up here without really meaning to.'

I'm nodding. 'That's true for all three of us.'

Sophie's pushing crumbs into her mouth and sounding typically impatient. 'But what happened next? Where is he now?'

Mum looks calmer. 'He saw a suitable property, bought it – and built the High Tides Hotel.'

Sophie chokes. 'What the actual eff, Mother! *David Byron is your long-lost love?*'

Mum gives an exasperated sigh. 'It would have been much more straightforward to get to know him without the history. But then I wouldn't have gone on a date with him in the first place, so maybe it *was* better we'd met before.'

I'm relieved and appalled in equal parts. 'So this is why you've been so cagey?'

She looks up at the beamed roof. 'You can't rush these things. I hadn't ever meant to come near the hotel at all, but you needed me for your ice-cream van evening, and when I saw David had spotted me, I had to do a runner. Then, on the spa night, I changed my tactics because I thought it would be useful for you, and we found there was a lot to talk about after all.' She gives a shrug. 'All this time later, we still haven't run out of things to say.'

I laugh. 'If you like each other enough to go skinny-dipping, in St Aidan's eyes you're together.'

'The swimming was only a bit of fun.' She pulls at the folds of her boiler suit. 'When I've had the luxury of pleasing myself as long as I have, giving up my independence will take a lot of consideration.'

I have tears streaming down my cheeks as I look at my lovely mum, who's done so well by us all our lives and always put herself last. 'Fun, happiness, love – it's your time to have them all. Whatever I've thought of David Byron in the past, I couldn't be more delighted for you.'

Mum gives a cough. 'There are a few drawbacks. He does have a tendency to want to pay for everything, but it's only because he's kind, and we're working on that. And his musical tastes are terrible. It's going to take a fair few St Aidan discos before he'll be dancing to the Arctic Monkeys.'

Sophie pushes the plate across the table. 'Cupcake, Mum?'

She hesitates. And then she takes one. 'The rules of a lifetime have gone out of the window lately, so why not?'

It's obvious Sophie's mind is moving at a hundred miles an hour. 'Are you and David going to get married?'

I let out a cry. 'Sophie, that's the kind of question Milla would ask!'

Mum's face breaks into a smile. 'I was wondering the same thing myself – I'm not sure I ever got the whole way with divorcing your dad!'

This is what I love about St Aidan and my family. Just when you think there are no more surprises, they bring out another one.

46

The bedroom at The Hideaway
Fishy tales and oyster catchers
Tuesday

'You're the only friend I know with a zillion pairs of bright stretchy shorts, so you were bound to be my first port of call.' Clemmie flicks through the pile of coloured Lycra on the bed and pulls out an acid yellow vest with purple swirls and a pair of lime green shorts. 'Perfect. I'll wash them after and bring them straight back, and I'll make sure Charlie has something matching.'

I've been helping Nell to organise this but I've no idea when I became head of wardrobe. 'If you hate the Lycra, Barbie also loves dresses, and long blonde wigs are available from Hardware Haven – Janice has bought a job lot specially.'

Clemmie's ticking off on her fingers. 'I'm lending you my skates.'

I nod. 'So long as you've bought your tickets, you're good to go.'

Clemmie blows out her cheeks. 'And now I need you to tell me all the goss in two minutes flat. It's my first time out without Arnie, I promised I'd be back in five.'

I grin. 'I'd better hurry then. Sophie is in a better place after the family chat you know all about, Rye no longer has Mum pegged as a gold-digging psycho since he realised she and David already knew each other, and apparently when David made his offer for The Hideaway, he was already aware who I was.'

Clemmie's eyebrows go up. 'Ignoring the stalker vibes, that explains why the offer was so generous.'

I shrug. 'I'm guessing he hoped it might help him reconnect with Mum.' I'm still trying to take it all in myself. 'As for the pool, that had always been in his mind, but the approach to the council was more to hide what he was up to than anything he was planning immediately.'

Clemmie shakes her head. 'It's all been for the best. Without that push you might never have hit on the idea of resurrecting the sea pool and that's going to be so good for the town.'

I laugh. 'Things are looking up at the hotel too. If we play our cards right, Mr Byron may make a donation to our fund.'

Clemmie gives me a searching stare. 'Do I sense you're warming to him?'

I roll my eyes. 'It's not going to happen overnight. But if he and Mum are in it for the long term, I'm going to have to make the effort.' I think about what's left to cover for Clemmie. 'As for the rest, Shadow and I are so busy we wouldn't have time for a social life even if we wanted one.'

Clemmie wrinkles her nose. 'Is your mum properly loved up?'

'She and David have both had a lifetime to change since the first time they met, so it wasn't a given.' I laugh. 'Mum's denying it madly, but she's head over heels.'

Clemmie hugs her arms around her. 'It's lovely she's having her happy ending.' She coughs. 'Is it too much to hope you'll grab the same for yourself?'

I screw up my courage to say the words. 'I'm only seeing Kit for business from now on, and that's not going to change. Regardless of anything else, he actively wants a girlfriend who can have kids.'

She lets out a cry. 'Oh, Floss, I'm so sorry.' She looks at me more closely. 'Are you *sure* about that?'

I pull a face. 'It's easier this way. If I know I'm a hundred per cent unsuitable anyway, it saves any soul-searching about the rest.'

She frowns. 'And how's that working out?'

I make my voice bright. 'I've done the moving-on sex, so I really have waved goodbye to Dillon. And it's a big relief not to be trying to hide Kit anymore.'

Her eyes narrow. 'But how are you doing *really?*'

I let out a long sigh. 'I'm currently eating my body weight in cookie dough, but I'm optimistic it'll pass.' Seeing Kit every day at the studio is agony. Watching him and pretending to smile and be happy for those other couples, my heart breaks all over again every day. But it can't go on for ever. I give a hollow laugh. 'Hey, Mrs, you need to go! We'll catch up soon. And don't forget your wig.'

And that's it for me for now. The next significant event in my life is the Barbie and Ken event next weekend. As I stand on the veranda and wave goodbye to Clemmie, it may as well be a century away.

47

The Barbie and Ken fancy dress day, The Promenade, St Aidan
Significant others
Saturday

'OMG you look just like my Hot Skatin' Barbie from when we were kids!'

Sophie is leaning up against the railings of the promenade swirling my shortest pearl-pink skater dress around her legs as she takes in my outfit, with Nate next to her in a pink gingham shirt, and Maisie, Marcus and Tilly like a cluster of mini-mes further along the prom.

I hope I wasn't mean keeping my brightest pink shorts for myself when people came to borrow outfits, but I already had the paint-splash print swimsuit and visor-hat to go with it. Now, as I spin around on my skates and look along the crowd milling on the wide pavement of the promenade, the bright July sun is supercharging the colours so much it's like Barbie land.

The curtain of platinum hair Sophie swishes back is way

longer than her own. 'Thanks to Janice, we're all rocking our peroxide waves.' She pokes my fluorescent yellow elbow-guard and gives my flaxen hair a flick. 'How is life as a blonde, Flossie-boots?'

I have to be honest. 'I'm the bounciest I've been for weeks.' I'm thinking I should embrace the skater vibe every day, when I see a figure in a fuchsia pink jumpsuit waving at us from beyond the bandstand.

Sophie nudges me as she waves back. 'Have you seen Mum and David over there? This surely has to banish any reservations you had about *him*?'

I'm not sure about that, but I wave anyway. 'He certainly gets the prize for best Hawaiian shirt.'

The day we talked to Mum, I made it clear to Sophie that I would not be going down the road of speculating about who my dad was, and since then we've successfully managed to put those few seconds of doubt behind us for ever and carry on as we were. I literally couldn't have coped if every time his name came up her eyebrows went up too.

We turn to Nell and George, sitting on the bench next to us, behind a Bugaboo the size of Waitrose. I'm looking at their shirts and shorts. 'Not being the outfit police, but what *are* you two wearing?'

Nell's laugh explodes. 'There wasn't time to pack the changing bag *and* get dressed, so we came in our pyjamas. At least we match!'

As Clemmie sweeps to a halt next to us all, snatches of The Beach Boys' 'Fun Fun Fun' are blowing on the breeze. 'All this buzz, and my two are sleeping through it.' She looks past Diesel's big head into her double-decker buggy, then smiles up at us. 'Rye must have got a free pass for the afternoon, too, because he and Plum were down by the harbour when I passed.'

Nell blows out her cheeks. 'Another win for the singles club.' She frowns at me. 'You and Kit are my biggest disappointment yet.'

I'm rising above it. 'We're a great match professionally, Nell.' Even though that sounds like an end to it, I hold my dog lead out to Clemmie. 'If you don't mind holding Shadow while the babies sleep, I'll have a whizz along the prom and catch you all in a bit.'

I didn't ever intend to *use* the ancient lace-up roller skates I borrowed from Clemmie, but as I glide to the centre of the pavement a feeling of freedom creeps into me. The long prom with its metal railings and light strings swinging between the lamp posts could have been made for skating. By the time I'm on my fourth circuit, I'm feeling like I could go on for ever. I make a turn by the harbour, wave to Nell and Clemmie on their seat as I speed by, and as a figure steps out from the crowd twenty yards further on I skid to a standstill and do a double-take.

Dillon at the Barbie day?

I swallow my surprise and as I land a quick kiss under his ear a strong blast of Dior Sauvage tells me I'm not mistaken. 'Hey, great to see you, Dillon!' There's only one reason I can think of for why he's wearing a ridiculously well-cut suit on a scorching afternoon at the seaside. 'You've come as Ken in Dubai!'

He smiles. 'Here on a flying visit! There was a last-minute meeting in London, so I hopped on a plane to Newquay on my way back.'

I'm shaking my head in disbelief. 'What are you like?'

He looks me up and down. 'I wanted to see how you were doing, and I got my answer. Flossy May comes to town, and sleepy St Aidan doesn't know what's hit it!' His face breaks into a grin. 'It's lovely to see you doing so well, and good to know I needn't have worried about you half as much as I have.'

He couldn't look happier, but I still have to ask. 'How are things working out for you?'

He gives a shrug. 'Dubai suits me, the projects are the kind I've dreamed of since I was six. I'm so grateful to you for having the insight to see that, and giving me the push to go.'

'You're welcome, Dill.'

He's in his element. And I can't help feeling proud of him for everything he's achieving. It's a relief that he's not only flying but soaring.

As I stand there blinking at him, it's hard to think we woke up next to each other every morning for all those years. That for almost a decade our hearts were beating to the same rhythm, that we shared the same dreams, and built our hopes together. I'm trying to work out if he's changed, or if I have.

He raises an eyebrow. 'They've offered me a shiny new job and a long-term contract. I wanted to check in with you before I accepted.'

And this is Dill. Still looking out for me.

All that time we spent together he was so full-on, I simply followed his lead and let him do the deciding. Seeing him now, I realise I'm not that person anymore. Having my own place and my own life here has given me a will of my own and I've discovered a drive I never knew I had. And now I've found it, I like it. Far from the shrinking I was terrified of, St Aidan has let me be a whole new version of myself – but best of all, I'm proud of what I've become.

I smile at him. 'When I used to drift through life, I'd look at other people and be amazed at how sorted they were. I admit it was circumstances that brought me back here rather than choice, but it's turned out that this is where I fit – the beach hut is my place and my purpose. Thank you for coming, Dill, but I'm surrounded by friends and family here, and I really am all good. The Emirates let you realise your potential, and St Aidan's done the same for me.' I grasp his hand. 'Go and enjoy your promotion – it's what you deserve.'

It's strange to think how close we once were, and how little by little we've separated since our paths have diverged, until now we're each our own entity. We're the same people we always were, but our time apart has made us different. And now we're each on our own distinct road to the future.

'Maybe we could catch up over the weekend and you could see Mum?'

He looks at his watch. 'When I said a flying visit, I meant it. I'm here for another two hours, and I've promised to touch base with Mum and Dad. But maybe next time?'

'In that case, I'll say "Goodbye and good luck", and let you get on.'

When I go in to hug him, his body feels strangely unfamiliar. Like I'm hugging someone I hardly know. Then he lets me go and I take a step back. And then another.

It's only as my foot fails to move that I know there's something wrong. By the time I look down and see the loop of my laces caught round a wheel, there's nothing I can do – the rest of my body is committed. My feet stay rooted, I put my arms out to save myself as I topple, but I'm like a tree that's being felled. My backbone crashes against the paving slabs and a second later there's a resounding thud as my skull hits too and a pain explodes through my head.

I hear Dillon's cry. 'Floss!'

Then as I look up at the blue sky high above me, there's another deeper, more familiar voice.

'Say something, Flossie, tell me you're okay?'

I mumble, and silently thank my lucky stars that Kit is here.

Kit starts again. 'It's Dillon, isn't it? I can probably take it from here.'

I prop myself up, and as Kit's arm slides around my shoulders, I can see Dillon looking down on us.

'I can see you're in good hands there, Floss.'

I shade my eyes as I look up. 'We aren't actually a couple, Dill!'

Dillon smiles. 'She's one in a million, look after her.' He's staring at Kit. 'Hang on – aren't you...?

Kit looks up. 'The one who made your rings, yes.' He laughs. 'A long time ago.'

This is an ideal opportunity, so I'll seize it. 'I still have those rings, Dill. If you don't mind letting them go, I've an idea to put them to good use.'

Dillon steps back. 'It sounds fine to me. They're yours to use as you wish.'

I give a silent cheer. If Kit melts them down, we can donate the gold for a ring-making day and run an online auction. My head might feel like my skull is cracking open, but I can still plan fundraisers for the sea pool.

There isn't time to say any more, because Plum comes

running over then, followed by Milla and all her friends, who all start bouncing around Dillon. As I stare up into the sea of faces Rye stoops down and puts his hand on my forehead.

'You can't be too careful with a bang on the head, Floss. Stay with her for twenty-four hours, Kit. If she gets blurred vision or is sick give me a shout, and we'll ring through to A&E.'

Twenty-four hours with Kit? I'm trying to think of anyone else. 'I could stay with Clemmie. Or Nell. Or Mum. Or I can go to Sophie's!' Once she'd have been my last resort, now she's my go-to choice.

As Clemmie steps out from behind the crowd, Shadow dives towards me and starts to lick my face.

She hands Kit the lead. 'It's a shame to miss the fun, Flossie. Why not sit with us as long as you feel up to it, then Kit can drive you home?'

Dillon laughs. 'In the meantime, the ice creams are on me.' He's immediately mobbed by Milla's group, and fighting off twelve teenagers.

As I untangle my laces and Kit helps me to my feet, I know I've got a couple of hours tops before I move on to the hardest night of my life.

It's one thing keeping my hands off Kit when he's in the studio. When he's in The Hideaway, it will be a whole different matter.

48

The Hideaway
Arm's length and an unfortunate playlist
Saturday

It's almost eight by the time we get back to The Hideaway. Kit walked along the beach to the hotel to collect his car, then we drove back from town without a word, with the Manic Street Preachers playing 'You Stole the Sun from My Heart' in the background. As soon as we're home I grab a bottle of Nosecco from the fridge, slide it into an ice sleeve, and put it down with two glasses on the living room coffee table. When I step over Shadow and sit on the opposite end of the L-shaped sofa to Kit, there's a decent distance between us.

He raises an eyebrow. 'I have two things to say now we're here.'

'Okay.' I look across at him, take in the shadows of his cheekbones, deepening in the fading light.

'First, please don't worry, I will be keeping my distance.'

'Great.'

'And...' he gives a cough '...I need to tell you I love you.'

My heart does a skip, then my mind catches up. 'That's *seriously* not allowed.'

'I know.' He pops the cork, pours the fizz and leans to hand me a glass. 'As we're going to be together for the next sixteen hours, I'm telling you in the interest of openness and honesty.'

I take a sip of fizz and watch the bubbles rise in my flute. 'Would you like some Wotsits?'

Kit shakes his head. 'I'm okay without, thanks.'

I go back to staring at my glass, then five minutes later I sit forward. 'How about honey-roasted cashews?'

I go to the kitchen without waiting for a reply, put the full bowl on the table and we both take a handful. I tuck my feet under me as I sit down and take a breath.

'You know I can't ever have kids?' I watch his eyebrows shoot upwards.

'Actually, I didn't.'

I'm taking this really calmly and slowly. 'Those scars on my tummy are from when they took all the bits and pieces away.' If I said the medically correct terms, there'd be no guarantee he'd have a clue what I'm talking about.

'Was that when you were ill?'

I nod. 'They went all around my body, chasing down every last nasty bit. The chemo had already wrecked my fertility, so there wasn't much to lose.'

'I'm sorry, I didn't realise.'

I shrug. 'HRT is out of the question, I have the hormone levels of a pensioner, which is why my sex drive is the size of a small gnat's.'

He smiles to himself quietly. 'I can't say I'd noticed that part either.' There's a puzzled look on his face. 'Why didn't you tell me this earlier?'

'It didn't go with the territory.' I try again. 'I'd hardly tell a casual date I'd had an early menopause after an elective hysterectomy. I'm only telling you now to explain why I'm not suitable girlfriend material.' I can tell from his expression he's still mystified. 'You mentioned you and Vee broke up because she didn't want children.'

His eyes narrow. 'Well, yes ... but maybe not in the way you're thinking.'

'How many ways are there?' Surely kids are either a deal-breaker – or they're not?

He takes a deep breath. 'As a business partner, Vee was hard-headed, astute, and glamorous, but those aren't necessarily qualities that make a great life partner. The moment she told me she didn't want kids, it hit me that we were never going to be happy as a couple in the long term. Before that I knew it wasn't working, but I couldn't pinpoint why. So, that was the catalyst to us breaking up, but it was more about her lack of warmth and empathy than the children themselves.'

I take a sip of fizz. 'Well, thanks for explaining that.'

'It's good we're finally talking about things that matter.' He hesitates. 'And I'm sorry if what I said about having kids was insensitive. I wouldn't have said it if I'd known your situation.'

I pull a face. 'I'm less sensitive about it than I used to be. I can't avoid little ones in St Aidan.'

His shakes his head. 'It was heroic of you to deliver Arnie given the circumstances.' His lips pull into a smile. 'When I see Milla and her friends mobbing Rye I find the whole idea of having kids terrifying, but I could go either way.' Then his frown deepens. 'So does knowing how I feel about children change anything for you?'

'Well, yes ... but no.' I owe it to him to at least try to explain. 'There's a lot going on in the background.'

'Evidently.' His legs are stretched out in front of him, and he uncrosses his feet. 'How about a slow, barefoot stroll along the beach? Strictly no holding hands.' Not only has he read my mind, but he's already kicking his deck shoes off.

As we walk down from the dunes the sun has already dipped below the horizon, and the wind is blowing our hair across our faces. We turn towards St Aidan, kick our way past the trail of high water seaweed and make our way down towards the ocean. As we hit the shine of wet sand the water pools around the outlines of my toes and Kit stoops to pick up a stick for Shadow.

He hurls it into the distance, and once we've fallen back into a regular stride with a comfortable gap between us, he turns to me. 'I'm listening whenever you're ready to tell me what the problem is.'

'I've told you before, I try never to think or talk about being ill, but it does have a big impact. If you haven't experienced illness it's hard to know what it's like, but the ripples it causes reach untold areas of your life.'

He nods. 'I imagine they do.'

I blow out my cheeks because these are the things I usually block out. 'When you're ill as half of a couple and then you recover, you know there are risks going forward, but because you're together you also know that you can face them as a team if they come up.'

A sideways glance tells me he's still listening intently.

'In many ways it's worse being the partner of someone who is ill than it is for the person themselves. What I'm saying is, you'd never choose to put someone into that situation if they weren't there already.'

He shrugs. 'I get that this isn't straightforward.'

It's my turn to take the stick from Shadow and I hurl it up to the drier sand and watch his back legs powering away before I turn back to Kit. 'Honestly, not being able to have children is the simple bit. I even have frozen eggs.' I roll my eyes. 'I don't have the money to pay for any procedures, because I used it to buy The Hideaway instead.'

'You've made a lot of brave choices.'

'I was simply being practical, planning my future as a single person because I don't have enough to offer a partner.'

He's still walking. 'That's the bit I still don't get. Why *can't* you be with someone?'

I blow out my cheeks again. 'Once you've had what I've had, it's not necessarily over. The cancer can jump around your body and start again somewhere else. It doesn't happen to everyone, but if you're one of the unlucky ones, you can't stop it coming.'

He's nodding. 'So there could be a relapse?'

I pull a face. 'If you look it up, you can find what the chances are but it's easier not to get hung up on the numbers. It's better to carry on and only worry about it if it happens. But it's a roller-coaster to hell and back. You go for the ride if you're already there because there's no choice, but you'd never willingly join in halfway through.'

He gives a gasp. 'Shit.'

I'm getting through to him at last. 'It's simply not fair to let someone fall in love with someone who could get ill again. If you're starting out, your best chance is to choose someone who is well.'

As he stops walking and turns to face me his eyes are shining, and as I stop as well his fingers catch mine. 'What if it's already too late?'

And this is the other thing about being ill. You have to be brave. To cope at all you have to toughen yourself, and never allow yourself to break. I've gone for years without crying for myself, but suddenly my face is soaking wet, and the tears are finally falling. I want this more than anything in the world, but I can't be that selfish. I've taken every knock along the way. I just never expected for it to hurt like this when the bad part should be over.

I swallow back the saliva. 'My prize was getting better, Kit. I'm well, I can't expect to have it all and fall in love too.'

His cheeks are wet with tears too. 'I need to hug you, Floss.'

I take a gulp. 'Please don't do that. The truth is, I love you too much to let you start any of this.'

His arms close around me, and then I'm burying my cheek in the soft folds of his T-shirt, digging my fingers into his beautifully muscled back. As he speaks his voice is reverberating through his chest.

'So, you do love me too?'

I nod. 'I realised it the day Rye told me you liked me. That's why I knew we had to stop seeing each other.'

Kit pulls back to look at me and his eyes narrow. 'And have you been happy since then? Because I've felt like shit.'

I have to be honest. 'I've felt awful too.'

He blows out a breath. 'So we could be two happy people, or

two unhappy ones? I think I'm going to have to overrule you on this.'

He pulls me closer. 'If you love me and I love you, we have to find a way to make it work.' He rubs his thumb on my temple. 'Nothing in life is certain. We may have decades or we may only have a year. But however long it is, I want to spend that time with you – the good bits *and* the bad bits.'

I sniff. 'I wish I could say "yes".'

His chest heaves under my face. 'I'd hate to be like your mum and David. I don't want to have to come back and find you when your life is almost over, I want us to live every moment together.'

What he says is resonating as I think of all those years of happiness Mum missed out on. 'Mum isn't one to talk about regrets, but I'm so pleased they're having their time now.'

Kit's looking down into my face. 'We need to be brave together, we need to take our chances and believe in the future.' He waits for a few seconds. 'I'm up for it if you are?'

I'm agonising, trying to let myself agree, when his lips land on mine, and the pulsing sweetness of his kiss draws me in. By the time he gently pulls back to look at me again, my head is spinning.

I have to protest. 'Making me see stars isn't fair.'

His laugh is low. 'Whatever it takes to make you say "yes", I'm going to have to do it.' He's rubbing his chin on my cheek. 'I fell in love with you that first day by the side of the road. It's not like anything I've ever felt before.'

I laugh. 'So what impressed you most? Me stripping off my T-shirt in a gale, managing to catch Arnie, or my banter with the fire brigade?'

He closes his eyes as he thinks. 'All of it. Especially your love for Clemmie. Not many people would have kept their nerve like you did. You were a total star and I was smitten. And your boobs of course.' He's biting his lip. 'I also have an insane admiration for your chocolate brownie puddings, the way you handle customers and your amazing pink shorts, but that all came later.'

If this is confession time, I've got some of my own. 'I did mentally undress you that first day – and every day after. And you buying me custard donuts was a game changer. Obviously you also saved The Hideaway from the out-of-hand teenage campfire, and you've made me feel sick every time I've seen you because of the outrageous tummy flips you cause, and I've lost count of the times you've come to the rescue for Shadow and me. As for the way you make me come...'

I'm about to say, no one's ever even come close, but I stop in mid-sentence when a rush of icy water hits my feet, and I jump back with a shriek instead.

'Jeez, that's freezing.'

Kit's laughing as he pulls me into another kiss as the water laps around our ankles. 'It's meant to be cold, it's the sea.'

We stand in the water, hanging on to each other, and I can already feel the happiness spreading through my body like a wave of warmth.

I'm about to bury my mouth in his again when he pulls back, puts a finger to his lips and gestures for me to look along the beach. As I turn and see what he's pointing at, a smile the width of the bay spreads across my face. A few feet along the beach, Shadow is standing, his big body motionless. There is water swirling around his legs, and his eyebrows are raised in the WTAF? position.

I whisper to Kit. 'I love that dog so much. He's like a huge dark brown hole of joy in my life.'

Kit laughs. 'He's not barking or running away anymore. He might be looking horrified, but he's in up to his elbows.' He looks down at me. 'Shadow in the sea – if ever there was a cosmic sign you need to say "yes" to our love, that's it!'

I laugh at Kit. 'I think you could be right.' I call across the water. 'Is it good in the sea, Shadow? What do you think, are we going to let Kit share our custard creams every night from now until the end of time?'

Shadow does a huge bark, dips into a play bow, snatches a mouthful of water then tears out of the shallows and off across the sand.

I laugh. 'And I think we got our answer. One thing is certain – us three escapees have all come a long way since we left London.'

Kit's hands are on my shoulders as he looks down at me. 'I have enough love for both of us and I'm ready to care for you. Whatever life throws at us, we'll face it together – is that okay?'

Put like that, there's only one answer. 'Absolutely.'

'Thank you, Flossie.' He laughs and pulls me into another dizzying kiss.

It's a long time later when he gets to speak again. 'Are we ready to go back?'

I lean into his warm body. 'I think we are.' And as we make our way arm in arm back along the sand to The Hideaway I feel like the luckiest woman in the world.

AUGUST

49

The Harbour Splash Day, The Harbourside, St Aidan
High stakes and high flyers
Saturday

I t's amazing what a non-organisational person like me can pull off with a whole community behind me. Thanks to so many willing helpers what is now known as the Harbour Splash fundraiser comes together, and three short weeks after the Barbie day, Kit, the mermaids and I are out on St Aidan's cobbled quayside, leaning on the stacks of lobster pots outside George's office, watching a throng of people in front of us.

Clemmie is gazing around. 'I can't believe there are so many stalls!'

'All thanks to Nell pulling in Dakota from the singles club.' She's a high-energy gym-princess who aced the marketing and publicity, and the stalls aren't all she's scored a hit with. 'There are roving reporters with TV cameras and live broadcasts for

Pirate Radio too, although she insists the sea pool is a very easy sell.'

Clemmie steers the pushchair into position, and slides onto a bench with Diesel beside her. 'From the very large banners by the jumping area, I'm guessing the High Tides Hotel are committed to the sea pool, rather than wanting their own?'

I nod. 'David must be trying really hard with Mum. He offered such a huge donation we couldn't refuse.'

Plum's nodding as she comes across. 'Look out for the High Tides stalls too, the beauticians are doing pedis and hand massages with advice on spa treatments, and they're giving out gorgeous samples in return for an addition to their email list.'

Sophie gives a cough. 'We've recently agreed with the hotel to feature our product ranges, so the goodie boxes on their stalls are bursting with Sophie May miniatures.'

Plum carries on. 'The splash will run nicely into the eating, drinking and – most importantly – the dancing.' She wiggles her eyebrows. 'I guarantee you an evening of first-class party bangers.'

Rye took charge of the sound system, and thanks to Plum doing the playlist, and insisting on playing every track to him before she added it, the gap between those two is now imperceptible. Obviously there are also *other* establishments in St Aidan, so the Hungry Shark are running the main bar, and there are lots of local businesses with food stalls and vans, but Dakota negotiated very favourable profit-sharing rates with all of them.

I'm looking up at the coloured bunting criss-crossing over our heads and listening to the cries of seagulls and the ring of the rigging on the masts of the brightly coloured boats moored along the floating pontoons. There are explosive splashes every couple of minutes as the participants hit the water, and cheers of the people watching them are echoing around the harbourside.

Nell appears in the doorway of the office where she nipped to change baby George, and points at the long line of people in board shorts and wet suits snaking along the far end of the quay-side, all waiting to hurl themselves off the harbour wall. 'Have you seen the queue? With that many sponsored jumpers we'll raise a bomb!'

I give her checked shirt a tug. 'Out in your real clothes *and* focusing on the bottom line – you *are* back in the game, Nelly-melon!'

She gives me a push. 'I'm not the only one! Truly, I'm over the moon for you and Kit.'

Kit hears her comment and leans in to kiss me. 'We're pretty happy too, Nell.'

Mum wanders over and joins straight in the conversation. 'Did you hear they went skinny-dipping, Nell?'

I let out a shout of protest. 'Mum, we didn't – *that was you!*'

She shakes her head. 'Well, whatever, sweetheart, we're all very happy for you both. Aren't we, David?'

David's looking down at her, his face full of love. 'We are. And we're looking forward to an afternoon full of surprises.'

I can't help but laugh. 'It might not be *that* thrilling – this is pretty much as good as it gets.'

Mum taps my arm. 'Take no notice, sweetheart, he's only excited because his High Tides banners are everywhere in town.'

Clemmie wipes the chocolate off Bud's hands. 'Don't undersell yourself, Flossie, it's a fabulous event, and it's all down to you.'

I can't take all the credit. 'It was my idea, but everyone else helped make it happen.'

Sophie gave me back my wig last week once Nikki at Force10 Hair had toned down her blonde, but she's still hung onto a few favourite playsuits of mine. She leans across to me. 'Your once-they're-gone-they're-gone cakes are going down a storm, Floss.'

I can't take all the credit for that either. 'I did the baking, but Milla and the gang are doing a fabulous job manning the stall. It was a great idea of theirs to bring out a different kind of cake every half-hour and push it out on socials with a running total of how much they're making.' I look around for Rye. 'Mars bar brownies are up next, if you're interested.'

He waves his ice cream and holds out his other hand to Plum. 'If you're coming, I'll finish this on the way, check on the staff and be first in the queue.'

David calls after them as they weave their way through the crowd. 'Don't be too long.' He gives a cough. 'Just saying!'

Mum rolls her eyes. 'What is he like?'

When I stand close to Kit, my shoulder tucks neatly under his armpit. I whisper into his ear, 'What's going on?'

He smiles. 'David's full of ideas for hotel publicity. You'll see very soon.' As he comes in closer and I breathe in his scent it makes me dizzy, like it always does. 'You look beautiful. I love those ripped denim shorts and that T-shirt.'

'Thanks.' I squeeze his hand and turn to Sophie. 'Remember your Libertines vest? Kit saw it falling out of the drawer earlier and asked me to wear it. I actually caught Arnie in this!'

Clemmie laughs. 'What an afternoon that was! He's grown so much, you wouldn't catch him in it now.' She pulls me into a hug. 'I'm so pleased you came back, and I'm ecstatic you and Kit are together. You look so well and happy.'

By the time we've reminisced about that, Rye and Plum are back, George has joined Nell, and Sophie, Nate, Milla and the kids are all tucking into whippy ice creams. As the distant sound of an engine cuts over the noise of the crowd, David points at the sky.

'Look, it's coming!'

As we all look up, a tiny aircraft comes into view over Comet Cove, and chugs its way towards us.

Nell calls out. 'It's pulling a banner! That's brilliant! Let's see what it says.'

David's reading it out as the aeroplane flies across the bay in front of us, with the banner furling behind it. 'HIGH TIDES HOTEL SUPPORTS ST AIDAN SEA POOL!'

Nell's chortling. 'I hope the TV crews get that!'

Kit's shading his eyes as he watches. 'Don't worry, the camera guys have been primed.' He looks down at me. 'You don't think it's too much?'

As I shake my head, I realise I've actually got goosebumps. 'No, it's amazing.'

As the plane flies out to Oyster Point we all wave, then it circles back inland, and when it comes across the bay for a second time we've all got our phones out to film it. When it disappears again, we all stare at the sky and wait for the next circuit. This time it takes a bit longer to come, but as it finally arrives Kit's hand tightens on mine. And then as the plane comes across the bay, Nell murmurs, 'They've changed the sign.'

The crowd around us gasps as I read the words:

WILL YOU MARRY ME, FLOSSIE FLAPJACK-FACE?

It takes a while for me to take it in, and by the time I do there are tears running down my face.

I turn to find Kit's down on one knee on the cobbles, looking up at me, his grey eyes soft against his dark lashes, and Shadow's beside him, giving his cheek a lick. 'So what do you think – would you like to marry me, Floss? I don't want to rush you, but I love you so much, I don't want to waste a day.'

I'm biting back the sobs, as I look around the sea of faces around us. Mum, David... Sophie is there, clenching her fists and gritting her teeth, Milla is jumping and down on the spot.

Then a lone voice nearby calls out, 'Say yes, Flossie Flapjack-face!' And the crowd around us takes up the cry too. Soon the whole of the harbourside is chanting, 'Say yes, Flossie Flapjack-face! Say yes, Flossie Flapjack-face!'

Kit is shaking his head as he looks up at me. 'Sorry, I didn't plan for there to be this much pressure.'

Nell lets out a huge whoop. 'It's St Aidan, Kit, everyone likes to help!'

The crowd are clapping and stamping now, so I murmur to Kit, 'Yes please. I'd love to marry you.' Then I shout it louder to the people around. 'Yes please! Of course I want to marry him! I can't think of anything better!'

And as the plane disappears, there's a general roar, and Kit hands me a ring.

'This is for today, until you decide on a proper one.'

As he slides the ring onto my finger, I can see the words engraved around the outside.

Will you marry me, Floss? xx

Milla's screaming. 'Omigosh, a dedicated proposal ring! *Grazia's* never mentioned them!'

And then the plane comes round again, and this time it's towing a new sign, saying:

*FLOSSIE SAID **YES!***

The roar of the crowd ripples right around the bay as the plane passes.

Kit's standing up, threading his arms around me, pulling me into a kiss. And by the time we break apart, the plane is passing another time, and it's back to towing the High Tides banner.

David's rubbing his hands. 'Well, that went well! Congratulations, Floss and Kit, and a great moment for the hotel too!'

Rye's holding up his phone. 'It's all captured on here!'

And then everyone rushes forward to hug us.

Nell's punching the air. 'The singles club have had proposals before, but this will go down in history as the most romantic one ever.'

Clemmie's smiling at Kit. 'I love how you knew what Floss was going to say, Kit.'

I laugh. 'As if I'd have said anything else.' As Sophie comes in for a hug I give her a huge squeeze and look at Mum. 'David was right about the surprises, Mum.'

Mum shakes her head. 'So what are we going to do now?'

I realise everyone is waiting for my reply, so I look at Kit. 'How about we eat our body weight in doughnuts to celebrate, then dance the night away?'

He grins back at me. 'This is St Aidan – what else would we do?'

PS

The next spring

The same night Kit asks me to marry him we see our first shooting star, but even before that, we both know it's what we want. We have a quiet wedding just before Christmas at High Tides Hotel, Kit makes our plain gold wedding bands, and Shadow carries them in a velvet bag tied around his neck. All the mermaids are there, and Milla, Tilly, Maisie and Bud are bridesmaids, Marcus is a pageboy and chief dog-leader, and the whole village comes afterwards and dances on the beach.

Yes, Kit looks amazing in a dark checked suit, and I wear a white satin playsuit, with platform shoes Plum's mum had in the seventies – just because I'm doing grown-up things, it doesn't mean I have to grow up in every area. Kit, Shadow and I move between The Hideaway and the Latitudes, and we're in no hurry to change that.

Not everyone abandons themselves to romance as fast as Kit and me. After some persuasion Mum concedes that she and

David can wear promise rings until she's ready to give up her independence more fully, so they split their time between the hotel and The Hermitage.

Thanks to the efforts of Clemmie's Charlie and the Chamber of Commerce, grants are secured to add to the substantial funds we've already raised for the sea pool. And thanks to David's drive and another very generous donation, there are diggers down on the beach as we speak, and we're all hoping to be swimming in the sea pool before the end of summer.

After my matriarchal upbringing I won't be acknowledging anyone other than Mum as a parent, but Kit uncovers an accidental clue to the question I never intend to pursue when he notices that David, Rye and me have hands that are uncannily similar. I'm confident that as a ring-maker he's the only person who will ever be close enough to make that comparison though, and also certain that for my benefit he will keep that information to himself. Now we've all come back together we're fine as we are.

Somewhere along the line my throat gets better, but I'm too busy to pick up my old job. And when we think of London or St Aidan, there's only one place we want to be.

There have been so many changes since the April afternoon last year when Shadow and I rolled into town. What felt like the end of the road that day turned out to be the start of a new and much better life. Not only do Kit and I look for happiness in every second, thanks to the strength we're finding together, we're also looking further ahead, daring to put our faith in each other and the future in the biggest of ways.

One of the happiest changes for me since I've been back is

what's happened between Sophie and me. When I first arrived, I was wary of being beholden to her, but working through our problems together we built a new understanding that's altered our relationship entirely. While I felt I was fully reconciled to not having children, I hadn't counted on seeing the man I love holding a baby in his arms. The day Kit stepped in at random to cuddle George while Nell sorted out the pushchair, Sophie was the one who saw me in pieces. A week later, when she suggested that she was the most natural person in the world to have a baby for Kit and me, using my frozen eggs, it took us by surprise, but it didn't take long for us to agree.

It's a huge sacrifice for her and the family to make, but they're all behind it and excited to share the journey with us. As Sophie says, pregnancy and birth come easy to her, and with her own family complete and her still being young enough, now is the best time. As my sister, she couldn't give me a bigger gift than a baby, but she insists that lately I've done things to make life inordinately better for her. Her baby bump is still small, but we're holding our breath, aching for it all to go well.

If you ever come to St Aidan to swim in the sea pool and walk far enough along the dunes towards Comet Cove, and look to see a washing line of baby grows blowing in the wind by the rickety beach hut with the wobbly tin roof, you'll know we've done it.

AUTHOR'S NOTE

To my readers...

St Aidan is a fictitious place, but I feel as if I live there, and some readers feel the same. If you've enjoyed your time in St Aidan, you may like to visit again. All my St Aidan stories are standalone reads. The books run chronologically, some characters appear in several books, but not everyone is in every story. For anyone who'd rather avoid accidental spoilers, this is the order they were written in:

The Little Wedding Shop by the Sea
Christmas at the Little Wedding Shop
Summer at the Little Wedding Shop
Christmas Promises at the Little Wedding Shop
The Little Cornish Kitchen
A Cornish Cottage by the Sea (aka Edie Browne's Cottage by the Sea)
A Cosy Christmas in Cornwall

Love at the Little Wedding Shop by the Sea
Tea for Two at the Little Cornish Kitchen
A Winter Warmer at the Little Cornish Kitchen

And lastly this one...
Happy reading and lots of love, Jane xx

ACKNOWLEDGMENTS

Thank you to all my readers. These stories come alive when you turn the pages. I love that you're as willing as I am to run away for a few happy hours in St Aidan.

When I began writing this story I was fit and well, and nervous about getting Floss's backstory right. Then a few chapters into the book a routine screening turned up a cancerous tumour in my bowel. With the cancer on the point of spreading through my whole body, I was incredibly lucky with the timing. As I went through my treatment I was spurred on by the knowledge that when this book was done, at least Floss's details would be authentic. My message to you all is – if you are offered health screening, do it. My pooh-stick saved my life. Yours could do the same for you.

In the course of this journey I've been helped by literally hundreds of wonderful and amazing professionals in the NHS, at Chesterfield Royal and Weston Park in Sheffield. I can't begin to express the size of the gratitude I feel to every one of them for allowing me another chance to live. I would not be where I am without them.

All through this time I've been surrounded by amazing support. Thank you to Charlotte and Amanda, (Ledger and Preston) for wrapping me up with incredible warmth and love. Thanks to the wonderful One More Chapter team, to Kimberly

Young and the wider Harper Collins team, to Rachel McCarron and the rights department.

To my friends who have travelled with me through this. To my sisters. For all the people who have wished me well. To my children, Anna, Indi and Max, and their partners, Aladdin, Richard and Izzy, for being there for the big stuff and the more enormous bits too. To Eric for doing star jumps outside my hospital window, to Theo for arriving and bringing the joy of holding a new-born. To Aladdin and Anna for the surprise delivery of Dahlia and Lyla-Rose.

To Jess and Ash, Lottie and Chris, Karl and all the Cushways.

Saving the last hugs for Phil. And of course, Herbie and Bear. xx

FLOSS'S RECIPES

In case this book has made your mouth water, here are a few of Floss's favourites from The Hideaway kitchen to try for yourself at home.

Floss's Lemon Drizzle Cake

Floss's Lemon Drizzle cake very easy to make for beginners in the kitchen, delicious at any time of year.

Glaze:
Juice from 1 lemon
50g of sugar (optional)
Cake Mixture:
100g Self-Raising flour
100g Soft margarine
100g Caster sugar
2 Eggs

Zest of 1 Lemon

Preheat the oven to 180C/160C fan, gas 4, and grease a shallow 19cm cake tin.

Grate the rind from the lemon onto a plate.

Sieve the flour in to a mixing bowl, add the caster sugar, margarine, eggs and lemon rind.

Beat the mixture until light and fluffy and well mixed.

Using a large spoon carefully put the mixture in to the greased cake tin.

Spread the mixture evenly and wipe the sides if mixture is around the sides of the tin.

Using oven gloves put the cake in to the oven for 15 - 20 min, or until golden brown and firm to touch.

Cut the orange/lemon in half and squeeze out the juice. Put the juice into a small bowl and mix in the small amount of sugar.

When the cake is cooked, loosen it from the tin using a palette knife. Turn it out on to a cooling tray.

If you are having the glaze with sugar option, put juice and sugar in a pan, and stir over a gentle heat until the sugar has dissolved. Pour the juice (or juice and sugar) carefully over the bottom of the cake a little at a time and allow it to soak in.

If you'd prefer Orange Drizzle Cake to Lemon Drizzle Cake, replace the lemon with an orange. If you'd like your cake to be deeper, use double the ingredients, and a deeper tin. Cooking time for this will be longer.

When the cake is cool, slice and enjoy!

Floss's Chocolate Brownies

Of all Floss's many brownie recipes, this is one of her favourites. She makes it in a tin that's 13 inches by 8 inches and 2 and a half inches deep. Some days she lines the tin with parchment, but if she's in a hurry she wings it and cooks without. Again, temperatures of different ovens may vary, and you may want to vary the cooking time to get a stickier brownie too. Remember the brownies will carry on cooking as they cool.

375g butter at room temperature

375g dark chocolate if you're feeling posh (cocoa is fine if you don't have that)

6 large eggs

1 tablespoon vanilla extract

500g caster sugar

225g plain flour

1 teaspoon salt

Preheat the oven to 180°C/160°C fan/gas mark 4.

Grease the tin or line with parchment.

Melt the chocolate and butter together in a heavy based saucepan and put aside to cool.

In a bowl, beat the eggs with the sugar and add the vanilla essence.

Sieve the flour into another bowl and mix in the salt.

When the chocolate mixture is cool, beat in the eggs and sugar.

Stir in the flour and beat until the mixture is smooth.

Transfer to the baking tin and bake for about 25 mins. Check often at the end to make sure not to cook it for too long.

When it's ready the top will have a paler brown crust, but the inside will still be dark and sticky.

Leave to cool and then slice into pieces.

Floss's Bakewell Tart Blondies

Some of Floss's favourite blondies, these are my personal faves because I love the jam. Yum yum.

250g butter
125g soft brown sugar
125g white granulated sugar
3 eggs (medium)
100g ground almonds
225g self raising flour
200g white chocolate, in chunks or chips (optional, but extra delish)
250g raspberry jam
50g flaked almonds

Preheat the oven to 180°C/160°C fan/gas mark 4.

Grease a 8 inch by 13 inch baking tin or line with parchment.

Put the butter and sugars into a heavy based saucepan, and stir gently over a low heat until all the sugar has dissolved.

Leave to cool for ten minutes.

Add the eggs one by one and stir.

Add the flour and ground almonds and beat for a short time until thick and sticky.

Add the white chocolate chunks or chips, and fold through the mixture if using.

Pour the mixture into the baking tin and spread out evenly. Dollop the jam in lumps across the surface, and gently swirl this through the mixture.

Sprinkle almond flakes evenly over the top, then bake in the oven for thirty minutes, until the surface begins to wave.

Once it's out of the oven let it cool in the tray. Then put the tray in the fridge to chill, before cutting into snack sized pieces.

Floss's M&M Cookies

Floss's go-to favourite, and one of mine too. There's nothing quite like an M&M cookie!

125 g unsalted butter/baking spread
175 g light brown sugar
1 medium egg
1 tsp vanilla
300 g plain flour
1 tbsp cornflour
1 + 1/2 tsp baking powder
1/2 tsp bicarbonate of soda
1/2 tsp sea salt
400 g M&Ms (or Smarties)

Put the butter and sugar in a bowl and beat until creamy.

Crack in the egg and vanilla and beat again.

Sieve in the flour, cornflour, baking powder, bicarbonate of soda, and salt and beat until it forms a dough.

Add the M&Ms (or Smarties) and beat until these are evenly spread through the mixture.

Separate your dough into eight and roll into even-sized balls.

Chill the cookie balls in the fridge for an hour (or in the freezer for 30 minutes).

Whilst the cookie dough is chilling, preheat your oven to 180°c fan, or 200°c regular.

Take your cookies out of the freezer/fridge and put four each onto two baking trays lined with parchment.

Bake the cookies in the oven for 11-13 minutes, then take out of the over and transfer a cooling tray.

Let the cookies cool on the tray for at leat half an hour. (They will continue to bake whilst cooling.)

Then enjoy.

These are best eaten on the day of baking, but will keep for a couple of days in an air tight container.

Love, Jane xx

ONE MORE CHAPTER

The author and One More Chapter would like to thank everyone who contributed to the publication of this story...

Analytics
Abigail Fryer
Maria Osa

Audio
Fionnuala Barrett
Ciara Briggs

Contracts
Sasha Duszynska
Lewis

Design
Lucy Bennett
Fiona Greenway
Liane Payne
Dean Russell

Digital Sales
Hannah Lismore
Emily Scorer

Editorial
Kate Elton
Arsalan Isa
Charlotte Ledger
Bonnie Macleod
Jennie Rothwell
Tony Russell
Caroline Scott-
Bowden

Harper360
Emily Gerbner
Jean Marie Kelly
emma sullivan
Sophia Wilhelm

International Sales
Bethan Moore

Marketing & Publicity
Chloe Cummings
Emma Petfield

Operations
Melissa Okusanya
Hannah Stamp

Production
Emily Chan
Denis Manson Simon
Moore Francesca
Tuzzeo

Rights
Rachel McCarron
Hany Sheikh
Mohamed
Zoe Shine

**The HarperCollins
Distribution Team**

**The HarperCollins
Finance & Royalties
Team**

**The HarperCollins
Legal Team**

**The HarperCollins
Technology Team**

Trade Marketing
Ben Hurd

UK Sales
Laura Carpenter
Isabel Coburn
Jay Cochrane
Sabina Lewis
Holly Martin
Erin White
Harriet Williams
Leah Woods

**And every other
essential link in the
chain from delivery
drivers to booksellers
to librarians and
beyond!**